FIRE CALL

In this job, especially on Rescue, you had to be prepared for anything.

Including plenty of false alarms.

When we arrived at the scene, Captain Stan Silfen
stood locked in an angry confrontation with the
construction foreman, a grizzled man whose giant
paunch protruded through a Day-Glo orange vest.

"You see a fire, calling us is fine. A bunch of rocks
and ashes doesn't qualify," Silfen said.

"Thing was blazing like the dickens when we got
here, Captain. It's not my goddamned job to take
chances."

Tracking the accusatory arc of Silfen's hand, I
froze.

Circle of stones. Smoke wraiths rising from a hill of
powdery ash. It was identical to the dying blaze we
found beside the Dolans' house the night we were
called to rescue Kitty from the roof.

The only thing missing this time was the victim.

MORE THAN YOU KNOW

by Judith Kelman

BANTAM BOOKS

NEW YORK TORONTO LONDON SYDNEY AUCKLAND

More Than You Know
A Bantam Book/February 1996

All rights reserved.
Copyright © 1996 by Judith Kelman.
Cover art copyright © 1996 by Mick McGinty.
No part of this book may be reproduced or transmitted in any form or
by any means, electronic or mechanical, including photocopying,
recording, or by any information storage and retrieval system, without
permission in writing from the publisher.
For information address: Bantam Books.

ISBN 0-553-56270-3

Published simultaneously in the United States and Canada

Bantam Books are published by Bantam Books, a division of Bantam Doubleday Dell
Publishing Group, Inc. Its trademark, consisting of the words "Bantam Books" and
the portrayal of a rooster, is Registered in U.S. Patent and Trademark Office and in
other countries. Marca Registrada. Bantam Books, 1540 Broadway, New York,
New York 10036.

PRINTED IN THE UNITED STATES OF AMERICA

OPM   0 9 8 7 6 5 4 3 2 1

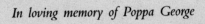

In loving memory of Poppa George

ACKNOWLEDGMENTS

For their generous advice and technical assistance, thanks to Deputy Chief Kevin B. Tappe of the Stamford, Connecticut, Fire Department; Burt Dubrow, executive producer of the *Sally Jesse Raphael* show; Dr. William Theodore of the National Institutes of Health; John Megaw of Bellevue Hospital's program for the Victims of Violent Crime, and Debbie Pauls of the Stamford Rape Crisis Center.

As always, I am indebted to my brilliant editor, Kate Miciak, and to my peerless agent, Peter Lampack.

MORE THAN
YOU KNOW

Chapter 1

DANA

At the entrance to the set, Dana Saunders hesitated. The topic of today's show gave her a rotten feeling in the pit of her stomach, a racing pulse. Like the onset of a sickness she was powerless to prevent.

As she stepped in from the wings, the audience exploded in a raucous round of applause. The waiting crowd had been preheated by Mickey Conway, a stoop-shouldered youth in a Princeton sweatshirt. The producer, a plump daffodil blonde named Lucy Breitmeier, had set forth the rules: No chewing gum or staring at the camera. Stand when selected and speak clearly into the mike. Keep questions and comments short. On command, be wildly enthusiastic. No cursing, nose picking, or scratching of private parts, unless you cared to have those acts immortalized. No unauthorized trips out of the seat. Such were the Ten Commandments of talk shows. Otherwise, anything went.

The boisterous clapping continued. The crowd was good, electric.

Dana scanned the rows of eager faces. The three rows of older women on the right were retired Ma Bell operators from Jersey City, her assistant had told her. On their left sat a church choir from Munich that was slated to perform this evening at Saint Patrick's Cathedral. This show should really get them in the mood, Dana thought grimly. From the sublime to the religious.

The survivors, nine women and three young girls, were planted in aisle seats along the center section. Dana caught the frightened eye of a teenager in the fifth row and smiled warmly. The girl was morbidly obese. Three hundred pounds, minimum. Poor thing was probably trying to hide behind the fat, hoping it might offer her a modicum of protection. The teen dropped her self-conscious gaze and gnawed a cuticle. Catching the producer's cue, Dana turned to read the scrolling text on the teleprompter.

"Every five minutes in this country, a woman is raped. In fact, one-fourth of all American girls have been sexually molested by the age of sixteen. Horrifying statistics? You bet. But numbers can't begin to describe the personal horror of this vicious, violent crime.

"What sort of person commits such a terrible act? Why does he do it? And above all, can the rapist be cured?

"Today on Back Talk *we'll examine these and other highly controversial questions. Stay with us."*

Dana's voice was swallowed by the rising chords of the show's musical theme. *Back Talk*'s logo filled the overhead monitors. Soon, it was displaced by the first thirty-second commercial in the two-minute introductory pod.

Lucy Breitmeier herded the day's principle participants toward the ring of armchairs on the elevated set. While the producer fiddled with the lapel mikes, Dana approached to greet her guests. To maintain the show's sharp edge, Dana always made it a point to avoid the greenroom. Given today's star attraction, she would have been glad to put off the meeting indefinitely.

First, Dana extended a hand to Dr. Marlene Mosher, an attractive, solid-looking woman with equally solid credentials. Over the past decade, Mosher, a psychiatry professor at the Yale Medical School, had studied over a thousand confessed sex offenders. She'd concluded that the underlying obsession was incurable. Her recent book, *In Sheep's Clothing: The Myth of the Reformed Rapist,* had stirred serious

dissension among mental health practitioners. It had also ignited enough public debate to propel the scholarly volume
to number one on the *New York Times* best-seller list.

The man on Dr. Mosher's right was Patterson Graham,
Ph.D., founder and director of the Cambridge Center for
Offender Treatment. Graham's program involved a pricey
three-month stay at a private clinic in Greenwich, Connecticut. His clients came by court referral or voluntary commitment. His "treatment" consisted of gourmet meals,
deluxe accommodations, and daily doses of what Graham
termed "Intensive Relatedness." From what Dana had been
able to learn, Intensive Relatedness boiled down to the
grown-up rapists' version of a naughty boy sitting in a corner, pondering his sins.

Somehow, Graham, whose doctorate was in botany, had
managed to peddle his snake oil to a startling number of otherwise prudent people. His program, in operation for nearly
thirty years, claimed a ninety-five-percent success rate,
though rapists were the most likely of all criminals to repeat
their violent acts. In the supposed interest of client confiden-
tiality, Patterson Graham's Cambridge program refused to
open its records to public scrutiny, so the lofty success per-
centage could be neither independently corroborated nor
disproved. Instead, Graham promised to publish his own
data, although to date, no book had appeared.

Patterson Graham had been packaged with an eye to
boosting his credibility. He sported a cozy gray cardigan,
mildly disheveled white hair, and the bemused expression of
a proud new grandpa peering through the nursery window.
His robust outdoorsy look was courtesy of a tan-toned
makeup base and liberal sprinklings of a ruddy blusher. The
artifice wouldn't show on camera. But Dana felt a renewed
determination to expose the rest of the man's phony face.

She nodded at Graham brusquely and moved on. Next
was the main event's attorney. Valerie Eckhard was unaffec-
tionately known as "Blowhard" by the *Back Talk* staff. A
brash, abrasive redhead, Eckhard had appeared on the show

several times, ardently espousing a variety of incompatible causes. Last time, the attorney played the superfeminist, outraged by private clubs and colleges that refused to admit women. Today, she was fronting for the monster on her right.

Finally, Dana forced herself to turn to the low-life creep himself. The rapist's image had been almost comically altered by a curly brown wig, mirrored sunglasses, and ponderous makeup. The nose was a bulbous blob. Circles of bright rouge plumped the cheeks. Pancake narrowed the lips, and thick, gray pencil made his eyebrows resemble lengths of dirty rope. But despite the clown mask, Dana felt a chill.

Valerie Eckhard had set firm conditions for her client's appearance. The lawyer would not reveal the man's name, not even to Dana or *Back Talk*'s in-house legal counsel. Mr. X would sign the necessary release form, but only if Blowhard could witness the signature herself and retain the form in her office safe. The camouflage makeup must be applied before he arrived.

On air, he'd be referred to as John. Dana could ask no questions that might hint at his identity. Nothing about his place of residence, his job or educational history, or his family status. The audience would be so instructed and reminded of this requirement whenever necessary.

The terms Valerie Eckhard demanded were vexing and unconventional. Dana hated flying blind. But her staff had embraced the idea and pressed her to proceed with it. Sexual assault was a hot issue. Many competing shows had featured known rapists safely ensconced in jail cells, and others who'd supposedly been rehabilitated after serving their terms.

Presenting a confessed molester who'd never been apprehended, her staff reminded Dana, added a fresh, titillating twist. Think of it, Dana, Lucy had urged: This nameless, masked creature functioned as part of some unsuspecting community. Viewers would not be able to escape the sinister implication. *Any* man could be a rapist: the helpful next-door neighbor, the trusted family physician, the kindly old pastor of the local church, any husband or father or brother or son.

Extra promotion had generated a large anticipatory buzz for the program, which would air at the end of next week. Record ratings were expected. The show's lawyer had voiced no serious objections. With mere moments to airtime, Dana saw no choice but to ignore the strident warning voice in her head.

"Good morning, John," she said stiffly. "Thank you for agreeing to do the show."

"My pleasure, Ms. Saunders." He spoke with a hiss that made her skin prickle. The makeup gave him a waxen, grotesque look. "Glad to be here."

Dana caught a double dose of her own uneasy expression in the gleaming, mirrored lenses of his sunglasses. Frown lines pinched her forehead. Her smile had the stiff, faded look of a pressed corsage. Worry dulled her large brown eyes. Turning away, she was grateful for the producer's next cue.

"We're on in ten seconds. *Places,* everyone. In five . . . four . . ." Lucy mouthed the final beats of the countdown. She held out three plump fingers. Two. One. The camera light blinked red. Once again the white-on-blue *Back Talk* logo filled the overhead monitors. The show's theme played over another burst of thunderous applause. Dana's next block of text flashed on the teleprompter. She stepped forward, eyes on the camera, and said:

"Can a rapist every *really* be cured? That is the question. To help us try to answer it today, we've invited a fascinating panel of experts. Please help me welcome them now."

Dana tried to keep her introductions of the four guests evenhanded. But the audience warmed at once to Dr. Mosher. The applause for Patterson Graham and Attorney Blowhard was tepid. John the Rapist drew a din of horrified murmurs and a smattering of boos.

Dana raised her palms for reason. "Okay, okay. John came here today to admit his crime and express his remorse. I think we should hear him out."

She turned toward the camouflaged face. "Twenty-five years ago, you raped a twelve-year-old girl, John. You were never arrested for the crime. In fact, you were never punished in any way. And yet, after attending Mr. Graham's Cambridge program shortly after the assault, you're convinced you would never, under any circumstances, rape again. Is that correct?"

Valerie Eckhard bristled. "John isn't on trial here, Dana. There's no need to badger him."

"I'm just trying to make things clear, Ms. Eckhard. Why don't you let John speak for himself?"

Blowhard was about to blow again, but John preempted her. Dipping his bewigged head and spreading his hands in a priestly gesture, he said, "That's exactly what I'm here to do, Ms. Saunders. I'm sorrier than you can imagine for what I did to that little girl all those years ago. I'd give anything—*anything*—if I could take back that one terrible night."

His tone was shallow and insincere. Dana felt a surge of fury. "I'm sure our viewers would like to know why you did it," she said.

"I was strung out. Totally screwed up. When I saw that girl, something just snapped inside me." John shook his head, as if trying to shake the ugly memory.

A horrific image formed in Dana's mind. Vividly, she saw this beast stalking her own precious child. A spark of rage ignited in her gut. The man deserved to die. Her fingers cramped with the sudden urge to squeeze the life out of him.

Drawing a breath, Dana forced herself back in control. She even managed to prod a snip of sympathy into her tone. Her job was to keep the show's fire stoked, not to charbroil the participants. "John, I can hear that you're sorry. I'm sure everyone can. But how can we be absolutely sure you could never slip into that strung-out, crazy state again? How can *you* be sure?"

Dr. Mosher smoothly took the ball. "Exactly on target, Dana. My study clearly demonstrated that sex offenders are compulsive personalities. They are driven by circumstance. Even after years without incident, the rapist might be set off by whatever triggered his prior attacks."

"Such as?" Dana prompted.

"For one man, it may be watching a pornographic movie. For another, it's getting drunk. The most trivial things can cause a relapse. I've had patients who said they were moved to rape by a fight with the wife or a bad day at the office."

Dana frowned. "You're talking normal stresses, Doctor. The kind all of us face every day."

"Precisely. Which is why we can never be a hundred percent certain that an offender won't repeat his crime," Mosher said firmly.

"Nonsense!" Patterson Graham bellowed his objection. "With all due respect, Dr. Mosher. It's obvious that the offenders you sampled lacked the benefits of a proven treatment program such as the one we offer at Cambridge. My clients benefit from intensive work, expert counseling, and long-term follow-up support."

"Then, why won't you allow outside investigators to confirm your results?" Dana asked.

"Because I refuse to compromise my work, that's why. Having outsiders poking around would be an intolerable disruption. Instead, I've laid it all out in my book, *The Road to Redemption,* which will be out next May. Our success rate is over ninety-five percent."

"But those remain *unconfirmed* numbers," Dana persisted.

"I have confirmed them, personally. Besides, our success speaks for itself."

Dr. Mosher consulted the computer printout in her lap. "As it happens, Dr. Graham, sixty-seven of my subjects were former Cambridge clients. Of those, twenty-two admitted to repeat offenses, fifteen reported near misses, and seventeen of the remaining thirty detailed disturbing, recurrent fantasies regarding sexual abuse. The majority of these fantasies involved children."

The audience stirred uneasily.

Graham chuckled, even as blotches of fury mottled his neck. He turned to Dana. "You know what they say. There are lies, damned lies, and statistics."

"Then, how do you explain Dr. Mosher's findings, Mr. Graham?"

"I don't *have* to explain them. *She* does. And, by the way, it's *Doctor* Graham."

Dana bit back a smile of her own. "Really? What exactly is your medical specialty, *Doctor*?"

Graham had that lovely trapped look that played so well on freeze-frame at a cut to commercial. "I'm a Ph.D., not a physician."

"I see. So you're a psychologist?"

The quack smoothed his cardigan and muttered an unintelligible reply. Reluctantly, Dana allowed him to slip the hook. It was way too early in the show to reel the fool in and leave him flapping. No doubt the audience would take care of that—and him—in the question-and-answer segment.

"The Cambridge program works," John interjected. "I sit here as proof of that. They taught me to view things from the victim's perspective. That makes all the difference."

Dana forced herself to face his hidden eyes. "Are you saying you've never had a disturbing dream or fantasy since participating in the program, John? Never a single instant when you feared you might lose control again?"

John the Rapist hesitated for precisely the beat Dana wanted. Before he recovered enough to respond, she flashed her signature best-friend smile at the camera.

"Stay right where you are, folks. *Back Talk* will return after these messages. . . ."

During the break, Dana slipped backstage. There, she

submitted to a swipe of fresh makeup and some predictable banter from her staff.

"You know when you mentioned that a woman in this country gets raped every five minutes, boss? Bet you anything some bozo in the audience asks how come the guy doesn't get tired," Mickey Conway said.

"Don't you dare even think of using that one in tomorrow's warm-up, Mickey," Dana warned.

Conway smiled meekly. Tasteless was his specialty. "Are you sure? I bet it'd get them going."

"*You* would be the one going," Dana replied crisply. "You read me?"

Crooked teeth and a dense crop of stubborn sandy hair gave Conway the look of an overaged Dennis the Menace. "Loud and clear. The PC police have spoken." He clicked his heels and saluted.

"Don't start with me, Mickey. Political correctness has nothing to do with it. There's nothing funny about sexual violence. People get hurt."

"Yes, boss. Whatever you say, boss." Rolling his eyes, Mickey loped off toward the projection room.

Dana watched him go. Conway was a computer whiz and a crack researcher. His services in those areas were indispensable to her show. They also brought him frequent job offers from the corporate sector. Mickey stayed on at *Back Talk* only because he adored playing stand-up comic for the fifteen minutes before each show began. Dana recognized the necessity of keeping him happy, but she could have done nicely without Mickey's dubious notion of humor.

"That John character gives me a major case of the geeks," commented Julie Westerman, the show's greenest production assistant. Jules, as she preferred to be called, was bright, eager, and impeccably organized. Promising, Dana thought. But the pretty young strawberry blonde needed toning down. Her voice was too shrill, her gait too brisk and bouncy. At times, Jules's explosive enthusiasms reminded Dana of a puppy in dire need of obedience school.

But Dana more than shared the assistant's revulsion for today's star guest. "Hard to feel otherwise when you consider he raped a twelve-year-old," she told Jules grimly.

The others lapsed in awkward silence. It was no secret among the crew that Dana's off-camera universe revolved around her twelve-year-old daughter, Rebecca. Becky was a terrific kid, upbeat, funny, remarkably unaffected by her formidable intelligence and prodigious talent for the violin.

The child also seemed entirely untouched by her mother's national celebrity. Dana fought hard to maintain her daughter's distance from the seamier side of fame. Becky went by her father's last name. At school and other functions, Dana, too, hid behind her ex-husband's surname and wore a hat and glasses that hid her identity. Dana well knew the risk of stalkers and other crazies. A frightening number of people were drawn to or delusional about public figures.

One highly unsavory character, a man named Lester Yurie, had been haunting Dana for years. Yurie was a seasoned criminal and Dana's self-appointed most ardent fan. On regular occasions, when he managed to breach Dana's security, the creep eagerly volunteered his services. "You need anything ripped off, Dana? Anyone taken care of? Give me a holler and I'll see to it. Be my pleasure. Make that my *privilege*."

Loyal staffers understood the need to protect Dana and Becky from characters like Lester Yurie. They cooperated in the information blockade, refusing to yield to frequent juicy bribes from the tabloids for tidbits about Dana and her family.

"Thirty seconds!" Lucy called.

"Okay, people. Let's get to it," Dana said.

"In five . . ." Lucy counted down as the camera lights flashed on the seated guests. Turning to the audience, Dana read the segment lead.

"Can the rapist be cured? That's the question before us

today. Our expert panel includes a confessed child molester."

A close-up of John's gargoyle face loomed on the monitor. He was caught in a satisfied smirk.

Approaching, Dana said coldly, "Is there something you
find amusing here, John?"

The rapist shifted in his seat. "Of course not. I was
just—"

"You say you learned to see things from your victim's
perspective. Is that correct?"

"Victim empathy, Dr. Graham calls it," John said eagerly.

"Do you honestly believe you can understand what rape
does to a little girl? Do you honestly expect *us* to believe
that?"

"Anyone can make a mistake, lady. I'm not a bad person."

The audience responded with boos and catcalls.

Dana silenced them with a hand and faced John squarely.
"A mistake? Is that what you call raping an innocent child?"

The crowd was riveted. They watched Dana with the fascination of watching a snake handler manipulating a cobra.

"Well, John. I'd say you still have a few things left to
learn."

The show ended with the audience on its feet. The applause was deafening.

As the crew stored cameras and equipment and the audi-
ence filtered out, Lucy herded the principal guests offstage.
Dana followed to offer thanks and farewells. As she spoke to
Dr. Mosher, she felt a prickle of unease. The rapist had re-
moved his mirrored glasses. His eyes were hard black beads.
They fixed on her, unblinking.

Dana shuddered. Anxious to be rid of him, she quickly
moved from Mosher to Graham to Eckhard. She couldn't
bring herself to meet the rapist's piercing stare. As she cast
a dismissive nod in his direction, Jules Westerman came
bounding in from the control room.

"Guess what just came over the wire? Becky won the

Lassiter Prize! Congratulations, Dana! Can you believe your daughter got an honor like that? I bet—"

Dana's stern look silenced the young woman at once. But the damaging words were out. Quickly, Dana turned to catch the rapist's response. The bastard's lips twitched. Was that a glint of amusement in his eyes?

Dana's fists clenched. The Lassiter Prize was big news, awarded annually to a violin prodigy. Stories about Becky winning the distinction were sure to run in the national press. Some of the pieces would reveal where the child went to school or other telling information. A confessed child molester now had the means to track her baby down.

There had to be some way to stop this, to back time up and reclaim those few lethal words. Maybe the creep hadn't heard what Jules said. Or maybe he'd failed to catch its significance. . . .

"Good show today," Lucy Breitmeier said, to break the awkward silence. "Thanks, everybody."

The others said good-bye. Blowhard Eckhard's parting nod was crisp and angry. John dawdled a step behind. Pinning Dana with his disquieting eyes, he proffered a hand.

Ignoring the hand, Dana tried to peer behind his glittering, impenetrable gaze.

"Thank you for having me, Ms. Saunders. A pleasure, *really*." Following his attorney, the rapist turned and headed out the door.

The Road To Redemption

by Patterson Graham, Ph.D.

(Advance Reading Copy)

The rapist *can* be cured. At the Cambridge Center for Offender Treatment, sex offenders learn to ana-

lyze their motives, to feel for their victims, and ultimately, to modify their destructive behaviors.

During my thirty years as founder and director of
the program, thousands of clients have tried and
proven the validity of our approach. John's* evolution
from offender to staunch defender of young children
ranks among our proudest successes.

As John describes below, his deviant behavior can
be traced to his formative sexual experiences at
home:

*I wanted the kid, so I took her. She was a pretty package to me.
Box of candy. A thing. Nothing at all.*

*My parents taught me to think that way. I could have whatever
caught my eye. No limits.*

*We didn't go by normal rules in my family. Laws, truth, right,
and wrong were for lesser people. "The trash," Daddy used to call
them. We were better, bigger, above all that. We could satisfy our
appetites, whatever they were.*

*My father's biggest hunger was for pain. He craved other people's
agony. Wanted it large, loud, and often. Daddy developed a whole
ritual around hurting me, so he could stretch it out. He wanted to
savor every moment.*

*First, he'd tell me what I'd done wrong. Recite the charges. His
voice stayed dead calm. Almost kindly. From the sound, you'd
have thought he was telling me a bedtime story.*

*Generally, my sin was not being good enough, not having
enough talent. Daddy revered any kind of brilliance, especially in
a kid. It drove him nuts that I was smart but no genius. Good but
not great. To Daddy, that was a terrible sin. Grounds for excruciating punishment.*

*After he expressed his displeasure, he'd light a fire in the circle
of stones. The burning ring was meant to catch the Lord's attention, to remind Him that I'd been found lacking. I had to look at
the fire while Daddy beat me. Forgetting to watch was a serious sin
in itself.*

*John is a pseudonym, used to protect client privacy.

The harder I screamed, the happier it made Daddy. I remember this one time when he broke my leg and three ribs with a two-by-four. One of the neighbors happened to pass by and heard me yelling. He knocked at the door and asked if everything was okay.

Daddy stayed perfectly calm. He claimed the noise was coming from the TV. After the neighbor was out of sight, he finished my beating. "Louder," he kept saying, when I cried. "That's the boy." Never saw that man so happy. You'd have thought he won the lottery.

He got this special slack-jawed, peaceful look on his face when he was making me suffer. You ever watch a person listen to achingly beautiful music? Or someone crazy in love? Pain was that for my daddy. Ecstasy.

Mother's tastes were more subtle. As a kid, I didn't even realize the things she did were for her own pleasure. I thought it was all for me.

After Daddy finished, Mother always stepped in to play nurse. She'd strip me down to see to the bruises. "Did he hurt you there, darlin'? How about there?"

The woman had velvet hands. The softest fingers in the universe. I can still feel how she'd dab a little antiseptic on this place and that, tenderly soothing away the sore spots with a damp cloth until I was tingling all over.

Afterward, she'd put me in soft, warm pajamas, fresh from the wash. She'd watch while I brushed my teeth. She'd supervise my prayers. Then, she'd take me to bed and lie down beside me.

Those soft hands knew how to rub away the pain. My momma's hands taught me 'most everything.

Chapter 2

LENNIE

As the fire engine swerved into Griscom Woods, Nick Marzullo killed the siren. Fine snow sifted through the spires of flashing light. Ice crunched like broken glass beneath the engine's giant tires. The wind shrilled, harsh and mournful.

"Where the hell's the fire?" Marzullo demanded. Short and squat, with squashed features and a belligerent mouth, Nick was humanity's closest answer to the bulldog.

"Slow down, Zulu. I can't see the numbers." Captain Joe Perriman squinted through the powdery haze at the mammoth house on the right, a French Normandy reproduction. "Keep going. The call was for Two-one-three Ledgebrook. We're still in double digits."

Formerly a private estate, the eighty-acre Griscom property had been sold to developers five years earlier. The builders peppered the land with artificial ponds and specimen saplings. Each two-acre lot held a gigantic house, as overblown and garish as a foolish kid on steroids.

Setting the homes at wide intervals had not curtailed the spread of that dread suburban malady: affluenza. The neighborhood reeked of excess. Luxury cars lined the driveways. Lavish pools and tennis courts crammed the manicured

backyards. Everything was too much and too new. Begging
for time and wear to dull the sheen.

"That's it!" Perriman barked. "Pull over."

The engine squealed to a wrenching stop at the curb
fronting a sprawling mock Tudor. Only a hint of smoke
tinged the air. The more obvious sign of trouble was the
distraught woman standing coatless in the snowy front yard.

Framed by a drizzle of porch light, her face was pinched
with fear. Her gaze and pleading screams were leveled toward the roof. Biting gusts billowed her black chiffon skirt
and cream silk blouse. Snow salted her honey blond hair,
but she seemed oblivious. You'd need a heart of stone to ignore the aching anguish of her cries. I hopped down from
the jump seat.

"Kitty, please!"

As the top-ranking officer on the rig, it was Captain
Perriman's place to approach the woman and assess the situation. Swiftly crossing the lawn, he questioned her briefly.
Then, frowning in disgust, he turned on his heel and
stormed away.

"My baby," the woman wailed after him. *"Please, you have
to help me!"*

Perriman was furious. "Woman expects me to risk my
people's lives to rescue her damned cat. She's nuts." He spat
his words like stones.

I stalled him as he headed back to the rig. "I'd like to do
it, Captain."

Perriman is all planes and angles: square jaw, hawk nose,
hay-toned stubble carpeting his head. He has a thick body,
blunt fingers, and a manner to match.

"Forget it, Finn. You go up there, you'll get clawed or
worse."

"I'll be fine, Captain," I told him evenly. "I'm good with
pets."

"I said, forget it. Damned cat'll come down when it's
good and ready. You ever hear of a kitty croaking up some
tree? On some roof? Doesn't happen."

"She obviously doesn't know that."

"Too damned bad," Perriman snapped. "I ought to have her arrested for pulling a false alarm. Let her learn the hard way. You see that? Dumb broad probably figured it'd cover the call."

Tracking his nod, I spotted the ring of stones at the corner of the house beyond the hedgerow. At its center, smoke ghosts wafted from a hill of charred debris.

Circle of stones? Smoldering ashes? The image was eerily familiar to me. But the connection stubbornly refused to gel.

Pushing the question aside, I focused on the more immediate problem. My heart went out to the woman on the lawn. She looked so lost, so desperate.

"Please, Captain. She's so upset. Let me bring the kitten down for her."

Perriman yanked his collar up and puffed his exasperation. "Finn, don't you ever goddamned listen? You're not paid to play hero to some cockamamie cat lover."

"It'll only take a minute—"

"Fire fighters fight fires and rescue people. This ain't the goddamned movies."

"Please."

"I said no. You go up there and get your fool neck broken, it'll be *my* ass."

"Please, Captain."

Perriman threw up his hands. "What are you, Finn? Part mule? Okay, damn it. Go get the stupid cat. But be quick about it."

"I will. Thanks!"

Before Perriman had time to change his mind, I returned to the rig for a ladder and a hand.

On the way, I doffed my helmet and enjoyed the cold wind ruffling my hair. The headgear went with the job, but it sat on my skull like a brick.

Even in full uniform, I know I fail to look the part. At barely five six, I'm considerably smaller than the typical fire fighter. My face would not play well on a recruiting poster.

The eyes lack that cold granite edge. The mouth is too soft, the complexion too fair to set beside any self-respecting Dalmatian. Several of my two-legged colleagues have their doubts about me as well. I'm too little. Too sentimental. I have breasts.

I was warned about possible problems when I signed on as the first woman ever to join the Stamford force ten years ago. But I honestly hadn't expected any. The ad in the local paper announcing competitive testing for the job appeared when I was at my restless worst, searching for some undefinable change in my life. I took that ad as an omen. When several of my friends challenged the idea as ridiculous, my overdeveloped stubborn side overrode all remaining objections.

A career in fire fighting sounded made-to-order. It was physical, risky, and held the heady potential for heroics. Saving people struck me as the noblest possible endeavor. The possibility of getting paid to do so, not to mention health and dental insurance and a dream pension plan, verged on perfection.

I'm a born tomboy; I have the battle scars to prove it. The slightly off-center set of my nose comes courtesy of a wild pitch in a regional Little League championship when I was in seventh grade. Other memorable incidents on and off the field have left me with a chipped front tooth and a faint scar, shaped like a sea gull poised for flight, above my right eyebrow.

My body is the athletic type, tending more to straightaways than curves. The breasts, outsized for the rest of me, loom much larger in the tiny minds of my infantile colleagues than in fact. Not that shape or gender even register in the S.F.D.'s emergency response uniform: oversized brown turnout coat with luminescent gold accents, baggy brown turnout pants, and knee-high black neoprene boots.

Marzullo had already reclaimed his place in the engine's elevated cab. "Wild Bill" Hitsig, the other fire fighter on the rig, had his long, lanky frame propped against the hose bed. Hitsig is hollow-cheeked and squint-eyed. Nasty as month-old milk. His breath formed visible plumes, like a dragon's. I gritted my teeth and approached him.

From my first day on the job, Wild Bill had signed on as my personal nemesis, determined to make my life miserable. The guy's world view was every bit as firm as it was idiotic. As he saw it, a woman's place was in housewares. Hardware, sports, business, and above all, notions (at least, the cerebral kind), were reserved for those with chest hair. Wild Bill couldn't imagine me as a bona fide human, much less an acceptable coworker.

"I'm going up for the cat, Hitsig. Grab the ladder with me, will you please?" Behind me, I heard the woman wail.

"Jeez, Finn. It's just a dumb animal. It's three in the frigging morning."

"Perriman okayed it. Now will you please give me a hand?"

Hitsig's leer framed a crooked span of yellow teeth. "Sure, baby. Where would you like it?"

Stifling a flash of anger, I looked him right in the beady eyes. "Speaking of dumb animals—"

"Watch your mouth, bitch."

"That's enough," Perriman snapped. "Get to it, Finn. Help her out, Hitsig. *Now!*"

Under the captain's watchful gaze, Wild Bill did his level best to impersonate a person. For a welcome change, he didn't try to undermine or override me. In short order, we had the ladder firmly propped against the roofline. Bracing myself against the bitter wind, I scrambled quickly to the top. By now, the woman's voice was scraped raw.

"Kitty, please!"

Scanning the shadowy roof, I searched for the missing cat. Snow ghosts formed and wavered in the wind. Otherwise, there was no sign of life on the forward slope. Treading cautiously over the slick tiles, I peered into the gutters. Rotted leaves, branches, and other debris packed the metal troughs. A small kitten could have slipped inside and gotten trapped in the litter. Chances were the poor little thing was dead by now. My heart sank.

But as I neared the end of the roof's forward valley, I picked up a muffled sound from the rear. It was a tiny cry, tinged with distress.

"Hold on, kitty. I'm coming."

Dropping to my knees, I scaled the pitched surface to the peak and eased slowly down the back side. Pausing to listen, I caught the muted whine again. Given the wind's fickle howling, it was impossible to pinpoint the source.

"Here, kitty, kitty. Where the hell are you?"

My hands stung from the cold. Standing, I inched lower. Despite the heavy ridges on my boot soles, the footing on the downslope was perilous. Icy squalls threatened my balance. My eyes watered.

"Come on, kitty. Have a heart. It's freezing up here."

I moved cautiously, calculating each forward step. But halfway down, a slate beneath my right foot broke away. I fell heavily on my back. In a dizzying slide, I plummeted toward the roofline. The sky abruptly wrenched out of focus. Swirled in a kaleidoscope of dizzy horror, I was skidding toward the cold, black void.

Desperately, I dug my palms and boot heels into the slick tiles. My body fisted. With startling clarity, I saw myself tumbling off the roof. Plunging into the darkness. Dashing against the rock-hard ground below.

No!

Suddenly, something snagged the collar of my turnout coat. My heels caught and held. Inches from the precipice, I came to a wrenching stop.

Shakily, I sat up and rubbed my aching hands together. My pulse was racing. Peering over my shoulder, I spotted the nail that had caught my collar, breaking my fall. Captain Perriman's warning echoed in my mind: *You go up there, you'll get clawed or worse.*

I coughed, struggling to catch my breath.

"Are you okay?"

Startled, I tracked the timid voice. It came from the slender figure rising from behind the wide brick chimney. A lovely child with pale eyes and a mouthful of glinting braces. Her cheeks were ruddy with the cold, her dark hair tousled. Dressed in a flowered flannel nightgown and fuzzy pink slippers, she was shivering hard.

"Who are you?" I asked.

"I'm sorry."

Funny name for a kid, I was tempted to crack, but the child's pained expression stopped me cold. And I suddenly understood what was going on.

"Your name's Kitty?" I asked.

She nodded stiffly. "Kitty Dolan."

"I'm Lennie Finn, Kitty. What are you doing up here, sweetheart? What's wrong?"

"Nothing. Just leave me alone!"

"What happened?"

The child cringed as if I'd struck her. "Go away, please!"

I rose and inched closer, squinting against the slap of swirling snow. A shudder shook the little girl like angry hands.

"You're so cold. Please let me take you inside."

"I can't. Mommy will kill me."

"No, she won't. She just wants you safe inside."

"Kitty, please!" the woman cried below.

"You don't understand." Tears welled in the huge eyes. "I was *bad*. That's why it happened. I'm not supposed to open the door to *anyone*. That's the *rule*."

I went numb inside. "Who was it, Kitty? Someone you know?" *Oh, God, don't let this be happening.*

The sobs deepened. "He said his car wouldn't start. He told me he needed to use the phone to call a tow truck. . . . He seemed so nice."

"Kitty, what happened?" But I knew what she would tell me.

The child stiffened. "He'll come back if I tell. He'll cut

me like he did that girl in the picture. I saw the knife. It was all bloody."

"He's not coming back. That was just to scare you."

Rapists aren't big on self-denial or delayed gratification. If the beast had an appetite for slashing, the child wouldn't be standing here now in more or less one piece.

"Why did I let him in? I'm so stupid."

She sank to the snowy tiles and buried her face in her hands. I sat beside her.

"The man did the bad thing, not you. Kitty, let me get you down from here, okay? Let me help you."

The crying stilled. There was a brittle silence. When the child broke it, her voice was barely stronger than the wind.

"He threw me on my bed. He stuck me with his—you know. I kept fighting. But I couldn't make him stop. I *couldn't*!"

I stroked her snarled hair. "I understand, sweetheart."

"He told me not to move, but I had to get away. I could hear him in Mommy's room, so I climbed out here."

"That was very brave."

"I thought he'd come after me, but he didn't. He kept calling me. Said, 'Come on. I have someplace special to take you.' I kept real quiet, and after awhile he stopped." She sobbed. "I feel so gross."

"You're not, Kitty. You're a beautiful girl. He's the gross one."

"I shouldn't have opened the door. It's my fault."

"You're not responsible for this, sweetheart. It's not your fault."

I slipped off my turnout coat and draped it across her shoulders. She looked so lost and tiny. A broken bird.

"Kitty," I said gently. "Let me take you down the ladder."

"Not with all those people. I don't want them to know."

"You can't stay up here forever." The snow had thickened, filling the sky like swirls of fog.

She considered awhile, then swiped at her eyes and

sighed. Tipping her head toward the roofline, she said, "My porch is down there."

Treading cautiously, I led the child to the edge. Kitty's mother kept calling her name. Clinging hard to the gutter, I lowered myself onto the wrought-iron chair perched on the terrace below. I helped Kitty down behind me, then hoisted her into the house through the open window.

Floral print paper covered her bedroom walls. The lacy lavender spread matched the pillow sham and dust ruffle. Tidy rows of costumed trolls and teddy bears lined the antique wicker desk and bureau. Children's books, CD's, and video game cartridges were shelved by size and category. Even the notes and mementoes tacked to her bulletin board were in rigid rows.

Everything looked equally clean and orderly as I led the frightened child downstairs. No soil, no clutter. I couldn't spot a crooked painting or a stray mark on the walls. Unfortunately, I knew too well the Dolans' world was about to get messier than they had ever imagined possible.

Opening the front door, I summoned Kitty's mother inside. By now, two other engine companies and several curious neighbors had gathered on the lawn. Wild Bill was strutting around, barking orders.

"Show's over, folks. Move along, now. Back to beddie-bye."

Mrs. Dolan looked dazed and disheveled. Copper hair escaped the bun at her neck. Spiders of smudged mascara rimmed her bloodshot hazel eyes. Her clothes were wet, and there was a ragged run in her hose. When she saw her daughter, what little was left of her control snapped.

"Kitty Dolan, what in the Lord's name has gotten into you? Have you lost your mind?"

"I'm sorry, Mommy." Kitty flinched at the fierceness in her mother's voice.

The woman seemed suddenly to remember I was standing there. She turned to me. "My husband's away on business. I was right down the street, playing bridge with some neighbors. When I got home a couple of hours ago, Kitty's bed was empty and the door to her porch was wide open. I called to her from the terrace, but she refused to answer. Then I climbed out there to try to get her down myself. Almost broke my neck doing it, but she wouldn't come in with me. She actually threatened to jump if I didn't leave her alone. To *jump*! Did you ever hear such craziness? Kitty, what on earth is the matter with you?"

"Don't be mad at me, Mommy. Please."

"Mad? You bet I am. What do you mean pulling a stunt like that? I have half a mind to—"

Edging closer, the child caught my hand. She clutched it like a lifeline.

I could think of no way to soften the blow. "Kitty was assaulted, Mrs. Dolan. Someone got into the house and molested her."

The words slowly sank through her careful facade. "What?"

"She survived. That's the important thing."

The woman's eyes widened with horror. "What are you talking about? That's impossible."

"You should take her to the Emergency Room," I urged. "They'll collect the necessary evidence and take care of her."

"What is she saying, Kitty? What did you do?"

"Your daughter didn't *do* anything, Mrs. Dolan. This *happened* to her."

"What's going on here, Kitty? I want the truth this instant!"

Whimpering, the little girl slumped on the couch and curled in on herself like a fading flower. I crouched in front of her and raised her chin so that her eyes met mine. "Stay here, Kitty. I need to talk to your mom alone a minute," I told her.

Grabbing an elbow, I steered the woman into the den and shut the door. "Kitty needs your love and support right now, Mrs. Dolan. She's been hurt. What she *doesn't* need is blame or guilt. This *wasn't* her fault. She's the *victim* here."

Stepping back, Mrs. Dolan brushed off the memory of my touch. "Look. I appreciate your getting her down, but I don't see that the rest of this is any of your business, Miss—"

"Finn. Lennie Finn. All that matters now is getting Kitty through this."

"I'll take care of my daughter," she huffed.

"That's what I'm afraid of."

"What's that supposed to mean?"

"The anger, the blame. If you're trying to twist the blade, you're doing a bang-up job."

She stiffened. Woman had finishing-school posture. Preppie arrogance as well. Minus the snow-soaked clothes and the scowl, she could have passed for an aging prom queen. She had a perfect manicure, salon highlights, and messy but unmistakably big-ticket duds. I couldn't help but wonder if this stiff, overprivileged person was capable of rescuing a wounded child from the sludge.

Without warning, the starch went out of her. She shook her head dully. "It's so unbelievable. She's just a baby. . . ."

"It's hard, I know."

"The Emergency Room, you said? Is that really necessary? We have an excellent pediatrician."

Patiently, I explained. In addition to saving important evidence, the child needed to be checked for possible physical damage or exposure to sexually transmitted disease. Emergency Room personnel would call in a volunteer from the Stamford Rape Crisis Center. Together, they were best equipped to offer the necessary tests, preventive medications, and supportive counseling.

"Kitty shouldn't change her clothes, wash, or bathe before she's examined, Mrs. Dolan. She'll probably want to, but you can't let her. It's important."

Her arrogance had utterly dissolved. Tears streaked the regal face. "How do you know all this?"

"EMS training is part of the job. Unfortunately, rape is not a rare emergency."

"But the hospital is so cold, so frightening. . . ."

"They'll take special care of her. I wish I could go with you, but I'm still on duty."

She dabbed her eyes with a monogrammed hankie. Damp mascara soiled the lace. "I'll take her."

"Good."

I checked my watch. More than half an hour had passed since I first hit the roof. Captain Perriman was likely hitting it himself by now. Not to mention Wild Bill, who had all the patience and understanding of a pit bull.

"I have to be going now, Mrs. Dolan. If there's anything I can do to help, please call." I gave her my number at the station house and the one at home as well.

"Kitty *can* get over this. I want you to know that."

Mrs. Dolan stared at me bleakly. She said nothing.

The child was sitting precisely where we'd left her. Once again, I squatted down in front of her.

"I have to leave now, sweetheart. Take care."

"You really *have* to?"

"I do, Kitty. My shift's not over. I'll check later to see how you're doing. Okay?"

She dipped her eyes. The child looked so worn and defeated, as if an inner candle had burned out.

Seeing her that way filled me with fury. The animal who did this had to be tracked and punished. He had to pay for hurting this little girl, for stealing her trust and her innocence.

With the right help and support, Kitty Dolan could heal, in time. But the monstrous events of this night would change her forever. The course of her life had been shifted irrevocably. She'd be forced to weather terrible storms on the choppy sea to recovery.

With gruesome clarity, I felt the child's pain. I could not mute or deny the facts. When I was close to Kitty's age, the same thing had happened to me.

Chapter 3

LENNIE

I'd set out that night to trap an angel.

A year had passed since my mother's death. A year since the sparse remains of my family gathered at a graveside to lower my mother's body into the ground. Her plot was beside my father's, who'd died three months earlier of a heart attack.

Officially, my mother's life had ended by reason of asphyxiation. She'd left our Buick station wagon running in the closed garage. When I came home from school that day, I found her splayed on the seat. Her face was chalk pale, her lips the color of a fading bruise. Her head lolled at a peculiar angle that caused my neck to ache in useless empathy.

Otherwise, she looked more peaceful than she had since Daddy's death. Her fingers were fanned, her dark hair spread in a lacy halo. A sly grin languished on her lips, as if the last thing she'd heard was a naughty secret.

No note was found, so the coroner chose to call it accidental. That finding suited me far better than the unthinkable alternative. Since Daddy's death, my mother had been drifting along, aimless and uncertain as a paper boat on a pond. Sometimes, she failed to hear me when I spoke. Some nights, she completely forgot about dinner or the baby's bath or my bedtime, all of which she'd previously observed with near-religious zeal. So it made sense that she'd somehow overlooked the danger and the fumes of a running engine in a closed garage. I pictured her deep in thought as her lungs absorbed the lethal poisons. In my heart, I could not believe she'd left us on purpose. I was sure she loved us far too much for that.

A year later, the smallest details of her burial still lingered in my memory. I could smell the loamy richness of the fresh-turned earth. Still feel the places where last year's too-tight Sunday dress nipped my waist and budding bosom. My ears rang with the jarring creak of the lowering pulley. The strike of dislodged stones against the coffin lid. Father Cleary's stooped presence and somber voice resounded in my mind: *Yea, though I walk through the valley of the shadow of death, I will fear no evil. . . .*

Afterward, the mourners straggled back to our house in Peoria, Illinois. Volunteer ladies from the church had set the dining table with platters of sliced beef and turkey, baskets of rolls, and mounds of freshly baked cookies. The men heaped their plates and wandered into the living room, where they indulged in whiskey shots and greedy helpings of selfish relief. Thankfully, Mary and Dennis Finn were the dead ones, not them. They could still enjoy their sandwiches and sweets, their liquor buzz, the rest of their seemingly unlimited lives.

I wandered among them, tugging my baby brother along like a pull toy, trying to ignore their pitying looks and hushed whispers.

"What'll become of the kids?"

"I suppose they'll go live with Mary's sister."

"That humorless snoot from Connecticut?"

"Seems she's all they've got, poor things. . . ."

A full year later, I refused to accept the impossible fact of my mother's death. With my father, it had been easier somehow. Certainly, I'd grieved. Cried myself dry and empty. But Daddy was a traveling salesman, Midwest rep for several lines of children's shoes and sneakers. He'd always been gone more than not. After the heart attack took him, I could easily pretend he was off calling on customers. Showing samples. Telling shoe jokes. Making deals.

Father Plunkett, pastor of the Westport, Connecticut, church we'd attended since coming from Illinois to live with Aunt Selia, swore that my mother's soul was still intact. Her spirit lived, the priest declared; it was readily available to comfort those of us who'd been left behind.

Hanging around after mass every Sunday, I pestered the portly priest for specifics. Were there special words I could use to summon Mother's soul? How would I recognize her spirit when it finally turned up? Most critically, how could I make sure Mom knew that her sister Selia had moved from her condominium in Norwalk to the prim three-bedroom Colonial we now occupied on Westport's Larkspur Lane? Was there some celestial change-of-address form?

Despite my gnatlike persistence, Father Plunkett refused to provide hard answers. Cradling his giant belly like a beachball, he stuck to his standard line about faith, patience, and the power of prayer.

For a time, I tried to play the game by his particular rules. I believed. I waited. I shamelessly implored. Though it felt strange to do so alone, not to mention on weekdays, I sang psalms and read endless Bible passages.

When all else failed, I offered truly enticing deals to the Devil. My soul. My soul and my skateboard. Soul, skateboard, the autographed Mickey Mantle rookie card bestowed upon me by my dad. Each day, I upped the ante, finally tossing in my prized baseball mitt, which was both seasoned to perfection and positively brimming with good luck.

What self-respecting demon could resist?

But nothing worked. After one final fruitless discussion with the priest, I concluded that I simply had to strike out in an entirely fresh direction.

All week, I slept fitfully. Awake in the dark, heart thumping, I agonized. What would be the most effective way to summon my mother's soul?

My loneliness aside, Mom simply must come back for my brother's sake. His name was Hubert Jamieson Arthur Eamonn Finn, which was far too large a mouthful for a boy of any size. Given our surname, someone had dubbed him Huck shortly after his christening. It stuck.

Fair and freckled with fine cinnamon hair, my little brother Huck was an achingly beautiful child. But puzzling. He was too good. Too still and silent. Mother often tried to engage him with songs and funny faces. Then, she'd wait expectantly for a smile or a gurgle. When none came, she'd shrug, pretending not to worry. "Seems the boy's away with the fairies," she'd tell me, smiling.

At the time, I fully accepted that comforting explanation. Until our mother died, I considered my baby brother the perfect plaything: adorable and amusing. For ten long years, I'd waited for a sibling. Politely requested one on every Christmas list.

When Huck finally arrived, he matched my imagined ideal. He made few demands. Rarely cried. Best of all, he allowed me to do whatever I wished with him. I could comb his silken hair, dress him in an endless array of costumes, place him in whatever pose or setting that struck my fickle fancy. Compared to other infants I'd observed, squalling and opinionated, Huck was a dream. I didn't care to consider that my compliant human doll might be defective.

But since Mother's death, Huck's behavior had deteriorated undeniably. Except for me, to whom he sometimes clung like a Chinese finger puzzle, my brother vehemently shied from people. He rarely talked, and when he did, I always wondered if he'd actually spoken or somehow planted his thoughts directly in my mind. His voice, as I heard it, was improbably manly and firm. And it had a strange, rusty quality, like the door to a long abandoned house.

But his speech, or lack of it, was far from the most disturbing thing. At times, for no apparent reason, Huck erupted in fits of furious shrieking. And lately, he'd taken to biting at the back of his little fist. My heart hurt from the sight of it, swollen and raw.

Huck was drifting away like a kite with a broken string. If I didn't find some way to stop him, I was terrified that he would soon be beyond my reach permanently.

My brother's peculiarities baffled and offended Aunt Selia. She had taken us in out of duty, not choice. My mother's sister had no knack for parenting and absolutely no interest in doing so. In her cool, distant way, I suppose she loved us. But children, even the standard kind, were noisy and messy. Unpredictable. Underfoot.

Selia would have preferred to ignore Huck's problems. Her practice was to store troublesome or unsightly things in the backs of cabinets or closets. She seemed to believe my brother's oddities could be similarly willed out of sight and mind.

But six months earlier, worn down by my fretful nagging, she'd had Huck examined by a specialist recommended by some friend of a friend twice removed. The doctor's fees were huge and we had to wait weeks for an appointment. To Selia, that meant the man's word was gold. She readily accepted his glib assurances that Huck would grow out of it, though "it" was never identified. Afterward, my aunt refused to discuss the matter further. Which left me with no choice but to tend to it myself.

Clearly, what Huck needed was our real mother, back as she used to be when Daddy was alive. I could still recall her comforting presence then. The musical lilt of her voice. Her laughing eyes. Her solid hips and firm square shoulders. The smell of the house at suppertime, thick and spicy and warm.

Even in spectral form, I was positive that Mary Finn could mother rings around her sister. Selia's nurturing instincts were limited to orchid plants and the Friends of the Philharmonic. My aunt meant well, but everyone knew which road was paved with good intentions. Each morning, when I took Huck downstairs for breakfast, she'd blink at us, as if we were scraps of foreign matter that had landed in her eye.

Our mother's return was the obvious solution. And conditions that night seemed ideal. The moon was plump and radiant. A brief afternoon downpour had polished the sky and planted a trail of puddles on the walk. Aunt Selia, dressed in a ruffly dinner suit and high heels, had left early to meet a friend in Manhattan for an evening of fine food, sensible conversation, and a show. She'd left me in charge with a businesslike list of instructions. With an air kiss and a look of anticipated relief, she strode outside and smacked the door shut behind her.

Dinner was the leftover cassoulet in the oven. Selia neither understood nor approved of child's food. I forced a few bites of mushy beans and mystery meat. If excitement hadn't squelched my appetite, the dish would have done the job. Knowing Huck would have no part of the pungent stew, I carved a chunk of cheddar cheese into precise cubes and arranged them inside a ring of Ritz crackers.

Huck liked his food symmetrical. He ate it precisely, too: cheese, cracker, cracker, cheese. Watching him eat was mesmerizing. Each bite was chewed six times and swallowed with a nod, like a poem.

Anxious to begin, I hurried Huck into his pajamas and read him an abridged version of *Green Eggs and Ham*. He wasn't listening anyway. Something invisible on the wall had captured his rapt attention.

"Night, Pumpkin."

I kissed his downy forehead and pulled the covers to his chin. Huck's sea-blue eyes remained riveted to the wall. He did not look sleepy.

Padding softly, I opened our closet door. My mother's old suitcase was on the floor at the back behind my soccer cleats. I pulled it out carefully. The mock leather trim was cracked and peeling, the embossed initials too worn to read.

But to me, the case was priceless. It contained everything I had left of my parents, except the memories.

After Mother's death, Aunt Selia had boxed up most of my parents' things and donated them to Goodwill. She'd set aside only a few mementoes for Huck and me. There was my father's Bulova watch, a brown leather wallet, and a dollar-shaped silver money clip engraved with his initials. I had my mother's gold wedding band, her cameo pin, and the azure lace hanky that had served as both the something old and the something blue at our parents' wedding. In addition, the suitcase contained a Bible, packets of soppy letters Daddy wrote to Mom when he was away in the army, and a pile of snapshots.

For bait, I chose Mom's ring, the corniest of Daddy's love letters, and a rare picture of Huck smiling. Gathering them quickly, I slipped out of our bedroom.

In the living room, I paused to put my mother's favorite song on the stereo. Stepping into that hallowed space took considerable courage. The living room in Aunt Selia's house was for anything but. Weekly, my aunt entered to renew the vacuum tracks and chase away the dust. Otherwise, everyone kept out, as if the room housed bats and vipers instead of ugly furniture.

Crocheted antimacassars protected the backs and arms of the sour green sofa and chairs, though no one ever sat on them. The knickknacks were arranged with geometric precision, though they were to be admired only from afar. The expensive stereo component system had never, in my experience, been used. Breath held, I pressed the power button and watched the arm approach the record in a tentative caress.

The music swelled, and a husky woman's voice crooned the familiar words. *More than you know——* I could hear my mother humming along in her soft, throaty way.

According to Aunt Selia's typed list of instructions, letting anyone or anything into or out of the house in her absence was strictly forbidden. That rule was sandwiched between the strict ban on dabbling with her cosmetics and the one about extremely limited viewing of educational TV programs *only*. (Fortunately, the definition of "educational" was left to my impeccable discretion.)

Ignoring a twinge of guilt, I ventured outside in my nightie. Listening intently to the music from within, I placed my angel bait midway between two shimmering puddles. The picture of Huck was reflected in the second moonlit pool. His image shone and wavered like a beckoning finger.

Irresistible.

Dear God, I closed my eyes and prayed my hardest, *please send our mother. Huck* really, really *needs her.* Then, from the darkened living room, I stood and watched in breathless silence.

For almost an hour, nothing happened. Hopelessness was setting in when the cluster of fireflies appeared. The lightening bug in the center was twice as bright as the others and abnormally large. But its size was not the sole giveaway. As the giant bug fluttered and danced, I caught the clear rhythm of my mother's favorite tune: *More than you kno-ow.*

Overjoyed, I raced outside carting the empty applesauce jar I'd readied for the occasion. I'd washed it six times, dried every bead of moisture, and poked plenty of breathing holes in the lid with Aunt Selia's tweezers. Fortunately, there was no rule on Selia's list about *wielding* her cosmetics.

On my first try, one of the smaller fireflies followed the angel into the jar. Attempting to free the extra bug, I accidentally released the spirit as well. For the next five minutes, I desperately chased the bright specter. But it kept flitting beyond my reach.

My feet were soaked, my hopes darkening. The bug's cruel teasing forced me to consider that I might have attracted the wrong angel by mistake. Likely there were countless dead women who'd had slim gold wedding bands, romantic soldier boyfriends, and smiling blue-eyed baby sons.

Forcing myself to be still, I waited for the firefly to settle down and approach me. When I was aching with despair, it finally did, hovering directly in front of my face. Slowly, I moved the jar in place beside it, and the luminous bug flew inside. Bursting with delight, I slapped the lid over the jar's mouth and screwed it tightly shut.

With enormous care, I ferried my prize inside, terrified I might drop the jar and harm the precious angel. Everything would be all right, now. Mother's spirit could do anything. Free me from my cloak of sorrow, cut Huck out of his stifling cocoon.

Suddenly, fearsome sounds split the air behind me. Low pulse of running feet. Jarring splash. Angry grunt.

Before I could set the angel down, steel arms clutched me from behind. Hot breaths stabbed my neck. My head filled with a peculiar smell: a mix of wood and chemicals.

Fiercely, clinging to the jar which held my precious angel, I struggled against the might and the fear. I wrenched and twisted. Tried to bite. But the intruder twisted easily out of reach. His grip was crushing. A burning cramp gripped my fingers, and the jar dropped to the floor.

My heart and will shattered along with the wretched sound of the breaking glass. Limply, I yielded to the terror. Rode it like a huge black wave to the other, distant side. The fear carried me to forbidding places, to hideous truths and questions I could never have fathomed on my own.

I did not come fully out of it for years.

The Road to Redemption

by Patterson Graham, Ph.D.

(Advance Reading Copy)

The sadistic rapist suffers from a learned fusion of pain and pleasure. At the Cambridge Center, examining the etiology of this sensual confusion is a critical step in the curative process.

John

Mother said she was doing it to ease my soreness. She'd start rubbing my scalp and slowly work downward. Out along my neck and shoulders. Over my arms to the fingertips. Along my back in lazy sweeps radiating from my spine. Farther. Deeper.

Her hands were indescribable. Electric velvet. I got hard the second she started. Sometimes before, from the mere anticipation. I remember kneeling at the side of my bed, asking God for new skates or whatever, and suddenly my little prick would spring to attention.

She always acted surprised when she got to it. Surprised and a little concerned. "Does that hurt you, darlin'? Did that mean old Daddy hit you on your wee-wee, too?"

By then, I couldn't have answered if I'd tried. My mind was bristling with expectation. I could barely breathe.

"Want Momma to rub it for you, sweetheart? There, now. Momma'll make it all better."

I understand now how that screwed up my mind. Made me mix up pain with pleasure so I got turned on by taking that little girl. Forcing her.

Understanding is the key. The way out. All you have to do is take it.

Chapter 4

LENNIE

News of my questionable heroics at the Dolan house spread through the station house like brushfire in a drought.

Shortly before the morning shift change, I slogged out of my cot. When we weren't out on call, everyone on night duty slept in a large room cut in cubicles.

I thought of it as a hive for idle worker bees. As the only female drone, my space was discreetly segregated from the others by a curtain. I had a separate toilet and shower stall, too. The arrangement provided tolerable privacy, but absolutely no sting protection.

I plodded down to the second-floor company kitchen. All I craved was the morning paper and a quiet cup of coffee. Instead, I was greeted by a dozen smirking faces and a chorus of meows.

A heaping bowl of cat food awaited me on the table. A ten-pound bag of kitty litter occupied my customary seat. My crudely sketched likeness was posted on the bulletin board. I took in the short brown hair, the trusting eyes, the crooked nose, and chipped front tooth. The breasts were the size of Alaska. Across them, someone had scrawled: CATWOMAN.

Next to smoke inhalation, nicknames are the clearest hazard of my chosen profession. Some, like Zulu, are meaningless variations of the person's name. Others reflect physical characteristics, as in the case of "Dumbo" Makowski and "Six Fingers" Bartell. Personality traits account for many of the rest, hence "Wuss" Elliot, "Studs" McElroy, and "Nervy" Carlone. Hitsig had earned his handle by regularly soaking himself in alcohol and imitating a wild bore.

Until now, I'd managed to escape the branding iron. But my alleged feline rescue was shaping up as a signature event. Silencing my childish colleagues certainly wasn't worth a breech of young Kitty Dolan's confidence. Determined to ignore them, I tossed the litter sack off the chair, sat, and buried my disjointed nose in the *Times*.

"What's wrong, Finn?" Nervy smirked. "Not your brand?"

Hitsig snorted. "Catwoman looks a little peeved, don't you think, boys? Maybe she's got herself a fur ball."

I didn't respond. If they failed to raise my dander (so to speak), they'd weary of the joke sooner. Besides, I was in no mood for games. My thoughts kept shifting to Kitty Dolan and what the poor kid was probably going through.

Chances were she was still at the hospital. Evidence collection and medical tests after a rape took forever, especially when the victim was a child. My rookie class on the squad had been walked through the standard procedures during our short-form EMS course. I'd learned more about the grueling process during the past year, after signing on to train for the company's Rescue unit. Vividly, I now pictured the little girl in a paper robe, splayed on her back like a helpless turtle.

Before each step in the legally mandated routine, a rape crisis volunteer would explain what was about to happen and carefully solicit the patient's consent. Rape is a hideous violation, an outright theft of the victim's self and dignity. Anyone with half a brain or a gram of sensitivity would try to avoid compounding the felony on the examining table.

Hitsig helped himself to a doughnut from the box beside

the coffee urn. Eyeing the bowl of cat food, he smirked. "What's wrong, Finn? Not hungry?"

"Cute, Hitsig."

"No, really. If you'd like, I'd be glad to order you up a mouseburger."

Almost everyone found that hilarious.

Larry "Red" Snapper, a charming sweetheart I dearly loved as a friend, gallantly rose to my defense. "Enough, you jerks. Joke's over."

"Not true, Red. The joke's still sitting right there," Hitsig retorted.

Red's boyish face tensed. As he set his jaw, a shock of ginger hair lolled over his forehead. "Shut up, Hitsig."

"You gonna make me?"

That was my signal to depart. I scooped up my coffee mug and got to my feet. As I left the kitchen, Red passed me a silent vote of support. His emerald eyes beamed empathy. I winked in grateful acceptance. Red was a perfect gem, no question. He knew exactly when to back me up and when backing off was more in order.

Purrs and catcalls followed me out to my car, a small white Toyota with a big attitude problem. I'd bought the crate six months ago at one of those government sales, where they auction vehicles impounded in drug deals and other crimes. It had cost next to nothing, and was worth every penny. For what I'd shelled out since on an endless string of minor repairs, I could have picked up the next lot on the block instead, a sweet little '65 red Mustang convertible. That auto was fully loaded. No extra charge for the bullet holes or bloodstains.

Sliding behind the Toyota's wheel, I nudged the cranky engine awake. My back and rump ached from the collision with the Dolans' roof. My head-on with Kitty's horror had kept me up and tossing for the remainder of the night.

I'd always kept my own rape a secret. If Aunt Selia found out, I knew she'd ship Huck and me off to some Dickensian orphanage. I'd broken my aunt's sacred rules. Brought the filth and horror on myself. I had to cover it up, to bury the nightmare under slabs of self-deceit and denial.

Time had blunted the pain. Mountains of time had dimmed the repulsive memory. As an adolescent, I'd acted out in what I later learned were painfully predictable ways. But for many years, aside from my morbid fascination with facts and stories about sex crimes, I'd considered myself pretty much over it.

Now Kitty's rooftop confession had brought the memory crashing down on me again. Once again, I was that foolish twelve-year-old, obsessed with my aching loneliness and the magical means I'd hit upon to cure it.

Finally, I'd captured the angel. In the darkened hall, my mother's soul flickered and glowed. My own spirit soared. Everything was going to be all right. Mother would fix whatever was wrong with Huck. Afterward, she'd patch my broken heart with her neat, invisible stitches.

Those were my thoughts one instant. The next, I was locked in the intruder's unbreakable grasp. Vicious arms squeezed my breath away and carried me to my room. Cruel force pinned me to the bed, mashing my cheek against the pillow. I felt the engulfing terror.

Struggling, I tried to turn and get a look at him. But I couldn't get past the sight of my baby brother's pale eyes, wide and unblinking. In the crib beside my bed Huck lay still as a forest creature in the night. Trapped by wonder and fear.

His frozen gaze gripped me hard. Before I was able to break free of it, my assailant wrenched loose the top sheet and stretched it tightly over my head. The air went dark and musty. I resisted the urge to scream. If Huck heard my terror and cried out, the faceless beast might hurt him, too.

Later, when my attacker was long gone, I lifted Huck from his crib and carried him to the chair. Humming, my cheeks wet with tears, I rocked him until his face went slack and his eyelids fluttered down like falling leaves. Such rabid evil couldn't possibly exist in the same world as this beautiful little boy. If I erased all physical traces, the horrible truth might simply cease to be.

Put it away, Lennie.

Hours later, I settled Huck in his crib and tiptoed downstairs. With a wad of paper toweling, I scrubbed away the trail of muddy footprints. The monster's tracks were nearly double the size of mine. At the center of the room, my footprints suddenly dissolved. That had to be where he'd caught me. My stomach lurched, remembering his inhuman grip, my useless struggles. The solid floor beneath me evaporating.

Put it all away.

Gingerly, I collected the shards of shattered glass and deposited them in the trash barrel outside the kitchen door. Venturing into the night again, even a single step, froze me in panic. Anything could be lurking there.

Anyone.

Breathless, I double-locked the door and slipped home the security chain. Then, I searched in vain for the lost angel. No sign of the spirit in the hall. Peering out through the dining-room window, my heart sank. The ring of fireflies had vanished. The sky looked glum as tarnished silver. Dense clouds had swallowed the moon.

Steeling myself, I raced outside once more to retrieve my angel bait. Everything was ruined. A muddy heel print marred Huck's smiling photo. My father's love letter was soaked, the ink blurred and dripping like cold, dark tears. Mother's ring was unharmed, but its shine seemed dulled somehow. Beside it on the walk, I spotted a gleam of red glass. A ruby, I thought. I picked it up carefully, pinching it by the roughened edges. Bloody remnant of my attack. I could not bear to look at it.

I soaked in the tub until the water cooled and my fingertips were blanched and wrinkled. Dried, I dressed in fresh pajamas and a robe. That done, I hid away the broken stone and my angel bait.

Put it away, Lennie. Put the whole thing far, far away.

Fogged by exhaustion, I forced myself to stay awake until everything looked normal enough to fool my aunt. Amazingly, on the surface, even I appeared unchanged.

Driving away from the station house now, I yawned broadly. Reliving Kitty Dolan's vicious assault and my own had left me dragging. I longed for a long, hot shower and a nap. Home beckoned.

But five minutes later, I found myself angling the Toyota into a narrow space behind Stamford Hospital's Emergency Room. Until I knew how Kitty was doing, I wouldn't be able to rest.

I managed to talk my way past the wall-eyed security guard at reception. Down the hall, Mrs. Dolan stood locked in heated discussion with bespectacled woman in a gray sweater set and pleated skirt. I waved, but they didn't see me.

I found Kitty seated alone in one of the curtained examining cubicles. The child was dressed in baggy corduroy pants and a homely plaid flannel shirt. Probably hospital issue, I thought. Her nightgown would have been claimed for evidence. So had the bodily fluids, scrapings, and samples sealed in the rape kit on the counter.

If her rapist had left behind any blood, hair, or semen, DNA profiling could help positively identify and convict him. The process was supposed to be as reliable as fingerprinting, maybe more so.

"Hey, champ."

She winced, but forced a small, brave smile. "Lennie, hi."

"How's it going?"

The terror in her eyes pinched my heart. "Now they want me to go look at some dumb pictures."

"That's important. You may be able to pick out the man who hurt you."

Her lip quivered. "Why can't I just go home?"

"Soon, sweetheart."

"But I'm tired." The child looked so mournful, I wanted to cry.

The two women returned. Kitty's mother had pieced herself back together artfully. Impeccable hair-do, beige designer sweat suit, brown cashmere swing coat, ballet slippers by Chanel.

Mrs. Dolan introduced me to the woman in the sweater set and pleated skirt. She was Cynthia Hebert, a volunteer from the rape crisis center. Behind fat-lensed silver glasses, the woman's green eyes swam like fish in a bowl. Her voice reminded me of whipped potatoes, smooth and reassuring.

"Kitty tells me you talked her down from the roof, Ms. Finn. She's very impressed with you."

"I didn't know they had lady firemen," Kitty said reverently.

I smiled at her. "There aren't many."

"Do you really go into burning buildings and everything?"

"Sometimes."

"That's cool. I think I'll be a fireman when I grow up."

"Time to go look at those pictures now, Kitty," Cynthia Hebert crooned.

"I want Lennie to come. Could you? Please?"

As I agreed, a storm cloud crossed the volunteer's amiable expression. Ignoring it, I took the small hand Kitty offered. We followed Mrs. Dolan and the volunteer outside. Kitty rode with her mother, and I trailed their tiny caravan to police headquarters.

The building was a two-story brick-and-block contemporary, lined with a claustrophobic row of slim, dark windows. Beside the entrance, Old Glory fluttered on the frigid wind.

The precinct staff had been alerted. A balding clerk quickly escorted us past the throng of waiting people and the bulletin boards crammed with notices and wanted posters. Our destination was a small interrogation room at the building's rear.

An unnecessarily handsome sergeant named Harry Kresky had been placed in charge of Kitty's case. His eyes were midnight blue, his dark hair dense and wavy. Worn jeans, a white cotton turtleneck, and a forest green crewneck showcased a gym-toned physique. Kresky greeted us with a terse nod, not bothering with introductions. Getting right to business, he installed Kitty at the head of a broad folding table capped with wood-patterned veneer. He excused himself and returned almost immediately with three thick albums crammed with mug shots.

Kitty's description of her assailant hadn't done much to narrow the field. White male. Average build. She described him as tall, about her father's height, which was six one. A low-slung cap with a broad bill had cast the rapist's face in shadow, leaving her unsure of his age or other distinguishing features. So far, shock had obliterated any further details. Kitty remembered only the man's awful threats. She said he spoke very slowly, but otherwise, nothing seemed odd or special about the voice. No distinguishing marks or scars on his face or body. Nothing distinctive about his clothing other than the cap, which was dark, had a larger than normal bill, and bore no insignia.

Any attempts Kresky made to prod the child's memory pushed her perilously close to the edge. Kitty was white-faced, having trouble handling the gentlest questions. The attack was still too raw and painful.

Kresky now hoped that Kitty might respond better to a picture. As the sergeant explained, all the men in these particular volumes were known Caucasian sex offenders residing in the area. Their sheer number was staggering. Add the unknowns and unreporteds, and it seemed miraculous that anyone managed to make it through a given day unscathed by sexual violence.

As Kitty opened the first book of mug shots, Sergeant Kresky ordered the rest of us to wait in the hall. He didn't want the child's perceptions colored by chance gestures or remarks.

I bit back a sarcastic response. I suspected that Kresky's presence might have a more profound effect on Kitty than anything we might say or do. Surely, under the circumstances, assigning a female officer made much more sense to me. But Kitty seemed perfectly comfortable in the company of handsome Harry.

Outside, her mother aimed directly for the pay phone. The crisis center volunteer fixed me with a kindly smile. The grin didn't falter as she kindly told me off.

"It's nice of you to be so concerned, Ms. Finn. But managing a child in Kitty's situation takes special training."

I bristled at her officious tone and the ridiculous implication. Picking up stray victims was hardly my notion of a good time. "I'm not here to *manage* anyone, Ms. Hebert. All I want to do is offer Kitty my support."

"I'm sure you do. But this is an extremely sensitive time for the child. She's highly vulnerable right now."

"I know that."

"Fine." She checked her watch. "I have to be going. Someone else from the agency will be assigned to Kitty's follow-up. It's a way to avoid *inappropriate* attachments. Good-bye, Ms. Finn. Take care."

I held my tongue as she ambled down the hall. Ms. Hebert had completed her "special training," and I'd had mine. *I've been there,* I ached to tell her. *I don't need you to tell me how it feels.*

A uniformed pair approached the interrogation room. Both men were pushing six feet tall. One had a moon face and the apple-cheeked complexion of an altar boy. The other swaggered. His practiced sneer reminded me of the old saw about avoiding nasty expressions. *Your face might freeze that way,* I was tempted to say.

"Kresky in there?" he snarled in my direction.

"Yes, but he's busy with a witness."

The sneer busted in anyway. His partner shot me an apologetic smile and followed. Before the door closed, I heard

Kresky introduce the two cops to Kitty. Their names were Garraty and Schmidt.

Feeling stiff and sore, I decided to walk around to ease the kinks. Nearing the end of the corridor, I was stalled by the sound of Mrs. Dolan on the phone around the corner. Her voice was muted, but I caught the angry gist.

"I was *not* checking up on you, Mark. I just thought you might be interested to hear that while you were out of town screwing your bimbo of the day, somebody molested your daughter."

Her tone squeezed tighter. "*I* was playing bridge, Mark. What—or should I say *who*—were *you* doing all night?"

I hastily retreated out of earshot. From the sound of things, the woman had her manicured hands more than full. Unfortunately, so did Kitty. Her rape seemed destined to bring the festering boil of her parents' marriage to a head.

Lousy timing.

Heading back toward the interrogation room, I sat on the bench in the hallway and flipped through my appointment book. As I did, the two uniformed cops emerged. Smooth Cheeks smiled meekly. The Sneer loped off without so much as a glance in my direction. He left behind the stench of someone with an allergy to soap and bathwater.

No wonder the face.

My schedule at the firehouse was straightforward. Normally, I was assigned to work three ten-hour day shifts followed by three fourteen-hour night shifts after which I had three days off. This week, I'd switched one night with Six Fingers, who wanted to attend his daughter's school play, and one day with Nervy, who was scheduled to have a root canal and a lube job, though not necessarily together. I was also on call to substitute for Vito Antinori should his wife finally decide to give birth. The woman was in her tenth or eleventh month, or so it seemed. Vito wasn't surprised or concerned. He claimed she always overcooked things.

Even with all the changes, the rotation left me ample time for moonlighting, which I did with a vengeance. With part of the proceeds, I made tiny weekly deposits to my dream fund. The dream was to buy a house of my own someday. Huck's needs, which were expensive, put the someday further off. But I kept assuring myself that I was getting closer. Recently, I'd taken to scanning the Sunday real estate section, familiarizing myself with the standard lingo and abbreviations. That much I could afford.

My brother's tuition at Bridgeport's Whitechapel School is astronomical. Before he turned twenty-one, federal law had forced our local school district to foot the bill. Five years ago, when Huck aged out of the system, his social worker suggested placement in a state-run group home. By her cheery description, he'd be living with a suitable peer group. The house was clean and well-supervised, she claimed, the clients continually instructed in independent living skills and engaged in meaningful work. Huck was ready for the change, the social worker glibly asserted. The whole thing sounded too good to be true. Predictably, it turned out not to be.

When I visited Huck after his first week at the Greenmeadow House in New Haven, he was upset and disoriented. The social worker blithely assured me he was going through a normal adjustment period.

By the following week, Huck could have qualified for emergency disaster relief. The back of his fist, which he'd ceased biting years earlier, had the look of steak tartare. He'd lost five pounds and several dozen yards of hard-won progress. I packed his things and got him the hell out of there. As soon as we exited the circular driveway, Huck's face lit up, as if I'd pulled a vexing thorn out of his paw.

I researched it and discovered that a variety of government programs would fund most of the weighty cost of Whitechapel. Compared to watching my brother's precipitous downslide in the group home, paying the rest seemed a breeze.

I love Huck with all my heart, though at times I've guiltily wished he would disappear in some quiet, nonviolent way. His life holds so much pain and frustration. His place in the world seems so small and tenuous. Worst of all, his future has always posed so many more questions than answers. Will he ever find personal peace? Where can he go when Whitechapel ceases raising their upper age limit to accommodate his mounting collection of birthdays? Who will care for and about him when I was gone?

At age five, after countless false leads and empty professional promises, Huck had been tested for autism. He'd passed with flying colors. In addition to the troubles he had communicating with and relating to people, his condition made it brutally hard for my brother to adapt to new situations.

For Huck, sameness was comfort. Anything strange or unexpected posed an intolerable threat. His face crumpled in horror; his shoulders hunched into the terrified posture of a passenger on a crash-bound plane. Normal reassurances had no power to soothe him. Words couldn't begin to penetrate the steel shell swaddling his soul.

I found it hideously unfair that my brother lacked the normal tools of human warfare. He had no meanness or sarcasm. He was incapable of scheming or subterfuge. He didn't even know how to curse his fates or rail at his oppressors.

The world isn't designed for anyone that innocent and pure. People like my brother are fun-house mirrors. In their wide, wondering eyes, you can't help but see your own ugliness. Some people react with rude stares or vicious comments. Most choose to simply look away.

Safely back at Whitechapel, where Huck had lived since he was five, he slowly regained the lost ground and started inching ahead again. The Whitechapel staff is caring and creative. They constantly seek new ways to get through to Huck, though the process is a lot like digging for oil with a spoon. My not-so-secret wish has always been that someday they might help my brother find a meaningful way to communicate. Part of the house dream is hanging out with

Huck there on holidays and weekends. Just shooting the breeze with my kid brother.

The door to the interrogation room opened; Sergeant Kresky's unfair face reappeared. "Kitty's doing a great job, but she's had enough for now, Mrs. Dolan. Why don't you take her home and bring her back after she's had some rest?"

"I'm Lennie Finn. Mrs. Dolan's making a phone call."

His mistake was understandable. Kitty's slim form and dark-on-pale coloring echoed mine. Swallowing a hard lump of feeling, I thought of all this happening to my own little girl.

The child appeared behind him. I smiled at her.

"Hi, Kitty. Ready to go?"

She dipped her eyes. "Where's Mommy?" she said softly.

"She's on the phone, Kitty. I'll take you to her. Have a minute, Sergeant? I'd like to speak to you."

"Sure. I'll wait here."

When I returned, the cop eyed me quizzically, then grinned. "Finn, you said? Thought you looked familiar. We met over a ground ball in last year's town league season opener. Ring a bell?"

As it did, I felt the hot flush rising. The Stamford Fire Department had been playing the Stamford P.D. I was covering first base. The score was tied at six all. Bottom of the ninth, bases loaded, two out. Harry Kresky was batting cleanup. On a full count, he grazed the corner of a low, inside pitch and sent it skipping along the baseline like a jumping bean. In my single-minded zeal to snag the thing and tag up, I accidentally kneed Sergeant Kresky in the groin.

Naturally, my infantile teammates were ecstatic. They believed in victory at any cost, especially when they weren't paying. By the time I managed to escape the frenzy of back-slapping and congratulations, the man I'd injured had ceased his agonized writhing and was gone.

"Sorry," I murmured belatedly.

His grin broadened. "It's okay. I've recovered. More or less."

"I honestly meant to call and see how you were doing—"

"It's never too late."

I've always been wary of excessively attractive men. Actually, I'm wary of most men. But in my experience, the pretty ones are the worst. They tend to be full of themselves and other things. Sergeant Kresky probably collected broken hearts for the sheer acquisitive joy of it. No way was I about to be lured to his crowded trophy room. Anyway, I was currently almost on the cusp of considering a possible relationship with someone else.

Though, maybe not.

My voice turned businesslike. "I wanted to ask how quickly you thought you'd be able to run down Kitty's rapist, Sergeant."

His grin faded. "As fast as we can."

"How long do these things *usually* take, I mean? A day, a week, a year?"

"Impossible to say. We'll do our best, Ms. Finn. That much, I can promise you."

The gnawing inside me was like an unscratchable itch. "How do you go about investigating a crime like this?" I demanded.

He sighed, and his midnight blue eyes hardened at my tone. "In a nutshell, we'll search the scene for prints and trace evidence. Send out any forensic traces for evaluation, hopefully get a DNA profile. We'll try to expand Kitty's description of the perp through a variety of standard procedures and match it to known offenders in the area. We'll interview neighbors. Look for other witnesses. The works."

"What if none of the works works?"

"We'll jump off that bridge when we come to i., Ms. Finn." His voice was flat.

I forced a long, slow breath. "Sorry. I don't mean to be difficult."

"Then, don't be," he said with a plastic smile. "Try to re-lax, OK?"

"Oh, I will, Sergeant. I'll be nice and relaxed as soon as you put the animal who hurt Kitty where he belongs."

"So will we all," Kresky said.

There was nothing more I could do here. I turned away. "See you, Sergeant."

"Yes, Ms. Finn. I'm afraid that's true," I heard Kresky say as I strode away.

Chapter 5

LENNIE

Dying for sleep, I drove directly home. My place is in New Canaan, fifteen minutes and a millennium removed from downtown Stamford's urban angst.

New Canaan is a picture-postcard New England hamlet. Despite its sprawling land mass, the town has a mere seventeen thousand citizens. Many of their pedigrees, politics, and/or wardrobes could be carbon-dated to the Mayflower. The place is heavy on prayer and tradition, light on poverty and crime.

Daily, in an astonishing number of the stately old homes, real-life episodes of *Father Knows Best* are reenacted. Many of the moms stay home to tend their perfect homes and flawless children. A disproportion of the dads commute to their seats on the stock exchange or in the boardrooms of cozy companies like AT&T or IBM.

No doubt the community's unsullied surface belies the facts. Neat hedgerows and madras trousers provide no real defense against debt, divorce, addiction, or the full litany of contemporary abuses. But from all outward appearances, the place is locked in a 1950's time warp. Approaching its borders, I often had the feeling I was about to be stopped and turned away.

The O'Callaghan house occupies half a block near the

center of town on South Avenue. In former incarnations, the rambling white Victorian served as a transient hotel, a tuberculosis sanitarium, a telephone relay station, and a school for wayward boys. Forty years ago, the oversized O'Callaghan clan arrived from Mallow, Ireland, and staked their claim.

Now, all eight children are grown and scattered and Mrs. O' is widowed. Unable to part with the big old place, the woman has elected to keep it filled with assorted renters, squatters, and strays.

My room is on the third floor, which also houses Mrs. O's sewing room, the sundrenched square where she does her daily meditation, and the room that contains her StairMaster, ergonomic rower, and free weights. In exchange for a variety of minor chores, my rent is a pittance. For entertainment value alone, my landlady is worth infinitely more.

Jane O'Callaghan is a very limited-edition original. For her eightieth birthday, she took up tap dancing. At eighty-five, she's planning either a culinary tour of Tuscany or an African photo safari. Knowing Mrs. O', she'll probably compromise and do both.

The woman has more friends than a lottery winner, more energy than a power plant, and a staggering supply of interests. She views life as endlessly diverting and keeps her keen mind open to its countless possibilities. Among her latest crop of quirky fascinations are yoga, macrobiotic cooking, and regression to past lives.

Aside from Huck and my oldest, dearest friend Miranda, Mrs. O' is the closest thing I have to family. When I turned eighteen, Aunt Selia emancipated me, or more accurately, herself. Ever since, she's called once a month or so to express her unfelt interest. A few times a year, when one or the other of us suffers a foolish bout of guilt or optimism, we get together for dinner. Invariably, the evening turns out to be a mistake: lost appetites coupled with indigestible conversation. Unfortunate memories bobbling up to mar the studied surface. Plenty of long, vacant stares.

With the help of scholarships, loans, and a variety of part-time positions, I'd managed to put myself through college. I met Mrs. O' on a job I would otherwise rather forget.

I'd been working all semester for a catering operation named "Elmer's Pantry." After logging two straight allnighters in preparation for a physics final, I'd been assigned by Elmer to work a party Mrs. O'Callaghan was hosting to benefit a local childrens' hospital.

In a semicoma, I got off to a literal roaring start by incinerating a hapless herd of pigs-in-blankets. Later, while attempting to pass the stuffed mushrooms, I bumped into two honored guests and a wall. Finally, after I overturned a tray full of drinks on her antique Oriental rug, Mrs. O' swiftly sized me up as a person in serious need of her particular brand of supervision.

Over the next several years, as I tried on and discarded a variety of ill-fitting life-styles and careers, Mrs. O' eased into my life and I slipped comfortably into hers. Mrs. O' makes no secret of her desire to see me off tending a noisy brood of pets and children. She's fiendishly determined to hook me up with likely marriage prospects. No luck so far, but this woman is not the sort to shy from a challenge.

I parked the Toyota on the circular bluestone drive. As I killed the ignition, the engine made a sound like automatic gunfire. I glared at the car, and the noise died.

Entering through the back door, I was accosted by Romulus and Remus, Mrs. O' s twin black Labradors, and Maniac, the mutt. One of my household responsibilities is purchasing the pet food, so my arrivals always inspire wild enthusiasm. The rangy trio wagged, barked, and bumped off me like pinballs until they realized I'd come home empty-handed. Dropping his tail like a rock, Maniac sneezed at me haughtily and led the others to the pantry, where the three canines sleep and plan their political uprisings.

A fire blazed in the kitchen's brick-faced hearth. Some creamy concoction bubbled on the stove. As I put the kettle on for tea, Mrs. O' came bounding down the stairs in gray sweats and aerobic shoes.

A riot of white curls framed her wizened face. Her jade eyes sparkled. She was flushed and energized from her morning workout: thirty minutes of cardiovascular exercise she variously termed Geriatric Jane Fonda or "Buns of Veal." Mrs. O' is unfailingly good-humored. But the sight of me today inspired a frown.

"What's the trouble, child? You're looking like holy hell." Worry thickened her brogue so she sounded like human bagpipes.

"Don't be shy, Mrs. O'. Just come right out and say what's on your mind."

"What's on my mind's not the issue here, Lennie Finn. It's clear to me you've got something heavy weighing on yours."

"Busy night, that's all. I'm just tired."

Bustling about, she fixed me a bowl of porridge and a steaming cup of aromatic tea. Carting the mug and bowl to the table, her scowl deepened.

"Lennie, it's no good to keep everything corked up like you do. Bet if Dr. Ruskin regressed you, he'd find you were a sphinx in a former life. Or that monkey with the zipped lip."

"I told you, there's nothing wrong, Mrs. O'. You shouldn't go to all this trouble. I'm really not hungry."

But the rich scent wafting from the bowl was irresistible. So was the pungent aroma of the tea. To be polite, I took a spoonful and a sip. When I looked again, the cereal and tea had disappeared. Delicious warmth radiated from my stomach.

"Not hungry and fine," she said with a knowing sniff.

"Someday, you'll learn to get things off your chest and the world will seem ever so much brighter, my young friend."

"There's nothing to tell," I lied. "Besides, your cooking cures all. What did you put in that oatmeal? Best ever. And the tea!"

She shook an admonishing finger. "Don't go trying to change the subject on me, my girl. Inquiring minds want to know."

Turning the faucet up full, I rinsed my dirty dishes and set them in the dishwasher. Finished, I wiped my hands on my jeans. "Thanks for the breakfast, Mrs. O'. I'm on tonight, so I'd better get some sleep."'

"You'll sleep better with a clear head, Lennie."

"There's nothing on my mind but that delicious break- fast. You should market that porridge, really. Mrs. O's *Oat*- standing Oatmeal. Has a certain ring to it, don't you think?"

And then I scooted upstairs, before she could pry any- thing further from me.

My room reflects Mrs. O's love of light and whimsy. The walls are a sunny yellow, the ceiling summer sky blue. The carpet, dense and green, has the look of a Lawn Doctor ad. On the bed sits an enormous teddy bear with button eyes and a scarlet bow tie. Mrs. O' sewed it herself and gave it to me for my recent thirty-sixth birthday. The accompany- ing card claimed it was high time I got used to sleeping with company. With her typical subtlety, Mrs. O' suggested I call the bear "Hubby."

As I greeted Hubby this morning, my phone trilled. My spirits immediately brightened at the sound of Miranda Connolly's smoky voice. Among my friend's countless vir- tues was her uncanny ability to call and catch me when I most needed to hear from her.

"Greetings from out nation's most glorious garden spot: Buffalo, New York."

"I thought you gave that honor to Hoboken."

"They'll just have to settle for second," Miranda replied.

"This is the first, and hopefully, last time I'll travel three hundred miles to play in three feet of snow and three-hundred-below-zero temperatures. And that's not counting the windchill. Or the crowd."

"But don't they have great cheese steaks or something?"

"That's Philly, my dear, not Buffalo. You want your ulcers to do the cha-cha in this town, it's killer chicken wings. Naturally, given my unfortunate tendency to commit gastronomical suicide, I ordered up a batch after the late show." She sighed. "Big mistake. Spent the rest of the night dodging a pack of wingless chickens, hell-bent on revenge. But enough about the glamorous life of an aging aspiring rock star. What's up with you?"

"Nothing much."

"How's the fire biz?"

"Hot, smoky, dangerous, and demanding. Just like singing with a band."

I told her about the emergency call to the Dolan house and my close encounter of the worst kind with Kitty on the roof. Miranda listened with her usual intensity. The connection between us was an electric current, the palpable flow of matter, energy, and affection.

Since we first met in junior high school, this woman has been the sister of my soul, my surest antidote against maladies ranging from laugh deprivation to crushing loneliness. Even now, when she travels ten months of most years performing, Miranda is virtually as close and familiar to me as myself. Maybe more so.

"Sounds like that kid really got to you, Len."

"Nah. I'm just pooped."

"There you go, hiding behind those walls of yours. It's okay to admit you have feelings, Len. I won't tell a soul, honestly."

"I do *not* hide my feelings."

"Right, and I don't care about whether my albums go platinum."

"I'm sure you don't. You never were the competitive type, after all."

Her sarcastic chuckle made me smile. But, most everything about Miranda had that effect. I pictured her as she was when we first met in seventh grade: a carbonated beanpole. Now, that vitality made Miranda a top draw on the concert circuit, and the leggy good looks, packaged in her signature all-black, were copied by countless guitar-wielding hopefuls, angling to garner some measure of her success.

"You haven't mentioned your new lover-boy," she said.

"He's not my lover-boy."

"Yet."

"Don't you need to rest your voice for tonight's concert, Miranda?"

"Maybe, dear heart. But what *you* obviously need is a nice roll in the hay. It's been what? A thousand years now?"

"What's wrong with celibacy?"

"Come on, Len. Sex'll do wonders for your disposition. Not to mention your complexion."

"Right. Don't mention it. Meantime, how's Tex? Or is it Saddlebag Sam this week? Or Chuckwagon Pete?"

"So happens my current flame's name is Clint, and he's to die for."

"Well, try not to let it go that far this time, Connolly. And please, when the time comes, no drowning your sorrows in Szechuan dumplings."

"Mmmm. Hot dumplings sound super."

"Forget I said that."

"I love you, too, sweetheart. Call you soon."

Hanging up, I flopped down on the bed beside Hubby. But the sleep I sorely needed refused to come. My mind kept swerving from Kitty to my own assault and back again until the two incidents were bound in a hopeless tangle. A single haunting image kept pressing in: *Circle of stones.*

Why had that odd ring of dying fire at the Dolans' house last night seemed so familiar to me? Had it been mentioned in something I'd read?

Dragging myself out of bed, I tugged open the swollen door fronting my maple night table. Inside, I housed the Lennie Finn Collection of Reading Material for the Incurably Obsessed. The space was crammed with recent magazine articles, newspaper clippings, and photocopied journal articles about rape.

Leafing quickly through my grisly hoard, I searched for some reference to a ring of stones. Rape is often ritualized, echoing elements of the attacker's sick sexual fantasies.

The variety and magnitude of the crimes never failed to horrify and amaze me. I flipped through harrowing accounts of urban "wilding," where packs of roving young beasts attack at random, beating and raping for sport. There were gruesome reports of mass rapes by soldiers in foreign battlegrounds.

I had articles about rapists as young as ten. Their victims come in all ages, sizes, and situations. Assaults have been made against severely retarded girls, comatose patients, nuns in full habit, and women in their eighties. To a rapist, nothing is sacred or taboo. Nothing matters but the sick urge and its violent fulfillment.

Nor is there a limit to the excuses offered by the accused. A football star claimed his battered victim had implied consent by asking for his autograph. A senator, fingered by six traumatized staffers, alleged that the women were suffering from mass hysteria. A pederast priest with enough young victims to fill a congregation blamed his sex crimes on an evil other personality, supplied by Satan himself.

Nothing about a circle of stones.

Delving deeper, I skimmed various expert opinions about what causes men to rape. Often, offenders have been sexually abused as children. Many have low intelligence and lower self-esteem. Disgusted, I tossed the stack of theories aside. I wasn't impressed by any of them.

For every abused offender, hundreds of abused kids turned out fine. Ditto for people of limited or skewed intelligence. And if low self-esteem could really be blamed for sex abuse, we'd be looking at armies of abusers, instead of mere platoons.

There is heated disagreement in the field about the most suitable and productive punishments. Historically, everything from medication to public humiliation has been tried. Sickeningly, rapists are among the most likely of all felons to repeat their crimes.

Some experts champion radical responses. I was particularly drawn to the suggestions by some that the only really effective solution for persistent sex criminals is castration. The idea is highly controversial and viewed by many as cruel and unusual punishment, but then I doubt any of those noble thinkers have personally experienced a rape.

My paper pile was running out. Maybe I'd only imagined that the smoky ring in the snow was familiar. The last several articles were about a high school fraternity in New Jersey that required members to have forcible sex with a classmate in order to be initiated. Several of the rapists' fathers claimed the case had been blown way out of proportion. "Boys have been pushing girls to do it since the dawn of time," one declared. "It's only natural."

Circle of stones?

The connection stubbornly refused to solidify or go away. Maybe it was from an article I'd read and failed to clip. Somewhere, I'd encountered that ring of dying fire before. And I sensed with chilling certainty that I hadn't seen the last of it.

Chapter 6

LENNIE

After a restless, sleepless day, what little was left of me reported to the station house for the night shift. Finding my friend Red Snapper in the locker room bolstered my outlook and energy considerably.

Red exudes boyish charm. I can't help but smile at the sight of his carrot-curl hair, warm blue eyes, and impish expression. Most would describe him as terminally cute, but that doesn't begin to cover the true range and depth of Lawrence William Snapper III.

Red is bright, funny, and dear. He's perceptive and insightful and unfailingly understanding. He sees right through my standard line of blarney about being an iron-clad, independent soul who doesn't need anyone for anything—ever. Whenever I finish one of those foolish tirades, Red smiles at me kindly and shakes his head.

When he first sought out my friendship several years ago, I was standoffish. I imagined Red might be some sort of a Hitsig in sheep's clothing. But soon, I came to appreciate the man. He's a real friend who shares an uncanny number of my tastes and sensibilities.

We laugh at the same absurdities, rail at the same injustices, distrust the same slick-talking, shark-toothed politicians. We also share a passion for comfort foods and cool, mellow music. Above all, both of us adore vintage movies.

We've each seen *Casablanca* so many times, we have the script memorized. Scraps of dialogue tend to slip into our conversations. I love to watch the look of pure befuddlement on Hitsig's face when he not-so-accidentally overhears us playing Rick and Ilsa or Ilsa and Sam. No doubt Wild Bill limits himself to movies starring swamp creatures and naked men in black socks. His type of guys.

"I thought you were off tonight, Red."

"Dumbo had a family emergency. I'm filling in for him."

"With those little ears? Forget it."

His eyes narrowed. "You okay?"

"Sure, why?"

He frowned and brushed a stray wave off my forehead. "You look beat. Why don't you try to get some sleep?"

"I've got equipment to check, Snapper. Places to go, people to see."

"I'll take care of everything. Go rest."

"You sure?"

"Go."

As usual, Red's diagnosis and prescription were flawless. I dropped off like a pebble in a well as soon as I slipped under the covers in my curtained cubicle on the second floor. When the voice from dispatch sounded over the intercom hours later, I had to fight my way up through sleep thick as molasses.

"Engine one, hose one, ladder one, engine two, report to structure fire at the corner of . . ."

The address was in a downtown commercial area shaped like and known as Bull's Head. The blaze had started in a Chinese take-out place at the bull's imaginary left ear and spread to the adjoining stationery store. When we arrived, sirens wailing, flames from the primary fire were starting to threaten the slim frame building next door. Spotting the sign out front, my stomach fisted: South Side Animal Medical Center.

Stepping down from the rig, I heard the desperate yips and meowing from inside. Animals have keen radar for impending danger. They were probably also reacting to some rise in the temperature as smoke and heat spread from the fire.

At two A.M., the burning shops were unoccupied. Perriman assigned Studs and Nervy to douse the raging flames in the Chinese restaurant. Lattimer and Glassband, a team from the Turn of River firehouse, went in to battle the blaze in the stationery store. Red, a rookie named Malloy, and I were dispatched to the veterinary center.

Hooking into the hydrant on the corner, Red and I donned our breathing apparatus and headed for the building's entrance. The plan was to wet down the interior wall abutting the burning building while Malloy soaked the outside through the tiny alleyway separating the structures.

Reaching the front door first, I removed a glove and reached out to test the knob. The move was almost a reflex. With the blaze next door, I fully expected the metal to be cold.

But before I could make contact, searing heat from the knob made me jerk back. Though there was no visible sign that the fire had spread to the animal hospital, it clearly had.

The sounds from the kennels at the rear of the building were growing more and more heartrending. A puppy's shrill plea sounded like the wailing of a frightened child.

"Drown it, Malloy. We've got to get in and save those animals."

With a nod, Red raised his ax and smashed a window fronting the waiting area. Ducking, he narrowly avoided the raging fireball that burst through the breech, gobbling air. I repeated the move on the other street-side window, dodging the ferocious roar of the liberated fire overhead.

In seconds the blaze dimmed and retreated. Peering into the square reception room a moment later, I saw nothing but low clumps of playful yellow flame and a few slender smoke wisps. Looked like daisies in a field on a cloudy day.

But I knew better than to be lulled by innocent appearances.

Like blind dates, any fire call has the potential to prove disastrous. My favorite rookie-year instructor taught me that it's critical to evaluate each fire carefully, to fully understand its mood and personality before you leap to any hazardous conclusions.

I'd embraced that sage advice and carried it a step or two further. I tried to take the full measure of every blaze in much the same way I sized up Mrs. O's parade of "perfect," eligible bachelors. The surface doesn't begin to tell the story. You have to sniff around. Stay alert. Trust your gut and your intuition.

This fire struck me as the most dangerous type of all. It was sneaky and underhanded. Full of nasty surprises. Definitely up to no good.

"Cover me with the hose, Lennie. I'm going in."

"Watch your back, Red. This one's not to be trusted."

With his heat-proof glove, Red opened the door. The piercing cacophony of terrified animals grew louder. Trailing Red, I trained the hose at the clumps of crackling flame. As I did, they dipped and darted out of reach. Damn things feinted and reformed, coming at Red and me in a rain of startling uppercuts and right crosses.

"Son of a bitch."

The fire refused to behave according to any normal rules of conduct. Through the billowing black smoke, I searched the room for a reason.

At first, nothing looked suspicious. There were chairs and couches, an empty parrot's cage, a broad desk fitted with phones and computers. Racks of collars, leashes, pet foods and vitamins, and grooming aids flanked the desk. The walls were hung with cunning pet posters and photos of loyal, four-footed customers. A few of the snapshots were beginning to curl at the edges from the heat.

The animals' cries grew more strident. I couldn't bear the naked terror in their screams. Red was at the door to the kennel area. But as he moved to open it, a spire of flame erupted, blocking his path.

Startled, Red drew back. "What the hell—?"

Horrified, I saw the raging blaze closing in on my friend. Encircling him. Bracing my legs, I trained the hose on Red, dousing him with the full force of the fire stream. The flames shot upward greedily.

Why wouldn't the damned thing die out?

Retreating, Red tried to beat down the burning spikes, but they kept coming. Shooting toward his neck. His face.

Dropping the hose, I wrenched Red back from the central force of the conflagration and wrestled him to the floor. Then I grabbed an extinguisher mounted on the wall and smothered the stubborn flames in a blanket of foam.

"It's out, Red. You all right?"

Sputtering, Red got to his feet. "Thanks to you I am. Thanks."

"Don't mention it."

"What the hell's up with this crazy fire?"

"I have an idea. Take the hose for a minute, will you?"

While he covered me, I fought my way to the desk. Flames rained sparks around me like firecrackers.

Approaching the display shelf on the right, I kept a wary eye out for the fire's dirty tricks. Red had the fire stream aimed behind me. I gestured for him to turn it my way.

As the hard spray hit me, another searing shot of fire leaped forth from the shelf. The instant it subsided, I grabbed the display rack, dragged it through the front door, and tossed it on the lawn.

"Drown those cans, Malloy. If that doesn't work, get the foam."

I didn't have to look at the labels to know that something in those flea and tick sprays was highly flammable. It could have been the contents or the propellant. Depending on the chemical composition, water might not be the solution.

But Malloy and Perriman would deal with the hazardous

materials. All I cared about at the moment was getting those animals out of danger.

Red and I hauled the cages two at a time, ferrying the frightened creatures out to the truck. The transfer took nearly half an hour, by which time the flea bombs on the lawn had been thoroughly defused.

And so was I. My muscles were screaming; my throat and eyes were sore and stinging from the smoke. I looked like burned toast. My scent was closer to charbroiled garbage.

As I was loading a shivering Siamese cat in a leg cast onto the rig, a van from the Humane Society arrived. Two strapping young men got out to relieve us of our evacuees. I said my farewells as the labeled cages were passed from the truck to the van.

"Good-bye, Cuddles Abernathy. Take care, Piewacket Pitrowski. *Au revoir*, Renoir Schwartz."

Perriman strode by and tipped his hat. "Nice going, Finn."

I masked my shock at the rare compliment. "Thank you, Captain."

Red came up beside me, draped an arm across my weary shoulders, and lapsed into his uncanny Bogart imitation.

"Here's looking at you, kid."

I was too exhausted to answer with more than a weak, little grin.

Chapter 7

LENNIE

Maniac and the twin Labs accosted me at the door, jumping on me and pulling at my clothes like crazed rock groupies sometimes did to my friend Miranda. Otherwise, the O'Callaghan mansion appeared deserted.

Not unusual. Mrs. O's days are crammed with classes, volunteer work, visits with friends. Stanley, the reclusive one-eyed sculptor who rents a room on the second floor, leaves early and returns late from his studio in nearby Bedford. Ivan and Bob, the gay couple who occupy the apartment over the garage, keep long hours at their downtown antique shop. The others act appropriately for transients: come and go.

With last night's real and remembered atrocities still echoing in my mind, the silence suited me fine. After filling the dogs' bowls, I fixed myself a tuna sandwich and sat on the rag rug amidst the furry trio for lunch.

Romulus and Remus chomped daintily at their portions, then settled at opposite ends of the fireplace to stare at the sputtering blaze. As usual, Maniac was in hearty appetite. The mutt gobbled her table scraps and kibble. After her bowl was spit-shined, she checked out the other bowls, then loped over, nudged aside my arm, and pressed her sturdy flanks against me like a bookend. As I scratched behind her ear, she shut her eyes and made sounds like a purveyor of phone sex.

Maniac and I are kindred spirits. Both of us have short fuses and long memories. We both play aloof but thrive on affection. Generally, both of us are able to pull off the cool, independent act. But every so often the frightened pup inside slips out.

The dog's neuroses are more comical and inventive than my own, but just as telling. Annually, Maniac, who'd been spayed a decade ago, experiences a hysterical pregnancy. For weeks after the phantom birth, she fiercely guards the tennis ball or pair of socks or Macintosh apple she's adopted as her hallucinatory offspring. Eventually, she gives up the baby ghost, but not without suffering a few days of excruciating embarrassment.

Mrs. O' discovered Maniac a dozen years ago, rooting in the garbage behind the house. Emaciated and skittish, the young dog had been abandoned and probably abused. Now, she was arrogant, overweight, and generally calm as rice pudding, but I recognized in her the lingering legacy of the badly wounded child. Mock pregnancies and other quirks aside, something in Maniac's rheumy eyes was a dead giveaway. At least, it was to me.

"So, girl. What's up?"

She yawned and dropped her mangy muzzle on my lap.

"Bored? Believe me, Maniac, there are worse things. This poor kid I met two nights ago was raped. It'll be years before she can be bored again. So many goddamned years."

The dog swallowed hard.

"What kind of inhuman bastard does a thing like that? How could anyone?"

Her tail thumped three shorts, two longs, mutt Morse code for *How the hell should I know?*

"Evil just is, buddy. Nothing anyone can do about it. Not a goddamned thing."

Kitty's nightmare weighted me like molten lead. I was dying for a nap. But as I headed for the stairs, the plants in the foyer clamored for my attention. They were drooping under the weight of my neglect. Guiltily, I fed and watered the Boston ferns, dead-headed and drenched the hibiscus, and breathed a bit of encouragement into the ailing amaryllis.

Mrs. O' claims she had no knack for plants or pets, but she persists in acquiring both in droves. I suspect it's all part of her calculated campaign to prod me toward a life filled with hubby, kids, and scads of domestic responsibilities. Somehow, I doubt that mealy bug and flea dips will ever send me charging to the altar. But persistence is one of Mrs. O's many middle names.

A shadow shifted. Startled, I jolted the watering can.

"Hey, watch it, Lennie girl. You're spilling."

Wheeling around, I took in the spongy form and apoplectic complexion of Frank Murphy.

"Damn it, Frank! How many times have I asked you not to sneak up on me like that? Can't you whistle or something?"

"Wasn't sneaking at all. You were just off in that other world of yours, daydreaming."

His feet were bare, his look nakedly smug. The man had planted himself on the O'Callaghan doorstep last May, down on his luck and fast approaching desperation. Frank Murphy is a distant cousin of the late Mr. O', some family branch that had snapped off and taken root in Chicago. Predictably, Mrs. O' agreed to take him in until he could find his footing. If you asked me, he wasn't looking for it all that hard.

Ordinarily, I approved, or at least comprehended, why Mrs. O' opened her door to visitors. But aside from the dubious bond of distant kinship, Frank Murphy seems without redeeming virtue. He has the personal hygiene, and aroma, of a yak. He is devoutly lazy. Most nights, he's out crawling the pubs. Then, he sleeps half the day away and fritters the rest on soaps and reruns. His contribution to the household is nonexistent, unless you count his mess. His tendency to pop up unexpectedly drives me nuts. Which was, I strongly suspect, the point.

I fetched a ragged towel from the mudroom and tossed it in his direction. "You caused it, Frank. You clean it up."

"In your dreams."

Snickering, he slogged into the den, ignoring the towel on the floor. I heard the drone of the television. The couch cushion sighed.

After angrily sopping up the spill and dousing the rest of my leafy charges, I headed for my room. Stripped to my underwear, I snuggled under the covers. Bed never felt better. Cool sheets, warm quilt, plump pillow.

Before I allowed myself to drop down the well to unconsciousness, I set the alarm. My dinner date wasn't until seven-thirty, but I felt a marathon snooze coming on. Two-ten express for oblivion now loading. Last call. All aboard.

Brrriiing!

The strident shrill burrowed into my budding dream. Clang of metal turning against the tracks. Breathy shriek of brakes catching. The conductor's voice droned from a distant car.

"Tickets. Tick-ets!"

Brrriing!

The sleep train was slowing down. Wrenching to a stop. Throwing me like an evicted vagrant.

Damned phone!

Fumbling for the receiver, I tried to find my voice.

"Yes!" I croaked.

"Lennie Finn?"

"More or less."

"I wake you?"

I caught an infuriating note of amusement. "Who the hell is this?"

"Kresky. Sorry to bother you, but I need your help."

The fog was lifting, but slowly. "Who did you say this is?"

"Harry Kresky. Stamford P.D. The Dolan case yesterday

morning, and last season on the way to first base, remember?"

"Now I do. What's up?"

"Your little friend Kitty's shut down. She's refusing to come back and finish looking at the mug shots."

Wide awake now, I fully sympathized with the child's resistance. Naturally, she'd try to set the ugliness aside.

"If Kitty wants out, that's her privilege, Sergeant."

"True. But I can't let it go at that. I think she might be able to help us crack this thing."

"So why call me?"

"From all the questions this morning, I figured you're interested."

"I am."

"Good. Kitty's mother tried to convince her and struck out. So did the head of the rape crisis center. My instinct says maybe you can get through to her."

"Your instinct's wrong, Sergeant. I met Kitty once. Under the worst imaginable circumstances. What makes you think I have any special influence over her?"

"Call it a hunch."

I was inclined to call it something cruder. "Even if you're right, it's Kitty's decision. If she's had enough, so be it."

"It's not that simple. You don't understand."

"Enlighten me."

Reluctantly, he did. As I listened, I regretted having asked. Kitty's rape wasn't the only one. The terror was spreading. So was the sour churning in my gut.

"All right, I'll see what I can do," I said dully.

"Thanks. I owe you one."

"Let's call it even, Sergeant."

Hanging up, I looked up the Dolans' number and dialed it. Kitty answered. She seemed pleased to hear from me. But when she heard the purpose of the call, her voice went shrill.

"No way. I'm not going back to that place, *ever*!"

Ten minutes of my finest wheedling failed to budge her.

For reasons the little girl could not or would not explain, she couldn't bear the thought of returning to the police station.

Left with only one feasible alternative, I phoned Kresky at headquarters and made the necessary arrangements. With a wistful glance at my rumpled bed, I dressed again and headed out the door.

Chapter 8

DANA

The clock on her desk read 3:36. Anxiously, Dana peered out of her study at the apartment's front door. Where was Becky?

Six minutes late, that's where she was.

Stop overreacting, Dana chided herself. But the events surrounding this morning's taping had left her jumpy as a tick.

Back Talk was deliberately designed to inflame. The show's controversial themes and dueling experts drew mountains of hate mail and scores of threatening calls. Most of the irate rantings were innocuous. But there was always the disturbing possibility that a deranged viewer or incensed panelist might prove dangerous.

Dana firmly believed in taking prudent precautions. Even in her own apartment house, she hid behind dark glasses, a hat, and her former husband's surname. She left Dana Saunders, celebrity and tempting target, at the studio door. She avoided public appearances and declined piles of tempting invitations.

In addition, she deliberately varied her daily work schedule to foil stalkers like her fanatic fan Lester Yurie. Dana had no idea what drew that lowlife to her in the first place. But clearly, the slimy worm was fixated. She shuddered, thinking about how he'd suddenly stepped out from behind the drapes in her dressing room two weeks ago.

"Must be something I can do for you, Dana. You want anything lifted? Someone out of the way? I'm your man."

Security had ejected him immediately, but Yurie's regular appearances were a reminder that Dana couldn't be too careful.

A driver delivered her to and from the studio's rear entrance and checked for lurking strangers before Dana exited the car. Her home address and phone number were carefully guarded secrets. So were the telling details of her personal life.

Until now.

Jules Westerman's foolish slip about Becky winning the Lassiter Prize had toppled the protective walls Dana had built around her daughter. The assistant's tearful apology couldn't repair the damage. Nothing could. Becky had been exposed. Endangered.

Eight minutes late.

Dana was a coiled spring. Crossing swiftly to the house phone, she buzzed the lobby. The doorman's cheery voice promptly came on the line.

"Hi, Jerry. It's Mrs. Meade. Would you mind taking a look around for Becky?"

"Sure, Mrs. Meade. One minute."

Sometimes a group of the building's kids loitered in the lobby. Dana willed Becky to be down in the mailroom or perched in the corridor near the elevators. Chatting. Safe and oblivious.

The intercom crackled back to life. "Sorry, Mrs. Meade. I don't see her."

"You sure?"

"Positive."

"Okay. Thanks, Jerry. If she comes in, send her right up, will you?"

"Certainly, Mrs. Meade."

What next? The police weren't likely to take her seriously if she called to report that her child was twelve minutes late. She could go out searching herself. But where? Anyway, that would leave no one in the apartment should Becky finally show up or try to phone.

Desperate to do something, Dana dialed Juilliard, the school for musically gifted children that Becky attended. No, the child wasn't there. At Dana's curt request, the secretary set down the receiver and asked around. She reported back moments later. As far as anyone knew, Becky Meade had left at the usual time and taken her regular van home. Oh, and congratulations. Everyone was *so* excited about the Lassiter.

Not everyone, Dana thought sourly. Under the circumstances, she wished the damned award had gone to someone else.

Becky was almost fifteen minutes late now.

Tension pounded Dana's skull. She pictured a deserted street steeped in shadow. John the rapist lurking out of view. She imagined Becky walking idly by, oblivious to the threat. Airy stride. Humming. Fresh and lovely.

Live bait.

Dana imagined urges like voracious worms consuming the rapist's reason.

Stop, Dana. Get a grip.

Her ex-husband, Adam Meade, was out of his office at a midtown import-export firm. Unreachable, according to his twit of a secretary.

He always was.

"Will you please ask him to call as soon as he gets in, Jeanette?"

"Okay, Dana. But I told you, I don't expect him for hours and hours."

Dana winced at the woman's high-pitched voice. The sound conjured the secretary's bump-and-wiggle body and her unfortunate passion for tight flaming dresses, overstated makeup, and flashy accessories. Amazing that Mr. Adam Proper Tightass III considered her suitable to occupy the elegant public space outside his office. He claimed that Jeanette's skills were excellent. But Adam was generally much more concerned about packaging than contents, especially when it came to his cherished business image.

Ironically, Adam's stony British reserve had been one of the things that drew Dana to him in the first place. She'd been reared in an emotional typhoon. Hot-tempered father, histrionic mother. Three siblings who shared her considerable flair for spontaneous combustion.

To Dana, Adam Meade seemed an exotic, alien life form. The man was totally unflappable. Adam's surface was as solid and smooth as freshly groomed ice. Unfortunately, Dana had never been able to breach the slick veneer. After ten long, frustrating years of marriage she'd stopped trying. When Adam didn't so much as notice that her remoteness had come to match his own, Dana tossed in the marital towel.

The divorce proceeded with near bloodless calm. No unsightly emotions or crude enmity. Dana had expected a cataclysm, but in reality, the change proved insignificant. Where they'd once been distant relatives, she and Adam now were distant friends.

Adam took Becky on weekends. Holidays and other special events were equitably distributed. When a business or parenting matter required extensive discussion, Dana and Adam made an appointment and met for dinner.

All quite civilized. And exasperating. Dana still fantasized sometimes about getting a rise out of Adam. Finding his elusive fuse and igniting it with a blowtorch.

How would he react to news of the current threat against their daughter? Better question: Would he react at all? Likely, he'd view the whole matter as another of Dana's tiresome little explosions. Somehow, she'd have to convince him to keep a closer than usual eye on the child, nonetheless.

Not that he wasn't a reasonably caring, vigilant father. Especially given the emotional coma.

Dana stood listening to the dial tone, searching her muddled mind for a plan.

She considered contacting the rapist's attorney, Blowhard Eckhard, then discarded that idea. A warning could backfire. Dana remembered Dr. Mosher's dire prediction: *Anything might trigger the offender to strike again.*

Dana's mind filled with the man's smirk. His smoldering eyes. Had she only imagined the devilish glint in them when he learned she had a daughter?

"Hey, Mimsy. Guess what?"

Becky stood in the doorway, grinning broadly. Framed by auburn curls, her freckled face was radiant.

Dana caught the child in a crushing hug. "Thank God," she breathed.

"Hey. You're squishing me." The girl giggled and squirmed loose.

A flare of anger edged out Dana's relief. "Where were you, Becky? You had me worried sick."

"At school. Where else would I be?" The child looked puzzled.

"It's three forty-eight," Dana snapped. "I expected you by three-thirty."

"Yell at the traffic." Tears pooled in the soft green eyes. "You don't even care about my news."

Dana stopped and drew a measured breath. "I'm sorry, honey. Of course I care. I was just upset, that's all. You know me: Mount Saint Helens in a dress."

Blotting her eyes on her jacket sleeve, the child went coy. "Guess who won the Lassiter Prize?"

"Hmm. I can't imagine. Is it somebody we know? Don't tell me it was that nerdy little nose-picker we met at that competition in Minneapolis."

Becky made a face. "You already heard."

Dana hugged her again. "I did, my darling daughter. And I'm proud enough to bust. The Lassiter Prize is a very, very big deal, and so are you. What shall we do to celebrate? Winner's choice."

"I can pick *any* place? You *mean* it?"

"Sky's the limit."

"Excellent! The Hard Rock Café."

Dana stifled a smile. This kid was so terrific. Upbeat, uplifting, but unfailingly down-to-earth.

"Okay, my love. I'll call right now and make us a reservation."

"Can Lisa come?"

"Sure." Lisa Kaplan was Becky's best friend. A virtual sister substitute, for which Dana was most grateful. Before the split, she and Adam had valiantly tried to provide the child with a real sibling. But three miscarriages and a stillbirth had convinced them it wasn't to be.

"Great! I'll go ask her."

The Kaplans lived around the corner on Sixty-seventh Street. It was only a two-block walk along busy streets in broad daylight, but suddenly the idea of Becky venturing out alone made Dana queasy.

"Why don't you call instead, Beck?"

The child frowned. "What's wrong with my going over?"

"Nothing," Dana replied, too quickly. "But I want to hear all about the prize. Who told you? What did they say? Did everyone make a big fuss at school?"

"I'll only be a few minutes. Then, I'll tell you *everything*. Okay?"

Dana kept her fears to herself and watched her little girl leave. After all, there was no real danger. Nothing about the prize had yet appeared in the papers.

Even after it did, Dana knew she couldn't hold her daughter prisoner, though she was sorely tempted to try. Thankfully, school, lessons, practice, and homework left Becky with little spare time for unsupervised roaming.

As added insurance, Dana decided to arrange for her driver to transport the child to and from her various activities for the time being. Becky loved the man, a gentle black giant named Nimrod Pierce. Roddy was a retired cop with a practiced eye and keen nose for trouble. Without arousing any unnecessary anxieties, he could look out for Becky.

For the first time since Jules's disastrous slip of the tongue that morning, Dana felt the knots of tension uncoil a bit. Roddy Pierce was the perfect antidote for her poison apprehensions. She didn't want to break her daughter's sturdy spirit. She didn't want Becky to view her world as dark and dangerous.

Deliberately, Dana had kept the apartment free of tabloids and newscasts with their graphic displays of city violence. Happily, Becky was too busy to watch the countless shows that highlighted humanity's underbelly, *Back Talk* included.

Becky didn't need to see the gore-spattered corpses. The body bags and decimated survivors. She didn't have to hear the horror tales and frightening admonitions. For as long as humanly possible, the child should be allowed to remain a child.

Crossing to the window, Dana stared at the milling crowd seventeen stories below. Searching hard, she picked out Becky's slender form skipping up Park Avenue. She watched intently until her daughter turned the corner and drifted out of sight.

Chapter 9

LENNIE

Heading toward the Dolan house, the Toyota bucked and stalled three times. For once, I couldn't curse the car. I was tempted to buckle and stall myself.

Meeting Kitty Dolan had sent me waltzing through my own private graveyard. Once again, I'd been forced to face the teetering stones and hollow epitaphs. I'd been made to feel the crumbling ground beneath my feet, to face the buried feelings poking forth like sun-dried bones. My pluck was an illusion. Built on sand.

More than anything, I longed to leave our tangled pain behind. And I intended to do precisely that, as soon as I could figure out the way.

A brusque young woman in tan slacks and a navy blazer greeted me at the door to the Dolan house. Her mousy hair had overflowed its bowl cut, so she had to raise her head to peer beneath the bangs. The eyes were mud brown, the mouth severe. Poor thing was having a bad face day.

"You Lennie Finn?"

"Yes."

"Clarissa Pratt. Sex crimes."

She gripped my hand and shook it once, which was more than sufficient. The squashed tendons would spring back in time. I had my doubts about the bones.

"You're with the State's Attorney's office?" I asked.

"Right."

"Does that mean there's a suspect?"

"Unfortunately, no. Kitty insisted on waiting until you got here. Say a quick hello and let her get on with it, will you? Then I'll take your statement."

The woman was sharp and short, like nail clippings. I hoped she kept a spare, more pleasant personality at the office. I hated the thought of porn czars and pederasts going free because jurors found them far more sympathetic than the prosecutor.

In grim silence, Ms. Pratt led me to the den. Sergeant Kresky sat next to Kitty on the couch. Clad in a clingy red jumpsuit, Mrs. Dolan entered from the kitchen carrying glasses and a ceramic pitcher on a tray. Despite an obvious attempt at camouflage, strain was etched on her aristocratic face. Her lids were puffy, the eyes bloodshot. The child looked sapped, too, hunched and drawn like an invalid. A rumpled shirt, faded jeans, and uncombed, sleep-flattened hair reinforced the sad illusion. My throat tightened.

Spotting me, Kitty brightened a bit. "Lennie, hi."

"Hi, yourself. Feeling better?"

"Okay, I guess."

"Well, she's *doing* great," Kresky said. "I wish all my witnesses were half as smart and observant."

The praise straightened the child's spine a notch. But not for long.

Settling the tray on the chrome-based glass cocktail table, Allison Dolan poured two glasses of lemonade. She handed one to Kitty. For Harry the hunk, she tossed in a peach linen napkin and a flirtatious hitch of her sculpted brow. She treated me and the prosecutor as if we were part of the furniture.

Noting the smug grin Kresky flashed her in response, my gorge rose. Men like that should be branded with warning labels, especially around the wounded wives of blatant philanderers. I longed to sit Allison Dolan down and give her a short course in the fundamentals of self-preservation. My favorite definition of insanity is doing the same thing over and over again and expecting a different result. I wanted to offer her that as a warning. And, should the caution fail, to drag the foolish woman out of harm's way.

Instead, I obeyed the commanding waggle of Clarissa Pratt's index finger and trailed the assistant state's attorney into the kitchen. As she walked, she scribbled something on a legal pad.

"Have a seat, Ms. Finn." Her voice was like rust. "Exactly what did Kitty say to you on the roof the night before last, Ms. Finn?"

"She told me about the assault."

Her mouth pinched tighter. "Can you be a *touch* more specific?"

"Why don't you ask Kitty?"

"I have. Now I want your version."

Her pen hovered over the legal pad like a guillotine.

"I don't *have* a version. I'm sure whatever Kitty told you is the truth as she remembers it."

The prosecutor shook her head once in the harsh negative. The bangs dawdled a beat behind. "We would appreciate your *voluntary* cooperation, Ms. Finn."

My scowl did not faze her. Apparently, the woman was accustomed to having things her way. Clarissa Pratt was my size, but like anything plumped with hot air, she gave a larger appearance.

"I was not a witness to the assault, Ms. Pratt. I don't see what I can add to Kitty's account."

She responded with a stony silence, timed to make me squirm. I stared back.

"Look, Ms. Finn," she said when that failed. "This is *not* to go any further, but we believe we're dealing with a serial rapist here. We're pretty sure this guy is the same one who hit once last spring in Putnam County and twice over the summer in upstate New York.

"Unfortunately, the incidents are accelerating. The first

was eight months ago, and the next couple were two months apart. Suddenly, he jumped to two weeks later. Only ten days between that assault and Kitty's."

She brushed the bangs aside. Fury narrowed her eyes to coin slots. "That's how it goes in these cases. The man's like any junkie—only violent sex is his drug of choice. The more he feeds his craving, the bigger it grows. At the rate this one is moving, expect another girl like Kitty to be attacked within a week. Maybe sooner."

I thought of Kitty's tearful account of the rape. The monster who assaulted her carried a bloodied knife and threatened to use it.

The prosecutor seemed to read my mind. "Sooner or later, it's likely rape alone won't satisfy him. The knife he carries and the grisly picture he showed Kitty are two of the things that helped us tie Kitty's case to the others. Creep might have slasher fantasies, or the girl in the photo might be his handiwork. You remember the Sharon Sue Davis case?"

"Of course."

The incident was unforgettable. Six months ago, the Long Island girl was snatched out of apparent thin air on the five-block walk from her home to her junior high school, where her mother happened to be principal. Thousands of volunteers plastered the country with posters and contributed to a giant reward fund for the child's safe return. Her parents' wrenching requests for her release aired countless times on local and national broadcasts and in print.

A horrific situation like that was bound to raise public outcry and a flurry of attention, but Sharon Sue Davis was a special case. The child had been a featured player in several Broadway shows, including a company of the hit show *Annie*. Shortly before her abduction, she'd been tapped for the lead in a major film. A flurry of stories touted her as having the superstar potential of a young Liz Taylor or Natalie Wood. But, as months passed without a hopeful

sign of the missing child, the buzz was drowned out by
grim murmurs.

"You think Kitty's case is connected to the Sharon Davis
abduction?" I asked Clarissa Pratt.

The prosecutor scowled. "There are some—similarities."

"Such as?"

"I can't share specifics with the general public, Ms. Finn."

"Don't, then. I'm only asking you to tell *me*."

Her scowl was a lethal brew of arrogance and bile. "At
the very least, we're talking about a mighty sick, extremely
dangerous sack of shit on the loose. Preying on our little
girls. You want to help out here, or not, Ms. Finn? Because
I'm too damned busy to join you in a pissing contest."

Her razor-edged tirade had the desired effect. I was no
fonder of Clarissa Pratt, but more than ready to do her bid-
ding. She'd made me feel small enough to slip under the
door and vanish. Which, at that moment, would have suited
me fine.

All the previous rapes had occurred in different jurisdic-
tions, the prosecutor explained, so no connection had been
made until the assault which took place ten days before Kitty's. If one man was responsible for all the attacks, there remained the cumbersome business of coordinating the
investigative efforts and compiling what little information
the various interested parties had managed to gather.

A special interagency task force had been established, Ms.
Pratt informed me, but the issue of who was in charge of
what had yet to be resolved. Meanwhile, the investigation
into the rapes threatened to bog down in a nightmare of red
tape and dueling egos.

Avoiding Clarissa Pratt's judgmental gaze, I hauled my
memory back up the ladder to the Dolans' snowswept roof.
I relived the perilous climb to the peak and my terrifying
slide toward annihilation. The frigid gusts. Kitty's spectral
appearance. I remembered the sound of the child's plaintive
voice and her words. As best I could, I recounted them for
the prosecutor.

When I finished, she eyed me strangely. "Are you an aspiring actress, Ms. Finn?"

"No."

"No dramatic training at all?"

"No, why?"

Her shoulders hitched and fell. "You put a lot into the story, that's all." Her voice chilled. "I have what I need for now. If you think of anything else, here's my card. I have your number."

I wished I could say the same. This woman rattled me to the bone. Much as I wanted to be done with her, I couldn't resist asking a few nagging questions of my own.

"How many others have there been?"

"Too many."

"Do you have any leads?"

"For a stone wall, you ask a lot of questions, Ms. Finn."

"You're doing some pretty nice stonewalling yourself, Ms. Prosecutor."

She attempted a smile, but her mouth seemed unfamiliar with the maneuver. "I'll be glad to tell you whatever you need to know, Ms. Finn."

"Fine. I need to know how many victims and whether you have any leads. I also need to know about the guy's M.O. Why do you think Kitty's rape might be connected to the Sharon Sue Davis case? Was that ring of stones at the Dolan house a signature?"

The rape in Putnam County sounded familiar. Could I have read something about that and the circle of stones in the papers?

"I can't discuss details, Ms Finn. I'm sure you understand that might compromise our investigation. I'd also appreciate your not discussing this with anyone. Until we're absolutely sure it's one perp, everyone's anxious to avoid general panic. Not to mention copycats. If this news leaks, I'll know exactly what hole needs plugging."

At least she didn't bother to disguise the threat. "Were

there connections between the victims? Have you checked that?"

"Why don't you put that in writing and mail it to our suggestion department, Ms. Finn?"

"I'm only trying to be helpful—"

"You call it helpful. I call it intrusive. Guess that's what makes horse races."

And horseshit. "I hope you got that temperament of yours at a big discount, Ms. Pratt."

Scowling, she turned her attention to the thick file she drew from her briefcase. Her bangs fell like a stage curtain as she skimmed a report. I'd been dismissed.

But I thought of several other things I needed desperately to know. If only the prosecutor could tell me why fate had dropped this particular bomb in my lap. Why me? Why exhume these long-dead demons? And most critically, how could I find the way to bury them again and make certain they stayed buried?

Why did little Kitty Dolan have to choose me, the unlikeliest of all possible prospects, as her lifeline? No way could I walk away from those pale pleading eyes. That tentative, frail smile. The last faint flickers of a child's dying hopes.

If Kitty felt better having me here while she went through the mug shots, I'd stay. But there was precious little I could really do to help her. My own emotional tonnage already had me riding dangerously low in the water.

The attack prosecutor was poring over her case file. Claiming a seat at the kitchen table, I settled down to wait.

Chapter 10

LENNIE

By the time I left the Dolans', day had yielded to a dreary dusk. The massive homes of Griscom Woods blazed like stage sets. Security spots illuminated lawns where children's footprints and dog droppings now freckled the day-old snow. A car packed with teenagers zipped by with its windows down, radio blasting. Heavy metal struck me like a bucket full of slush.

As the silence settled again, a tidal wave of exhaustion bashed me. Accustomed to odd hours and sleep in stingy portions, I couldn't remember the last time I'd suffered such numbing fatigue.

To stay alert, I played some jarring music of my own. Despite several trips to the shop, the Toyota's wayward radio picked up only two stations, both country/western of the worst kind. The tape deck worked, but the only cassette I had on board was a specially prepared one Miranda had bestowed upon me before she left. Hearing her sing right now would only intensify my loneliness. And her current tour wasn't slated to end for another four months.

Damn her for being so good and so successful. Why couldn't she be a wannabe like ninety-nine percent of all singer/songwriters? Growing up, I'd envisioned us pushing prams together, spending gobs of quality time. I was confident that my plan to be the first female third baseperson for the Yankees would not interfere. Nor would Miranda's ambition to work in large-animal veterinary medicine, preferably on the racetrack circuit. Our husbands would be glad to fill any resultant gaps at home. They'd be wonderful cooks, specializing in French pastries and Chinese food, and simply fabulous with the kids.

Funny how things turn out.

To stay alert, I flipped on the radio. On the ride home, I listened to all five verses of that timeless classic: "I Thought My Heart Was Broken, But It Was Just A Nasty Sprain," followed by a personal favorite: "Ain't No Way To Grow No Roses In The Mud."

It seemed forever before I rolled into the bluestone drive and eased to the end of the circle. Through the window, I spotted Mrs. O' and Frank Murphy huddled in the kitchen. Like the trio of dogs, Frank's nose was always fine-tuned to a potential feed. The jerk aimed all his charm, though Lord knew it was precious little, in Mrs. O's direction.

Several silhouettes drifted behind the living-room shades, where assorted guests and boarders generally gathered before dinner. Mrs. O' encouraged socializing with nibbles and a well-stocked bar. In true Irish tradition, she believed a good chat helped clear the lungs.

Not feeling in the least bit sociable myself, I stole around to the far side of the house and climbed the rickety wooden fire stairs. My labored steps crushed the snow hills on the risers. My grip displaced the frozen powder frosting the rails. By the second flight, I was puffing like a locomotive. I was more out of steam than out of shape, but the net effect was identical.

From inside came the sound of Maniac's irate howling, which everyone knew to ignore. In addition to phantom pups, the mutt had a problem with imaginary intruders. Her paranoia stripped the dog of all credibility. The Labs were too lethargic to bother guarding anything on the property but their food bowls. So, when it suited me, I could generally slip in or out unnoticed.

The O'Callaghan house offered an abundance of most everything, but solitude was in desperately short supply. Someday, when I'd saved enough for a down payment on my own place, I planned to spend months reveling in the seclusion. Dressing or not at will. Behaving as I pleased. If it struck me to do so, I'd talk to no one for days at a time. Being congenial was fine to a point, but I had no yearning to make a habit of it.

At the third floor fire escape landing, I stomped the snow off my shoes and shook my gloves to dislodge the ice beads. As always, the door was locked from the inside. But on the job, I'd received extensive training in the fine art of forcible entry.

For occasions like this, I'd left a rusty old Halligan tool at the back of the window box. Digging under packed snow and a crisp tangle of dead geraniums, I felt its comforting metal heft.

The device, named for the Chicago fire fighter who invented it, has a picklike structure at one end and a two-pronged prying mechanism on the other. Its crude look belies its efficiency. No self-respecting cat burglar should leave home without one.

The door was designed to challenge: solid core slab construction with a rabbeted jamb. Fortunately, age had deformed the wood, leaving a slim space at the level of the lock. Slipping in the pick head, I was able to grab the bolt and slowly urge it out of the keeper.

There were two messages from Jack Chambless on my phone machine. Rehearsing my excuses, I dialed Jack's number. I hated to back out on him at the last minute. But I barely had the stamina left to chew. The need to do so groomed, upright, and in public seemed altogether beyond me.

No answer. After the sixth ring, I hung up. Jack's machine wasn't on, which probably meant he was puttering in his shop or taking a shower. I stripped to my underwear. I decided to rest my eyes and try again in a few minutes.

In my dream, Jack's shop was attached to a huge lecture hall, and I'd been invited to attend. Arriving early, I took a seat among the thousands of eager, adoring students awaiting Jack's appearance. Ten minutes after the class was slated to begin, there was still no sign of him. The murmur of disappointment was building to a roar when he finally arrived. While scores of envious young beauties looked on, he headed straight for me.

Feeling a trifle embarrassed, I stood and made for the exit. But my friend Miranda blocked the way, strumming her guitar and singing about rolling in the hay with a monk.

Next thing I felt was a startling chill. My eyes snapped open to the sight of a florid Frank Murphy tugging off my covers.

"What the hell do you think you're doing?"

"That gentleman friend of yours is downstairs. Mrs. O' asked me to come up and fetch you."

"Give me the damned blankets and get lost, Frank. You've got some nerve."

"You were sleeping like the dead, Lennie girl. I tried calling your name, shaking you. This was a last resort. Believe me."

His eyes were glued to my chest. My bra was a cotton cover-up number, ditto the underpants. Careless laundering had tinted both a tepid pink. The ensemble was about as sexy as fried fish, but the slime still looked entirely too interested for my comfort.

"The blanket, Frank. *Now!*"

With a rakish grin, he dropped the covers to the floor. "Oops."

"You S.O.B. Get out of my room this minute!"

Not a move. Not a blink. The crooked grin sat on his face like a dare.

"Get the hell out, Frank. I mean it."

"But your professor sweetie's waiting. Man's dressed to the nines. Has that can't-wait-to-see-my-lady look about him. Can't say I blame him, Lennie girl. Just look at you, all pretty in pink."

"GET——OUT!"

I took aim with the pillow. Ducking out quickly, he slammed the door behind him, and the pillow hit with a breathy whomp.

Fully awake now and seething, I slogged out of bed. Someday, I'd murder that little shit. But right now, I didn't have the time. I brushed the fuzz off my teeth and took a quick shower.

The mirror wasn't fogged enough to mask the sorry facts. I smoothed taupe shadow over the sinkholes that were formerly my eyes. A swipe of blush eased my pallor from death gray to a charming sickbed green. My hand was far too shaky to trust with a liner brush or mascara. The hair was hopeless. I raked a comb through it and let the dips fall where they may.

In the full-length mirror behind the door, I eyed the large bruise blooming like a prize hydrangea on my left buttock. Lucky thing that nail had caught my coat collar. Though, given little Kitty Dolan's effect on me, I might have been better off taking my chances with wingless flight.

That child had crept under my skin and stuck there. I could still see her mournful expression as she finished viewing the mug shots. Kitty was terribly upset that she couldn't identify her assailant. Before I left, she confessed her desperation.

"What if the man comes back again? I'll die if he does, Lennie. Honest."

"He won't, sweetheart. Try not to think that way."

I'd had nothing to offer the child but empty assurances. Facile bits of phony optimism. For years, I, too, had been haunted by the same hideous worry that tormented Kitty.

The creature who attacked me is out there somewhere. What if he's watching? What if he's waiting for a chance to steal any scraps he might have left behind?

I threw on black slacks, a teal silk blouse, gold-buckled belt, a choker of mock pearls, and faux pearl earrings. Giving myself a final once-over, I was thankful for Jack's apparent infatuation with me. Hopefully, if love was blind, a crush was at least seriously nearsighted.

Though I hated to admit it, especially to myself, I cared about this man. After a long string of disastrous relationships, I'd sworn off romance indefinitely. I'd said as much to Mrs. O'. But she remained determined to see me paired, like a shoe.

She had picked Jack up a couple of months ago at a benefit performance of the Stamford Symphony. Before the final number, she had also learned enough to ghost the guy's autobiography. If I'd been a sphinx in a past life, Mrs. O' was probably the clever soul in charge of chipping features from the stone.

Jack Chambless was in his late forties, a widower with a grown son and a young granddaughter. Born, reared, and educated in the South, he was a recent Stamford transplant.

In Jack's native Charleston, his father had founded a successful string of retail clothing stores. Jack had been expected to take over, but a few summer stints convinced him that the business gene had skipped his generation. Instead, he'd followed his academic inclinations and taken a Ph.D. in philosophy. After graduation, he worked his way to a full professorship at the University of Virginia. Four years ago, he took a leave from the university to see his wife through her long and ultimately losing battle with ovarian cancer.

Two years after her death, Jack moved north to be nearer his son, who lived across the state line in New York's Westchester County. Jack, whose writings and commanding presence on the podium were celebrated and widely respected, was offered several endowed chairs in the area. He accepted a position at NYU which offered him the most freedom and flexibility.

In addition to teaching, he wanted time to pursue a number of personal and charitable interests. His father had left a considerable estate, and Jack was determined to see the money put to positive use. His particular passion was helping inner city kids stay out of trouble and in school. In Charleston, he'd been one of the first to adopt a high school class, guaranteeing college scholarships to anyone who graduated with at least a C average. When he came north, he took on another group of fifty needy kids from South Norwalk. Determined to brighten their future, he'd bought a big house downtown, which the kids were helping him convert into a recreation center.

The man was bright, attractive, charming, and accomplished. According to Mrs. O', all he lacked was a suitable companion. This she immediately set out to provide. Employing her favorite ambush tactic, she invited Jack home for dinner.

Our first date was six weeks ago. Since then, Jack and I had gotten together whenever our crazy schedules allowed. On all occasions, he proved unfailingly attentive and interesting. And considerate. When he promised to, he called. When he said he would, he showed. His sense of humor was droll and entertaining. He made good company and better conversation. Finely tuned to the vagaries of my temperament, he deftly accepted my prickly nature and my tendency to brood. Noting my reluctance, he hadn't pressed for sex or, failing that, excuses.

Before Jack, I'd considered myself the Goldilocks of romantic relationships. Every man I met was too something. Too warm, too cold, too medium. Too self-centered or not centered at all. Power-crazed or tepid as tapioca. Over the years, I'd suffered evenings with every imaginable variety of emotional dwarf: dopey, grumpy, stuffy, selfish, grabby, chintzy, and dull.

Many of the men I'd dated were damaged goods. Not that I wasn't. But dealing with my own dents and bruises kept my hands more than full. Mrs. O's wishes aside, I had firmly concluded that being alone was preferable to being hitched and saddled.

Then came Jack.

Now, I smiled at the prospect of seeing him. Quickly, I

slipped on low suede boots and grabbed my black wool coat. Downstairs, I found Mrs. O' and Jack in deep discussion in the music room.

Jack and my landlady have a great deal in common. Both enjoy classical music, culinary arts, and ballroom dancing. Both have a way with people. Both are talented at crafts.

As a child, Jack had learned woodworking from a favorite uncle. He had single-handedly renovated his vintage stone house, restoring the original sheen to the carved moldings, oak plank floors, newel posts, and balusters. He'd patched and painted. He'd replaced rotting windows. Repaired antique moldings. He'd even modernized the antiquated kitchen and baths, doing everything but the electrical work himself.

Once the house was completed, he started on the half-dozen small outbuildings dotting his wooded property. He was even fitting one as an elaborate playhouse for his granddaughter, a five-year-old named Cara.

Several weeks ago, Jack took me on a tour. The playhouse's sunny, single room had parquet floors, lace curtains, a dining set capped by a mock crystal chandelier, and a dozen small hurricane lamps fitted with pink candles. Its kitchen featured a refrigerator that lit like the genuine item when the door was opened. The doll corner was fully stocked, the toy chest crammed with a tempting array of blocks and games.

I'd gravitated toward the dressing area immediately, irresistible with its rack of costumes and trayful of sparkling costume and cast-off jewels. A glance regressed me thirty years. I wrapped myself in the pink boa and the floppy felt hat with the wide fuchsia bow. In the jewel tray were sufficient rings for every finger, including a very tempting diamond solitaire and a broken college ring just begging for a neck chain and an invented boyfriend.

I noticed a large can of solvent near the window. "That's a fire hazard, Mr. Chambless," I chided.

"Thank you, ma'am. I'll see to it immediately."

"You do that," I ordered. "This place is much too wonderful for any bad thing to happen."

I was thoroughly enjoying myself when an odd, unpleasant feeling gripped me. Replacing the rings and costumes, I hoped the malaise didn't show. If Jack noticed, there'd be questions, and I honestly couldn't explain my sudden mood shift.

I was probably just feeling sorry for myself, grieving for my parents and the childhood that had been lopped off at its knees. How the lonely little girl in me would have loved to have a doting grandpa like Jack and a fantasy place to play in such as this. If things didn't otherwise work out between us, I'd decided to offer myself to him for adoption. But first I had to get through this evening without falling asleep in the food.

"Sorry to keep you waiting," I said.

Jack looked up and his smile lit his eyes. "Not at all. I was enjoying Mrs. O'Callaghan's company. Anyway, you're worth waiting for, Eleanora. You look lovely."

Normally, I hate being called by my given name. Coming from most mouths, Eleanora sounds like an accusation. But on Jack's drowsy drawl, the name floated like a pond lily.

"Thanks. So do you."

Jack has my favorite kind of good looks. Strong bones, generous mouth, deeply etched lines that confirmed his willingness to display emotion. His dark hair is graying in distinguished patches. Everything about him says class, but not at a scream. He is unquestionably sexy, but not in that self-aware, heavy-lidded way that makes me want to splat some men with a cream pie. In fact, he seems entirely oblivious to the panting attentions of countless ripe young beauties in his classes.

When he strode over and walked me out after a lecture I sat in on, several eager crush bunnies tried to bump me off with poison eye darts. But Jack didn't so much as notice. That moment alone was enough to guarantee him the presidential suite in my heart.

Tonight, he wore a double-breasted navy blazer and soft gray slacks, a bold blue-and-silver geometric tie, and a matching pocket silk. The stark white shirt complemented his swarthy complexion and near-ebony eyes.

"Care to join us for dinner, Mrs. O'Callaghan?"

"You're a dear to ask, Jack, but no, thanks. I've a roast in the stove and a houseful of hungry mouths to feed. Run along now, you two. Have yourselves a grand time."

Jack's forest green Jeep was parked at the end of the circular drive.

"Bad day?" he asked.

"I'm fine. Just a little tired."

He brushed a drooping wave off my forehead and gently traced the wing-shaped scar.

"Tell you the truth, I could use a hair-down, feet-up sort of evening myself, Eleanora. I was up half the night puttering in my shop. How about I fix us a nice dinner at Chez Jack?"

"I wouldn't want you to bother. . . ."

"No bother at all. I'd prefer it, really. Bottle of wine. Warm fire. My specialty chicken and dirty rice with a salad and candied yams. How's that sound?"

"Wonderful, except for the filthy rice part."

"That's *dirty* rice. A South Carolina low-country specialty. Don't worry. Since it's your first time, I'll only use a little bit of mud."

Twenty minutes later, I was posed like Cleopatra on the plump leather couch in Jack's snug wood-paneled den. Bare feet on the armrest. Head propped on a hill of needlepoint pillows. Sipping a rich red wine.

Jack's house is in Wilton, ten miles north of the meandering New Canaan line. Two hundred years old, the place is as sound and elegant as its owner. Centered on a dozen wooded acres, it's also a world removed from the three-ring circus I call home. The lights were dim. The silence dense and intoxicating.

Delectable aromas wafted from the kitchen. Fragrant

warmth emanated from the hearth, where Jack had set a crackling blaze.

He'd refused my offer of help. While dinner cooked, I accepted his offer of a foot rub. The man had magic fingers. Closing my eyes, I couldn't help but wonder how they'd feel on other select parts of my anatomy. I could already feel the squeeze. The heat.

When he had finished turning my feet into cream soup, Jack leaned over and pressed his mouth to mine. Melting kiss, gentle as a sigh. The rest of me clamored loudly for the same attention. But the sudden shrill of the stove timer drowned me out.

Dinner furthered the sensual symphony. Moist, tender chicken; delectable blend of spices and herbs; rich red wine.

By the time I finished his incredible pecan pie, my stomach was packed like a Japanese subway car at rush hour. Since he still refused my offer of help, I relaxed on the couch while he went to do the dishes.

Steeped in drowsiness, I stared at the leaping flames.

When I snapped awake some time later, the fire had burned to cold white ash. Jack had killed the lights and covered me to the chin with a lavender-scented quilt. The house was dead still. According to the kitchen clock, it was after one in the morning.

Struck by a rare but irresistible naughty notion, I padded up to the second floor. There were four bedrooms. All empty. The bed in the master suite was rumpled but unoccupied.

Too bad.

All my protective instincts were temporarily out of service. I felt no trace of the usual fear. None of the typical doubts shrilled in my ear. My icy coating had melted.

I wanted to be held. Touched.

Peering out the bedroom window, I spotted the light leaking from the rear of the garage where Jack did his woodworking. A devout insomniac, he said he found the hobby restful. But I had other ideas tonight for how the man could spend that pent-up energy. Bent on seduction, I braved the night's chill.

Wordlessly, I opened the door to his shop. Jack looked up from his finishing work on a small table and smiled. The jeans and sweatshirt he'd changed into set off a most appealing body. Broad shoulders, slim torso, long legs ending in a charming butt. Just a hint of incipient love handles. Six feet plus of intriguing unknowns and possibilities.

"Sorry to interrupt you, Jack. But it's bedtime."

He searched my face for the fine print. "You sure, Eleanora?"

"Positive."

His smile intensified. His dark gaze was so penetrating it made me shiver. "Go on inside before you catch your death, darlin'. I'll join you soon as I clean my hands."

In his room, I quickly stripped to the basics and slipped between the sheets. Happily, I'd decided against my everyday undies in favor of a more attractive silky set edged in lace. This was right. I was ready.

Repeating those phrases like a mantra, I tried to drown out the rising objections. What if there was ugliness beneath the artifice? What if my judgment here was wrong? How many times had I closed my eyes to kiss a prince only to open them again facing a frog?

Firm footsteps mounted the stairs. Jack stood framed in the darkened doorway. My reservations evaporated as he neared the bed. Slow, lazy walk. No hurry.

"Want a back rub, Eleanora?"

"Mmmm."

I rolled over, inhaling his musky cologne on the pillowcase. With practiced moves, he kneaded the tension from my neck and shoulders. Easing lower, he liquefied my spine. Gently, he soothed the soreness from my lower back, trailing his fingers with his lips. His tongue. Easing down my panties. Slipping them over my feet.

I was drowning in relaxation, electric with desire.

He paused for a minute and stood. I heard the snap of his

jeans opening, the scratch of his sliding zipper. Fabric crumpling to the floor.

Before I could turn to face him, he lowered himself on top of me. Gripped me hard. I felt his urgent press. Warm breaths stabbed the back of my neck. His faceless weight was terrible, suffocating.

"Jack—"

The pillow muffled my words. Moaning, he pushed harder.

"Oh, darlin'. That's so good."

Driving piston, pressing at me. Invading.

"NO!"

Bucking furiously, I wrenched free. Sprawled on his back, Jack was panting. Startled. Shrinking.

"What's wrong, Eleanora? I thought—"

My panic receded. Hot humiliation flooded in to take its place. "I'm sorry. I'm so sorry—It's not you."

His eyes were on mine, searching, confused. "That's all right. Doesn't matter."

"Yes, it does. You must think I'm crazy—"

"Shh. Not at all. You get some rest now, darlin'. Don't give it another thought. I'll go sleep in the guest room."

The man was so dear and thoughtful. As he turned to leave, I impulsively leaned over and kissed his cheek. Drawing me lightly toward him, he pressed his mouth to mine.

My hunger came back like a riptide. I parted my lips, seeking a deeper kiss.

It was then I caught the odd smell on his breath. Wood and chemicals. The stench of nightmares. Evil's scent.

My rapist's signature cologne.

The Road To Redemption

by Patterson Graham, Ph.D.

(Uncorrected Page Proofs)

The Cambridge program promotes victim empathy through a unique process called Intensive Relatedness.

To prepare for this highly charged, emotionally challenging procedure, the offender completes a series of exercises designed to foster sensitivity and compassion. These traits have often been stunted or underdeveloped in the sexual sadist, but the seeds of his humanity remain to be sown and nurtured. Below, John re-creates an offense in preparation for empathic transfer to the victim's perspective.

I was cruising around when I spotted the girl. Just thinking. I'd smoked a little dope, but I wasn't stoned or anything. I felt pretty mellow, or so I thought. Looking back on those days, my mellow was probably the normal guy's Fourth of July.

Things were tough. My wife and I weren't getting along. The baby had colic. Kid was up screaming the whole night. I hated what I was doing, where I was, all of it. What I wanted most was change, a way out.

When I saw that girl, I read her as an engraved invitation. At the time, that's what went through my head. What a sweet coincidence, I thought. She's here. I'm here. Simple addition puts us together.

I was looking for relief, escape. I understand now that I was trying to recapture the confusion of pleasure and pain I used to get from my parents. It wasn't really about sex. Sex was the least of it.

When you ask me to see it through that little girl's eyes, that night comes right back to me. It's as clear and real as this minute.

I become that girl. I can feel her terror. The trembling inside. The dizzying heat.

Who is this man? What the hell does he want?

"Stop," I scream. "Please don't."

He won't listen. He roughs me up and pushes me down on the bed. I'm struggling my hardest, but I can't get away from him. He pulls my clothes off. Help! Stop!

I can feel that poor kid's pain, now. Feel everything I did to her. How did I ever get off on a thing like that? What the hell can I do to make it right?

Chapter 11

LENNIE

Shocked mute and trembling, I watched Jack stride down the hall to the guest room. His door shut with a soft clack. Darkness settled like a shroud.

My thoughts raced.

Could this man be the faceless beast who invaded my home and body twenty-five years ago?

Impossible.

Or was it?

The acrid woody scent he exuded was identical. Burned on my memory. So was his overpowering approach from behind. The strength. The weight of him. All echoes from my blackest nightmare.

Could the rest of Jack Chambless be a calculated act? The courtly manners, the solicitous attentions, the gentlemanly respect for my maddeningly changeable mind?

Not likely.

Poor Jack had reaped the full benefit of my overdeveloped doubt. Despite my toughest scrutiny, I'd found nothing to distrust in him. Nothing in the least bit suspect or disturbing.

Anyway, why would the man who raped me a quarter century ago choose to reenter my life? I couldn't imagine a reason, sane or otherwise.

Surely he couldn't have deliberately engineered meeting Mrs. O' at the symphony? And even if he had, how could he know she would promptly invite him home for dinner to meet me?

Psychic powers?

It would have taken that at least. Aunt Selia's last name was Malone, not Finn. The man who raped me had no way to learn who I was, much less find out where I'd come to live. The pieces didn't fit.

Turning the issue on its head, I found piles of compelling evidence in Jack's favor. He'd spent his entire life in the South. A doctorate took four or five years, minimum, which meant that at the time of my assault, he was still a student. Already married and the father of a baby son. I could hardly picture him taking off once in a full moon and winging away to Smalltown, Connecticut, in search of a careless young victim.

Jack came nowhere near the image of my attacker I'd gripped in my secret soul all these years. This man was gentle and considerate. Kind and giving. A proud, attentive poppa. A doting grandpa. A dedicated teacher and mentor who reveled in his students' enlightenment and respect.

I thought about the playhouse. No monster's hands could create such fanciful wonders. No monster would hang a wall full of family pictures in the den and smile whenever he passed them as Jack did.

Fear loosened its grip on me. The crowd of doubts quieted. This wasn't the first time my darkest imagination had wrestled my common sense to the ground.

My sleep was restless. Crammed with vivid dreams. In one, I was chased by a cloud of swarming bees. I ran, lungs bursting. Tripping over a rock, I lay hurt and weeping while they circled overhead. Taunting. Dipping one by one to hover and sting.

Original, Lennie. Freud's estate could likely sue for plagiarism.

I awoke to the sound of rushing water from the bathroom down the hall. Early morning light spilled over my rumpled bed. While Jack showered, I tossed on a robe and hurried downstairs to fix breakfast. By the time he appeared, shaved and dressed, I had the coffee perking and a gourmet feast of Cheerios, skim milk, and orange juice set out on the dining-room table. I would have liked to make an omelet or pancakes, but I'm cooking-disabled. Instead, I used the good dishes and fan-folded the napkins to distract him from the food.

Ever the gentleman, Jack acted as if last night's lunacy had never happened. Sitting opposite him, eating in companionable silence, I felt certain that my crazy misgivings had been just that.

By some miracle, our budding relationship seemed to have survived my stupid hysteria. When I was ready to leave for the temporary agency where I worked when I had any spare time, Jack walked me to the door.

"How's dinner tonight, Eleanora?"

"I don't know. I'll have to see if the agency needs me later. Saturday night can be busy."

"Think they'd consider sending you out to baby-sit a lonely old coot?"

"Maybe. But you don't qualify."

His kiss relit my pilot. But the thought of another unfortunate scene spooked me. I drew back. "Speak to you later, Jack."

Crea-Temps operates out of a converted gray-blue Colonial on New Canaan's Park Street. The owner, Shelby Burkhardt, inherited the building and the business from her parents when they retired to Boca Raton.

While the elder Burkhardts ran the place, it was a standard temp agency, providing fill-in secretaries, gofers, and receptionists. Shelby, whose astrological sign is neon, quickly bored of that. She sought out more unconventional assignments. Now, Crea-Temps fields a steady stream of typical and offbeat requests from as far away as Massachusetts. Since signing on to work with them three years ago, I've subbed as an aerobics instructor, a party clown, a limo driver, a clambake chef, and on and on. My most frequent assignment is product demonstrator for Sassy Susan's Sassiest Salsa Supreme.

Entering the building's dim foyer, I wondered what dear Shelby had in store for me today. We'd been wary allies since high school, where we'd been assigned adjacent lockers. Like alien species in adjoining zoo cages, Shelby and I spent endless time observing each other. Circling around.

Senior year, a swaggering tough tried to amuse his pals by shoving a hand up Shelby's abbreviated skirt. Shelby, who didn't get the joke, hollered for help and screamed obscenities. I caught the jerk squarely in the face with my book bag.

The history text alone weighed two pounds. Add Contemporary Literature, Calculus, Physics, gym shoes, baseball mitt, lunch, *Great Expectations,* and a jammed three-ring binder, and the tough's imitation of a felled tree was not surprising. Neither was Shelby's newfound fondness for me. I felt the same for her when she swiftly gathered her dignity, strode out of the building, crumbled a leftover bran muffin from her own lunch; and shoved the mess into the gas tank of the tough's Harley-Davidson.

Shelby's talent for retribution has always far exceeded mine. The creep's broken nose healed in time; his bike never recovered.

Smiling at the memory, I hung my black wool coat in the Crea-Temps hall closet and passed through the living room\reception area to my boss's bedroom\office.

When I entered Shelby's office, she was on a call. Her brown suit, purchased during a liquid protein low, gave her the look of a bumpy back-country road. The orange shoes, purse, nails, and lipstick blazed forth like traffic cones placed to mark an accident site. Covering the receiver, she mouthed something I couldn't decipher.

"What?"

She tried again, but I still didn't get it. Sensing my puzzlement, she stood and dramatically gyrated her generous hips. The message came through that time, though not without a touch of confusion. Someone was looking for either a belly dancer or a truck to mix cement.

Shelby wound up the conversation. "Yes, Mr. Bronzini. I'll get right on it. Should have an answer for you by noon. *Ciao.*"

Hanging up, she tossed her boot black hair like a bullfighter's cape. As she flipped through her daily order cards, she lit a Kool. The cigarettes were for effect only. Shelby didn't inhale, except people. Eyeing me slyly, she spoke on a cloud of minty smoke. "Silk blouse, pearls, screw-me boots. Didn't get home to change last night, did we, pal?"

"Not that it's any of your business, but I was tired. I fell asleep on Jack's couch, and he didn't wake me."

Her brow peaked. "His *couch*, is it? Now, that's one I haven't heard before. Exactly how big a *couch* does the man have?" She ventured an estimate with her fingers.

"Jack and I are friends, Shelby. That's all."

"Very *close* friends, I'd guess. Suits you well, toots. You're positively glowing."

"And you're positively wrong."

Veiling the smirk with her fingers, she peered into an imaginary crystal ball.

"Madame Shelby sees all, knows all, tells all. There. It's getting clearer now. I see a man in your life. Tall, dark. Rhett Butler type but without Clark Gable's fabled halitosis."

Anticipating a lengthy performance, I sat. To the best of my knowledge, Shelby had been born without an off button.

"This man is falling for you, hard. And you for him." She frowned. "But wait. I see a cloud forming. Miz Scarlett isn't sure she wants to get involved. Yes, I see her running. Terrified of commitment. Slow down, Scarlett. Stop! Grab this one, and, as God is my witness, you'll never be horny again."

"Aside from unsolicited advice, do you have anything else for me today, Madame Mouthpiece?"

Her frown deepened. She spewed a minty vapor trail. "Seriously. What's wrong with the guy? He's rich. Single. Smart. Only has one head. What more could a girl ask?"

"Nothing's wrong with him. I just don't believe in rushing into things, that's all."

She aimed her crystal-gazing stare my way. "You're scared, Lennie. Admit it."

"What's the point, Shelby?"

"Just say it. Come on."

"Okay. I'm scared."

She threw up her hands. "What the hell is there to be scared of?"

"Where shall I begin?"

Puffing like a locomotive, she paced behind her desk. "I hate to say it, but this is a definite pattern with you, missy. Girl meets boy. Girl likes boy. Girl puts on track shoes and hits the road. I've been watching you cut bait and bolt since high school. Don't you think it's time to change the tune?"

"Let us not forget that this golden advice come from one who's been down the aisle and back again five times."

Shelby hatched a batch of smoke rings. One for each of her failed marriages. "So happens it's only four. Brian was annulled. Anyhow, I'm not the issue here. What's the deal, Lennie? Are you afraid he's a cheat, a cheapskate, a closet queen, a druggie, a philanderer, what?"

"It's nothing specific. I told you. What's wrong with being cautious?"

Leaning toward me, she propped her pudgy elbows on the desk. "How about I have him checked out?"

"You mean investigated?"

"Absolutely. Since Brian, I do it all the time. This private eye I use is very discreet, very thorough. Say the word and I'll call him. My treat."

"The word is no."

"I thought you said you were cautious."

"Too cautious for belly dancing. What else have you got?"

Ten minutes later, I was stationed behind the counter adjoining the deli section at the Food Emporium. Dressed in a cobbler apron and a chef's hat, my mission was to distribute low-fat taco chips stuffed with mock guacamole, "lite" sour cream, and Sassy Susan's Sassiest Salsa Supreme.

Assignment to supermarket salsa duty was Shelby's version of a rap on the knuckles. Consequently, it was my most frequent assignment. Of course, I never let on that I found the work reasonably enjoyable. Hungry shoppers, grateful for the free snacks, lavished me with thanks and compliments. I imagined saving some of them from desperation junk food purchases at the checkout counters. The task was mostly mindless, allowing me unlimited thinking time. Ordinarily, I welcomed that, but not today.

Every girl I saw reminded me of Kitty. Every tall, dark man brought troubling thoughts of Jack. I couldn't bear all the cozy couples. The chatting friends. The relentless parade of pert, retired prom queens pushing shopping carts crammed with gourmet groceries and gorgeous kids.

I was thirty-six. Single, childless, and likely to remain so. I had no home to call my own. Precious little family. In my chosen job, some still viewed me more as a punch line than as a professional. Considering how disappointed my parents would likely be, I hoped heaven wasn't equipped with one-way mirrors.

A pudgy little boy charged the counter and grabbed a fistful of taco treats. He stuffed them in his mouth and chewed furiously.

Spotting him from the deli, his mother wailed, "Billy, those are *fattening*!"

Next to the woman, the child looked emaciated. Under her barber-pole turtleneck and red tights, rolls of flesh undulated like the tides.

"Hunh-uh, Mommy. Look. Low-fat." Spraying chip

crumbs and salsa bits, little Billy read from Sassy Susan's nutritional analysis sheet. "Only three milligrams."

"Everything you put in your mouth is fattening, Billy Wolkowitz," she said, ogling me for affirmation. "Isn't that so?"

"Whatever it says on the sheet," I replied with the company's recommended diplomacy.

"Air and water aren't fattening," Billy challenged. "You put *them* in your mouth."

"Fine. Be a know-it-all. Eat this crap and you'll turn into a house like your mom someday. That what you want?"

The rest of the day passed without incident. At quitting time, I decided against calling Crea-Temps for an evening assignment. I'd had more than my daily fill of Shelby's meddling. Dinner with Jack was far more appealing. Maybe I could make up to him for last night's temporary insanity.

We met at a small candlelit café on New Canaan's Elm Street. Jack had called ahead to reserve the back corner booth and a bottle of fine merlot.

He was waiting when I arrived. Standing, he caught me in a gentle hug and set a gossamer kiss on my neck. Every one of his moves set me tingling. The man seemed hardwired to my nervous system. Suddenly rubber-kneed, I sat and pretended to study the menu.

Dinner passed in a lusty haze. Jack's dark gaze made my heart stutter. The press of his knees was a candle flame, melting me to drips of weeping wax.

"Want dessert, Eleanora?"

I met his dangerous dark eyes head-on. "Nothing that's on the menu."

His expression became grave. "You sure?"

"Positive. I'd like to throw myself on the mercy of the court for last night, Your Honor."

"No need. You're more than worth waiting for, darlin'. I don't want you to push things on my account."

"I'm pushing them on my own account, Jack. Honestly. Let's get the hell out of here, shall we?"

The drive to his house seemed endless. Everywhere he touched—cheek, arm, knee, shoulder—started an intense blaze burning.

As soon as he shut the front door, I lifted my lips for his kiss. Barely brushing my mouth, his touch filled me with waves of pleasure. His fingers traced my eyes, trailed down my neck. Worked me into a frenzy of aching need.

Afterward, I reveled in a dreamy fog. I felt no trace of the standard regrets. Sex for me had been many things, but never like this. Never close to this pure rush of exquisite sensations.

"That was nice, Jack. Extremely," I murmured into the crook of his neck.

He sighed and drew me closer. "All I want is to please you, Eleanora. That's everything to me."

Chapter 12

LENNIE

As soon as my bones hardened sufficiently, I sat up and started dressing.

"You're going?"

"I've got a full night ahead of me, Jack. I'm planning to do some highly disreputable dreaming about you."

"What's wrong with doing that right here?"

"Wouldn't be the same."

"No way I can convince you?" His finger started tracing school figures on my back. A giant shiver engulfed me.

Scooping up my discarded clothing, I retreated to the armchair. "Several. But it's better if I go. Really."

His naughty grin faded. "Whatever you want, darlin'."

My car was still parked in the restaurant lot. When Jack braked his Jeep to let me out, I was startled to see that the place was still open. In under two hours, the world had changed beyond recognition. At least, mine had.

The rape hadn't destroyed my sex drive, but it certainly marred the way with perilous curves and treacherous potholes. As a teenager, I'd readily acquiesced to any and all advances. Saying yes meant no one could force the issue. Anyway, I was used merchandise. What was left to protect?

I found it excruciating to hear my friends agonizing endlessly over their virginity. Mine was a phantom limb, a mammoth, unreachable ache.

Most times in bed, I felt little or nothing. My senses were stone, my skin dried rubber. At will, I could disengage my mind. It would soar off to circle the broad, blank sky or perch at a distance in still, uncaring observation.

Later, when I finally emerged from the numbness, when I started to value myself again, I swore off intimacy altogether. Sex was difficult, messy, dangerous. It had a way of confusing simple relationships and turning complex ones astray. Adding sex to the mix was like adding a storm to a journey. You were much more likely to get lost or sidetracked. Not to mention damaged or destroyed.

But with Jack, it was different somehow. I felt clear. Easy. As Miranda had predicted, my mood was mightily improved. Ditto the complexion. I could feel the drowsy glow.

He caught my hand as I moved to open the car door.

"Let's go somewhere for a nightcap."

"I shouldn't, Jack. I'm more than fuzzy enough already."

"Coffee, then. I'm just not ready to let you go yet."

When he put it that way, I found myself fresh out of arguments.

Five minutes from town was the Manchester Arms, an elegant country inn with a dozen guest rooms perched above a fine continental restaurant. We claimed a vacant table in the crowded main floor lounge, where a man in a tux was teasing cabaret and show tunes from an ebony baby grand. The lights were dim, the atmosphere languid. To keep from nodding off, I ordered a double espresso. As the bitter brew sliced through me, a striking woman in black stepped to the mike.

With a pinch of irrational envy, I was glad that Jack was sitting with his back to her. The woman was ageless, lithe and graceful as a cat. And she exuded a cat's raw sensuality. Sculpted mouth, almond eyes, high-boned cheeks, and a long sinuous neck. Her moves were fluid, her poise firm and commanding.

The piano player riffed through the opening chords of "Just My Bill." The singer joined in, crooning in a lush, throaty voice that reminded me vaguely of Miranda's. Instantaneously, the crowd was hooked. Conversations halted. Everyone turned to watch.

But her effect on Jack was nowhere close to what I would have predicted. He eyed the singer for a beat, then turned away in rude dismissal. Signaling the waiter, he motioned impatiently for the check.

"Ready to go?" he mouthed.

Leaning close, I whispered, "Let's stay for the set, okay? She's terrific."

He shrugged. During the next several numbers, he sat stiffly, suffering obvious discomfort. I could not bring myself to go along with his unspoken wishes and walk out. She was that good.

In the thunderous applause at the set's end, Jack tossed a bill on the check and rose to leave. Mystified by his reaction, I followed reluctantly. We were halfway through the inn's lobby, when the singer came up behind us in a breathless rush.

"Jack? I thought that was you."

At close range, she was even more arresting. Her cat's eyes glinted as she wrapped Jack in her long, liquid arms.

He drew away abruptly. "Eleanora, meet Sally Deane. Friend from way back."

"Has been a century or two. What brings you up this way? Business?"

"No. I have a place in Wilton."

"A northerner? You?" She turned to me. "Jack and I met an age ago, when he was at Yale. Boy was edgy as a caged bird. Thought what you needed was to be down Dixie way with the other rebs, Jack."

Jack chuckled dryly. "I was young, Sally. I got over it."

Her eyes tracked him boldly. "Looks like a fine recovery to me. Stop by and see me sometime, why don't you? Be fun to catch up."

"Sure."

She slinked off. Jack led me out to his car. As we trudged across the slushy lot, I tried to make sense of her disturbing revelation.

Why hadn't Jack told me he'd lived in New Haven?

Don't get carried away, Lennie. There has to be a simple explanation.

As I framed the question, I willed my heart to stop its fretful thumping.

"You never mentioned you went to Yale, Jack."

He shrugged. "No? I did some postdoctoral work there after I finished up at U.Va. It was that or Vietnam."

The chill air thrummed with other unspoken questions. Shrill accusatory doubts I couldn't bring myself to voice.

Where were his wife and baby while he studied in New Haven? Wouldn't the wife and child have exempted him from the draft? And why had he led me to believe that New England was entirely new to him?

A horrifying fact crept over me like a fever.

When I was raped, Jack lived no more than twenty minutes from the house I shared with Huck and Aunt Selia. If he hadn't kept that from me deliberately, why was he so anxious to avoid that accidental run-in with the singer?

Easy, girl. There could be plenty of other reasons. Maybe their "friendship" hadn't been strictly kosher. Even if it was, the presence of a drop-dead sexy woman like Sally Deane could surely inspire any man to imitate a squirrel.

All the twists and reversals made my head spin. How well did I know this man? Did I really know him at all? Jack avoided talking about himself. Was it out of modesty, as I'd always assumed, or did he have something dark and ugly to hide?

When he stopped the car, I deflected his kiss. His troubled eyes begged for reassurance, but I had none to offer.

"Dinner tomorrow?"

"I don't know, Jack. I'll have to see."

He opened his mouth to say something, then thought better of it. "Okay, Eleanora. Sleep well."

At home I hurried up the back stairs, trying to outrun my dizzying suspicions. But they trailed me to my room and prodded me toward the phone.

Before I could lift the receiver, however, it rang. Miranda's smoky voice barely pierced a roar of background noise.

My volume rose in sympathetic reflex. "Connolly, where are you?"

"Between sets. Can't remember the name of the town, but it's someplace extremely hostile to the human life form as we know it. Couple of polar bears were sitting fifth row center during the first show, I swear it. And they were wearing sweaters."

"What's up?"

"That's my question. I keep catching these Lennie vibes."

My recent suspicions caught in my throat. "It's nothing."

"What kind of nothing?"

"I don't think nothing comes in different sizes and flavors, Miranda."

"Okay, don't tell me. Just go on keeping all that poison inside until it eats holes in your lining, Len. See if I care."

I smiled. "You *do* care."

Her voice went grim. "Enough to keep playing the same old broken record. If you can't open up to me, fine. Go see someone you *can* talk to."

"For the millionth time, I *do not* need a shrink, Miranda. I'm small enough as it is."

"I'm not kidding, Len. Everyone needs to open up and air out once in awhile. Even you."

"Isn't that your introductory music I hear in the background?"

"The polar bears can wait. Promise me you'll think about it."

"About polar bears waiting? Sure."

Her voice became stern. "I mean it, Len. What do you have to lose?"

"Time and money. Not to mention a perfectly wonderful bunch of neuroses it's taken me decades to perfect."

Miranda puffed her disgust. "You're hopeless."

"And you're missing your cue."

"At least promise me you'll be good to yourself. Deal?"

"Deal."

"And careful." Miranda knew, all too well, my long, sorry history of turning accident-prone under stress.

"You'd better go, Miranda. Polar bears are not known for their patience."

There was no answer at Crea-Temps. Dialing Shelby's home number, I wondered how quickly her tried and trusty private eye could get the investigation done.

Chapter 13

LENNIE

The Whitechapel School occupies six ivied brick buildings, circling a tidy green near downtown Bridgeport. The main house at the head of the snow-capped square contains the dining room, social hall, classrooms, therapy rooms, gym, and chapel. Flanking that are four small dormitories, where the students are placed by age.

During his two-decade tenure at Whitechapel, my brother Huck has made the full circuit. He's also spent his fair share of time recovering from assorted bugs and mishaps in the homey infirmary at the campus's diminutive foot. Aside from Whitechapel's founder, Arthur Crandall Myers, Huck has logged more years at the place than anyone. I suppose that qualifies me as the school's most seasoned visitor.

When I'm off duty, I come to see Huck during the standard Sunday visiting hours. Today, arriving ten minutes early, I was fifth in the line of cars rolling into the unpaved lot.

The D'Allessios, whose ten-year-old twin sons were housed in Junior II, parked beside me. As usual, they came equipped. The rear of their van was crammed with commercial-sized food containers. Mr. D'Allessio opened the hatch, unleashing a toxic blast of oregano and garlic.

Though the school officially bans food gifts, the staff is inclined to look the other way. They recognize that the so-called normal relatives of disabled kids need their own quirky coping mechanisms. Mine are stubbornness and extra-thick insulation. Gae D'Allessio attempts to salve her grief with oceans of homemade sauce and acres of lasagna.

To kill the remaining few minutes until visiting hours began, I scanned the real estate section of the Sunday *New York Times*. I savored the feast of MBR's, EIK's, and formal DR's. I noted how the prices were stated to make them sound as tiny and innocent as possible: "Only 200K." "Reduced to low 3's." "A real steal in the low seven figures."

Hard not to leap on that one immediately. But it was time to see my brother.

The mess hall was at the rear of the main house. And at the end of a typical Sunday dinner, quite the mess it was. When compared to the eating habits of some of his schoolmates, Huck's manners seemed downright elegant.

Theo Carrington, a fourteen-year-old blond stringbean, considered all round foodstuffs suitable for throwing. Kitchen personnel eliminated obvious hazards such as peas and new potatoes from his plate. But that didn't stop Theo from balling up other packable substances and pitching them at every opportunity.

Vanessa Gould was finger-painting with her mashed potatoes. Gary Southworth squirreled his leftover meatloaf, gravy and all, in his pockets. A couple of students preferred hands to implements. Several chose to dine under their tables. Add the standard complement of tantrums, shrieks, and flailing, and the scene was a lively one, indeed.

Huck sat at the head of the senior table, finishing his dessert of applesauce and oatmeal cookies. *Spoon, chew chew chew. Spoon, spoon chew. Chew chew chew chew——spoon.* The complexities of his rhythms had grown with the rest of him.

My brother is over six feet tall now, handsome and husky. His hair has darkened to the color of wet sand. Near-black brows and lashes set off the wide blue eyes. His complexion, pale as bisque, belies his sturdiness. Huck is built to last and moves with the force and velocity of a freight train.

Though it was nothing new, the feel of whisker stubble on his cheek still startled me when I bent to kiss him. Who'd given my beautiful baby permission to become a man?

"Hey, good-looking. What's up?"

He shook his head sharply, protesting the interruption. I waited out two more verses of Ode To Applesauce And Cookie before daring to speak again.

"So, bro. What do you think of those Giants?"

The line is part of my stock monologue. Huck never fails to watch the games, though I'm not convinced he follows the action. He might as soon be entranced by the blur of rushing behemoths or the dizzy play of cameras over artificial turf. In his skewed universe, there is no way to determine exactly what or how much passes intact from sensory organs to brain.

Some describe autism as a state of perpetual overload: a flood of sights, sounds, and experiences from which the sufferer protectively withdraws. If that is the case, I can't imagine why Huck and so many of his fellow space travelers gravitate toward raucous music and contact sports. To be honest, what I don't understand about Huck's condition could fill a much larger volume than any I've ever read on the subject.

"Earth to Huck. Come in, Huck."

Twisting in his chair, he bravely bore the indignity of my hug. Several guttural grunts said he was glad to see me. Or so I chose to believe.

A bell sounded, signaling the official end of the meal. Huck rose and started neatly stacking the dessert plates from his table. Being elder statesman had its privileges.

The final dish he retrieved was larger than the others. Placing it atop his stack, Huck uttered a squeal of distress.

"They must have passed out a lunch plate by mistake," I told him.

Fixated, Huck pushed the offending dish from side to side, struggling to make it match the others.

"It's okay, sweetheart. Don't worry about it."

But Huck was growing more agitated by the second. He set the plates down with a crash and wildly shook his hands at them. A pulsing cry rose from his throat. Soon it stretched to a piercing wail of anguish.

"Shh, Huck. Take it easy."

I tried to calm him with a hug, but he wrenched loose and flailed harder. The screams intensified, and his face blazed a furious scarlet.

I stood helpless, desperate to stop the tantrum. Nothing I said or did got through to him. After what seemed to be an interminable time, one of the staff finally came to the rescue.

She raised a hand directly in front of his ashen face and spoke in a sharp, demanding tone. "Stop, Huck! No!"

His shrieks dimmed to a whimper.

"Stop!" she repeated.

That broke the spell. Mute and focused, Huck lifted the stack of plates, ignoring the mismatched one, and loped off happily toward the kitchen.

When he returned, I suggested a walk. We were on the way to the coatroom when we ran into his speech therapist.

Actually, Huck ran into her. I reached out and grabbed the woman before she went careening into a display of student artwork.

Rosemary Keaveny is a petite blonde in her forties, a Tinkerbell look-alike with the force and determination of a backhoe. Ten years of hard, often thankless work at White-chapel haven't dimmed her enthusiasm. She is constantly testing new methods. She remains ever vigilant to her client's mostly unspoken needs. Nothing ruffles her. Not even my brother, the tank.

"Sorry, Rosemary. You okay?" I asked.

"Fine. So happens you two were just the people I came

to see. We have a surprise for your sister, don't we, Mr. Finn? Hope you didn't give away our big secret."

"If anyone can keep a secret, it's Huck. Isn't that so, sweetheart?"

"Wait until you see this, Lennie. You'll flip."

The therapist had to jog to keep up with my brother's breakneck stride. Moving at a near run myself, I trailed them to Rosemary's second-floor office.

The windowless rectangle was furnished with a child-sized table and chairs, a battered brown sofa, a braided rug, and plaid curtains. Warped wooden shelves held toys, games, puppets, books, a tape recorder and tapes, electronic communication aids, and assorted testing materials. Student drawings and photos festooned the wall behind Rosemary's gunmetal desk. Her computer was on, its cursor working like a nervous tic at the corner of the otherwise blank blue screen.

With rare eagerness, Huck hurried across the room and plopped into the desk chair. Flapping his hands impatiently, he squeaked like a trapped mouse.

Rosemary laughed. "Okay. I hear you, Huck. You're as anxious to show her as I am."

Standing behind him, the therapist placed a hand beneath Huck's right forearm. "Go on. Do your stuff, sir."

His index finger dipped like a divining rod. Barely eyeing the keyboard, Huck started punching letters. "HAIT-MEET"

"Look at you. You can type," I said.

Rosemary silenced me with a look. Huck pressed the enter key and dipped down a line. "HAITM," he typed again.

"Remember to space," Rosemary prompted.

This time he pressed the return key twice and started over. "HAIT MEET LOFE"

Rosemary beamed at me. "Get the message, sis?"

"*He* said that?"

"His spelling needs work, but the sentiment's all Huck's."

While Rosemary was looking in my direction, Huck added a line for emphasis. "MEET LOFE SUCKS"

Not knowing whether to laugh or cry, I did both. "But how? I don't get it."

"How remains a mystery. It's called Facilitated Communication. I went to a workshop over the summer to learn the techniques. With the slightest touch on the arm, some kids like Huck are able to type or use a word board."

"It's incredible. You sure you're not helping him?"

"Hard to believe, I know. And I have to tell you there are plenty of esteemed skeptics who say it's all wishful thinking, strictly in the mind of the beholder. Unfortunately, the method has been near impossible to prove in controlled studies. But from everything I've seen, it works."

She turned away again. Facing the side wall, there appeared to be no way she could see what Huck was typing or influence him in any way. "Tell us something else, buddy."

Slowly, he pecked at the keys again. "SULVANS GAY"

"Let me know when he's finished," Rosemary said.

Huck nodded firmly.

"I think he is."

Looking at the monitor, the therapist stifled a grin. "You don't know that. Your brother's a born gossip, I'm afraid, Lennie. He's been making that claim ever since the music teacher had his ear pierced."

"RITE EAR MEENS GAY," Huck persisted.

"Not necessarily. Anyway, what difference does it make if Mr. Sullivan is gay or not?" the therapist chided.

"VANESSA LIKES SULVAN," Huck typed. "SULVAN GAY SHE SHUD FORGET HIM"

Rosemary ruffled Huck's hair. "I'm afraid we've created a monster here."

Huck squeaked in protest and groped wildly. He wanted the therapist's helping hand again.

"LENNIE TELL MYERS NO MORE MEET LOFE"

"You have a suggestion for our esteemed headmaster?

Tell him yourself," Rosemary said. "How about saying something to your sister, Huck? Lennie's waited a long, long time for this."

I held my breath. I willed him to say he loved me. When he was little, I often imagined I heard his phantom voice. *Love you, Lennie,* he intoned in my fantasies. *Can I have a great big hug?*

Huck's brow furrowed with concentration. I tensed. The wait seemed endless. Another twenty-six years. Finally, his fingers played over the keyboard.

"GIANTS SUCK," he wrote.

After a few additional remarks about the state of professional sports and the food at Whitechapel, Huck turned off the computer.

I wanted to press for more, but Rosemary warned against the dangers of overload. Other clients had regressed when pushed too far, she told me. One had shut down altogether, refusing to go anywhere near the computer again.

With my brother coming along so well on the system, the therapist didn't want to risk that. With my heart already full to overflowing, neither did I. Huck had spoken. It was a miracle of mythic proportions. I felt like running home and filling in the long-standing blank in his baby book. *First words:* "I hate meat loaf. Meat Loaf Sucks."

Rosemary stayed in her office to catch up on some paperwork. I followed Huck down to the day room, a generous square crammed with comfortable chairs, books and games, a Ping-Pong table, a jukebox, a player piano, and a large-screen TV.

Grabbing the remote control, Huck tuned to the pre-game show. Whatever his opinion of the home team, my brother seemed eager to catch the kickoff. Soon, several other residents, visitors, and staff drifted in and clustered around the set.

After the first quarter, a voice came over the loudspeaker to announce the end of visiting hours. I kissed Huck and said good-bye, half expecting him to dispatch me with a witty comment. But my brother had reverted to his standard self. Stone face. Unseeing stare. Deafening silence.

It was eerie to think of him composing at the computer. Expressing himself. I assured myself the cataclysmic event had really happened. I didn't dream it. At least, not this time.

A celebration was definitely in order. I considered my options for dinner company and dismissed them in turn.

The person I most wanted to mark the occasion with was Huck. But restaurants threw my brother completely. Too much noise. Too many strangers. And no matter how good the food, the menu was inevitably arranged without the least regard for rhyme or meter. Even the minor mania of the O'Callaghan house disturbed him. Whitechapel was chaotic, certainly. But it was familiar chaos. Comfy pathology. The devil Huck knew.

Jack came packaged with too many disturbing questions. Mrs. O' spent most Sundays visiting relatives. The only other housemate whose company I tended to single out was Maniac. But I doubted the mutt would appreciate Huck's accomplishment. Maniac wasn't big on conversation. Typically, when I attempted to confide in her, she propped her muzzle on her paws and promptly fell asleep.

I saw enough of Shelby at the office. Make that too much. Ditto most of the men on the squad.

There was one notable exception. Inspired, I stopped to call Red from a pay phone. No answer, but he spent much of his off-duty time tending bar at Ernie's, a comfortably seedy spot two blocks from the firehouse.

Claiming a stool at the scarred oak bar, I waited while Red blended a batch of margaritas, tapped a keg of Bud, toted a couple of checks, and doused a conflagration between two patrons. In the ensuing lull, he drifted my way and tossed me his best Bogart.

"Of all the gin joints in all the towns in all the world she walks into mine."

I answered him in kind, though my Bergman was

soundly second-rate. "Was that cannon fire—or just my heart pounding?"

His grin was infectious. "To what do I owe the high honor and distinct pleasure?"

I bragged about Huck's newfound skill on the computer.

"Fantastic news. I'd say a spot of bubbly is in order." Red popped the cork on Ernie's lame excuse for champagne, an ancient bottle of sparkling something-or-other he found gathering mold at the back of the cooler. Raising his empty glass, he clinked mine.

"To Huck."

"Here's looking at you, kid."

Many wines improve with age, and this one seasoned with striking speed. By the time I finished the first glass, the swill tasted much better. Halfway through the second, my brain was fizzing nicely, too. When Red tipped the bottle to pour me yet another refill, I slanted my palm atop the glass to ward him off.

"Enough, Red. Any more, I'll have to walk home."

"No, you won't. I'm off in an hour. Red Snapper's personal driving service, at your service, ma'am."

"That's sweet. But I need my car tomorrow morning."

"No problem. I'll drive you in your bomb and have one of the guys from here follow in mine. Then, I'll come back here, get him to his car, and—"

I made a time-out sign. "Stop. You're making me dizzy."

"Sorry, milady. Let's leave that to this fine bottle of Chateauneuf du Crap, shall we?"

I sipped my way through another glass and a half, which more than did the job. Hoping to neutralize the wine, I ordered a burger and fries. While I ate, Red regaled me with jokes and stories. For some reason, everything he said struck me as hysterically funny. I laughed until my sides ached. When his relief finally arrived an hour and a half later, I floated out beside Red on a nice fuzzy cloud.

He pulled my Toyota to the end of the O'Callaghan

drive. His buddy from the bar had followed in Red's Blazer and sat idling at the curb.

"Thanks, Red. I had entirely too good a time."

"You're entitled. That's really great about your brother. Nice to see you up where you belong for a change."

His solemn caring brought unexpected tears to my eyes. "You're the best, Red. Don't know what I'd do without you."

"Feeling's entirely mutual, my dear."

I reached across the seat to kiss his cheek. He turned, and in one of those awkward missteps, my lips grazed his mouth instead. The friendly little gesture turned into a long, dizzy, penetrating grope.

Flustered, I yanked away. "Whoa. Sorry. I guess that wine got to me even more than I thought."

"Right. Me, too."

"You didn't have any."

"You sure? Feels like I did." His grin broke the tension. "I'm really glad about your brother."

"Thanks. Good night, Red."

" 'Night, Lennie."

Mounting the fire stairs, I felt him watching from the driveway. *Great, Lennie. Nice going. Perfect way to kill a perfectly good friendship.* Hopefully, Red would write the incident off and forget it. Things between us had been fine for two years. Verging on perfect. I didn't want our pleasant, easy friendship warped or strained.

Forgetting suited me fine as well. I refused to let a moment's foolishness or anything else spoil this incredible day.

Thinking of Huck, I couldn't help but smile. *Meat loaf sucks.* Music to my ears.

Chapter 14

LENNIE

My phone was ringing as I stepped out of the shower. Wrapped in a towel, I ran to pick up before the machine. Seven-thirty in the morning was too early for anything good. Given the hours she kept, Miranda rarely managed to roll over and dial before eight. I steeled myself for disturbing news or an emergency. But I was mistaken. It was both.

"Ms. Finn. It's Clarissa Pratt."

The prosecutor's tone had lost its starch. She sounded overwhelmed. My scalp prickled.

"What's wrong?"

"Looks like our man's struck again. Late last night in Ridgefield. Kid was only ten."

Less than a week had passed since Kitty Dolan's rape. The prosecutor's dire prophesy about the rapist escalating his attacks was coming true.

"Who's the victim?" I asked. "Can she add anything to the profile?"

"Not likely. I just came back from paying her a visit at the morgue."

The Assistant State's Attorney tersely described the crime. While her parents vacationed in St. Croix, the little girl had been spending the week with her grandparents. Last evening, the trio enjoyed dinner out at a seafood place. Returning home, they watched a *Star Trek* movie video in the den. Shortly before ten, the girl went to sleep in the guest room. After the late news, the grandparents locked up as usual and turned in themselves.

Sometime during the next five hours, the perp slipped into the granddaughter's room through an unlocked window. He raped the girl and slit her throat, though not necessarily in that order. When the grandmother awoke at four A.M. to use the bathroom, she looked in on the child. Found her lying in a pool of blood. With the window left open, the room was refrigerator cold, so the coroner hadn't been able to pinpoint the time of death.

The prosecutor's sudden willingness to share specifics of a case with me raised my suspicions. "Exactly why are you calling me, Ms. Pratt?"

"We picked up a possible suspect. Slimeball with a sheet as long as your arm. No rapes we know of, but I wouldn't put much past him. He was stopped for speeding a few miles from the scene at two this morning. Could be a coincidence, but I'm praying it's the lucky break we've been waiting for."

Which made the purpose of her call painfully obvious. "You want Kitty to come in and identify him?"

"We need a positive ID in an unimpeachable lineup. Whoever did this was *very* careful. Cleaned the relevant parts of the body. Even took the kid's panties. We found them near the road. Guy must've dropped them there by accident. Unfortunately, they're useless."

"Why? Was the specimen too stale for DNA testing?"

"No. They can lift a profile decades after an attack, but only if the sample's well preserved. Unfortunately, the victim's underwear fell in the slush."

According to the prosecutor, Kitty was the most recent and by far the most promising witness in this string of heinous crimes. Two other girls had repressed details of the trauma or been shielded from the cops by wary parents.

The victim before Kitty was mildly retarded and unable to offer a credible, consistent version of her attack.

"The girl before that one agreed to cooperate," Clarissa Pratt told me grimly. "Seemed like a good prospect. Bright and articulate, like the Dolan kid. Unfortunately, on the day she was scheduled to work up a composite with the sketch artist, she locked herself in the bathroom and slit her wrists. She's still in the hospital, and although the attempt failed, her parents blame us for the pressure of the investigation. They won't let her talk to us. I've tried to change their minds. They won't budge."

Kitty's sad eyes loomed in my imagination. "So now you're asking me to push another victim in the same direction."

"Give me a break, Finn. I'm one of the good guys here, remember? Kitty's already agreed to view the lineup, but only if you'll come along and hold her hand. We're on for nine A.M. today at headquarters. What do you say?"

What I wanted to say was no. I didn't like the prosecutor or the situation. Kitty's dependence made me feel flimsy and inadequate.

"I'll be there," I told her.

"Good. Meet me outside the building at ten of."

The line went dead. Ms. Pratt had no use for pleasantries.

My thoughts swerved again to Kitty. The little girl hated the police station. Consenting to return and attempt to identify her assailant showed tremendous courage.

Inspired by her example, I phoned Shelby at home. I told her I'd be unavailable for snake charming or road paving or whatever else Crea-Temps had in mind for me this morning. I had urgent business, I said. Unavoidable.

I braced myself for an explosion. Shelby did not deal well with disappointment.

"Great, Lennie. Swell. I give you the prize assignments. Do you personal favors. And what's my thanks? You leave me in the goddamned lurch, that's what."

"I'll see you this afternoon, Shelby. Maybe later this morning, depending."

"So happens I count on you, Lennie. This is a *business* I'm running here. Not some drop-in day care center. What am I supposed to tell the clients? Maybe I'll help you and maybe not, *depending*?"

"See you later, Shelby."

"What's so goddamned important, anyway? At the very least, I deserve an explanation."

Whether or not she deserved it, the truth stuck in my throat. "I'm having my nails done."

"You, Lennie? You mean it? That's fabulous!"

"Thanks. I knew you'd understand."

Shelby chuckled. "You live long enough, you see everything. Listen, don't rush in on my account. Give yourself plenty of drying time. Nothing worse than a smudge."

The Toyota glistened with frost. Ice glazed the windshield. I left the engine idling while I scraped. Chilled to the core, I climbed in and revved the heater. A puff of noxious steam spewed from the vents. Smelled like barbecued hair with a side of baked rubber. Huddling deeper into my coat, I backed toward the road.

As threatened, Clarissa Pratt awaited me outside police headquarters. The prosecutor was dressed to distress in a mock beaver coat, barber-pole striped scarf, and fur-lined ankle boots. Her bangs were clipped back by a gold barrette, which might have been an improvement had the change exposed someone else's face.

"Glad you got here first, Finn," she said brusquely. "Kid's a nervous wreck. I don't want her to freak out and go blank on us."

A black Mercedes sedan turned in and coasted to a space at the front of the lot. Mrs. Dolan slipped out and circled to the passenger side. She looked elegant as ever in a pale cashmere coat, Hermès scarf, fawn ostrich Kelly bag and matching pumps. Opening the door, she tried to coax her daughter from the car. Her breaths rode the frigid air like smoke signals. After a few minutes, she cast me a pleading look.

Approaching the car, I spotted Kitty huddled hard against the leather seat. Bent knees walled her chest.

"I can't do it, Mommy," she whimpered. "I changed my mind. Take me home. Please!"

"Shh. It's okay, darling. Look. Lennie's here."

With a pleading glance my way, Mrs. Dolan stepped aside. I slid in and sat next to the terrified child.

"It's up to you, sweetheart. If you don't want to do this, nobody will force you."

Tears trailed Kitty's cheeks. Her nose ran.

"I want to. I just can't. I hate it here."

"Why, Kitty? Did something bad happen when you were looking at the pictures here?"

"No."

"You sure?"

"I just want to go home."

"The men in the lineup won't even know you're looking at them."

"I know. I know," she wailed.

I wiped her drippy nose with a tissue. "What, then, sweetheart? What's scaring you?"

She snuffled. "Will you stay with me?"

"That's what I'm here for."

"The *whole* time? You promise?"

"Promise."

Kitty shuddered, then slowly unfolded. "Okay. I'll try." She took my hand and held it hard.

Sergeant Kresky stood beside the reception desk, eyeing the jumble of notices tacked to the bulletin board. He asked Mrs. Dolan to wait in the lobby, then led the rest of us to the rear of the second floor. A conspicuously armed guard was planted in the center of the corridor. Kresky directed us into the narrow room next door.

Inside, a line of wooden chairs faced a mirrored wall. Kitty took the chair in the center. Since she refused to release her grasp on my right hand, I claimed the logical spot at her left. Clarissa Pratt and Kresky stood behind us. The sergeant's voice was tuned to extra-gentle.

"When I flip the switch, Kitty, you'll be able to see and hear the men behind the mirror. But they can't see or hear you. You understand?"

"Yes."

Her fingers tightened on mine.

"I can talk to the police officer through this microphone," Kresky continued, pointing to the hand mike mounted on the wall. "But he wears an earphone, so only he can hear what I'm saying."

Kitty nodded, but I felt the steely terror in her grasp.

Kresky's upbeat smile bounced back at me from the mirror. So did Clarissa Pratt's dour face. There was a long, expectant hush.

"Okay, Kitty," the sergeant said. "When the lights come up in there, you'll see six men standing in front of a wall marked to show their height. Each man has a number. I'm going to ask them to step forward one at a time and repeat what was said to you. I want you to wait until all of them finish before you decide whether or not you recognize anyone. If you do, you tell me his number."

Kitty was silent.

"You sure you understand what to do, Kitty?" Pratt's attempt at a softer tone made her sound like a cartoon chipmunk.

"Yes."

"You're sure you have no questions?"

"She *said* she understands." I smoothed Kitty's hair. "You'll do fine, sweetheart. Try to relax."

"Please refrain from making any comments until we're finished, Ms. Finn," the prosecutor barked. On the downslide from chipmunk to attack dog, her voice squeaked like a rusty hinge.

With her free hand, Kitty covered her mouth to squelch a nervous giggle. Her hold on me eased a notch. But it tightened an instant later when Kresky leaned toward the control console and pushed a silver lever.

His action abruptly exposed the room behind the mirror. Harsh fluorescents cast a garish glare. The unsettling effect was heightened by the stark white walls, polished floor, and absence of furnishings.

Six men stood facing us. According to the oversized growth chart, they ranged in height from five eleven to six one. All were white and of medium build. Each wore jeans and a plaid sports shirt. Low-riding caps masked their features. Off to the side two uniformed cops stood with their backs to us. One sported a headset.

Leaning over, Kresky spoke into the microphone. "Okay to start now, Schmidt. Take it slow."

I recognized the name. Garraty and Schmidt were the officers who'd barged into the interrogation room while Kitty was viewing the mug shots. The head wearing the earphones was shaped like a bowling ball. So Schmidt must be the pleasant, moon-faced cop. I wondered if the slouchy back beside him belonged to Garraty, the sneer.

"Number one, step forward. Turn to profile and back. Then read what's on the sheet."

The first man took two stilted paces toward us, showed his side view, and faced front again. Squinting, he eyed the printed page in his hand. "You tell anybody about this, I'll cut you like I did her."

He read without emotion, as if he were ordering from a menu. I watched Kitty, searching her face for any hint of recognition.

Nothing.

Schmidt repeated the process with the other five men. Each spoke the threat in an awful dry monotone. Rules of the rogue's gallery, I presumed. Kitty stared and listened intently, but her expression didn't waver.

"Any of them familiar, Kitty?" Kresky asked.

"No." Her voice was pinched.

"Take your time, dear. Try to remember," Clarissa Pratt

urged. "Have them take off the caps, Kresky. You never know."

Kresky leaned into the mike again. "Ditch the caps one at a time, Schmidt."

Starting with number one again, the men stepped forward in turn and bared their heads. I focused on Kitty, hoping.

When the final man was called, I shut my eyes and prayed. *Let him be the one.* As the man stepped forward, my throat tightened. *Please, let this be the end of it.*

Slowly, he lifted his hand and removed his cap by the bill. I studied the child's features. No change.

"Anything, Kitty?" Kresky asked.

"No." She turned to me, her eyes pooled with sorrow. "I really, *really* tried."

"I know, sweetheart." I longed to hug her and squeeze away the disappointment. "Don't feel bad."

Kresky leaned into the mike. Crisply, he said, "That's a wrap, Schmidt. No sale."

Patting Kitty's hand, I watched the line of men shuffling toward the exit. Number six was nearly out the door when he turned to say something to Schmidt. Bristling with shock, I watched as he listened to the cop's response.

Kitty didn't have to name her assailant. I'd be only too glad to do it for her.

Chapter 15

DANA

"No way, Mom. Absolutely not!"

Dana clenched her fists and held her temper. Why did Becky have to pick this, of all times, to become an adolescent?

"I understand you'd rather ride the van, Becky, but the arrangements are made. Roddy will be here any minute. I'm afraid you'll just have to live with it."

"You don't want me to have a life. That's the problem. God, Mom. I'm almost thirteen!"

"Age has nothing to do with it, honey. The van is always getting you home late, that's all."

"What can Roddy do if there's traffic? Sorry to have to break it to you. But he can't fly."

Life in the talk show trenches had imbued Dana with near-perfect public restraint. Blowing a fuse on-air could taint her professional image. But doing so in the privacy of her home was another story. Emotions were meant to be aired. Denying them as Adam did made no more sense to Dana than buying lovely jewelry you were too afraid to wear. Off camera, Dana prided herself on erupting with the force and regularity of Old Faithful. But right now all she cared about was getting her daughter to accept the necessary new order.

"You've always been crazy about Roddy, Beck. What's the problem?"

"You just don't get it, Mom. Showing up at school in a *limousine* with a *chauffeur*. Everyone will think I'm a total geek."

Reluctantly, Dana found herself sympathizing with the child's dismay. To a teenager, even one in basic training, being in any way conspicuous was deadly.

Dana recalled the painful adolescent indignities her own parents had inflicted. No lipstick until the eighth grade. No dating boys with cars until junior year. They'd even prohibited her from wearing a strapless gown to the senior prom. Even now, she could conjure the unbearable weight of those pink spaghetti straps on her shoulders. Stupid things felt as cumbersome and humiliating as handcuffs and leg irons. As soon as she got to the party, Dana hurried to the girls' room and tried tucking the offending strings into the bodice of her dress. But for the indomitable force of gravity, it would have been a brilliant solution.

"Blame it on your mother, Beck. Tell your friends the truth—that I'm completely unreasonable and totally uncool."

Becky planted her hands on her hips. "All parents are like that. Nobody cares."

Dana searched her hat for a different rabbit. "How about if I ask Roddy to let you out at the corner?"

Becky scowled. "Somebody's bound to see anyway. Come on, Mom. Give me a break!"

Other remembered adolescent trials trampled Dana's resolve. Zits that loomed large as Vesuvius. Her period's surprise arrival during an assembly when she was wearing a white skirt. And what about that interminable week in tenth grade when everyone, absolutely *everyone,* thought she had a crush on the class Einstein, Mark Dunstable. Oh, the agony!

"How about if he drops you around the block? You can slip out of the car when no one's looking."

Becky's slim shoulders dropped a notch. But she wasn't raising the white flag yet. "What if one of the kids walks that way or one of the vans drives by? It just won't work, don't you *see*?"

Dana did, but the overriding image in her mind was a monster stalking her little girl. Grabbing her. Doing her terrible, irrevocable harm.

The buzz of the house phone forestalled further negotiation. Roddy Pierce was downstairs. Dana managed to prod Becky out the door. As soon as she heard the elevator bell, she raised Roddy on the car phone.

"Hey, Mrs. Meade. What's up?"

"Becky's temper, I'm afraid."

Suddenly, there was a clatter, followed by the sound of angry muffled voices.

"Sorry, ma'am," Roddy said when he came back on the line. "Caught that Yurie jerk hanging around again. Probably wanting to tell you he'll be glad to bump off your competition for you."

At the thought of that man getting anywhere near Becky, Dana cringed. "You got rid of him?"

"Sure did. You can't imagine how fast the little sucker can run when he's got a good reason."

"Good. Here's the deal with my aspiring teenager."

Roddy agreed to deposit Becky around the block from the school and then tail her at a discreet distance until she safely entered the building.

"Thanks, Roddy. You don't know how much better this makes me feel."

"Glad to oblige, Ms. Saunders. Can't be too careful these days."

As Dana feared, the Metro section of yesterday's *New York Times* had run a front-page feature on Becky and the Lassiter Prize. The piece mentioned that "this budding prodigy attends the prestigious Juilliard School." It described her as "unassuming and outgoing." Most disastrous was the final paragraph: "Rebecca Meade is the daughter of Adam

Meade, president of the Stark-Elliman Import Company, Inc. Her mother, who chooses to remain anonymous, is a prominent television personality."

Some mouth at Becky's school or the station had sprung a lethal leak. Dana groaned. How difficult would it be for an interested party to fill in the blanks? So much information was public record. Given a computer and a seasoned hacker, most of the rest could be accessed instantaneously.

Mickey Conway, *Back Talk's* researcher, had demonstrated everyone's vulnerability hundreds of times. Armed with little more than a name and address, Mickey could dig up a staggering pile of personal information. Shameless show-off that he was, he always tossed in a little extra spice when asked to compile routine background data on a subject. Dana marveled at what Mickey was able to learn on-line: net worth, credit rating, medical history, sexual preferences, college transcript, drinking habits, shoe size. You name it.

Anyone who'd ever registered to vote, married, owned property, operated a motor vehicle, filed tax returns, joined the military, applied for government jobs, or opened a charge account was vulnerable to such invasion. Dana had committed many of those sins against obscurity and probably a host of others. So had Adam.

Not even children were exempt. Becky's birth certificate, social security number, school and medical records could all be accessed by a skilled operator. From any of those, a snoop of Mickey Conway's caliber could follow the trail right to the girl's homeroom or apartment.

Thank heavens for Roddy Pierce.

Dana clung to that comforting thought as she ventured into her cavernous closet to choose appropriate outfits for today's taping. Two shows were scheduled back to back, with only a brief time-out for a quick change of wardrobe and studio audience. Happily, both topics were light, the kind the producer called "Twinkie" pieces.

The first was coyly titled "Reheating Your Romance." A

variety of guests were slated to present segments on cozy weekend getaways, setting the mood at home, sexy overtures, and guaranteed bedroom boredom busters. The latter, involving racy lingerie and suggestions for fantasy play, would be introduced by a three-time *Penthouse* pet with incredible legs and Grand Canyon cleavage.

The second show was an evergreen: "Best Holiday Gift Ideas." Three personal shoppers would appear to present their favorite selections from the mountain of seasonal catalogues. All Dana had to do was look and act properly enthusiastic. Kid-in-a-candy-store face, liberal sprinklings of *ooh*'s and *aah*'s. After ten years in the business, she could pull that one off in a sleepwalk.

For the holiday show, she quickly chose a belted red suit, a white blouse with ruffled cuffs and jabot, dark stockings, and midheeled black suede shoes. A black crepe cocktail dress with a fitted bodice and high illusion neckline would do for the romance gig. She quickly selected the necessary accessories, packed everything in a garment bag, and settled on the bed to await Roddy's return.

Cruising the channels, she checked the morning talk shows. Dana religiously watched her competitors in the crowded field. She followed their Q-scores, the critical measure of a celebrity's public recognition. She monitored their ever-shifting mannerisms, hemlines, hairstyles, set designs, interview styles, and topical preferences.

Dana had been popular with viewers from her first on-camera stint as a weatherperson in Milwaukee a dozen years ago. When *Back Talk* was in development, her audition tape caught the producers' eye. From its debut, the show's viewership and syndication swelled. On one or two heady occasions, Dana had even edged out Oprah in the mighty Neilson ratings.

Still, she was often pressured to change something or other. Over the years, various handlers had urged her to shed the extra ten pounds, add blond highlights, lose the midwestern twang, hide the obvious liberal leanings. She'd been advised to lower her guard and raise her profile. Public relations types offered to reconstruct her past and private lives to appease the public's insatiable appetite for scandal. As they saw it, every self-respecting celebrity needed a lurid sex life, a checkered childhood, and a backup supply of sizzling skeletons to pull out of the closet when media interest flagged.

So far, no one had suggested that Dana adopt a visual trademark on the order of Sally Jessy's red glasses or Jane Pauley's road-kill hairdo. But she imagined the oversight would eventually be caught and corrected.

She filed the day's revelations in her mind under "miscellaneous." Katie's hair was shorter, as was Kathie Lee's skirt. Paula's contact lenses had gone from green to blue. All three women were still as perky as popping corn. Watching them felt like a workout.

While she waited impatiently for Roddy's return, Dana decided to tackle the mountain of reading material on the cabinet behind her desk. A veritable paper avalanche. She was forever buying more books and magazines than anyone could find the time to read. So many things intrigued her. If only the average day were made of elastic . . .

She skimmed an article about biophilia, the inborn human urge to merge with nature. That would certainly account for the times she found herself staring longingly at the scraggly maple on the corner or the lush plantings along the Park Avenue median. Living in the city was necessary, given Dana's work and Becky's music lessons, but no one could convince Dana that it was in any way natural.

A provocative piece on date rape claimed that the current emphasis on the problem put women in a victim's mindset. Fleetingly, Dana wondered about the ultimate effect of her current fears on Becky. Quickly, she convinced herself that no amount of overprotection could be half as damaging as a sexual assault.

Halfway through a poignant essay on disabled children, the house buzzer sounded.

"Your car's here, Mrs. Meade," the doorman said.

Dana put on her camel coat, dark glasses, and a velvet porkpie hat. Carrying her wardrobe, she headed for the door. Before she could reach it, the phone rang.

"Mrs. Meade? This is the attendance teacher at Juilliard. You didn't call in, so I'm checking. Is Becky sick?"

"No. She's at school. Someone just dropped her off."

"Strange. Her name came down with the absentees. Let me double-check."

Dana heard the woman speaking over the intercom. Soon, she came back on the line. "She *is* out, Mrs. Meade. Becky didn't report to homeroom, and none of her classmates saw her this morning."

Dana's heart squirmed. "Hang on a second." She punched the hold button with her finger and rang Roddy on the car phone.

"Ready when you are, Mrs. Meade," he said cheerily.

"Where's Becky, Roddy?" she demanded brusquely. "Is she with you?"

"No, ma'am. I dropped her off at school. Followed her to the door just like you told me."

"The school's on the line now. They claim she never arrived."

"Can't be, ma'am. I saw her go in with my own eyes."

"My God. Where is she?"

Dana raced to the car. At her shrill urging, Roddy drove at breakneck speed to the school. He veered wildly around a stopped cab and narrowly avoided a collision with a crosstown bus.

"Hurry, Roddy!"

"Don't want to get you killed, ma'am."

"We have to find Becky!"

They left the car doubled-parked and hurried to the school. The principal and several staff members nervously awaited them in the main office.

"We have guards canvasing the building, Mrs. Meade.

Becky's probably practicing or whatever and lost track of the time," the principal assured her.

"That's not like her at all."

Dana stormed out of the office with Roddy at her heel. The principal followed, urging her to keep calm.

"Relax, Mrs. Meade. Our people will find her."

"I have no intention of sitting around until they do, Mr. Waltham." Turning on her heel, Dana headed down the hall with Roddy to conduct a search of their own.

While Roddy checked the boys' rooms, Dana canvased the girls'. She looked under stall doors and inside storage closets. But Becky was nowhere to be found.

"Any chance she ducked out?" Roddy asked.

Dana considered Becky's recently acquired rebellious streak. "Anything's possible. But until we find her, we keep looking."

"Fine with me. Only—"

"Only what?" Dana demanded. Her nerves were raw and jangling.

"Suppose you might want to call the show, is all."

Eyeing her watch, Dana shook her head. "Five minutes to taping and the show honestly hasn't crossed my mind. Thanks, Roddy. I'll call Lucy. You wrap up here and I'll meet you in the basement."

Lucy Breitmeyer sounded frantic. "What's going on? We're four minutes to the opening credits."

Dana struggled to hold herself together as she recounted Becky's inexplicable disappearance.

"I'm so sorry," Lucy said. "Don't worry. I'll take care of everything at this end."

"Thanks."

"Let us know as soon as you find her, okay?"

"Oh, I will."

Access to the building's basement was through a ponderous fire door. Dana wrenched it open. Her steps resounded on the metal staircase. The thump and wheeze of the furnace filled the air.

"Roddy?"

No answer. So she'd gotten here first. Too anxious to wait for the big man, Dana started searching the vast, machinery-jammed space.

"Becky? Are you here?"

She scanned the shadows behind the furnace and the slender space between the water tanks and the wall. Ducking, she peered beneath the scrub sinks. She checked behind and inside the large commercial washer and dryer. "Beck?"

The furnace's harsh thumping matched the cruel pounding in her skull.

"Honey, please!"

Nearing the janitor's room, Dana caught a scratching sound. Cringing, she pictured mice scurrying inside. Or worse, rats.

Swallowing bile, she twisted the knob.

It was locked.

"Anyone in there?"

"Any sign of her?" Roddy had come up behind her.

"Not yet. Try this door, Roddy, will you? Force it if you have to."

"You sure? I could go up and ask for the key."

At the moment, Dana had no use for propriety or protocol. "I'll get it fixed. Just do it!"

"Yes, ma'am."

Roddy backed up and butted the door with his shoulder. It flew open, revealing a small room cluttered with supplies and shabby furnishings.

"Check the closets. I'll search the room," Dana ordered.

Quickly, she looked under the couch. As she was nearing a row of tall buckets, she heard the scratching sound again. Squelching her revulsion, Dana crossed to look behind the buckets.

What she saw there made her scream.

Chapter 16

LENNIE

The bastard was getting away. If he wasn't stopped now, he'd probably leave town. Why would he stick around and give the cops a second chance to nab him? Any place could meet his simple needs. Cover of night. Families under the flimsy guard of false security. A limitless supply of unsuspecting young victims.

Desperate, I grabbed Kresky's wrist and yanked him toward the viewing room door.

"What the hell—"

"I have to speak to you alone, Sergeant. Now!"

As we exited the small room, I spotted the men from the lineup ambling off down the corridor.

"Number six is your man, Kresky. I *know* him. You have to stop him before he gets away. Hurry!"

Handsome Harry raised his hands. "Whoa. Slow down. You have evidence?"

"It's him. Trust me."

He scowled. "Evidence. That's what I trust."

The last of the six turned the corner. "Damn it, you idiot," I spat. "You're going to lose him!"

Taking after the animal myself, I sprinted down the hall. A stainless steel coffee cart appeared as I rounded the bend. Swerving madly to avoid it, I skidded on a polished tile. Every step after that drove a searing spike of pain down my leg. I slowed to a lurching hobble.

Kresky caught up, huffing.

The men were nearing the station house door. "Stop him," I gasped. "Please!"

The sergeant shot me a venomous look. "You'd better be right, Finn."

As he took off, the prosecutor appeared in the hall with Kitty in tow.

"What's going on here?" Clarissa Pratt demanded.

I hated to upset Kitty, but there was no time for delicacy. "I recognized one of the men in the lineup. Kresky's running him down."

"Which man?"

The child went pale.

"Kitty should wait somewhere out of the way," I urged.

"Which?" the prosecutor persisted, oblivious to Kitty's terror.

"Number six."

Pratt shook her head. "Wrong answer, Ms. Finn. That wasn't the suspect."

"You don't understand—"

"No, *you* don't understand. Follow me. Both of you. In here, quickly."

Clarissa Pratt herded us toward a conference room across the hall. Kitty entered first. As I girded myself to follow, I spotted Kresky. He had my man in handcuffs. Frank Murphy's doughy face was mottled with rage.

Hurrying inside the conference room, I shut the door behind me. Then I faced the prosecutor.

Her voice was strangled with fury. "Apparently you've never heard of constitutional rights, Ms. Finn. There's this little thing called presumption of innocence. Not to mention just cause for arrest or detention."

"Frank Murphy is a sleazy bum. He's been freeloading in my landlady's house for months. Eight months to be precise. Does that ring a bell, Ms. Pratt?"

The prosecutor herself had told me the rapist's first attack was eight months ago. All the rest fit neatly, too. Frank was often out half the night. I'd imagined him haunting the bars. But now, I could as easily picture him stalking deserted neighborhood streets. Seeking out vulnerable little girls.

Kitty moaned.

"It's all right, sweetheart. Don't worry. They'll lock him away where he can't hurt anybody ever again."

"Give it a rest, Finn," Clarissa Pratt snapped. "Ms. Finn is mistaken, Kitty. If you'll excuse me, I need to go get Mr. Murphy released and offer him an apology." She shot me a harsh look and wheeled toward the door.

I grabbed her wrist before she could turn the knob. "Apologize? Didn't you hear me? I know this man."

She wrenched free of my grip. Her eyes were blazing. "Is that so? Then I suppose you know he works as a volunteer for the men's shelter on West Main Street. This so-called *sleazy bum* of yours patrols the downtown area during the night to bring in mentally ill homeless who might otherwise freeze to death on the streets."

"I don't believe it."

The prosecutor puffed her exasperation. "We often use men from the shelter to fill out lineups. When I stopped there early this morning, they were short one Caucasian six-footer. Your Mr. Murphy offered to take the space."

"He offered?"

"Exactly. Seems your so-called *freeloader* is quite the civic-minded individual. Father Harrington told me he's never had a more dedicated, reliable volunteer. Murphy even waived the standard twenty-five-dollar lineup fee. Asked us to donate it to the soup kitchen. Still think he's the guilty party?"

"Doesn't sound that way," I said dully.

"You'd better hope Mr. Murphy's charitable instincts extend to us, Ms. Finn. If he sues the city, I'll make sure you pay big time." Clarissa Pratt stormed out and slammed the door.

Kitty looked stricken.

"Sorry," I told her.

She wrapped me in a hug. I was struck by the fragile feel of her. Meager padding. Spindly frame. The child gave off the clean, honest scent of a rain-soaked garden.

"Don't feel bad, Lennie. I hate that dumb Miss Pratt. She's so mean."

"She's right, Kitty. No one should be accused without proof. I shouldn't have jumped to conclusions."

She stepped back, her lip quivered. "I wish it *was* him. Then I could stop being so scared."

"Oh, sweetheart, I know. They'll find the man soon."

Her eyes gleamed with tears. "Can I ask you something?"

"Sure."

"How come they think I'm crazy?"

"No one thinks that."

Brokenly, Kitty explained that her mother and the prosecutor were pressuring her to go for counseling at the Rape Crisis Center. On the phone last night, her father had pushed therapy, too.

"That doesn't mean you're crazy, Kitty. They just want you to feel better."

Bury your feelings, and they'll push up bitter roots, I wanted to warn her. *You'll be trapped in a forest of treacherous doubts and brambled secrets. Stumbling blindly in the dark, it could take years to find a clearing.* Painfully, I remembered my own slow, labored emergence. Even now, the blazing light of remembrance could make me shrink and look away.

"You think I should go, too?"

"I think it'll help you, yes."

"But all the kids'll tease me."

"No one will know unless you tell them, sweetheart."

She studied my face. "Okay. I'll try it—once."

The knot in my back had slackened a notch. Kneading the sore spot with a knuckle, I eased the screaming spasm to a whine.

Nearly ten minutes had passed since Clarissa Pratt's angry departure. By my calculations, she'd had ample time to kiss Frank Murphy's ruffled butt and make it all better. Hopefully, the jerk was gone by now.

Treading cautiously in case he wasn't, I led Kitty toward the reception area, where we'd left her mother waiting. On the way, we spotted the prosecutor and Sergeant Kresky.

Handsome Harry's cheeks looked hot. Pratt hung on him like a cheap suit. As we neared, I caught a few of her choice tidbits.

"How does foot patrol sound to you, Sergeant? Better yet, how about a new career? Something that doesn't take the common sense you were obviously born lacking."

I cleared my throat to divert her angry attentions. If looks could kill, my wake would be this evening.

"It wasn't his fault, Ms. Pratt. Sorry, Kresky. Looks like I did it to you again."

The prosecutor scowled harder. "If you'll *excuse* us, Ms. Finn."

But I refused to leave Kresky flapping in the breeze. "Whatever happens, I take full responsibility. There's no reason to blame the sergeant."

"Maybe you didn't understand me clearly, Ms. Finn. I said, take a hike!" The woman came on like a riot hose. I could even feel the spray.

Kresky's expression urged me to respect her request. With reluctance, I took Kitty's hand and kept walking.

Allison Dolan was not in the reception area. The officer on desk duty remembered her asking where in the neighborhood she could go for a cup of coffee.

We waited five minutes, which Kitty used to pump me for fresh promises. Would I go with her to her first counseling session at the crisis center? When I agreed, she brightened. She'd feel *so* much better if I was there. She didn't think she could do it without me. The child made me sound like an essential nutrient.

Fortunately, Mrs. Dolan appeared a beat later, before the

little girl had a chance to request my pancreas or a chocolate-coated chunk of the moon. I didn't know how to refuse her.

"Mommy, guess what? Lennie's gonna come along when we go to the counselor."

"Only if it's all right with you, Mrs. Dolan," I hastily added.

"Sure. I guess. How'd it go?"

Kitty wilted. "I couldn't pick the guy out. I did my best, Mom."

Mrs. Dolan stroked her daughter's cheek. It was the first tender gesture I'd seen her bestow on anyone except Kresky. "Of course you did, darling. Let's get you to school, now. If we hurry, you'll be on time for music. Mrs. Echenthal hates it when you miss her class." Pride squared her shoulders. "Kitty has a wonderful voice. Last Christmas, she was chosen to sing with a special childrens' choir at Saint John the Divine. She had her own solo."

Kitty blushed. "Only one line, Mommy. No big deal."

Allison Dolan huffed. "No big deal indeed. Only one of the world's foremost cathedrals. There was even a piece about it in the *Times*."

I walked them to the parking lot. As their Mercedes floated out of sight, I tried to nudge a spark of life into my testy Japanese import. Damned machine was playing coy. With every hopeful hitch of the ignition, it hacked a few times and died.

"Come on."

I forced myself to wait out a slow ten-count. Goosing the gas, I turned the key again. As the motor finally caught, the passenger door flew open. I was hit by a rush of cold air and the disheartening sight of a smirking Frank Murphy.

"Headed my way, Lennie girl? I could sure use a lift home."

"Actually, I'm late for work, Frank."

"That so? Well, I'm sure you wouldn't mind going a bit

out of your way. Especially seeing how you put me through so much mental anguish and public humiliation and all."

Steeling myself, I managed to get out the words: "I'm sorry, Frank. Let's forget it, okay?"

He sighed gustily. "If only I could. But I took a hard blow to my good name and reputation in there. Bet I'll have trouble getting the food down. Problems sleeping. I think we may be talking permanent damage to my health here, Lennie girl."

The worm was having a grand time. Only the obvious need for damage control kept me from matching him shot for shot. The prosecutor wasn't the type to make idle threats. If Frank Murphy brought a lawsuit against the city, Clarissa Pratt would see to it that my losses matched or exceeded theirs. No doubt she had nasty friends in high places who could scuttle my career in the bargain.

"I was mistaken, Frank. I apologize."

"Lucky for you I'm not a petty person. Long as you admit you're wrong and make amends, I suppose I'd be inclined to let bygones be bygones. . . ."

The devilish twinkle in his eye stung me like a cattle prod.

"Make amends how?"

"You can start by driving me home," he announced blithely. "Then, we'll see."

I made the trip in seething silence. At the foot of Mrs. O's driveway, I braked the car.

"Good-bye, Frank."

Frowning, he ticked his tongue. "Seeing all you put me through, I figure the least you can do is drive me to the door."

Six feet from the back porch, I came to a screeching halt. The driveway surface would probably never recover. "Will this do, or you want me to carry you the rest of the way?"

"Hmm?" he mused. "Nope. Don't think that'll be necessary. Like I told you, I'm a reasonable man. You can rest assured I won't be asking for anything that isn't due me."

"I can't tell you how relieved I am, Frank. Really."

As he opened the door, he waggled his fingers at me. "You take real good care of yourself now, Lennie. Hurry back."

He shifted his bulk out of the car. Fuming, I watched him swagger toward the house. Maniac's crazed barking filled the air like buckshot.

"Good girl," I muttered. "Sic the son of a bitch. Kill!"

Circling the end of the driveway, I vowed to ignore Frank for the rest of my life. In time, he was bound to weary of the game. This thing could only go so far.

Chapter 17

LENNIE

Shelby sat in her office, stockinged feet propped on the desk blotter, poring over a fat sheaf of papers. Stuffed into a scarlet knit sheath with a fluffy white collar, she reminded me of some lucky kid's Christmas stocking.

Whatever she was reading looked like serious business. Three neglected cigarettes burned in the ashtray, raising a peppermint fog. Her voice mail was poised to intercept any calls. Shelby had even traded her contact lenses for a serious set of wire-rimmed glasses. There wasn't a spark of acknowledgment when I entered. Never had I seen her so engrossed. Normally, Shelby had the attention span of a hyperactive flea.

I rapped my knuckles on the door frame. "Anybody home?"

Flinging down the papers, she made a noise like a sucking chest wound. "My Lord, Lennie. I didn't hear you come in."

"What's so fascinating?"

She flushed. "Oh, nothing. It's the report you wanted on Jack Chambless. My investigator dropped it off for you."

"So how come *you* were reading it?"

"I was not *reading* it. I was just checking to make sure the pages were in order."

"How considerate."

She pushed the paper stack toward me. Hesitantly, I picked it up. This was the electronic equivalent of rifling Jack's drawers. Going through his wallet. Eavesdropping on his calls.

But I had to find out whether my suspicions about the man were real or groundless. After all these years, I simply *had* to know.

The detective's key findings were summarized on the top page. I was not surprised to learn that Jonathan "Jack" Roy Chambless was a forty-seven-year-old, white, unaltered, American-born, heterosexual male. The investigator had found no indications of mental illness, criminal activity, or substance abuse. No hidden second wife or secret second identity. Jack was a registered Democrat with an organ donor card.

A comprehensive credit report listed his liquid assets, the status of his charge accounts, the size of his home mortgage, and his bill-paying habits. Everything was in model-room order.

A medical checkup six months ago also found him to be in excellent health. His bad cholesterol was good, his good better. His blood type was A positive. He had a clear colonoscopy and no significant enlargement of the prostate. Normal EKG. No hypertension. His doctor had recommended increased cardiovascular exercise and prescribed an anti-inflammatory medication for a recurrent knee injury. No report of excretory, sleep, or sexual dysfunction.

All systems go.

I found no revelations in his family profile, either. As claimed, Jack was widowed three years ago when his wife succumbed to stage-four ovarian cancer. His son lived in the town of Mamaroneck with his wife and young daughter and commuted daily to Manhattan, where he worked as an investment advisor.

I marveled at the details Shelby's pet investigator had managed to unearth. There was a list of Jack's organization memberships. A full account of his charitable contributions. A log of his recent travel. An account of his major purchases. Nothing appeared in the least bit unusual.

Skimming the report's conclusion, my heart sank.

"What's with the long face?" Shelby demanded. "The man's squeaky clean."

"Yes, but this is all current information."

"No kidding. What did you expect? A rundown on how he was potty-trained?"

"Forget it, Shelby. Thanks anyway. What's the job situation? I traded on-duty days, so I have today off."

Shelby snatched the report from my hands and shook it at me. "I will *not* forget it. Jack Chambless is a grade-A certified gem. What'll it take to convince you? His marks in elementary school? Who his great grandpa *shtupped* in the old country? I know unreasonable when I see it, Lennie. And you're the genuine article. I will *not* stand idly by and watch you toss this one back in the pond."

"I'm not planning to do that."

She eyed me warily. "You're going to keep seeing him? You mean it?"

"Yes, Shelby. I am."

After a night of brutal doubts, I'd come to that inescapable decision. I couldn't turn my back on the truth, whatever it turned out to be. And I couldn't let Jack out of my life if there was any chance he might take that truth with him.

Shelby beamed. "Great. Since that's settled, let's get your meter running, shall we?" She paged through the order slips for today. "Can you take an S.A.T. class?"

"Take them where?"

"Cute. How about working the phones at Fat Blasters?"

"Isn't that the program guaranteed to take off the weight and give you gallstones?"

"The very same."

"No, thank you."

Shelby tossed her hair. "We really have to do something about that conscience of yours, Lennie. It's so impractical."

She continued thumbing through the pile. Finally, her trigger finger popped up like the timer on a frozen turkey. "Got the perfect gig for you, Lennie old pal. How about a quick run out to Kennedy Airport?"

"To pick up who?" Dealing with Shelby, I'd learned to get all the details before agreeing to take a job.

When she hadn't answered after a suspiciously long pause, I said, "To pick up *what*?"

"Nothing much. A couple of teeny, weeny, little pythons."

"Forget it, Shelby."

"Why? They're only babies. Bet they're cute. Not to mention caged and sedated."

"Go get them yourself and then you tell me all about it. What else is there?"

We finally settled on the afternoon's round of toddler gymnastics classes at the Y. I was always happiest when my temp work had something to do with athletics. I enjoyed moving myself and others. Aside from occasional Kodak moments, such as my waitressing debacle years ago at Mrs. O's, I'm strong for my size and, most of the time, reasonably well-coordinated. My agility only fails me when I'm under severe stress. Then, I become a one-woman demolition derby.

Though no allowance was made for gender, I placed third out of four hundred on the performance section of the fire fighters' qualifying exam. I scored highest in both dangling from a ladder and the dummy carry, skills I've had ample opportunity to practice over the years.

I seriously doubted I'd do as well if there were a similar entrance test for basic adult existence. But a crowd of tumbling, bumbling children sounded right up my alley this afternoon.

The kids turned out to be cute, loud, proud, and exhausting.

"Watch me, way-dy!" "Hey, lookit!" "I did it. Yay for me!"

Their mothers were another story. When I tried to pry the little ones loose at the door, several of the moms suffered acute bouts of separation anxiety. One took me aside to soberly confide that her Tiffany was a budding Mary Lou Retton, though to me, the similarity ended with the kid's fireplug physique. Another insisted that her Christopher Jason, who was prone to ear infections, wear his stocking hat in class.

After an hour of mindless mayhem on the mats, a dozen boisterous three-year-olds replaced the twos. The fours followed, striking me as remarkably sophisticated by comparison. At that advanced age, they rarely rolled into or atop one another. They pretended to listen while I spoke. Not one of them smelled like the men's room at Grand Central Station.

But they still took the vigilance of a spy satellite and limitless patience. Operating as I was on no sleep and a surplus of anxiety, I found their boisterousness jarring. By the end of the final class, my energy level had dipped dangerously into emergency reserve.

When the session ended at three, I headed for the Town Center. Shopping occupies a special place in my heart, right up there with root canal. But Huck's monumental achievement deserved special recognition.

For an endless half hour, I prowled the rows of stores. The line between product promotion and outright mugging had been virtually obliterated. My senses were assailed by garish displays, ear-splitting music, and SWAT teams armed with semiautomatic perfume atomizers.

On the main level a store specialized in authentic reproduction athletic gear. I selected a Giants jersey and matching sweats in size large. The hulking teenage clerk eyed me strangely when I asked him to iron on the word "suck" beneath the team name, but he obeyed without a word.

From the phone in the parking lot, I called Crea-Temps.

The evening's job prospects weren't exactly enticing. I passed on the chance to instruct a group of first-degree black belts in tae kwon do, though Shelby blithely assured me I could fake my way through it.

Next, I retrieved a message from Jack on my phone machine. How about dinner somewhere nice and relaxing where we could talk? He sensed that I was upset with him for some reason. Whatever it was, he wanted to clear the air.

His honeyed voice heightened my confusion. The Jack I knew was incapable of harming a fly, much less a child. I'd found him intensely appealing for the gentlest reasons. He loved his granddaughter. He reveled in his son. Every one of the kids he taught or sponsored held a special slot in his affections. How could I possibly doubt him?

On our second date, we had stopped in at a high school science fair where several of "his" kids had projects on display. Jack didn't disguise his pride and regard for each of them. And the sentiment was obviously returned. This wasn't some arrogant rich cracker spreading his crumbs. Mr. "Champ," as the kids called him, was a genuine friend.

It struck me then that genuine was the operative word. This man wasn't afraid to get teary-eyed over a soppy film or a sad story or a moving piece of music. He readily admitted his fears and failures. He was a whole person, not a dick with ears like Hitsig.

But what about the Jack I didn't know? In a brief, terrifying flash, I was certain I'd glimpsed another side of him. He had secrets. A hidden past.

Sounds familiar, Lennie. Sounds like you.

The next voice on my tape was a child's. Please, Kitty begged, could I call her back *right away*? It was *very, very* important.

I dialed the Dolans' number. Kitty answered on the first ring.

"Lennie. I *knew* you'd call. I just *knew*."

Her mother had made an appointment with a rape crisis

counselor for five o'clock that afternoon. I agreed to meet them at the center's home base on Summer Street. With the proper help, Kitty would get the chance to rid herself of any lingering guilt or shame. She'd be encouraged to air her feelings, to talk the demons away. Gradually, she could learn to trust again.

I couldn't help but think how different my life might have been if I'd been able to do the same: lance the wound and release the poison.

Maybe it wasn't too late.

If I could solve my own toxic puzzle, maybe I'd finally be able to set it aside.

Chapter 18

LENNIE

During rush hour, Stamford's business district is an asylum without walls. Kamikaze pedestrians and lurking potholes make the driving perilous. Protesting the speed bursts and wrenching stops, my Toyota finally gave up the ghost. The engine expired, and a steamy specter wafted tauntingly from the hood.

While I worked to revive the stubborn heap, night fell. Passing cars pelted me with angry honks and curses. There was the squeal of tortured brakes. As I stepped outside to flag down help, a city bus whizzed by, splattering me with filthy meltwater.

Several long minutes later, a pickup truck angled in and stopped behind my car. A spindly kid in leather pants and a studded denim jacket hopped out of its cab. He had long stringy hair and a lazy eye. A nut-sized chaw of something was packed in his pitted cheek. Swaggering toward me, thumbs hitched in his low-slung waistband, he struck a pose.

"Problem, lady?"

"Thanks for stopping. The motor conked. Can you give me a push?"

"Think a push'll do it?"

"Yes. It'll usually take off from a rolling start."

He snickered. "If you ask me, what that car of yours needs is a new car."

In no mood or position to argue, I forced a smile. "Maybe so. In the meantime, how about that push?"

My knight in shining leather looked me over as if I were for sale, paying special attention to my hood ornaments. His leer reminded me of Wild Bill Hitsig's. My composure hung by a thread. One suggestive crack from this little hood Samaritan, and I'd be doing the pushing.

"Ten bucks," he said.

Those were not the words I expected. "For a *push*?"

"Take it or leave it."

I took it, mutely handing him two fives.

As the truck nudged my bumper, I worked the gas and prodded the ignition. Half a block later, the motor stammered and caught. I offered a prayer to the great god Toyota. To signal the kid, I hefted my upturned thumb out the window. He backed his truck away, gunned his souped-up engine enthusiastically, and pulled alongside to pass me on the right.

"Thanks," I called.

"No problem," he hollered. "Now you can get that shit heap off the road, you old bitch!"

I answered with a rakish hitch of my middle finger. Twerp had some nerve insulting my car.

Stamford's Rape Crisis Center occupies half of a nondescript two-family house on Summer Street. Arriving ten minutes late, I found a solitary man pacing the beige Berber carpet in the reception area. His brown suit and white shirt were rumpled, the dotted red tie loose and lolling down his chest like a dog's tongue. Despite his burly build and dark coloring, his eyes were a dead giveaway.

"Mr. Dolan?"

"Yeah?" Wheeling toward me, his tight lips curled. "Don't tell me. You must be the famous Lennie Finn my daughter keeps carrying on about."

"You should be proud of Kitty, Mr. Dolan. She's a terrific kid."

"Thanks for the news flash. Now, here's one for you. You're late. You want to play hero, I can't stop you. But Kitty's had enough aggravation. She doesn't need to sit around waiting for some fireman in drag who can't get it up to show on time."

I was wrong about his eyes. Kitty's weren't freeze-dried. "Nice meeting you, too, Mr. Dolan."

Distancing myself as best I could, I claimed one of the blue vinyl chairs ringing the perimeter and paged through a back issue of *Newsweek*.

Kitty's father resumed his pacing. From time to time, I caught the restless pass of his long, slim, coffee-colored wing tips. A full ten minutes lapsed before he paused in mid-orbit and tossed up his hands.

"I didn't mean it, okay?"

I raised my eyes. "Are you talking to me?"

"This hasn't been a picnic for me either, you know. Here I put in half a day on the goddamned plane. Five hours stuck at goddamned O'Hare by lousy weather. And all I get for my troubles is a barge of grief.

"My wife's on my case because I've been out of town trying to handle a company disaster. My boss is busting my balls for coming home earlier than I planned. I figure I should be with my daughter. And when I finally am able to get home to her, all she can talk about is *you*."

"Kitty's having a rough time, Mr. Dolan. Sometimes, dealing with a stranger can be easier."

"I'm the one who rocked and held her, for God's sake. I'm the one who gave her bubble baths and told her stories. *Goodnight Moon*. That was her favorite. 'Read it again, Daddy,' she'd say. 'One more time—please!' I must've read that book to her a thousand times." His voice quivered.

To my dismay, he started sobbing. "What the hell kind of animal could do this to my little girl?"

"I wish I knew."

Letting the tears flow freely, Mark Dolan balled his hands

in bloodless fists. "I'll kill the rotten bastard. I swear I will. I'll squeeze the life out of him with my bare hands."

Entering in a blaze of crimson silk, Allison Dolan caught the tail of the tirade. Posed with hands on hips, she fixed her husband with a look of utter disgust.

"Don't you think it's a little late for the macho savior act, Mark?"

His jaw twitched. "What the hell do you want from me, Allison?"

"Nothing anymore. Not a single thing."

"Great. All I need right now is more of your bullshit."

"That from an expert on the subject," Mrs. Dolan huffed. She slipped off her silk-lined red coat, exposing the matching skirt and sweater underneath. Her accessories were ocher ostrich, her hair was cinched back in a swingy silken tail. Thick door-knocker earrings, a chunky gold choker, and several large bangle bracelets completed the lavish look. Folding her arms, she raised her haughty chin like a drawbridge.

I wished I could turn off the set or change the channel. Disappearing would have worked for me, too. Unfortunately, I was bound by my promise to Kitty. Talk and traffic had made me too late to see her before she started her counseling session. I had to be waiting when she got out.

"I'm so sick of your Miss Perfect act," Kitty's father hissed. "This wouldn't have happened if you hadn't left the kid alone."

"If you're such a model parent, why weren't *you* home with her instead of off somewhere screwing around as usual?"

A wormy vein wriggled at his temple. "For the millionth time, Allison, I was *working*. Making the money to pay your goddamned bills. You want me home more, quit shopping like it's about to become illegal."

A single tear defied her flawless makeup. "Don't worry, Mark. I won't spend another nickel."

"Right," he sniffed. "That's all for today, folks. Tune in same time tomorrow at Neiman-Marcus."

An inner door opened. The woman who appeared was every inch as plain as Allison Dolan was fancy. Soft brown waves framed her face. Her hazel eyes, unadorned except for clear-framed glasses, radiated intelligence. She exuded a welcome air of patience and equilibrium.

"Mrs. Dolan? Nice to see you. I'm Lila Sperling, director of the center." The keen gaze lit on me. "Ms. Finn?"

"Yes."

"Glad you're here. Kitty won't be finished with her counselor for a few more minutes. Mind stepping into my office for a chat?"

"I'd be glad to." If it meant escaping more of the Dolans' wedded blitz, I wouldn't have minded stepping in for an injection.

She led me down a long, narrow corridor. Passing a closed door, I heard the hum of voices. Another, standing open, was spare and neutral. A pair of taupe armchairs faced a leather couch. Framed diplomas lined the slender strip of wall space between a mullioned window and a bookshelf packed with texts.

The director's office was a very different story. Here, inspirational posters and kids' art crowded every spare surface. Battered dolls and well-loved stuffed animals huddled on the windowsill. Mingled among the reports and correspondence on her desk were yo-yos, decks of cards, plastic Slinkys, Lego pieces, even a debonair Mr. Potato Head in a top hat, smoking a pipe.

The director explained. "We conduct very serious business here. Having a little fun around seems to help, especially with our youngest clients."

"Like Kitty."

A shadow crossed her face. "We've had them as young as two, Ms. Finn. Incest victims, little girls abused by neighbors, teachers, babysitters. You name it. If infants could talk, I suspect we'd have them coming in from birth."

I sat in the swivel rocker opposite hers. "How do you stand it?"

"The only possible way. I keep my distance. Fortunately, that's best for the clients, too. Letting them form inappropriate attachments only backfires in the long run."

Inappropriate attachments.

Exactly what Cynthia Hebert, the crisis center volunteer, had warned me against when I met her in the hospital emergency room.

"Are you trying to tell me something, Ms. Sperling?"

"No. I'm *asking* you to be careful, for Kitty's sake and your own. Rape victims, especially children, tend to latch on to whatever helps them escape the pain: food, fantasies, drugs, psychosomatic illness, promiscuity. It seems Kitty's chosen you."

Recalling my own misguided escape attempts, I winced. During my agonizing adolescence, I tried most everything the director listed. And more.

My lowest, loneliest point was after Aunt Selia and I delivered Huck to Whitechapel for the first time. Since the day Selia made the decision to place him there, I'd dreaded the separation. I imagined Huck terrified, screeching in anguish as strangers wrenched him from my love and protection.

Before we left home that morning, I bathed Huck and dressed him in his best striped overalls. As I fussed over his hair, his cornflower blue eyes looked webbed with worry. When he caught my wrist, his grip felt stiff with fear.

But five minutes after we arrived at Whitechapel, he took the director's outstretched hand and trotted off without a backward glance. It was as if I'd ceased to exist for him, as if he were leaving nothing at all behind.

Aunt Selia openly rejoiced in Huck's leaving. Driving away from the school, she was as garrulous and giggly as a child at a slumber party. Happier than I'd ever seen her. As soon as we got home, she headed for the den with a book and a glass of dry sherry. At her insistence, I went to the kitchen to fix myself a cheese sandwich. I hadn't eaten all day, but I had no appetite. Food could not begin to fill the yawning void inside me.

Mechanically, I took the bread, cheese, and mayonnaise from the refrigerator. For a long time, I stood at the sink beside the sandwich fixings, clutching the paring knife. The cheddar chunk was oddly shaped, missing the geometric bits I'd carved out for Huck's dinner the night before.

Suddenly, the facts hit me like a crushing blow. There would be no more fixing Huck dinner and watching him eat in rhythmic sweeps. No more walks, no bedtime stories. Since the day our mother died, I'd viewed myself as her best substitute where Huck was concerned. I'd believed I was the crucial link between that little boy and oblivion.

Now, I knew the bitter truth that it wasn't so. I was easily replaceable. Forgotten in a breath.

Stunned, I poised the knife and sliced the shiny hill of flesh beneath my thumb. There was a sharp sparkle of pain. Seeping ooze of angry tissue. Warm sticky rush. Not at all what I'd expected.

What had I expected?

Maybe I was trying to breach the numbness, to feel real again. To feel *something*.

Returning to the moment, I ran my finger over the hard-packed scar below my thumb. "Somehow, I can't put friendship in the same category as gorging on junk food or sleeping around, Ms. Sperling."

"Nor do I. But anything that gets in the way of Kitty facing what's happened to her is a negative. Keeping the feelings locked up only prolongs the healing process."

Tell me about it. "And exactly how am I supposed to turn her off?"

"Gently. The point is, if you pull away, she'll seek support elsewhere. From her parents, and hopefully, us."

I mulled that over for a minute. Caught the obvious flaw. "So she latches onto someone here. What's the difference?"

"The difference is what I mentioned earlier: We're *trained* to keep our distance."

My anger flared. "Let me tell you something. I don't need Kitty's dependence, and I certainly didn't ask for it. But I'm not going to rub salt in that little girl's wounds. If you're such a well-trained expert, *you* figure out how to let her down gently. *You* take care of it! I've had enough!"

Her calm didn't waver. Neither did her scrutiny. The smart eyes studied me. Squirming like a specimen on a slide, I forced myself to stop my chair's incessant rocking. When had I started that?

The director let the silence settle. I tried to ignore it, but the stillness kept building. It was flooding the room. Threatening to drown me.

"What!" I demanded. "Why are you looking at me like that?"

"Sorry. I should have seen it sooner. Obviously, Kitty picked it up on some level."

"Picked up on what?"

"It happened to you, too. Didn't it?"

Numbly, I looked away.

"We don't only deal with children, Ms. Finn. And we don't restrict ourselves to new cases. Plenty of clients come to us many years after an assault."

I felt her expectant gaze.

"That's okay," she said softly. "It's entirely up to you. When and if you're ever ready, I'd be glad to help you talk it through. Meanwhile, you're right. We can certainly work on this end to ease Kitty's reliance on you."

Finally, I was able to look at her. "Don't get me wrong, Ms. Sperling. The last thing I want is to harm Kitty. If you honestly think—"

"Not at all. There's nothing wrong with answering her pleas with kindness. When Kitty's ready, she'll let go. She'll get back to the critical business of becoming her old self."

Her unspoken words hung in the air. *When and if you're ever ready, Lennie, you'll do the same.* She was challenging me to stand and slay my ancient dragon.

The Road To Redemption

by Patterson Graham, Ph.D.

(Uncorrected Page Proofs)

After the offender masters the victim empathy phase of the Cambridge program, Intensive Relatedness is again used in the curative modeling phase.

At this critical juncture, the client selects a subjective ideal (real or imagined) to emulate. The chosen model provides the reformed offender with a blueprint for permanent recovery.

In John's case, discovering the model marked a crucial advance.

Finding my ideal wasn't easy. As a kid, the people I loved and looked up to were monsters, perverts. That was normal to me. Admirable.

My counselor knew I was having a hard time. He suggested the answer would come to me if I stopped trying so hard. He told me to put it out of my mind.

Worked like a charm. Two days later, I came up with the perfect curative model. Actually, I found him right here at the Cambridge program. He was there for me all along, but until I eased up the way the counselor suggested, I didn't see it.

The man couldn't have been better if I'd designed him myself. We're amazingly alike in so many ways. He's my size. Same age. Comes from a similar town and background. The only major difference is that I still have to think of myself as an offender, which, of course, he's not.

If I watch him closely enough, do what he does, I know I can use what I've learned at Cambridge and control myself. No one else has to get hurt. Finally, there can be a permanent end to it.

Chapter 19

DANA

Dana bent and kissed her sleeping daughter's brow. Becky looked so frail. Her face was pale and pinched. Vivid nightmares played beneath her lids. Shadows from the metal rails of the hospital bed sliced her slender frame.

For Becky's comfort and safety, Dana had brought every scrap of her considerable influence to bear. She'd pulled strings to have the child admitted to the eleventh floor at Mount Sinai's newly renovated Klingenstein Pavilion. For a considerable premium, the private wing offered the posh accommodations, impeccable service, and flawless discretion of a five-star hotel.

Dana had arranged for Becky's transport from the school to the hospital by private, unmarked ambulette. The attendants, hand-picked from the city's finest personal security firm, had spirited the child out of the school basement through the service door. Their instructions were to draw as little attention as possible. Becky's identity and the circumstances of her injury were to be kept secret. Dana had persuaded school officials to put off calling the police.

"No!" Becky cried out in her sleep.

"Shh, Baby. It's okay. You're safe, now." Dana stroked her daughter's troubled brow. "Mimsy will keep you safe, don't you worry."

Whatever it takes, Dana vowed in grim silence, *I'll get that rotten son of a bitch. I'll see that he pays for every bit of pain he caused you.*

Roiling with fury, she thought about the terror Becky had been forced to bear at that animal's hand. When Dana discovered her little girl in the janitor's room, Becky was unconscious, but still scratching wildly, trying to defend herself.

Before the ambulance arrived, Becky had come around long enough to tell Dana what had happened. A stark portrait of the attack lingered in Dana's mind.

As planned, Roddy had dropped Becky off two blocks from the school. Seeing none of her friends, Becky had gone the rest of the way herself.

Walking toward the school, Becky mentally reviewed a problem passage in a new piece she was learning, humming the rush of notes as her imaginary bow caressed the strings.

The Lassiter Prize was to be conferred during a hundred-fiftieth anniversary gala next month at Lincoln Center. A stellar cast, including the President, First Lady, and several star players in the classical music community were slated to attend. After accepting the honor, Becky had been asked to perform a special selection for the packed house. She'd chosen an excerpt from Sibelius's devilishly difficult Concerto in D minor, opus 47.

The stranger appeared without warning. The child heard no anticipatory rush of footfalls. She didn't have a hint of his approach.

Suddenly, Becky was grabbed from behind. Before she could cry out, the assailant clamped a hand over her mouth and forced her around to the rear of the school building. The man dragged Becky down the stairs to the basement and shoved her into a room deep with shadows.

There, he forced the child facedown on the concrete floor. One relentless hand still muffled her mouth. With the other, he reached beneath her. Becky tried to fight him as he worked her denim jeans over her hips.

His stifling weight crushed her hard into the floor. Positioned as she was, her flailing arms were powerless. She groped for something she might be able to use as a weapon. The only thing within reach was the case containing her violin.

The man was breathing hard. Groaning in low, harsh pulses. Becky couldn't bear the pressure of his monstrous weight. He was crushing her bones, scraping her skin raw. Desperately, she searched for a way to break loose. But she was trapped. Immobile. Drowning beneath a giant wave of terror.

Suddenly, his grip eased a notch. His weight shifted. Reaching out in a blind rush, Becky grabbed the handle of her violin case and slid it nearer. When it was close enough to afford her decent leverage, she whirled around and bashed the hard frame into the stranger's face with all her strength.

Blood gushed from the attacker's nose. He doubled over, clutching his face. Scrambling to her feet, Becky raced toward the door. But it was locked.

She was desperately trying to open it when a hand grabbed her. Becky flailed and fought. She scratched her assailant's arm. When he drew back, she raced to the door again. This time, she managed to twist the lock open. Becky thought she could escape, then. She was halfway through the door.

But suddenly, he caught her in a grip as hard as granite. Furious, he lifted her and flung her hard across the room. Becky must have hit her head when she fell. Next thing she knew, the man was gone and Dana was crouched over her, screaming.

Compounding the horror, the child had lost her precious violin. When Dana arrived, there was no trace of the instrument.

The violin, a 1732 Antonio Stradivari, had been entrusted to the child by her beloved teacher, Jacob Brinmann, when illness forced his retirement six months ago. A treasure like that was rarely to be found at any price. Even if Dana managed to track down an equivalent, the love and legacy attached to that particular instrument was irreplaceable.

Wrong, Dana admonished herself sharply. The only thing that's irreplaceable is this beautiful child.

Becky's pediatrician, Gwen Jaffe, had come by to examine the child. Thank the Lord, she'd confirmed that the child had not been raped. Fortunately, the blow to her head had not resulted in a concussion. Aside from lumps and bruises, there was no apparent physical damage. Spending the night in the hospital for observation was strictly a precaution, Gwen assured Dana.

If only the same could be said for Becky's emotions. A horrific experience like this was bound to leave scars. The child would probably show behavioral changes, the doctor warned. Dana should expect some regression, the return of babyish habits or demands. Dr. Jaffe also counseled her to expect Becky to be moody and difficult for awhile. Once she had had a few days to recuperate from the immediate trauma, Dana and the pediatrician would explore counseling and other means to help Becky over the worst of this.

Before she left, Dr. Jaffe had left orders for a mild tranquilizer for Becky and a stiffer one for Dana. When the nurse arrived, Dana had declined hers. She wanted nothing to dull her roiling fury. Becky needed to sleep and heal. What Dana needed most was revenge.

She padded out of Becky's room and shut the door. The suite's sitting area had been equipped, at Dana's request, with a multi-line phone. Her first call was to Marian Doyle, her longtime personal secretary. Marian retrieved the numbers Dana needed from her Rolodex. The secretary asked no questions about the rare cancellation of today's taping or Dana's reason for requiring these particular numbers. From long association, Marian knew that Dana would 'ell her what she cared to and no more.

Pausing only to check that Becky was still asleep, Dana

spent the next two hours on the phone. Accustomed to going directly to the top, she started with New York City's Police Commissioner, Joe Halliburton. Through his office, she traced him to Astoria, Queens, where he was attending the funeral of a fallen officer. After she explained that the call was urgent, Dana was patched through to the car phone in his limousine as he was being driven from the service to the cemetery.

"Joe, it's Dana Saunders. Sorry to intrude, but it's an emergency."

When he heard about Becky's assault, Halliburton made the appropriate sympathy noises. "Love to help, Dana. And I'll certainly see that things are expedited once there's a suspect. But at this point, this is more a matter for the D.A.'s office."

Dana made the call to Fred Parmenter, who was holding a press conference at his office at One Hogan Place about a recent rash of antigay bias crimes. Parmenter called back in ten minutes offering apologies, but little else.

"You're asking me to go after someone with no evidence, Dana. Getting access to privileged medical or lawyer-client records is near impossible under any circumstances. No judge is going to issue a warrant allowing you to search for this 'John's' records on the strength of your hunch."

"It's more than a hunch. I saw that man's eyes, Fred. They were guilty as hell."

"I don't doubt you, Dana. But law demands much more in a case like this than instinct, no matter how sound. So sorry to hear about your little girl. Is there anything I can do?"

"Apparently not." Frustration was heating Dana's temper to a boil. The D.A. was hamstrung by politics and procedure. Dana suffered no such stifling limitations.

Parmenter cleared his throat. "I don't think they'll give you a different answer, but since the Cambridge Center is in Connecticut, you might want to check in with the State's

Attorney's Office there. Bill Magnussen's an old friend of
mine. Tell him I suggested you call."

"I will, Fred. Thanks."

Magnussen was at a conference in Scottsdale, Arizona.
Dana tried to reach him there, but his aide reported that
he'd be touring correctional facilities statewide and out of
phone contact for the rest of the day. Too edgy to wait for
evening, she dialed the State House.

Connecticut's governor, had been a guest on *Back Talk*
shortly before his race for reelection. Dana had given the
incumbent a forum for his controversial tax reform proposal. Andrew Elliot's appearance on the show was widely
credited with ensuring the bill's passage. The program's success had bolstered Elliot's popularity and given him a large,
essential boost with the voters at the polls.

Dana was more than ready to call in the debt.

But Elliot wasn't paying. The governor returned Dana's
call promptly and patiently heard her out. But when she
asked him to help her get into the records at the Cambridge
Center to learn "John's" true identity, he balked.

"You're asking me to authorize an illegal search of privileged medical information."

"I'm asking for your help, Andrew."

"And I'd be glad to give it to you, if I could. But what
you're asking for are impeachable offenses. Serious viola-
tions of civil rights and public trust."

"This man tried to rape my twelve-year-old daughter.
Why the hell should he have civil rights?"

"Blame the system."

"I'd rather blame someone I can kick."

Dana made a few more legitimate tries. She got as far as
the U.S. Attorney General, Royce Larrimore, a friend of
her brother's from law school. Like the others, Royce was
sympathetic and attentive, but discouraging. There seemed
to be no legal way to unearth the masked rapist's identity
and get him charged with the assault against Becky.

Hanging up, she heard a tiny cry from Becky's room.

"Mommy? Mom!"

Rushing in, she found the child whimpering and wide-eyed with terror. Dana lowered the side rail and scooped the little girl in her arms.

"Easy, Beck. I'm here."

"But the man came back, Mims. He had these long, ugly teeth. And his eyes were all bloody."

Becky's skin was clammy. The hospital gown was soaked with perspiration. "That was just a bad dream, honey. He's not coming back. Not ever."

"But it was so real, Mims. So real. . . ."

Dana rang the nurse for a fresh gown. She helped Becky off with the old one and sponged her down with cool water on a cloth. The child's slim arms were limp as a rag doll's. She barely had the strength to hold her head.

"There. That's better," Dana crooned.

"Would you sit with me until I fall asleep, Mims?"

"Sure, honey." Becky hadn't asked for her comforting presence at bedtime since she was a tiny thing.

Soon, the little girl's eyes fluttered shut and her breathing settled. She looked so relaxed and peaceful. If only Dana could kill the nightmares and bury them in the dim distance.

Slipping back to the sitting room, Dana made another call.

Chapter 20

LENNIE

I entered Gates Restaurant through the ponderous iron portals for which it was named and followed the din to the bar.

This proud New Canaan institution dispensed more anesthetic by the glass than any other proprietary establishment in southern Connecticut. People of all ages and persuasions flocked here in desperate droves. Weekends brought heat-seeking singles and naughty pretenders on the make. At six-thirty on a Monday, lust took a backseat to the great American quest for oblivion.

This was serious merrymaking. Many of the patrons sported funeral suits and Windsor-knotted nooses. The faces behind the beer-foam mustaches were grim. And the conversational drift was definitely southward. Waiting for Jack, I caught snippets on unemployment, tragic accidents, acts of God and terrorists, and terminal disease.

"Would you believe she's got Hodgkin's, and the face-lift's not even paid for."

"You think that's bad? Will's father has a spot on his lung, and just last year he lost his shirt in condominiums."

A hand circled my waist. A breathy whisper in my ear made me shiver. "Hi, Eleanora. So glad you called."

The crowd soldered us together. I drew back, suddenly stifled by the crush.

"Hope this is okay," I managed.

Jack had suggested a quiet, relaxing place. My overriding desire was for neutral ground. Somewhere public and predictable where I could try to escape the maze of confusion I'd blundered into on the Dolans' snowy roof.

I needed to search Jack's dark eyes for sincerity. I wanted to penetrate his lake-smooth surface, to toss him all the hard, open questions and watch for telltale ripples in his response.

"Anywhere you are is perfect," he said. "Want to sit?"

We cut through the jungle of bodies to a clearing. A willowy brunette in a flowing ankle-length dress and espadrilles presided over the dining room. Here, the decor was soft and settling. Quarry tile floors, lush plants, large oil renderings of outsized flowers. Ceiling fans circled lazily overhead. We were shown to a cozy booth overlooking a small fenced garden. Sparkling snowdrifts capped the lawn. Tiny lights jeweled the ice-sheathed shrubs.

Jack looked tired. His eyes were puffy and vague. After choosing a cabernet from the wine list, he leaned back and braced his hands on the table. The sleeves of his pale blue shirt were rolled to the elbows. His forearm bore a staff of ragged scratches.

"What happened?"

He stifled a yawn. "Oh, that? I was puttering in the shop. Dropped a set screw. When I bent to pick it up, I scraped against the table I was finishing for Cara's playhouse."

Odd. To me, they looked like claw marks. I'd been similarly stamped by a bruised stray tom Mrs. O' brought home for a bout of rest and recovery several months ago. But Jack didn't have a pet.

Stop, Lennie. Next thing you'll be dodging evil aliens or hearing voices beckon you from the toaster oven.

"What's wrong, Eleanora? You seemed so put off Saturday night."

"I was just surprised to find out you went to school here. You act as if you don't know this area at all."

"I don't. I was at Yale for two terms. Less than a year, all told. Spent most of that going through the motions."

"Why was that?"

"I'd rather talk about what's troubling you."

"What's troubling me is I hardly know you, Jack. If I ask you anything personal, you change the subject. Like you did just now."

Wasn't that precisely the same accusation Mrs. O' had leveled at me? Felonious subject changing. Hiding emotions in the first degree. Inwardly, I cringed. Maybe Jack's biggest sin was being far too much like me.

His smile was rueful. "Can't see as I'm much worth discussing, that's all. Anything you want to know, ask away."

The opening was ideal, but the possible consequences of slipping through it gave me pause. If Jack was all right, I wasn't. If he proved not to be, my judgment about him had been dangerously flawed. I couldn't afford any more strikes in the trust department. I wasn't like Shelby, able to bounce back and blithely risk making the same mistake over and over and over and over again.

Get on with it, Lennie.

"I did, Jack. Why do you say you were going through the motions?"

"Had my mind full of other things, I guess. The baby. Liz." A wistful cloud crossed his expression. "She was a wonderful woman. Way better than I deserved."

"Why do you say that?"

He mused awhile. "Most people tend hardest to their top layers. What shows. Liz was good clean through. Managed to find some good in most everyone else, too, no matter how deep she had to dig."

"And you?"

"I do my best. Can't say I'm always proud of the results."

"Join the club."

"What else do you want to know, Eleanora? I want everything clear between us."

Without hesitation, Jack answered my barrage of questions. What emerged was the portrait of a shy, gangly boy, reared by two affluent icons of Charleston society. While mother lunched and Daddy did business, a string of revolving nannies cared for Jack and his younger sister, Jillian.

"Guess that's why I was always so set on being there for Liz and Michael," he told me earnestly. "Can't help thinking Jilly might have turned out differently if she'd had more attention from our folks."

His sister suffered from severe emotional problems. The diagnosis was borderline personality disorder, an aptly named condition that kept her walking a tightrope at society's fringes.

Periodically, Jillian dropped out of sight. When she turned up again, weeks or months later, it was generally in a jail, psych ward, or homeless shelter.

He shook his head sadly. "Such a waste. Jilly's a beautiful girl. And talented. Always starred in school plays and the like. Teachers thought she had a real future in classical dance. When she turned fourteen, she went to study with the American Ballet Company in New York. Things started off all right. But she couldn't hold it together.

"That was the first time she ran off. Police couldn't find her. After a couple of days, my folks and I went up to look on our own. The investigator we hired finally traced her to this topless joint she was working in, in Times Square. God, how she looked when we found her. All done up like a two-bit baby whore."

His sadness seeped under my skin. I knew the helpless heartache that came from watching a loved one sink.

Interesting that we shared that particular pain. But strange that we hadn't shared it sooner. I always told new people in my life about Huck right away. I couldn't imagine trying to hide him like an unsightly rash or the fine print on an underhanded contract.

Jack seemed to read my mind. "I'm not ashamed of Jilly, but I still find it hard to talk about her illness. My folks didn't believe in hanging out the family wash. Never forget

the time I accidentally let on about my sister to some of
their friends at the club. Made Daddy so mad, he couldn't
wait to get home and express his displeasure. Stopped on
the way to whip me. Used a fence post he found on the
side of the road."

"That's terrible."

"Got his point across. That was his main concern. He
figured a boy's bones would knit soon enough once you
fixed his mistaken opinions."

"Didn't it ever occur to him that he might be mistaken?"

Jack sipped his wine. "Don't think so. Not that he let on
anyway. My father meant well enough, but he was old
school. Believed he had the Word and the sacred responsibility to pass it on. Mother eased the blows some. At least,
she tried."

In high school, Jack came into his own. Freshman year,
he sprouted nine inches, making him the tallest in his class
and one of its top athletes. His brains, for which he'd been
teased mercilessly, now won him respect. The shyness that
had plagued him evaporated.

Following his father's wishes and footsteps, he attended
the University of Virginia. There, during the screwiest of
the psycho sixties, he grew his hair to his shoulders, dressed
in beads and Birkenstocks, and took up the acoustic guitar.

"If I do say so myself, I did a pretty mean Travis pick."
With a flourish, he raised an air guitar and demonstrated his
remembered technique to a chorus of "Puff, The Magic
Dragon."

I air-clapped my approval. "Nice voice. But I think the
instrument could use a little tuning."

"Doubt I would have noticed in those days. Spent too
much of my time circling Jupiter."

"Drugs, you mean?"

"Soft stuff. Mostly grass. It was like beer back then. Nobody gave it much thought until years later when they were
running for office or seeking confirmation for Supreme
Court seats."

Studying my face, he went grave. "Don't get the wrong idea. I was just a kid doing what all the other kids were, dumb as that might seem. Suppose I enjoyed tweaking my old man some, too. Lord knows he deserved it."

"When did you clean up your act?"

Leaning closer, he caged my hand in his. "Who says I have?"

I flushed, remembering his lips. His tongue. "I don't mean that way."

"Hard for me to think of much else. After my wife died, I thought that part of my life was over. Never imagined I could find those feelings for another woman. So glad I was wrong."

Peering hard into his eyes, I couldn't help but feel the same. What was this man really guilty of, after all? Living in New Haven? Getting an advanced degree?

But the man went to Yale, Your Honor.

Off with his head!

"Come home with me tonight, Eleanora."

"I can't. I have a gift to deliver to Huck, and then I really need some sleep. I'm back on days tomorrow."

"Mind if I tag along? I'd love to meet your brother."

"I don't know, Jack. He's not too hot with strangers."

To be honest, Huck wasn't all that terrific with friends or relatives, either. My brother did best with things inanimate, imaginary, and prerecorded.

"That's okay. I'd still like to meet him."

And so, Jack paid the check and we went to Whitechapel together.

By the time we arrived, the junior dorms were dark, the parking lot nearly deserted. A few lights still blazed in the main house area, where some of the staff treated private clients after hours.

Frigid temperatures had capped the snow on the green with a glinting sheath of ice. As we picked our way along the narrow path cleared toward my brother's dorm, I grew increasingly uneasy.

"Anything unfamiliar sets him off. Try not to take it personally."

"I won't."

"Chances are he'll pretend you're not there. But he might head for the hills. A couple of years ago, I showed up with a new hairdo. Nothing radical, mind you. It was just a little shorter than usual and parted in the middle. Huck took one look at me and ran off screaming. I couldn't go back to see him again until it grew in."

"Stop worrying, Eleanora. It'll be fine."

This close to lights out, most of the Senior II residents were already in their rooms. We found Huck alone in the lounge, splayed in an armchair, dozing. He wore his favorite blue striped pajamas and a pair of worn cabin slippers that he'd put on inside out. Sitcom characters cavorted on the large-screen TV in front of him, but the sound had been muted by remote. I ruffled his hair, and his eyes snapped open.

"Hey, handsome. I brought you something. It's the first annual Huck Finn Excellence in Communication Award."

I held up the shirt and sweats. Huck flailed at the garments angrily and grunted. The nerve of me, blocking his view of the television set.

"All right. I read you. I'll get out of your hair in a minute. But first, I want you to meet somebody. Huck, this is Jack Chambless."

The program broke for commercials. I seized the opportunity to draw Jack into my brother's line of sight. The move inspired a predictable response. Huck tossed his head in protest.

"Come on, bro. Be nice. Jack's a friend."

Suddenly, Huck went dead still. His mouth gaped.

"Huck? What's wrong?"

Strangled cries escaped him. They were sounds I'd never heard before: a shrill, unearthly mix of rage and fear.

I gripped his arms. "What is it, Huck? Are you sick?"

His cries continued, harsh and unnerving. I tried holding

my hand up in front of his face and ordering him to stop as I'd seen one of the staff do when he threw a fit over the mismatched plate in the lunchroom. But his tantrum raged unabated.

Desperate, I scanned the room, trying to figure out what had triggered the violent outburst.

"You don't like the Giants' stuff, sweetheart? Is that it?"

Hurriedly, I balled up my gift and stashed it in the hall outside the lounge. But that didn't stop Huck's shrieking. Grabbing the remote control, I tried changing the channel on the TV set. I flipped the sound on and off again.

No change.

I felt his screams like stabs, sharp and piercing. My teeth clenched so hard my jaw ached. There had to be some way to stop him.

"Wait outside, Jack. Please."

He hesitated a beat, then left. Kneeling, I swaddled my screaming brother in my arms.

"Shh, sweetheart. Easy now. It's okay."

Slowly, Huck settled down. His cries grew fainter and finally stilled. Sweaty and breathless, he heaved a massive sigh and went limp as a rag doll."

"That's better, champ," I murmured. "Come. Let's get you to bed." I helped him up and walked him down the hall to his room. Huck leaned on me heavily. He was as slow and sluggish as an invalid. But when I tried to slip off his robe, he shook loose vehemently. Moving like a launched torpedo, he lurched across the room, grabbed his coat, and tugged it on over his pajamas. Then he bent and pulled on his boots.

"Uh-uh, slugger. I think you're a little confused. You're supposed to stay here, now. It's bedtime."

Grabbing my wrist, he charged out of the room, bolted down the hall, and lunged out of Senior II, dragging me with him. I saw no sign of Jack on the way. Wise man had probably decided to sit out the storm in the car.

"Slow down, Huck. Where are we going?"

He hurried across the path toward the main house and butted his way through the door. Powerless to do otherwise, I followed him up the stairs and down the hall to Rosemary Keaveney's office.

The door was unlocked. Without pausing to turn on the light, Huck crossed to the desk and powered up the computer. The screen lit, and the cursor pulsed. Huck shoved his hands at the keyboard and thrashed, filling half the screen with angry gibberish.

Squealing in frustration, he backed off and tried again. This time the computer whined in protest and the keyboard seized.

"Easy. Let me help you."

I turned the power switch off and on again. Trying to match the moves his speech therapist had made during her Sunday demonstration, I set one hand lightly beneath Huck's forearm. Magically, his clumsiness evaporated. He pointed a purposeful finger and started pecking at the keys.

"BEDMANHEER"

"Remember to space, Huck."

Frowning with purpose, he started again. "BEDMAN HEERGOWAY"

"Bedman?"

"BED MAN"

"What's that, Huck?"

"BED MAN BAD"

My throat closed. "You mean Jack?"

"BADMAN BAD BEDMAN GOWAYGOBACK"

"Easy, Huck. Are you talking about Jack?"

"GOOOOOOOOOOOOOOOOOOOOOOOOOOOOOOOOOO"

Breathless, he leaned over and switched off the computer. Before I could flip it on again, he bolted from the chair and dashed out of Rosemary's office.

Racing to keep up, I trailed him back to Senior II. As soon as we got to his room, he dropped his coat on the floor, shed his boots, and sank on his bed like a stone.

His breaths were short and labored. His nostrils flared, and his ribs beat beneath his pajama shirt like the frantic wings of a trapped bird.

"Shh, sweetheart. You can rest, now. I know what you were trying to tell me."

He stared at me, hard.

"It's okay, Huck. I'll take care of it."

Fear glinted in his wide blue eyes.

"I promise."

Turning toward the wall, he hugged his pillow. His muscles relaxed, and his breathing settled in a low, whistling rush.

"That's better. Rest now. Sleep tight."

There is no silence deeper than Huck's. But in that infinite, bottomless hush I found the answer I'd been seeking. Finally, I saw a path to the truth. Dousing the lights, I left my brother to his dreams.

Chapter 21

DANA

Leaving Becky at the hospital under her father's cool but capable supervision, Dana hurried to the studio.

By the time she arrived, Lucy Breitmeier, Mickey Conway, Heather Warren, and Stacy Raybuck had gathered in the conference room. Heather, a highly decorated veteran of the talk show trenches, was *Back Talk*'s executive producer. Stacy, a waifish blonde, was a top-flight production assistant and a rich source of inventive ideas.

Dana had declared this inner circle gathering a level-six emergency. To date, none of the show's crises had ranked above a level five, and that weighty designation had been invoked only once.

It was during last November's sweeps. In one unforgettable week, two of five scheduled celebrity guests canceled. Another was arrested for cocaine possession with presumed intent to sell.

In November, Stacy's brilliant bailout proposal was for Dana to hold "town meetings" on a number of sizzling issues. With unprecedented speed, the necessary arrangements were made and the show went on the road.

First, *Back Talk* traveled to a redneck southern town to debate forced busing and affirmative action with Mayor Jim Crow and the large local chapter of bigots anonymous.

From there, Dana visited a group of Bible-thumping fundamentalists to discuss abortion rights. Finally, she brought the issue of gun control to a rabid group of paranoid survivalists in northern Idaho.

All three of the shows generated considerable heat, a ray or two of light, and superb share numbers.

This time, however, much more was at stake than advertising rates. Dana had to uncover the identity of Becky's assailant. Once she did, she would see to it the bastard was put out of commission, permanently.

She was still reeling from the sting of being rebuffed by every one of her influential contacts. When push came to shove, all the fawning bureaucrats and politicians were interested only in promoting and protecting their own hides. Dana might be *their* best friend when they had books or bills or candidacies to peddle. But when she needed something, the only best friend she could really count on was herself.

But then she'd always known that.

Mickey Conway finished chugging his Sprite and set down the can with a belch.

Dana shot him a withering look as she claimed the chair at the head of the conference table.

"Sorry for canceling today," she said grimly. "It was unavoidable."

"All that matters is Becky," Lucy replied. "How's she doing?"

"She'll be fine. I want the bastard who assaulted her. What are the chances Valerie Eckhard will roll over and give him up?"

"You're convinced it was the kiddie diddler?" Conway looked surprised.

"I can do without the word choice, Mickey. But yes, I am convinced. Unfortunately, that's not enough to get the son of a bitch what he deserves."

Lucy frowned. "Eckhard wouldn't cooperate for anything short of a *People* cover. Maybe not even then."

Heather Warren smoothed her boxy tweed jacket and nodded agreement. The executive producer was a trim, green-eyed brunette. "Forget Blowhard, Dana. Give that bitch any rope, she'll find a way to hang you with it."

"What's the alternative?"

"Can't the police help?" Heather asked.

"I've tried the official route. Forget it. How about you, Mickey? Any way you can dial John up on your magic keyboard?"

He frowned. "Easiest would be if the law firm's computers were on-line. I'd probably be able to nail down the baby boffer from time slips and such. But seeing that the lady lawyer specializes in tooting her own horn, I doubt she's got much use for any of the legal research networks. There must be something else. I'll have to think on it."

Dana's teeth clenched. "I *told* you to watch your word choice, Mickey. This man is a child molester, a sick, repulsive animal who tried to hurt my little girl. You will show some sensitivity or I'll show you the goddamned door. You got that?!"

Biting back a nervous smile, Conway held up his hands. "Whoa. Easy, boss. Sorry."

Dana rolled her eyes. What the hell was wrong with Conway? In certain respects the guy was a true genius. But he could say the most inappropriate, most irritating things. Could Mickey's warped personality be the sign of something darker?

Conway knew where Becky went to school. He had full access to Dana's schedule and the little girl's. What if "John" wasn't the perpetrator after all? Why hadn't she considered that Becky's assailant could be someone much closer to home—like Mickey Conway?

Drawing a breath, Dana asked herself that horrifying question. But the obvious answer came to her at once. When Becky was attacked, Mickey was right here at the studio, working on the preliminary subject reports for a number of next month's shows. The reports he had generated during that time were stacked in front of Dana, a full morning's work to be sure. Furthermore, a dozen or more people would have noticed and reported Mickey's absence immediately. *Back Talk*'s grapevine was too small and active for anyone to go AWOL without raising voices and eyebrows.

Dana forced her thoughts back on track. "Stacy? I could definitely use one of your brainstorms here."

The assistant searched the acoustical ceiling tile for answers. Suddenly, her face brightened. "How about the Cambridge Center files? Our anonymous John was a client, right? Maybe Mickey can tap in and get the dope on him there."

"Great idea." Dana turned to Conway. "What do you think?"

"Hate to rain on your parade. But John went through Patterson Graham's program over twenty years ago. Way before computers were in common business use. No reason I can see they'd spend the time and money it'd take to upload all their back records. Stuff's probably been trashed or stored somewhere."

"Didn't Graham mention long-term follow-up?" Dana asked.

"Group stuff, I think." Mickey frowned. "Can't imagine how we'd pick our guy out of a list."

Dana blew an exasperated breath. "There has to be a way."

"How about we put a tail on Blowhard? Watch her office. Hope that leads us to the guy," Conway proposed.

"Too iffy and too slow," Dana snapped. "I want that bastard now. I want him where he can't hurt any more little girls—ever! Becky needs to feel safe again—whatever it takes." A bitter lump filled Dana's throat. She swallowed it down and tried to piece herself together.

"I'll keep plugging at it, boss. See what I can do," Mickey said.

"Me, too," Stacy promised. "We'll think of something, Dana. Don't worry."

"Until we bring John in, worrying's all I can do. Keep me informed, will you?"

"Absolutely." Heather said.

"And don't worry about pulling any punches. I don't care what it takes to nail him. Just *nail* him. I'll clean up after you if necessary."

Dana's enormous L-shaped office was divided into work and sitting areas. Normally, she found the pale mauve carpeting, cream drapes, and abundant fresh floral arrangements calming. Today, however, nothing short of a tranquilizer gun would do the job.

Which was just as well. She needed to be alert. On guard. The man who's attacked Becky could be anywhere. Anyone. The best Dana could hope to recognize were the eyes. She conjured them now, hard lumps of lifeless coal.

A pile of message slips and a stack of urgent memos awaited her on her desk. Pushing them aside, she dialed the owner of Watch Link, the private security firm that had transported Becky to the hospital.

Crisply, Dana arranged for round-the-clock armed guards outside Becky's suite at Mount Sinai. After her discharge tomorrow, things would get trickier.

"I want my daughter watched whenever she leaves the apartment, but I don't want her aware of the surveillance. Can you arrange that, Mr. Rostron?"

"Whatever you want, Mrs. Meade."

"I'm talking about *close* and *constant* observation. Becky is not to go anywhere alone. That includes the latrine."

"No problem. We'll put our best female operatives on it. I'll arrange for them to pose as visitors to your daughter's school, student teachers perhaps. Trust me, Mrs. Meade. Watch Link has handled personal security for major celebrities, even heads of state."

"This is more important. This is my little girl."

Pacing restlessly, Dana agonized over what more she

could do to bring this horror to a quick and certain end. Every button she could think of had been pushed. Her powerful friends were useless. Her key staffers would do their best, but what if that, too, proved insufficient?

Even the tightest security could be breached or compromised. Bodyguards were human and, therefore, fallible. If Roddy Pierce had failed to keep the child safe, how on earth could Dana rely on anyone?

Once she knew John's identity and where to find him, Dana was certain she could twist arms to get the case against him pushed to the top of the glutted trial calendar. She'd have him behind bars in a heartbeat.

No matter where she began, she ended back again at the urgent need to unearth the rapist's true identity. And fast.

Suddenly, Dana hit on the most direct means to that priceless information. Picking up her private line, she set the filthy wheels in motion.

Chapter 22

LENNIE

Leaving Whitechapel, I felt swallowed by an eerie calm. Cloud wisps veiled the fulsome face of the moon. Lush shadows cushioned my steps. The wind urged me forward like gentle fingers prodding a stage-shy child.

As I slipped into Jack's car, his face tensed with worry. "Your brother okay?"

"Fine. He's sleeping."

"You were right Eleanora. I shouldn't have come."

"No, Jack. I'm glad you did. Really."

His mouth pressed in a grim line. "All I did was upset the boy. That's the last thing I wanted."

Battling revulsion, I forced myself to look at him. What *did* this man want? Reassurance? Absolution? A ticket to the Kingdom of the Born-Again Squeaky Clean?

Or was Huck mistaken?

All my brother had to go on was the fragile dust of distant memory. Crude impressions etched on a grainy ground of terror, youth, and shock. At the time of my rape, Huck was only a baby. Still in diapers. Tethered to the world by a slim and fraying thread.

My own case against Jack wasn't built on much more. Flimsy scraps of circumstance and supposition. Lies so small they would pass for mere evasions. Nothing nearly sound enough to fill my aching void.

The prosecution rests, Your Honor.

Dismissed! Next case.

I thought of Rosemary Keveany's disclaimer. Huck's messages might be an illusion. Wishful thinking. Could my fingers have guided him ever so subtly in his damning accusations? Were his fears and charges really mine?

The ride home was awkward and interminable. Silence loomed between us like some hulking stranger we'd picked up along the road. Jack kept glancing anxiously my way. His dark eyes brimmed with sorrow and confusion. I pretended not to notice.

Finally, he dropped me at my car. Idling alongside, he waited to make sure the crate started.

I drove off in the direction of home. Jack's Jeep trailed me for a couple of blocks, then veered northward toward Wilton. I watched in my rearview mirror until his taillights evaporated in the distance. Swerving onto a side street, I turned around and doubled back through town.

Traffic was sparse. My Toyota moved with rare enthusiasm. Arriving at the place with unexpected speed, I nearly breezed past the modestly marked approach.

Entering the foyer of the Manchester Arms, I caught the haunting strains of Sally Deane's voice from the lounge. The song was "Killing Me Softly," the rendition so boldly seductive the bar's featured drink should have been sailors on the rocks.

As I stepped through the archway to the lounge, my eyes were stabbed by the sharp shine of a misdirected spotlight. Blinking hard, I stared through the dense swag of smoky air. The sultry singer was nowhere to be seen. In her place beside the baby grand piano was a cassette player hooked to a set of speakers.

Retreating to inn's foyer, I approached the slick-haired, dark-suited clerk behind the desk.

"Will Sally Deane be here tonight?"

"Sally?"

"The singer?"

"Not tonight, no. I don't think so."

"Do you know where I can find her?"

Stroking an imaginary beard, he frowned. "Sorry. Can't say I do."

"Please. It's urgent."

"I suppose Stuart Long might know. The piano player. He stepped out on a break. Should be back in ten minutes or so."

I perched impatiently on one of the floral chintz window seats flanking the door. Through the mullioned glass, I watched the road.

Fifteen minutes passed before a set of approaching head-lights slowed and bumped into the inn's driveway. Ducking out quickly, I intercepted the piano player as he trudged up the cut stone walk. His hands were thrust deep in the pock-ets of his trench coat. An upturned collar walled the bottom of his craggy face. The top was dominated by a sharp slop-ing forehead and small, suspicious eyes. Straps of yolk yel-low hair rode the strident breeze like windsocks.

"Mr. Long? I'm looking for Sally Deane. The man at the desk said you might know where she is."

His eyes narrowed. "What do you want with Sally?"

"It's personal. I'm a friend of a friend."

He sniffed. I smelled bourbon on his breath. "Isn't every-one?"

"Please, Mr. Long. It's important."

He looked me over. Shrugged. "I think she has rehearsal tonight in Stamford. You know the community house on Cascade Road?"

"Yes."

"That's the place, but it's late. Session's probably over by now."

"Thanks. I'll try to catch her."

I navigated the twisting back streets at a restless clip. At the wishbone-shaped intersection of North Stamford and

Cascade, I skidded on an unseen patch of black ice. The car swerved wildly, lurching sideways up the steeply inclined road. At the peak, the wheels spun out, setting me on a collision course with a towering oak. I jammed the brakes. They slipped. Made a hideous grinding noise. Finally, with a jarring squeal, they caught, inches from the tree.

"*Good* jalopy," I crooned with a grateful pat on the dash. "*Nice* pain in the ass."

The community house was a squat stone structure with a waffle weave door and a small porch girdled in wrought iron. Cars crammed the minuscule dirt lot beside the entrance. The overflow occupied several slots fronting the darkened clapboard church across the street.

Entering, I found a dozen middle-aged men and women clustered at the far end of the long, single room. They stood stiffly, their mouths agape and expectant like hungry hatchlings. All eyes were trained on the prim woman standing before them. Perched behind a music stand, she held one arm aloft. Her brow was hitched, lips pursed in concentration.

Dipping her hand, she unleashed a harmonic burst of varied voices. The piece began with a rousing "Hallelujah" and proceeded from there in an alien language in a mournful minor key.

Scanning the room, I searched for Sally Deane. On a table near the door, a stainless coffee urn burbled beside a half-eaten mound of oatmeal cookies and a scatter of soiled Styrofoam cups. A heap of coats, hats, purses, and mufflers warmed on the broad boxed radiator. There was no sign of life in the small, open storage space at the building's rear. Not a hint of the singer anywhere. Discouraged, I was about to leave when the choir director tapped the stand, halting the song in progress.

"Ease up on the bass, would you, Marty? And try to keep it crisper, Ruth. Like this."

At the sound of her voice, my jaw dropped in astonishment. The woman leading the chorus was the sultry songbird from the lounge. Sally Deane was virtually unrecognizable in a prim black calf-length skirt, celery green sweater set, pale stockings, and sensible black flats. Her raven hair was corralled in a velvet headband. Large tortoiseshell glasses with an amber tint defused the striking eyes.

Practice continued for ten minutes more. Finished, the chorus claimed their coats and shifted toward the door in a chatty mass. Sally Deane ushered them out, dispensing nuggets of praise like a human Pez machine.

"Great job tonight, Merle. Sandy, that solo is coming along beautifully." Catching a plump woman by the elbow, she chided jokingly, "No leaving us for the Met, now, Ida. Remember, we saw you first."

After the last of the pack was out the door, the singer turned toward me. She proffered a graceful hand.

"Jack's friend, right? Afraid I didn't catch your name."

"It's Lennie Finn. Stuart Long said I might find you here. Sorry to barge in on you like this."

"Not at all. Nothing oils the pipes like an audience. That bunch never sounded better. Care for coffee?"

"Thanks. Black's fine."

Crossing to the urn, she filled two cups from the clean inverted stack. She handed me mine, added two sugar lumps to hers and stirred with a wooden stick. Her eyes studied me.

"What can I do for you, Ms. Finn?"

"You said you knew Jack while he was at Yale. What was he like?"

"You're involved with Jack?"

"In a way, yes. What I'm trying to figure out is what way."

"It's been a very long time. I can't see why Jack's ancient history would make a difference to you now."

"In this case, it does."

"May I ask why?"

I groped for a neat explanation. And I came up empty.

Lousy liar that I was, I should have tired to concoct a decent story in advance.

"I really can't tell you, Ms. Deane."

Her brow peaked.

"I guess that sounds strange," I faltered.

"True."

"All I can say is that it's important to me. Very important."

She was silent, considering. I tried to appear calm and offhanded, though my insides were fizzing like a shaken can of Coke.

Finally, she removed her glasses and rubbed the narrow bridge of her nose. "Not much for me to tell, I'm afraid. I met Jack when I was starting out, assisting in a congregation in New Haven."

"You're a minister?"

"No, a rabbi. I'm with a small group in Stamford now. We're in the process of raising money for a temple building. Meantime, we've been renting space from the church."

"It's hard to believe you're not really a singer."

"In a way, I suppose I am. Actually, I planned on a stage career, but somebody up there changed my mind along the way. Originally, I trained as a cantor. That's the temple official who sings the liturgy. When they eased up on ordaining women rabbis, I went back to school."

"But you looked—"

"Not very rabbinical?" Her smile was good-natured. "You're right, of course. Inside this dowdy old lady lurks a frustrated lounge lizard, I'm afraid. Once in awhile, I let my friend Stuart talk me into letting her out. In exchange, he fills in when our regular organist is out."

"You're wonderful."

"Thanks. I'd like to say I do it all for the sake of the congregation, but that wouldn't be entirely true. Performing's always had a powerful pull on me. Still does, though the basic act's changed considerably."

I remembered Sally Deane at the mike. Her raw sensual

power was difficult to reckon with this level, low-heeled servant of the Lord.

"Where did you meet Jack?" I asked.

"At the synagogue. For awhile, that down-home Southern Baptist boy was one of our best customers. More active than some of our diehard regular congregants. He showed up at services, special events. Worked in our volunteer programs. Even took a few classes in our night school."

"Strange."

She sipped her coffee. "Happens from time to time. Some people seem to be plain uncomfortable in their own skin. So they go fishing. Bait whatever hooks they can find, trying to land something that fits better."

"Was his wife active, too?"

The brow peaked. "Didn't know he had a wife."

"He did."

She shrugged. "Jack was very young. Couldn't have been married long. Some have trouble getting used to the concept."

"Do you think he was planning to convert?"

"Maybe, but I think he finally realized his religion wasn't the thing that needed changing."

"What was?"

Her eyes narrowed. "Can't say for sure. Seemed to me he was running from something, though I honestly don't know what. Jack wasn't much of a talker. At least, not to me."

My hopes plunged. I'd counted on this woman to lead me to Jack's hidden past.

"I'm afraid I haven't done much enlightening."

"I appreciate your time anyway, Rabbi Deane."

Rising, she unplugged the coffee urn, tossed the soiled cups in the trash can, and shrugged into her wool tweed coat. I followed her into a night gone suddenly bleak and discouraging.

Her car was parked two rows behind mine in the church lot across the street. We walked together, treading cautiously over the ice-slicked pavement. At the edge of the lot, we shook hands and parted.

While I fumbled through my cluttered purse for car keys, the chameleon clergywoman slipped into her Volvo wagon and started rolling toward the road.

Where were the keys? I checked my pockets, searched the seat. Finally, I found them in the open zippered section of my purse.

As I nudged the ignition, I was startled by the sudden blast of a horn. The rabbi had backed her car up next to mine. She was motioning for me to roll down my window.

"Something just occurred to me, Ms. Finn. One of our volunteer projects that year was a community outreach program. Helping families in crisis.

"One case was especially tragic. A local woman was killed in a convenience store robbery. She was an innocent bystander. Widowed mom with five kids. Social services wanted to ship the younger ones out to foster care, but the oldest daughter insisted on holding the family together. Remarkable young woman. She managed to pull it off against some *very* long odds.

"Our congregation helped out until the girl finished school and landed a decent job. Your friend Jack took particular interest. Got pretty close, I think. You might want to talk to her."

"She's still around?"

"Oh, yes. With a vengeance. Her name's Eden Hilliard."

"Like the department store?"

"Yes, Ms. Finn. Exactly like that."

Chapter 23

LENNIE

Frantic scratching at my door awakened me. Burrowing under the pillow, I sought to work the percussive rasping into a dream.

My fuzzy mind wove a lovely fantasy. Hitsig was scrabbling a chain link fence. Below, a pack of slavering dogs hurled themselves at the thick metal mesh. As his burning muscles threatened to give way, Wild Bill screamed for me to help him. But my nails were wet.

Nothing worse than a smudge, Shelby kept yelling. *Nothing worse than a smudge.*

Maniac kept whimpering and pawing until I hauled myself out of bed and poked my weary head into the hall.

"Go back to sleep, girl. It's too early."

The mutt looped in fretful circles, pausing once each orbit to nose at the stairs. Her whining stretched high and thin, like the menacing shrill of a live wire. My skin prickled.

"What's wrong, Maniac? Show me."

The house was dead still. No sound but the syncopated tick of the grandfather clock in the hall and the dog's sharp, shallow breathing.

Tracking her through the hall, I tensed. I imagined one of the boarders blue and lifeless from a heart attack. Or my beloved Mrs. O' in a pool of blood on the kitchen floor. But when Maniac finally led me into the pantry, her agitation peaking like clicks on a geiger counter, all I found was a spreading yellow puddle and a heap of droppings near the kibble sack.

At the corner of the room, Romulus and Remus slept in a slick ebony tangle. Outraged, and clearly refusing to take the rap, Maniac loped over to them and barked in shrill, accusatory yips.

"All right, Maniac. Forget it. No harm done."

I cleaned the floor with paper toweling, though the mutt kept nosing my hand away as if I were trying to squelch evidence in a homicide. When I finished, she eyed me balefully.

"What can I tell you? Life's not always fair."

"You can say that again, Lennie girl."

Frank Murphy's abrupt appearance unnerved me, but I refused to let on and give him the satisfaction. Cold polished his skin to the watery sheen of a winter tomato. He smelled like the dogs did after a drenching romp in the rain.

"Good morning, Frank."

"Looking up nicely, now I see you're here. How about fixing a weary soul a nice, hot breakfast? Couple of eggs, bit of sausage, toast, and coffee would surely hit the spot. Get my mind off my *troubles*, if you catch my drift."

I considered frying him up a nice, hot batch of dog droppings, but he wasn't worth even that much effort.

"I don't cook, Frank. But if you'd like to go to Hell, I'll gladly write you a recommendation."

"You'll be sorry you said that, Lennie Finn."

"Actually, it feels pretty terrific."

"When I get through with you, you'll be singing a different tune, you arrogant little harpy."

Dressed in her sweats, Mrs. O' walked in and caught a whiff of the tension.

"I won't be letting anyone fill this dear old house with

ugly vibrations. Go on. Set things right, now. The two of you."

Frank stood glowering at me. "She's the one with the nasty mouth, Auntie Jane."

"Go on, Lennie, my love. Tell the man you're sorry."

"But I'm not."

She frowned. "Do it for me, then, child. Can't abide bad feelings."

Mrs. O' rarely asked me for anything. For her sake, I caved in immediately. "All right. You have my insincere apology, Frank."

"I accept."

His smile was so smug, I itched to pry the damned thing off with my Halligan tool.

The day had gotten off to a lousy start, but it rapidly changed for the worse. As I entered the station house, the overture from *Cats* boomed over the intercom. Moments later, Hitsig's nasty voice chimed in with his sorry notion of parody lyrics.

> *"Midnight, not a sign of a fire.*
> *Has old Finn lost her marbles?*
> *She's up chasing a cat.*
> *In the—"*

A blast of static was followed by an angry amplified burst from Captain Perriman: "This sound system is official equipment, Hitsig. Department property that happened to cost ten big ones. It's for transmitting critical information, not a goddamned toy, you read me? Now haul your stupid butt out of here and get to work."

Suddenly, things were looking brighter.

Checking the duty roster in the hall, I was reasonably pleased to note that my assignment for the day was Rescue Company One, where I'd be assisting Dumbo and Red.

Hopefully, my friend Red had disregarded my moment

of tipsy foolishness in Mrs. O's driveway Sunday night. The memory of that far-too-friendly kiss made me very uneasy.

Craving distraction, I plunged hard into the morning routine. Upstairs, I relieved Wuss Elliot, my counterpart on last night's shift. Wuss was a large lumbering man with a terror of even the tiniest animal, hence his nickname.

Working Rescue, Wuss had been known to dive into fifty feet of bone-chilling water to retrieve a drowning victim. I'd seen the big lug battle dangerous chemical spills and pull people out of burning vehicles that threatened to explode at any instant. But the very mention of a mouse would send the grizzled galoot ducking for cover like a cartoon character in a panic.

Wuss glanced at my face and frowned. "You okay, Finn?"

"Fine, why?"

"You look beat."

"That's because I am, Wuss."

"Me, too." Mighty yawn. "Can't wait to get home and catch some Z's. Think I'll sleep straight through 'til tomorrow. Day after maybe."

"Sounds wonderful. Catch a few for me."

I retrieved my turnout gear from the storage room and stowed it on Rescue One. Operating as a full member of the special emergency response team involved considerable extra training, including scuba certification and a full two-year EMT course, but I was determined to complete the requirements.

I had signed on for the program a year ago, after watching Red and Wuss pull a four-year-old out of the North Stamford reservoir. While her father was fishing off the bridge, the pudgy cherub had slipped through a battered section of the fence and tumbled down the rain-slicked embankment. Standing idly by while the others dove to save her had been unbearable. I felt as if I were flailing in the water myself, small and helpless.

Rescue was considered elite duty. It was reserved for the strongest, bravest members on the squad. Several of my fellow fire-creatures, specially Hitsig, found my ambition to join them laughable. That skepticism was more than enough to spur me on when the additional demands felt too demanding.

Retrieving my uniform from the locker, I headed toward my walled-off sliver of the restroom. Hitsig spotted me as I passed the gaping entrance to the men's side. Smirking like the fool he was, he charged for the bank of urinals and let fly. Over the waterworks came Wild Bill's charming color commentary:

"That's one six-pack down. Ah, sweet relief. That you out there, Catwoman? Not very neighborly today, are you? Least you could do is stop in for a nice piss good morning."

It occurred to me that Hitsig and Frank Murphy had probably been separated at birth. From their brains.

Roll call is at eight. We're required to line up in order of seniority, which places me ten spots from the head. Red is eight places lower. Seeking reassurance that our friendship remained unspoiled, I tried to catch his eye. Before I could, Captain Perriman showed up to log us in and make the day's announcements.

"First up: Vito Antinori is the proud papa of a bouncing baby boy. Eight pounds, two ounces, born last night at Saint Joe's. Mother and son are doing fine. Vito told me he cut the cord himself."

"Not the one between him and *his* momma, I bet," Nervy cracked.

"Number two," Perriman went on, ignoring him. "The marshall is setting up a series of visits to local elementary schools to talk about the Tot Finder program and hand out decals. He's looking for volunteers."

My hand went up with a pack of others. The glow-in-the-dark stickers placed on the windows of kids' room helped us locate and rescue the little ones first in a fire.

"—Last and definitely least, if any of you haven't seen this morning's paper, there's a very disturbing story about a serial rapist in the area. Man's hit at least six times in the past eight months. All kids."

"Busy boy," HItsig muttered. "Better hurry and make your appointment, Finn."

Perriman caught the aside. "I think you're the one who needs an appointment, Hitsig. Sounds to me like you need to get yourself an IQ lift."

There was a nice round of derisive laughter. Hitsig turned a fetching shade of hypertension pink.

Scowling, Perriman continued. "Needless to say, I want everyone on the alert, especially those of you with daughters."

The news raised a chorus of outrage. Silently, I rose to my own defense. Given the number of people involved in caring for the rape victims and investigating the crimes, it was amazing that the story hadn't broken sooner.

Hopefully, Clarissa Pratt would see it that way, too. I remembered her furious threat to pin any leaks on me.

Perriman finished the announcements and commenced the customary five-minute morning location drill. We are required to know the entire city by rote, including all street and hydrant locations. If that sounds trivial, imagine being trapped in a burning house while the people with the hose and ladders are bumbling around lost in the wrong neighborhood or scratching their heads searching for a water source.

Often, we reviewed the streets by theme. Today's was trees.

"Carlone? Where's Mayapple?"

"North off High Ridge, West of Sunset, Chief," Nervy offered.

"Maple Place, Hitsig."

"That's a hard one," Wild Bill whined.

"So's your head," Six Fingers intoned.

I gazed at the window. The sun was glowing brighter and brighter.

After Perriman dismissed us, I headed down to the garage. My in-house detail for the morning was to check the apparatus. Red arrived at the rescue truck a beat behind me. Wordlessly, he climbed aboard and started testing the equipment.

Working the hind end of the rig, I endured his silence for a brief eternity. Finally, I gave up and joined him in the cab. There was an odd squirming in my chest.

"What's up, Red? You mad or something?"

"At what?"

"I don't know. You just seem a little frosty."

"To you? Nah." He chucked my chin. "I was thinking about what Perriman said, that's all. Raping a kid. Christ."

"You're such a sensitive soul, Red. It's one of the many things I love about you."

Straightening, he affected his Bogart face. "You know I came to Casablanca for the waters."

"Waters? What waters? We are in the desert."

Red winked. "I was misinformed."

We were still friends. With a swell of relief, I finished examining my half of the truck. That done, I checked out my SCBA, the compressed air breathing apparatus we were required to wear in any fire. The day's first alarm sounded as I tested the final gauge.

"Engine one, hose two, ladder two, Rescue one: Report to construction site at Two-four-six-six Tresser Boulevard."

In seconds, we were out the glassed bay doors, sirens wailing. Makowski was behind the wheel of the rescue truck. Red rode shotgun. Perched in the rear, I mulled over the possibilities. Construction calls covered a broad range of hazards. Could be a cave-in or explosion. A worker or passing civilian might be trapped under a fallen crane or concrete block. There was always the possibility of a chemical spill. I pictured the escape of toxic fumes. A slice of the city cordoned off while we braved exposure in the cleanup. In this job, especially on Rescue, you had to be prepared for everything.

Including plenty of false alarms.

When we arrived at the scene, Captain Stan Silfen stood locked in an angry confrontation with the construction foreman, a grizzled man whose giant paunch protruded through a Day-Glo orange vest.

"I see a fire, I call you guys. You don't like it? Tough."

Silfen, tall, trim, and imposing, faced the foreman down. "You see a fire, calling us is fine. A bunch of rocks and ashes doesn't qualify."

"Thing was blazing like the dickens when we got here, Captain. It's not my goddamned job to take chances."

Tracking the accusatory arc of Silfen's hand, I froze.

Circle of stones. Smoke wraiths rising from a hill of powdery ash. It was identical to the dying blaze we found beside the Dolans' house the night we were called to rescue Kitty from the roof.

The only thing missing this time was the victim.

Chapter 24

LENNIE

Sergeant Kresky and Clarissa Pratt arrived at the scene simultaneously. Moments later, two other unmarkeds, three patrol cars, and an envoy from the mayor's office rolled up.

"Let's fan out and do a full sector search of this erector set," Kresky ordered. "Resnick, Mahoney, Feighan, Silvera, take the top level. Wilson, Vanneman—"

"Who's in charge here?" Clarissa Pratt demanded.

"I am." The foreman lumbered forward, his monumental gut leading the way.

"Get your bozos out of here before one of them contaminates important evidence," the prosecutor snapped.

The foreman cocked his head like a lost dog.

"Have to ask you to call your people down, sir. Clear the area," Kresky translated for him.

"Time's money, Detective. I can't just shut down on your say-so."

"Do it on mine, then," Clarissa Pratt shot back. "We need this area cleared. Fast."

"Who the hell are you?" the foreman snarled.

"Devil or angel, porky. Your call."

The man's fists curled. For an instant, I thought he would strike her. Then he snorted and turned away. Cupping his hands like a megaphone, he called up to a pair of men perched several skeletal levels above.

"Get those beams secured, Malozzi. Biggerstaff, set the platform for the crane. We got work to do. Chop, chop!"

Clarissa Pratt issued a weary sigh and turned to address the slim, balding cop standing beside her. "Cuff this fat fool and haul him in for obstruction, Sanderson," she said curtly. "Anyone else gives you trouble, do the same."

"Yes, ma'am." Sanderson pulled out his cuffs and approached the foreman. "Hands together, please."

The fat man backed away. "Okay, okay. Real funny—"

"So how come I'm not laughing?" Clarissa Pratt snapped.

Sanderson edged closer. "Get off me," the foreman mewled.

The prosecutor was enjoying this. She ticked off the charges on her stubby fingers. "Obstruction. Resisting arrest. Want to go for a hat trick, slim?"

The foreman was still retreating from Sanderson's outstretched cuffs. Looking up, he bellowed, "Everyone clear the area. Go hang out at Dunkin' Donuts. I'll let you know when we're ready to roll again."

"Thanks *ever* so much for your cooperation, sir," Clarissa Pratt mocked. "Get to it, Kresky. Go!"

"We'd be glad to help out," Red offered.

Kresky nodded. "Sure. We can use the extra hands."

"I don't think that's wise," the prosecutor said icily. "Liability."

Handsome Harry faced her down. "I'd think we'd have more to answer for if we turned up some poor kid a few minutes too late, Ms. Pratt. Especially after we refused help from our willing colleagues. But *you're* the lawyer."

Red, Dumbo, and I were dispatched to the rear of the site. Inching forward, we examined the knee-high litter piles for any sign of a victim.

Kresky had cued us to keep a close watch for articles of clothing or even the tiniest scrap of torn fabric. Stay alert, he'd told us, for small items such as jewelry, buttons, or hair ornaments that might have come loose in a struggle. Any footprints, hairs, or even the vaguest possibility of blood-stains were to be reported, ASAP.

If we came upon anything significant, our orders were to lay off and signal Kresky or one of the other cops. Misguided handling could destroy valuable prints or evidence, Handsome Harry patiently explained. Clarissa Pratt tartly seconded the motion, but coming from her, the advice was impossible to distinguish from a threat.

My heart sank. The building site was awash in fast food wrappers, beer and soda cans, crumpled newspapers, cigarette packs, bent nails, splintered wood chunks, twisted metal beams, and endless dusty blocks of broken concrete. Mouse droppings, crack vials, and empty pints of rotgut turned up at intervals.

Following Kresky's suggestion, I tested the debris with the toe of my boot first to spare my hands any nasty surprises. The sergeant explained that rats or other unsavory squatters would likely vacate after a well-placed kick.

Comforting.

Kresky didn't need to mention what else might be lying beneath anyone of the rubbish heaps. Cold flesh. Bloody slashes. A smooth, young face contorted in the silent scream of death.

The only sounds were the scratchy relentless shifting of filth and waste. Feet shuffling. Hacking coughs. "Hello?" I called to cut the dreadful silence. "Anybody here?"

Red was several steps ahead of me in the adjoining lane, sweeping his own slow swath through the rubble. Dumbo was scanning the strip beyond. Kresky strode over to check our progress. He was coated with dust and grime. Hardly suitable for framing at the moment.

"Doing okay, Finn?"

"Yes. Find anything?"

"Not yet." Kresky frowned and placed a hand on my shoulder. "Sure you're all right? The stress can be tough to take."

"I'm fine."

I pressed on, trying to outpace the garish images. Broken angels. Faceless monsters. Wide, still, bewildered eyes.

Two more litter piles lay between me and the far end of the unfinished building. I kicked at the first one, raising a choking fog of grit. Picking apart the rubble, I found none of the items on Kresky's wish list.

Approaching the final mound, I indulged in a trace of reckless optimism. Maybe the smoldering ring of stones was a simple coincidence, an innocent blaze set to keep some homeless person warm.

Or the copycat fire could have been built by a sicko trying to cause a commotion. If news of the rapes was now public, specifics surrounding the crimes may have leaked out as well. Clarissa Pratt had refused to tell me whether the stone-bound fire was part of the rapist's M.O., but maybe someone else associated with the case had tipped the press about it.

Warming to that idea, I toed the final heap. The now familiar grainy puff rose and settled. Kneeling, I pawed through the tangle of trash. Near the bottom of the mess, I came upon a dried-out leather glove perched on a menacing shard of glass. Thinking it might be of interest to Kresky, I kept hands off and looked around for the sergeant or one of his boys in blue.

There were no cops in sight. I started sifting through the remains of the pile, taking care not to touch the glove. As I scraped toward the concrete, I spotted Kresky off to Dumbo's left and called out to him. In a careless sweep, I speared the heel of my hand on the spike of glass.

"Damn!"

The wound was a gusher. Trained to deal calmly and professionally with such emergencies, I assessed the damage, compressed the area with the flap of my turnout coat, and promptly fainted.

When I came to, Red's troubled frown swam over me. I caught a woozy glimpse of Dumbo's wobbling ears and Kresky's cover-cop face. The latter undulated like the innards of a lava lamp. Clarissa Pratt hovered behind the three of them, muttering furiously to herself, "I told him, but would he listen? Fat chance."

"Look, she's coming around." Red's fingers brushed my cheek. "Hey, you. You had us worried."

"I'm okay." I raised my hands. A handkerchief now bound the ugly gash.

Red helped me to my feet. "Come on. I'll take you to Emergency."

"Not necessary, Snapper. The cut's deep but clean. Doesn't need stitches."

"Sure you're not hurt?"

"Just my image, Red. But that'll have to heal on its own. Go finish your search."

"You sure?"

"Positive. Go."

Red edged away, checking me over his shoulder as if unsatisfied that I wasn't about to take another header.

Clarissa Pratt scowled. "It's probably best if you go to the hospital, Ms. Finn. We want to be absolutely sure you're all right."

"How sweet of you to care, Ms. Pratt."

I knew what the prosecutor was thinking. No matter how noble the reason, she'd allowed a bunch of untrained people to assist in an official search. If my wound proved serious, she'd have plenty of explaining to do. *Liability.* Word had a nice ring to it.

"Come on. I'll take you to Emergency," she ordered.

"Hmmm. I don't know. Why don't I give it a few days? If there's a problem, I can always have it looked at then. Unless it's become seriously infected or something."

Her gaze went murderous. "Exactly what game are you playing, Finn?"

"I think it's called two-handed back-scratching, Ms. Pratt. You climb off my case and Kresky's—cut the threats—and I suspect this injury of mine will heal nicely without my having to report the whole, unfortunate incident to city authorities."

Her eyes blazed. I was about to get the tongue-lashing of my life. But, to my surprise, she threw up her hands. "All right. Okay. Go wash that off before you really foul up my day and get infected. Fetch some antiseptic and a Band-Aid for Ms. Finn's boo-boo, Kresky. And get that goddamned smirk off your stupid face."

There were two portable toilets near the sidewalk. I stepped into the one on the right, groped through the dim light to the sink, and twisted the taps. No water.

The door on the second unit was locked. I waited several minutes, then knocked with my good hand. Silence.

"Anybody in there?"

No answer. Seemed the door was stuck. Butting with a shoulder failed to budge the stubborn latch. Rattling the knob and cursing worked no better. My injured hand was throbbing, chipping through my always slender patience to raw nerves.

Crossing to the rig, I rummaged through the gear bin. Beneath the jumble of hooks, flares, and lines, I found a Halligan tool.

The pick head quickly broke the jam. In the glum interior, I waited for my eyes to adjust. As they did, I spotted the paper propped behind the sink.

"So you're out of order, too. Great," I griped.

As I turned to leave, something fluttered to the ground beside me.

I was busy relishing my minor triumph over Clarissa Pratt. But in a rush, the chilling message pierced my reverie. The writing was crude and childish. And the dark blot at the corner looked like blood.

Chapter 25

LENNIE

Kresky and the prosecutor were still huddled at the rear of the building site. When I handed the sergeant the note, he blanched.

"I found it on the sink in the Portosan," I told him.

"What the hell did you touch it for?" Clarissa Pratt howled. "God sakes, Finn. Use your head!"

Kresky scowled at the prosecutor. "It's okay. No harm done. We'll have to take your prints for elimination purposes, Finn. Chances are the perp never laid a hand on this."

He pulled a plastic bag from his pocket and gingerly dropped the bloodstained page inside.

"Chances are," the prosecutor raged. "What the hell do you know for a goddamned fact, Kresky?"

"Only that you're a nasty pain in the butt. Know what they call you behind your back, Clarissa?"

"What?"

"Nothing you don't deserve."

The prosecutor bared her pointy teeth. "Here's a news flash, pretty boy. I don't give a damn what anyone thinks of me, especially you. Just stop staring in the mirror long enough to solve this goddamned case."

Kresky dismissed her with a look, then turned to me. "We're about finished here. Thanks for pitching in."

I was haunted by the note. All it said was "Help." The word ended in a long, wavering line, as if the victim had wanted to write more but ran out of courage or time.

I felt sick at heart. "Where do you go from here?" I asked.

Kresky shrugged. "We finish combing the area, take the note to the lab. After that, we sit tight and wait for a relevant missing person report. Maybe a witness sighting, if we get really lucky."

"Just wait? Do nothing?"

"Nothing much we can do. If it's a kid, the parents probably won't miss her until school's out."

"Can't you check with the schools? Find out who's absent?"

"We wouldn't know where to start."

"She can't be from too far away, can she?" I could see Kresky's irritation building, but I couldn't make myself stop. "What could it hurt to check absentees?"

Kresky sighed. "This might be nothing, Finn. We might be dealing with a runaway or a practical joke. Calling schools would be wasted wheel spinning."

"Not to mention adding fuel to the unnecessary panic started by the bigmouth who leaked news about the case in the first place," Clarissa Pratt huffed.

I caught her poison sneer and returned it. "At this point, I'd think you'd *want* the public to know, Ms. Pratt."

"Look at that. A half-hour search, and she's an expert in the nuances of criminal investigation. I'm impressed. Really."

"People have a right to protect their children."

"My word. Finn's also the last word in constitutional law and soap-box oratory. Better hurry back to your firehouse, Mr. Finn. Bet the brass doesn't dare make a move without you."

Kresky glowered at her, then turned to me. "I know

you're anxious, Finn. We all are. But we're doing everything
we can. Honestly."

"I'm sure you are, but—"

"I'll keep you posted. Okay?"

I glared, then shrugged. It was clearly the best I was going to get.

"I'd appreciate that," I said lamely.

"And *I'd* appreciate your remembering she is not a part
of this investigation, Kresky." The prosecutor was boiling.
"Go take care of your boo-boo, Ms. Finn. We'll see to
ours."

By the end of the day, we'd logged three more calls. One
was a malicious false alarm. A panicky-voiced man dialed
911 to report a flash fire in a small frame Colonial on
Belltown Road.

When we pulled up eight minutes later, the house was
picture peaceful. The only hint of trouble was the blond
surfer type who charged out from the rear, vaulted a hedge,
and bolted up the adjoining driveway. He pulled up his
pants as he ran across the snow, shirttails flapping. A hiking
boot was wedged under each muscled arm; a ski jacket was
tossed over his shoulder. His barefoot gait was the syncopated sprint of a scared rabbit.

"Carlone, Makowski, after him!" Perriman howled.

The pair, department record holders in the hundred-fifty-
pound victim carry, caught the fleeing man before he could
circle the neighbor's garage. As they marched him back to-
wards Perriman, a second floor window flew open. A woman's head popped out. Her indignant face was framed by a
manic froth of coppery hair. She shrilled:

"You let go of him! *Now!*"

"False alarm's a serious offense, ma'am," Perriman warned.

"Nobody here pulled anything like a false alarm. We
were much too busy. Weren't we, tootsie puss?"

"Shut up, Louise," the surfer hissed.

"We'll see about that when the marshall investigates." Perriman was mad.

"I can save him the trouble," the woman trilled. "If anyone called in a falsie, I guarantee it was Bernie Trupin, my none-too-soon-to-be ex. That's *T-r-u* and *pin* as in pin. First name: Bernard. He's in the book."

Perriman made note of the name.

"Bernie's insanely jealous," she went on. "Stops at nothing to keep me from getting a little—you know. Last time, it was ducks. Bernie got wind I was having company and had half a truckload of ducks dumped at the door. God, the stench. And just as I was about to—"

The surfer was still barefoot in the snow. His face was the picture of misery. "Enough, Louise."

"Talk about killing the mood." Her hand fluttered, dispersing the phantom smell.

"You'll excuse me, ma'am, but we did not come to see about your love life," Perriman said.

"Great. Then why don't you run along and let me get on with it?"

Perriman shook his head. "You'll hear from the marshall." Get Romeo's name, address, and phone number, Makowski. Let's roll, people."

"Come back, tootsie baby honey sweetie," crooned the woman. "It's cold out there. Cold in here, too."

"Forget it, Louise. Tell Bernie he wins. It's not worth the aggravation." The blond guy hastily pulled on his boots and crossed the street to his waiting Miata.

"No. Don't go," whined Louise. But tootsie folded himself into the small white car and took off down the street like a streaking comet.

"Damn you, Bernie!" the woman wailed. "I hate it when this happens."

The other two calls were minor. First came a car fire in the parking lot of the First County Bank. The owner had taken his Buick in for recent servicing. From the dense, acrid smell, excess lubricant had been left under the hood.

Heat from the engine was enough to set the gunk aflame. The blaze looked impressive, but a few shots of an extinguisher were enough to put it out. The owner's temper was another story. Guy was pacing furiously. His face was the color of rare meat.

"Damned country's so full of incompetents, we might as well give up and start over."

"Yes, sir," Dumbo said, vainly trying to placate the guy.

"Incompetence and mediocrity. I'm so sick of it, I could bust. I could just goddamned up and bust."

"Go right ahead, sir," Dumbo said agreeably.

Our final outing was a condominium on West Main. A dense cloud of black smoke wafted out the window, which the tenant, a tiny gray-haired woman in a housecoat, had thrown open before stepping outside to safety. She stood on the lawn, clutching a towheaded boy of three or four.

"Don't be scared, Brendan. Everything'll be fine now the firemen are here."

Hitsig was revving up to do one of his dash-and-trash numbers. Wild Bill loved splintering everything in his path with an ax and then drenching the premises beyond any hope of recognition. But while he was grabbing the hose, I caught the child's response.

"But, Granny Bea? What about our cuppy cakes?"

"Sorry, honey. They're all burned up, I'm afraid. We'll whip up more later, soon as these nice firemen make sure it's okay for us to go inside."

I blocked Hitsig's cavalry charge. "Easy, Rambo. It's burnt food. That's all."

"Oh yeah? You got a crystal ball, Catwoman?"

I didn't need one to see that the smoke had cleared. The last pale wisps breezed out the kitchen window.

While Hitsig dealt with his disappointment, Red and I entered to check the premises. The only visible damage was a charred muffin tray, a sooty coating on the stove, and a dark dusting of ash over the checkerboard linoleum.

Back at the station house, I called police headquarters for

the fourth time. Handsome Harry's world-weary tone warned me he was not thrilled to hear my voice.

The news remained discouraging. They'd still received no relevant missing person reports. No witnesses had come forward. The lab hadn't finished testing the note I'd found for prints or other clues, but Kresky doubted they'd come up with much.

"I told you, I'll let you know soon as anything breaks, Finn."

"Sorry if I'm being a pest, Sergeant. I can't get that poor kid out of my mind."

"Who can?"

"If there's anything I can do . . ."

"Actually, it'd help if you'd lighten up a little. To be honest, I've got more than enough guns aimed at my head at the moment."

"I know. I'm trying."

"Try harder. Okay?"

"Okay."

He breathed his relief. "Oh, and thanks for trying to smooth things over between me and the she-beast. But I'm afraid you're wasting your energy. It's an old story with us. One of those hate-hate relationships."

"I know them well."

Hilliard's department store in New Haven had been closed earlier in the day for inventory. Dialing the main number now, I was patched through to voice mail which routed me back to the switchboard which bumped the call to customer service which patched me through to the executive suite for transfer to the president's office where I was placed on hold.

Eden Hilliard's receptionist, was a human moat complete with snapping alligators. Miss Hilliard's schedule was booked months, sometimes years in advance, she crisply informed me. My claim of urgency didn't budge her. Neither did my mention that I'd been referred by Rabbi Sally Deane.

"If you'll tell me the *nature* of your business, I'm sure someone else on staff will be able to assist you, Miss Finn."

"I told you, it's personal."

"And *I* told *you*, I handle *all* Miss Hilliard's concerns. Please be assured, your request, whatever it may be, will be relayed with the *utmost* discretion."

"All right. Tell Miss Hilliard it's about Jack Chambless."

I was put on hold again, briefly. When the receptionist returned, her tone had softened considerably. Miss Hilliard was due to leave shortly for a sales conference in New Orleans, she told me. When the boss returned late tomorrow evening, she'd be glad to meet with me.

I took directions. "Thanks. See you tomorrow."

"Delighted to help," the receptionist crooned. "Miss Hilliard said to tell you she's looking forward to it."

Chapter 26

DANA

After she finished taping the last of the day's promotional announcements, Dana hurried toward the studio exit. She stalked past Stacy Raybuck, Heather Warren, and Mickey Conway, all armed with "urgent" matters to discuss.

"Sorry, people. I'm late for an appointment. Whatever it is will have to wait."

"But, Dana," Heather wailed. "The archbishop called on that 'Pedophile Priests' show. He's talking lawsuit."

Dana kept walking. "As I understand it, truth is still an absolute defense against libel."

"Maybe so, but the church is claiming that our inside informant is delusional."

"If that young priest is delusional, I'm the Easter Bunny."

Heather sighed. "I think they're prepared to call you a lot worse than that."

"Can't hurt our ratings. Be sure to let them know we'll be glad to have the pope himself on to refute us. Big guy can name the day."

When Heather stepped aside, Mickey Conway inserted his lanky form between Dana and the door.

"Just need a minute of your time, boss. I've got an exclusive bead on a really neat theft-of-service scam. Cellular phone numbers are being captured by remote. Hackers zap the stolen codes to thousands of buyers instantaneously on-line. Tons of calls go through before central billing computers have a chance to catch the extra volume. We're talking huge losses. Zillions. I've got a guy willing to appear in disguise and lay out the whole thing, step by step. Sound great or what?"

Dana groaned. "For the *zillionth* time, Mickey. *Back Talk* is not a how-to show for crooks and con artists. Now please, get out of my way."

As he did, Stacy Raybuck meekly claimed his spot. Dana's annoyance evaporated as she caught the young woman's desperate look.

"What's wrong, Stacy?"

"It's private."

With a wave of her magic arm, Dana cleared the area.

"Sorry to hold you up," Stacy began. But I just fielded a call on your private line. It was a man's voice, low and muffled. Wouldn't say his name. He told me to tell you the kid got lucky. He said her luck's about to run out."

Dana's gut churned. But she managed to maintain the calm veneer. A decade of on-air experience had superbly schooled her to preserve appearances.

"That's all he said?"

"Yes. Can I do anything? Want me to report it to the police?"

"Not necessary. Everything's under control."

That statement was about the farthest Dana could leap from the truth. The attack had changed Becky almost beyond recognition. The child's airy optimism and adventurous spirit had evaporated. She'd ceased pushing for independence. Now, she sought the constant reassurance of Dana's company, the way she had as a toddler.

Last night, Becky even wanted the lights left on, another comfort she hadn't craved since infancy. And with that, she woke up screaming several times, bathed in chill perspiration, reliving the horror of the attack.

Dana refused to tell Stacy or anyone about her plans for

reprisal. She would allow nothing to get in the way of seeing that Becky's assailant got what he deserved. She harbored vivid, murderous fantasies toward the man. Grisly scenes of the sort that usually made her flinch and turn away. But the beast who'd hurt her baby deserved to be spit-roasted, flayed, castrated, and worse. Dana wanted to set the stage herself and sell tickets. She'd personally supply the applause. Not to mention the laugh track.

Roddy was waiting beside the car outside the studio door. "I won't be needing you anymore today, Roddy," Dana told him. "Someone's picking me up."

"Anything you'd like me to see to?"

Dana had been looking for a means to get the big man out of her way. The opening was perfect. "Actually, if you don't mind, I need this memo delivered to corporate headquarters."

"Be glad to."

Dana watched Roddy drive off, then she circled the building. Camouflaged by her hat and dark glasses, she flagged a cab.

Normally, she loved the city's energy, but now, everything had a squalid, hangdog feel. Thick gray clouds soiled the sky. The sidewalks were banked with the sullied remains of last night's snowfall. A bumper crop of fresh potholes slowed crosstown traffic to a maddening crawl.

But Dana barely noticed. Her thoughts were fixed on her destination. She'd arranged to meet her nemesis at the Festival Theater on Fifty-seventh Street. She had chosen the place carefully. The current feature was a low-budget art film, unlikely to attract large crowds at any time. For a midweek show, the auditorium was sure to be empty or nearly so, which suited her purposes exactly. She'd be able to conduct this rotten business in a safely public place with the fewest possible witnesses.

By the time she bought her ticket and entered the theater, the lights were out, front credits rolling. As her eyes adjusted to the stifling darkness, she suffered a fleeting panic.

Half a dozen people were scattered in the center section. But she saw no one seated at the extreme left, where they'd agreed to meet. What if he'd given up waiting for her and left? What if he'd had second thoughts about the whole business?

But then, she spied the small mound protruding above a seat halfway down the aisle. Sleazy worm had slumped so low, all that showed was the top of his balding pate. Dana approached and slipped into the adjacent seat. She winced at the scent he exuded, a pungent stew of dirty hair and onions.

At close range, Dana took in the hawk beak, rheumy eyes, pitted complexion, and pouchy receding chin. He was dressed in a garish plaid sportscoat over a black shirt and gangster white tie.

"Hello, Mr. Yurie."

He yapped in delight. "It's actually you in the freaking flesh. Can't believe it. Didn't, in fact. When you said it was you on the phone, I figured it hadda be some kinda joke."

"Thank you for coming."

"Hey. Don't thank me, Dana. Can I call you Dana? Sure you can, Lester. That's the lady's name, ain't it?"

"Dana's fine."

"Good, great. Anything I can do for you's my pleasure. I'm a *big* fan. Got every single one of your shows on tape. Wanna guess my favorite—?"

"If you don't mind, Mr. Yurie. My schedule is tight."

He clapped a hand to his forehead. "Lissena me, goin' on and on like a dumb *goombah*. The lady's busy, Lester. So shaddup and let her tell you what she needs."

Dana had weighed exactly what and how much this lowlife needed to be told. Becky's name definitely would not enter into it. A modified half-truth would suffice.

"There was a guest on the show recently. He set strict conditions for his appearance, and we complied. But apparently, he wasn't happy with the way things turned out. At the end of the taping, he threatened me."

Her thoughts swerved to the real threats. *Kid got lucky. Luck's about to tun out.*

"The freakin' nerve." Yurie jiggled in his seat like a hyperactive child. "Don't tell me. Lemme guess. Was it that killer who offed the whores? Or the guy with five wives?"

"This particular show hasn't aired yet."

Yurie chuckled. "There you go, Lester. Jumpin' the gun again. Now, stop flappin' your lips and let the lady talk, for chrissakes." He flashed a crooked grin. "Go on—Dana. I'm all ears."

"This man has a history of sex offenses. Because of that, his attorney insisted on keeping his true identity a secret. She has the appearance release form with his true signature in her office safe."

Yurie's head bobbed like a spring toy. "So you want me to find out who the scumball is and take care of him? Consider it done."

"I don't want him taken care of, just identified."

The ugly face fell. "You sure? Be no problem."

"I'm positive. It's important that he not be harmed in any way. Once I have the information, I'll see that he's dealt with."

"Serve the asshole right if you drop his sorry ass in hot oil. An eye for a tooth. Right?"

Dana gritted her teeth. Could she really trust this dumb rodent to deliver the necessary information?

"May I ask how you plan to go about this?"

Yurie's yokel grin yielded to a diabolical smirk.

"Simple. I case the lawyer's office. Scope out the employees' schedules, check for alarms. Once everyone's out of the place, I disable the system and go in. Then, I go into the safe. Soon as I have the perp's name, I'll call you."

"And if you're caught?"

He calculated on his little fingers. "Biggest they could get me for is breaking and entering. Figure I plead that down to a D misdemeanor. No room at the inn, so I'll probably walk with time served."

"What sort of . . . compensation . . . would you expect?"

"Money, you mean? Not a nickel. This is an honor for me. A freaking privilege."

"You understand I won't be able to protect you, Mr. Yurie."

" 'Course I do. You got your good name to consider. Important work to do. Last thing I'd want is to see anything get in your way."

"I understand that, but—"

"You know that show you did about that really gross-looking kid who came from Romania to get a face? That was brilliant. Art almost."

Dana persisted. "We're talking about illegal acts here, Mr. Yurie. I want you to consider that could mean imprisonment."

He shrugged. "I've gone up two dozen times, give or take. If the state decides they want me back for another little visit, no biggie."

"And what would you give as the reason for your illegal entry, should you be caught?"

"The usual. That I'm scum. Looking to rip something offa someone. Not that they usually bother to ask. All you gotta know is I won't give you up, Dana. No way. No time. No how."

As satisfied as she'd ever be, Dana filled Yurie in on the particulars. The man's lawyer, Valerie Eckhard, had offices on Park Avenue South.

"You said the ambulance chaser taped the show with this shithead?"

"Yes," Dana said. "Why?"

Yurie grinned broadly. "Figure I'll check limo, cab, or car receipts for the date of the taping while I'm at it. Might get us his home address."

That clever idea did nothing to ease Dana's disgust. She never imagined sinking this low. Seeking the assistance of a degenerate like Yurie. She felt soiled. Sickened.

She knew the potential consequences. Yurie's promises

aside, she might be facing disgrace, dismissal, not to mention criminal charges for conspiracy and Lord knew what else.

But the horrific image of Becky trapped in terror on that cold cellar floor pushed all other thoughts aside.

Kid got lucky.

"How long do you think it'll take?" she asked.

"I'll get on it right away. Any luck, I should have what you're looking for in a coupla' days. Big luck, sooner."

"The sooner the better, Mr. Yurie. You know how to reach me."

Chapter 27

LENNIE

At the close of the day shift, I called to retrieve the messages from my answering machine. Sergeant Kresky had checked in as promised.

He had no promising news. So far, there had been no pertinent reports of a missing person. The blood on the note I'd found was human, type A positive. The pen used to scrawl the desperate message was a garden-variety ball-point. The long-grain twenty-pound bond paper could be found in any school or office. A single latent print had been lifted by the lab, but a check of the national computer registries, including the child safety data bank, turned up no workable match.

The next caller was Kitty, wanting to say hello. Hearing her voice gave me a start. Since finding the note, I'd been picturing Kitty's face on the unknown new victim. Hearing Kitty's unheard cries for help. All the hurt little girls were hopelessly knotted in my mind, myself included.

Jack's voice came next. He sounded strained, almost brittle. "Hope your brother's okay, Eleanora. I feel terrible about how I set him off. There must be something I can do to make it up to him. And to you. Please call."

Short of stripping bare his mind and soul for my inspection, I couldn't think of a thing Jack could do to smooth the situation. I was going to have to iron these particular wrinkles out on my own.

The last three messages were from Shelby. With each call she sounded increasingly miffed and desperate. She knew not to phone me at the station house. Moonlighting was widespread and tolerated, but it was still officially against department rules.

Setting aside my better judgment, I called her back at Crea-Temps.

"Lennie. Thank God! Where the hell are you? Why aren't you here?"

"Sorry. I must have the wrong number."

"Don't be a wiseass. I need you. Right now. Desperately."

"For what?"

"Damn it, Lennie. Didn't you hear me? It's an emergency. Just get that inexcusably small butt of yours over here!"

"Not until you tell me what for."

Shelby had a slightly skewed view of what constituted a crisis. Global hunger was about a two on the Burkhardt Richter scale. The Big One was the time Saks ran out of store-brand off-black control-top panty hose in size Tall. Shelby could wear nothing else. By every other manufacturer's unthinkable reckoning, she was a Large.

"I'm asking you as a friend, Lennie. No—make that *begging*."

I can always tell when Shelby's being manipulative. The dead giveaway is that she opens her mouth.

"Is it the Ginzlers, Shelby?"

"Would I turn you down if you were in a bind, Lennie Finn? Tell me that."

"All right. You can give it up, now. I'll go."

Babe and Harvey Ginzler ran a large entertainment booking operation. In an average week they supplied the bands, disc jockeys, *karaoke* players, mimes, magicians, balloon artists, face painters, clowns, go-go dancers, and fortune tellers for over a hundred tristate area weddings, bar mitzvahs, and assorted other festivities. Babe, a longtime

Burkhardt family friend, threw a great deal of the company's inevitable fill-in business Shelby's way. Naturally, Shelby was reluctant to refuse when Babe occasionally asked her to take care of "a little something" in return.

The little something's name was Wendell "Dell" Ginzler, age nine. Young Master Ginzler was a bright, imaginative child, given to behaviors that ranged from the merely unsavory to the frankly grotesque. The boy was particularly taken with decaying things, disagreeable bodily fluids, and foul odors (their production, advertising, packaging, and distribution). Ginzler nannies averaged about half the shelf life of homogenized milk.

Aware of the child's reputation, I'd anticipated our first evening together, almost a year ago, with more than a touch of apprehension. But as soon as we were introduced in the Ginzlers' gilt-and-mirrored foyer, I knew I could relax.

To me, the little boy was transparent. The faked flatulence and inverted eyelids were a smoke screen. Ditto the stink bomb and the charming rubber hairy thing he'd set out for my amusement on the kitchen counter. This little boy was lonely, scared, and totally down on himself. I suspected he held himself responsible for his parents' constant absences. Poor kid thought himself unloved and unlovable.

In Dell's misguided quest for compensatory attention, he'd pushed all potential surrogates away. I doubted he did any better in the friend department. All of which made him more desperate, and consequently, more obnoxious.

Sad, vicious cycle.

Babe Ginzler was a piece of gold Lurex-coated work. The woman's hair was a platinum hornet's nest, her features sharply outlined and filled in as if her face were a paint-by-numbers kit. Bustling about the foyer, spewing non sequiturs, she had swaddled herself head to toe in white mink.

"Stuff's in the fridge. Be home whenever. Don't forget, Dell. Ba-bye now. Have a good."

Harvey, the short, portly husband, had followed in her Shalimar-scented wake. Harvey was fifty-something to

Babe's thirty-five. The stogie corking his sausage-lipped mouth reduced whatever he said to a string of guttural grunts. Leaving, he rapped Dell's skull with his stubby knuckles. Babe's farewell was a waggle of long scarlet nails.

As soon as his parents had gone out the door, I faced the child squarely. "Here's the deal, Dell Ginzler. I like you, and I'm going to continue to like you, no matter what you do."

That promise would be sorely tested during the next couple of hours. The boy tried everything he could think of to change my mind and turn my stomach. The evening's truly memorable highlight came when he stomped upstairs to use the bathroom. Moments later, I heard a horrific scream. Racing up, I found Dell stooped over a toilet bowl full of extremely convincing fake blood. Fortunately, the kid's explosive giggle kept me off the phone to 911.

After that, I plunked him down for a long, tough heart-to-heart. I told him about Huck and the other kids at Whitechapel, who couldn't help behaving in ways that made people cringe and recoil. I pointed out that he'd been blessed with a good healthy mind, enormous creativity, and fine looks to boot, and it was a total sin to waste all that. Not to mention chicken.

That got through. Dell Ginzler was no chicken. He still wasn't prepared to let down his defenses entirely. But where I was concerned, he stopped hiding his light behind a barrel of rubber barf.

Naturally, I let Shelby continue to think that minding Dell was a huge imposition. The economic balance of our relationship had always hinged on the passing of a critical number of bad checks.

The boy had stretched out since I last saw him six weeks ago. His soft contours were giving way to the gangly legs and taffy-pulled arms of a fledgling adolescent. His freckled face looked older, too. The cheeks had slimmed so a small shelf of bone was beginning to show through.

Most telling of all, the kid had started to take obvious pains with his appearance. The stubborn brown mop was

damp and scored by comb tracks. Instead of his typical patterned boxer shorts and T-shirt, Dell was nattily dressed in
khaki pants, a woven leather belt, and a crisp plaid button-
down shirt. I even thought I caught a whiff of soapy cologne, though it might have been a case of stingy rinsing.

He belched hello, but I knew that was for his parents'
benefit. The minute Babe and Harvey hit the road, Dell
dragged me up to his room to show off several finer accom-
plishments. I offered my undivided attention as he slew a
slew of monsters on his Sega Genesis system. I watched him
log on to an on-line service and breeze around the electronic superhighway with the speed and certainty of a seasoned pro. He was doing better in math and proudly
displayed back-to-back 90's on his latest trials by long division. Then came the second-place ribbon he'd won for the
fifty-yard dash in gym class and the honorable mention he'd
gotten for his art show project, a "family" portrait of Babe,
Harvey, and their beloved Porsche.

"You're a very good artist," I said, forcing the words past
the lump in my throat.

Dell ignored the compliment. "Ready for game time?"

"You're the boss, boss."

"Okay. First, I'll be the pirate, and you be the coast guard
guy who tries to bust me for bringing in the dubloons."

"Got it."

His hand popped up like a tollgate. "Only, when you try
to board the ship, I come up behind you with my sword
and chop your head off before you can put on the cuffs."

I made a face. "Sounds painful."

"I promise I'll chop easy. Come on."

Game time had become the highlight of our evenings together. Dell loved inventing skits and planting himself in the
victor's role. Having a playmate of any size was a treat for this
kid. A willing one like me was especially irresistible. I meekly
accepted the bonds, beheadings, holdups, assassinations, inter-
rogations, financial reverses, dread illnesses, and whatever other
dire entertainments the dear child had planned.

In truth, I got a huge kick out of his energy and imagination. Dell never repeated a scenario, and he always had all the necessary props and costumes ready and waiting in the playroom. For the pirate/coast guard bit, he'd fashioned a cardboard sword covered in aluminum foil, a paper eyepatch, and a cape. He'd even readied a stake to hold my decapitated cranium. Clever child had removed the hoop and basket from his Nerf basketball set for the purpose. The foam ball, already fitted with clay features, would double as my *gently* chopped-off head.

After pirate/coast guard came traffic cop/incensed motorist. I was assigned to play the furious blond lady in the Porsche. Dell claimed the part of a very large, mean, humorless cop, who not only refused to accept the twenty-dollar Monopoly bill rakishly propped in my wallet, but threatened to arrest me for an attempted bribe.

Some of Dell's playlets were obviously lifted from life. Others were inspired by tabloid TV, the news, his large personal library, and tidbits he learned at school. Several of the fresher combinations were Dell's own. A particular favorite of mine was the antifur activist trying to wrest the coat off Bugs Bunny.

The boy had prepared exhaustively for tonight. After cop/motorist came waiter/irate patron followed by snoring husband/exasperated wife. I thought the wife's idea to cure the din by suffocation with a pillow was particularly inventive. Maybe that accounted for Harvey Ginzler's squashed face.

There followed a manic round of sumo wrestler vs. tuna-destined-for-the-sushi-bar that left me in a breathless sprawl on Dell's beanbag chair.

"I need to take five, Dell," I puffed. "Talk amongst yourselves."

"But I have a really great one left, Lennie."

"Unless it's about an undertaker and a dead lady, you'd better give me a minute to regroup."

"One minute, coming right up."

While I recovered, Dell hurled Velcro darts at a bull's-eye.

Thoughts of the unidentified victim slipped in to fill my vacant brain. Somehow that clever, courageous little girl had found a way to pen that desperate note. She'd gotten her assailant to let her use the portable toilet. Who was she? And where the hell was she now?

Suddenly, Dell raced up and tackled me from behind.

"Hey. Easy."

He growled menacingly. "I'm the raper, you're the girl. Now, stay still."

"What?"

"I said I'm the raper. You stay still and I'll get you."

"Cut it out, Dell. I mean it."

He was giggling wildly, hurling himself at me. "Shut up, little girl. I told you, I'm the raper."

"Stop that!"

I shoved him roughly away. Tossed off balance, he tripped over the prop pile and landed hard on his rump.

I rushed over. "Hey, I'm sorry. Are you okay?"

Tears puddled in his eyes and spilled over. "Why'd you have to hurt me?"

"Oh, sweetie. I didn't mean it. You just surprised me, that's all."

"I thought you liked to play. I thought you were my friend."

"I do. I am. I just don't like that particular game. Okay?" I bent to help him up.

"The guy on the news talked about a raper," he wailed, refusing to take my hand. "What do you want from me?"

"Nothing, Dell. I'm sorry. Let's play make up—all right?"

"Get *away* from me." He drew away. "Leave me alone!"

I couldn't get through to him. Still weeping, he stomped off to his room and slammed the door. I tried to coax him out, but he wouldn't budge. I'd done exactly what he feared the most from people. Found him repugnant. Pushed him away.

Poor kid didn't even understand the nature of his offense. "Raper" was a meaningless word to him, a juicy-sounding term he'd heard on a newscast. Dell's only sin was taking a misstep in my personal minefield. How many people had I annihilated over the years for the same innocent sin?

Would I ever find the way to stop?

The Road To Redemption

by Patterson Graham, Ph.D.

The reformed rapist has broken the bonds of destructive impulse. He is a man reborn and remade in his own best image. While the curative model serves as an external standard, it is the internalization of that ideal that insures against repeat offenses. John describes that personal epiphany below.

Finding my model cleared up all my questions, I could slip into his mind and know exactly how to behave. In a way, I became my model. Weird as it sounds, the line between us turned invisible.

The counselor said it would work that way. You picked the person you wanted most to be. Someone you related to and respected. Then, when you found yourself hungry for a wrong thing, like wanting a kid, you did exactly what your model would do under the circumstance. Think of it as being the other person's shadow. Strictly under his control and not your own.

For me, it worked like a charm. I'd heard enough from my model to know how he'd react to things, what he'd do. I patterned myself after him completely, down to the smallest detail.

Through him, I found an entire other side of myself. He opened my eyes to brand-new ways to satisfy my appetites. Deeper, more ecstatic satisfactions than I'd ever dared to imagine.

I don't need to worry about stopping anymore, about losing control. The whole thing is entirely out of my hands.

Chapter 28

LENNIE

I was halfway out Mrs. O'Callaghan's door when the phone rang. Charging upstairs, I picked up before the machine.

I'd plastered the psychic airwaves with urgent messages for Miranda. Over the years, I'd found that more efficient and far less frustrating than trying to reach my friend on tour. Miranda was forever between sets or cities. She generally opted not to stay in the hotels prebooked by her manager, preferring small inns and bed-and-breakfasts that happened to catch her eye. Worse, she never went to sleep until she was leveled by exhaustion. At that point, it took something closer to an air raid than a phone bell to wake her.

Fortunately, she could read me flawlessly by remote.

"Hey, Len," she yawned. "What's up?"

"From the sound of it, not you."

Second yawn. "I'm fine. You work things out about that Jack business yet?"

"Funny you should ask."

I told her about Huck's reaction to Jack and my conversation with the singing rabbi. Cringing, I recounted last night's horror show at the Ginzler house.

"Sounds to me like you're just the teensiest bit off the wall, Len."

"You could say that."

"I did. So how do you plan to put Humpty Dumpty together again?"

"Very carefully. How's Clint?"

"Clint who?"

"Your latest cowpoke."

"You're a poke behind. The latest lone ranger's name is Dakota."

"North or South?"

I always did my best thinking out loud to Miranda. By the time we hung up, I felt clearer, surer, and more in control than I had in days. Dangerously close to sane.

That stability came in handy at the station house. Perriman was on the brink of flashover about my five-minute-late arrival.

"Seven-thirty means seven-thirty, Finn. You read me?"

"Yes, Captain. Sorry."

"Discipline. Dedication. Reliability. Those words mean anything to you?"

"Yes, Captain." I was also familiar with the terms "over-reaction" and "anal-retentive," but I saw no point in fanning the man's leaping flames.

Without any help from me, Perriman's temper continued burning through roll call and morning announcements. He kept shooting incendiary looks and heated asides my way.

"I've assigned two-man teams in shifts for tours of the new Greystone Chemical plant in Research Park starting first thing tomorrow morning. That includes you, Finn. *If* you can find time in your busy schedule, of course."

At a quarter to nine each morning, most of the squad congregated in the kitchen for a coffee break. Hitsig, still intent on milking every possible drop from the Catwoman gag, had set my regular place at the table with a squeeze toy and a box of catnip. He made purring sounds while I fixed myself a bowlful of Rice Krispies and banana. His irksome noise continued as I ferried the cereal to the table and left again to draw a cup of coffee from the electric urn. When

I scooped my first spoonful, I exposed a strikingly realistic-looking mouse.

My stomach lurched.

"Eat up, Finn. Yummy, yummy." Hitsig guffawed.

"You think so, you have it." I pushed the bowl across the table toward him.

He pressed it back. "It's all yours, Catwoman. After all, you need your vitamin M."

"No, Hitsig. I insist." I shoved the bowl hard. It skidded across the table and flipped, showering Wild Bill with milk, soggy cereal, rubber mice, and banana rounds. Wild Bill howled.

Before he had time to collect himself and retaliate, however, the alarm sounded. Dispatch reported a structure fire in the Revonah Woods section of town.

The house was a large Colonial faced in weathered cedar shakes. Greasy smoke billowed through the open double doors. Tongues of flame lapped the ground-floor windows. A young brunette in a robe and slippers stood on the lawn, dandling a fretful infant.

Deputy Chief Will Raines questioned her briefly, radioed an update to dispatch, then crisply briefed us and dispensed preliminary orders.

Raines was a full-time, full-tilt professional. Walking procedure manual. His stance was square, his uniform crisp and polished, his look earnest, and his features forthright. I'd never once seen the man crack a smile, bend a rule, or lose his temper.

"The owner says no one's inside. Origin's suspected to be a space heater in the living room. Hitsig and Bartell, lay a line. Snapper, Carlone, take the interior. Brewster, Boggs, and Wilcox, work from outside. Finn and Makowski, go up top and get this baby vented through those skylights."

Dumbo and I hauled an extension ladder from the truck, did a flat raise, and set the safety hooks at the roofline. I clambered up first while Dumbo heeled the base, then I steadied the roof section while he followed.

This blaze had a manic quality. Big voice. Large, effusive gestures. Nothing about it appeared to be the least bit shy or reserved, yet I detected something off. A sneaky quality, reminiscent of Frank Murphy, that put me on my guard.

Given the active flames and dense dark smoke, I could tell it was still in the free-burning phase. Gobbling oxygen. Spewing puffs of heated gas. Stoking its ravenous appetite.

I decided to name it Shelby.

Like her human namesake, Shelby was a busy, bossy conflagration. At the moment, she was in the process of sucking all the searing hot gases upward. Cooler air would then be forced out and down, igniting everything it encountered on the way. Left to her own devices, Shelby would keep up her frantic bingeing until she consumed all available oxygen. Eventually, her leaping flames would have nothing to sustain them and subside. But this brazen fire would continue to smolder, churning out smoke and combustible gases at temperatures as high as 1000° F.

That was the perfect setup for a lethal backdraft, where an air-starved fire erupts in massive, instantaneous combustion as soon as it can lay its greedy hands on an oxygen source. The dreaded condition announced itself in a number of characteristic ways: muffled sounds like ghosts playing racketball, smoke-stained windows, the absence of flame, black smoke that turns a grayish yellow.

We're trained to recognize the signs, but every once in a while, a careless cohort fails to pay full attention. On most jobs, the direst consequence of sloppy work is dismissal. Act careless in this business, and you might very well get taken out in a dustpan.

Venting the gases through the roof would help keep the lid on Shelby's volatile temper. But I sensed this girl held other nasty tricks up her smoldering sleeve.

Three glass-domed skylights clustered near the flat center of the mansard roof. Approaching, I tested the tile surface for sponginess, a sign that the blaze had weakened the structural members below. Once, I'd blithely walked onto the roof of a burning ranch house and taken a nasty fall right through to the family room. The footing this time seemed firm, but I progressed with caution. No reason to make the same mistake twice, especially given my talent for inventing fresh ones.

My mind turned to little Dell Ginzler. How could I have erupted like I did last night when all the boy wanted was to play a silly game?

Keep your mind on business, Lennie.

When we arrived at the center skylight, Dumbo bowed from the waist, granting me the honor. Poised on the bubble's windward side, I braced my feet and brought my ax down hard. The glass shattered. Shelby shot a blast of acrid smoke and roared her displeasure. As the fumes thinned and the clamour died down, I caught a heart-stopping sound from below.

A cough.

I called down on my walkie-talkie. "Deputy Raines! Someone's in there."

"You sure?"

"Yes, sir. I heard someone."

Raines quickly conferred with the brunette holding the baby. Soon his voice played over the portable unit I was holding.

"Could be the owner's kid brother. Boy sometimes stays out past his curfew and crashes here without her knowledge. Finn and Makowski, get inside and help the search team. You, too, Hitsig. Work the line, Snapper. Careful, people. This one's a scorcher."

Dumbo and I hustled down the ladder and entered the house through the front door. Visibility was near zero in the smoke-filled hallway. Fumes stung my eyes and made them water.

No big change, I thought. *I haven't seen anything clearly in days.*

The interior team was still canvassing the ground floor. Smoke obscured everything.

"Living room's clear," came a voice.

"So's the kitchen."

"We're going up," Dumbo sang out. I trailed him through the dense black fog hugging the stairway. Gulping fresh air through my mask, I blinked to drive away the tears.

At the landing, Dumbo headed left. I took the right side, ducking through the first open door. The nursery. The heat up here was more intense. Moving in a crouch, I held to the cooler air hugging the floor. Squinting to see through the smoke, I circled the crib. I checked the closet, groped behind the wicker dresser and toy chest.

"Anyone here?"

Satisfied that the room was empty, I moved on. The next door was shut. Cautiously, I turned the knob. I held back a beat, in case Shelby had planned any nasty surprises, then pushed the door open.

The bedspread was ablaze. Worms of flame climbed the sheer white curtains. Fiery arms circled a basket of folded laundry at the rear of the room. I checked under the bed. Searched the bathroom. Nobody.

Minus the smoke and flames, the house reminded me of the Dolans'. Everything so neat and orderly you'd think that horror liked this wouldn't dare to intrude.

But you'd be wrong.

Through the adjacent door was a small room fitted out as a study. Here, chaos reined. Papers were strewn everywhere. Piled on the desk, perched precariously on the floor, spilling over out of the wastebasket. The bookshelves were crammed to bursting with books and magazines. One spark in this room, and everything would go up in a ferocious rush. So far, Shelby the inferno hadn't made her grand entrance, but the floor was hot, the walls wavering.

The space had been heated to the brink of spontaneous ignition, also known as flashover. Any moment, when the crucial temperature was reached, the room and its contents would explode in a searing ball of flame. At such a time, you definitely did not want to be part of the contents.

I thought of firefighting's basic commandment. *If it doesn't feel right for any reason, get out.*

Ducking out quickly, I headed back toward the stairs. Dumbo was still searching the other side of the floor.

"Find anything, Makowski?"

"Not yet, Finn. Still have one more room to cover."

While he did, I poked through the broom closet, prodding the spare blankets and linen piles. Could my ears be playing tricks on me? Had I really heard that cough?

My brain and senses hadn't operated at peak since I met Kitty. Everything felt so odd and muddled. Normal certainty seemed as distant and unattainable as the peak of a forbidding mountain.

Great, Lennie. If you got everyone in here for a figment of your imagination, Deputy Raines will not *be amused.*

As if in answer, a compulsive choking sounded behind me. I tracked the noise back to the study. Spooked by the impending flashover, I hadn't checked the room thoroughly.

Rushing in now, I shielded my face against the searing heat. The whole room shimmied like an exotic dancer. Ready to blow.

"Talk to me, kid brother. Where are you?"

Frantic, I threw the mess off the smoldering couch and wrenched free the cushions to check beneath. The dense smoke and seething heat had me working blind. I circled the desk, slogging through the paper piles. At the far end, my foot struck something.

Groping around, my fingers touched a flaccid arm. Quickly, I dragged the limp body toward the hall. As we passed through the doorway, a thunderous mass of flame erupted behind us. With a furious pull, I tugged the inert form out and locked the door shut.

The teenager was unconscious, streaked with soot. He was a hulking kid like Huck, same willful hair and whisker stubble. As I moved to lift him over my shoulder, I spotted the wavering blanket of flame climbing his legs.

Horrified, I rolled him on the carpet. I beat the stubborn

flames with my glove, but the fire kept spreading. My head filled with the stench of charred flesh and fabric.

"Help! Somebody!"

The boy was being sucked into a tunnel of leaping flames. Desperate to help him, I slipped off my turnout coat and tried to smother the blaze. As soon as I did, fiery trails shot from the boy's clothing and gobbled up my shirtsleeve.

Deadly mistake.

"Somebody! Anyone, help!"

Shelby was getting the upper hand. I tried to beat her back with my coat, but she feinted, ducked, and grew fiercer. As the first bites of pain nipped my forearm, I fought a rising panic. Panic, I knew, could kill us both.

"Hang on, kiddo. I'll think of something."

Miraculously a burst of frigid water pelted me. The flames on my sleeve sizzled, then died. Soon, the icy stream extinguished the boy's fiery clothing and drenched the wall and carpet around us. The face behind our savior's mask was Red's.

"Okay. Enough, Red. It's out," I sputtered.

"Be right back. Stay there!"

Red dropped the hose, hoisted the kid, and carried him out of the house. As I was getting to my shaky feet, he bounded up the stairs again and tossed me over his shoulder.

"I can walk, Red."

Still, he carted me down the stairs and across the lawn where medics were examining the injured boy.

"I'm okay, Red. Please—let me go."

He set me down gently, as if I'd break. His frowning face was grime-streaked, his breaths short and sharp. "Let the medics take a look at you."

"I'm fine."

"No, you're not," Red shot back. "You're a damned id-iot!"

His face was taut with anger, reddening to match his hair. I'd never seen the guy so mad.

"What was that for?" I sputtered.

"You know better than to take off your coat. You could have gotten yourself killed, you dumb jerk. You could have—" His voice broke.

Drawing a stammered breath, he shook his head. Muttering furiously, he turned on his heel and stormed away.

On the return ride to the station house, my mind fixed on the weird encounter with Red. I decided to take him aside immediately and straighten things out. I couldn't imagine what had set him off, but I didn't want whatever it was to fester and build. I cared too much to lose Red's friendship. My heart already had far too many painful vacancies.

I memorized the words I'd say to start our conversation. But when Dumbo turned the ladder truck into the garage, I found a large distraction waiting.

Chapter 29

LENNIE

As soon as I climbed off the truck, Kresky caught me by the elbow. He propelled me out of the equipment bay and through the station house lobby toward the door. His mouth was running in overdrive.

"Call finally came in. Our missing kid is a ten-year-old from Hastings, New York. Her name's Wendy Lister. Parents thought she was sleeping at a friend's house. When she didn't show at school, the friend figured she'd stayed home sick. Whole thing finally came together when she didn't turn up at some practice she was scheduled to attend at six o'clock this morning."

He shook his handsome head in disbelief. "Kid's a figure skater. Potential world-class, they tell me. Of course, that hinges heavily on whether and how soon we find her. Not to mention in what condition. Let's get going, Ms. Finn. My car's out front."

"Whoa. Wait up, Sergeant. So happens I'm on duty." I was also soaked, soiled, singed, confused, and exhausted, but suddenly none of that mattered.

"I've already cleared it with your captain. Come on."

"What do you need me for?"

"Kitty wants your hand to hold. We've called in a hypno-tist to pull out any details she might be forgetting. A sketch artist is on call to work any new information we get into a composite. We've been trying to get the Dolans to go along with this for a couple of days, but the father's refused. Said Kitty's done enough, had enough. When we told him about the missing girl, he finally changed his tune. Kitty's only condition was you."

Pausing for breath, he seemed to see me for the first time. "Maybe you'd better clean up first."

"Good idea."

I showered, gingerly washing the raw, blistered spots on my forearm. My uniform shirt was fireproof, but I'd gotten behind on the laundry, so I'd tossed on a clean cotton blouse. That was error number one. Goof two was removing my fireproof turnout coat in strict violation of the basic rules. Three was not exploring that study thoroughly on my first pass, allowing Shelby the scorcher to intimidate me and consequently get the upper hand. Four was getting out of bed this morning. Five was not going to medical school, when all I'd lacked was the money, time, grades, interest, and scientific bent.

I could have gone on and on, flagellating myself for my sudden and complete lapse in common sense. But my friend Red had already claimed that privilege. Thankfully, I'd more or less gotten away with it this time. Better yet, according to the medics at the scene, the kid brother's injuries didn't look nearly as grave as I'd initially feared.

Kresky activated his siren and drove like a man pursued. When we arrived at headquarters, Kitty and her mother were waiting in the parking lot.

Mrs. Dolan, suitably garbed for a Chanel ad, acknowledged my arrival with a crisp nod and angrily addressed her daughter.

"There. Lennie has finally arrived. *Now* can we go inside?"

"Okay, Mommy."

Mrs. Dolan rolled her eyes. "Well, praise be."

She reserved her larger enthusiasms for Kresky.

"Good *morning*, Sergeant." She preened. "So nice to *see* you again."

Kresky deftly slipped the woman's reins. "Thanks for coming, Kitty. It's a big help."

Kitty was pinched with terror. I set a hand on her slim shoulder. Kresky hustled us to an interrogation room. The others had already assembled.

Frowning, Clarissa Pratt gazed up from her case file. The prosecutor's costume was as dark as her expression: ash-toned skirt, blouse a fetching smog shade, dense black stockings, storm trooper boots.

Black was great on my friend Miranda, who'd made black clothing a trademark in her act. All Ms. Pratt needed to complete the look was a nice executioner's hood.

Kresky introduced us to the sketch artist, a bookish brunette named Wanda Hough. The hypnotist, Paul DeMott, was a Boston-based psychologist. Slight and soft-spoken, he looked to be in his late fifties. Thin graying hair and a trim white beard framed his craggy face. His deep-set eyes were cottony blue, his mouth was bowed in a permanent look of kindly bemusement. He was casually clad in a pale yellow cardigan over a navy knit shirt, gray flannel trousers, and well-worn rubber-soled boots. His gaze and manner were disarmingly direct. He focused both on Kitty.

"First off, I'd like to clear up a few mistaken ideas people have about hypnotism. For instance, I have *never*, under *any* circumstances, asked anyone to imitate a chicken."

Kitty giggled nervously. "I once saw this hypnotist guy on TV who made a lady's arm so strong, he couldn't even bend it."

DeMott nodded. "No chickens. No unbendable arms. No suggestions that when you hear a bell, you'll start barking like a chihuahua or singing the Star-Spangled Banner in Chinese. People who get other people to do those things are party hypnotists. Performers. My job is to help subjects remember important things they may have forgotten."

"Do I have to go to sleep?" Kitty asked anxiously.

"Not regular sleep, but it's similar. You'll be very relaxed, with your eyes closed. But you'll be able to hear what I say and talk to me when you want to. I'm not going to *make* you do or say anything against your will, Kitty. Is that clear?"

She frowned. "What if you wanted to do those other things? Make me cluck like a chicken or get my arm stiff? Could you?"

"I might know how. But I don't believe in those things, so I wouldn't."

The little girl's eyes dipped. "What if I say something . . . embarrassing?"

"You won't tell me anything unless you decide you want to, Kitty. That's the way it works."

That seemed to satisfy her. Kitty kicked off her sneakers and settled back on the cot that had been rolled in for the purpose. DeMott took the chair beside her. He signaled Kresky to dim the lights.

"Okay, Kitty. If you could go anyplace in the world. Anywhere at all. Where would it be?"

"That's easy. The mall."

DeMott squelched a smile. "Fine. I want you to close your eyes, now, and picture yourself at the mall. You're coming in from the parking lot, riding the elevator. Getting off at—"

"Seven. I'm meeting my friend Jennifer. We're going to Chi-Chi's for tacos and then we'll hang out near the Gap."

"And then you'll hang out," DeMott smoothly put in. "And you'll see people you like. And you'll talk to them and have a wonderful time." The psychologist's voice was so soothing, I felt my own bones turning to mush.

"You're at the mall, now Kitty. Eating a delicious taco. Can you taste the cheese?"

"Mmm." Kitty ran her tongue over her lips. Her face was so slack, the purposeful gesture surprised me.

"What are you drinking?"

"A Coke."

"Have a sip."

She pursed her lips and swallowed. "Good."

"Sweet and cold, isn't it?"

"I love to chew the ice."

"So crunchy. You're very happy, now, Kitty. Completely relaxed."

She nodded "Totally."

"Tell me what your friend is wearing."

The child pointed, enumerating. "Jen's got on her work shirt with the Mickey Mouse on the back and these really cool blue leggings with patches at the knees. And her cowboy boots. And her hair's tied back in a scrunchy. I really like it better down."

"Wonderful remembering. Now, you're going to leave the mall for a little while, Kitty. I'm going to take you back to the night that stranger came to your house."

"The bad man?"

"Yes. I want you to tell me what he's wearing."

Beyond the dark cap with the oversized bill, Kitty hadn't been able to remember anything about her attacker's clothes.

Her face tensed. "He's got this black cap pulled way down. Jeans. Except there's this red mark on the leg. Looks like a paint smear. Or ketchup, maybe. And he's wearing this short black jacket."

"Is it zipped?"

"To here." She touched the center of her chest.

"So his shirt is showing through?"

She nodded. "A T-shirt."

"Can you see anything on the front? A picture or a word?"

"Just two letters." Her lids scrunched as if she were squinting to focus. "*I——N*. Or maybe *I——M*."

"What color are the letters, Kitty?"

"Red."

Kresky and the prosecutor exchanged a look.

"Can you see his shoes?"

"Brown loafers. With dangly things near the toes. They're kind of muddy. Yuck."

"Excellent. Now tell me about this man. What does he look like?"

She arched her neck, peering at some imagined vision overhead. Watching that, I realized she must have seen her attacker's face. Given the discrepancy in their heights, the bill of a cap couldn't possibly have obscured the intruder's features, as Kitty mistakenly recalled. Fear and self-protection had walled off the details of the attack. Now, Kitty was confronting them head-on.

"Tall. About like Daddy. But thinner. And pretty old. At least forty."

"What about his mouth?"

"Kind of mean."

The artist had a sketchpad propped on her lap. Her pencil worked feverishly as the child described her attacker.

"Does he have a beard? A mustache?" the hypnotist prompted.

"No. But his face is smudgy like Daddy's gets when he doesn't shave on Sundays."

"Any marks on his face? Scars or moles?"

She strained as if to get a clearer look. "No. Nothing like that."

DeMott drew out the rest of the description. Dark eyes, verging on black. A straight, almost aquiline nose. Strong chin, high cheekbones. Straight teeth. None missing or visibly marred. Despite the baseball cap, Kitty could see his dark hair was graying.

"What else can you tell me about him? How are his hands?"

"Big, with long fingers. A couple are scraped a little like mine got that time I cut through those brambly bushes to get to Jen's house."

Other details floated up from the little girl's subconscious. The stranger's car had been parked across the street in the shadow of a neighbor's spruce tree. Kitty described the car as big and dark, though not as large or deeply colored as her parents' Mercedes. She was fairly sure it was foreign and fairly new. No dents or scratches, at least, not on the side facing the house. She hadn't seen the license plate, but she recalled the small silver emissions-testing seal posted at the left of the windshield.

Kresky made note of that. From the color, size, and position of the sticker, the car was probably registered in Connecticut.

"I want you to back up a few minutes, Kitty," DeMott said. "It's right before the man comes. What are you doing?"

Her look hardened. "Watching TV. That commercial just came on where the little boy bangs on the piano, but his mother drinks some kind of tea that makes him sound like Beethoven. The lady slurps when she drinks, like the tea's too hot. You know that one?"

"Yes," DeMott said. "Then what happens?"

"The doorbell rings. I figure it must be Mommy coming home early from her card game. Sometimes she gets really fed up with Mrs. DiStefano, so she leaves. That lady is so dumb, it's amazing. She actually believes yellow teeth are stronger. And she swears you can smoke all you want and not get cancer as long as you gargle every day with hot water and peroxide. Is that dumb, or what?"

"It is indeed. What happens after the bell rings?"

"I hurry to open it up and let Mom in. But it isn't her. It's the man who—" She cried out, then hid her face in her hands.

"It's okay," the hypnotist soothed. "You're safe now. This is just telling the story, Kitty. Nothing but words."

The child's chest heaved. Slowly, the fear subsided.

"He's standing on the porch. 'Hi,' he says. 'Sorry to bother you, honey. But my car's broken down.'"

"Does he tell you his name?"

"No. Wait, maybe. He sort of mumbles something. I'm not sure."

"Does he say why he's in the neighborhood?"

"No. Only that his car's not working. Something about an injection."

"Fuel injection?" DeMott asked.

"That's it. He needs to use the phone to call a mechanic. Only take a second, he says. It's so cold out, he could freeze if he has to wait 'til someone comes along to help him. We don't get many cars on our block."

"And then what?"

"He walks inside and pushes the door shut. His face gets so mean all of a sudden. There's a phone in the kitchen, I tell him. But he keeps walking toward me. He's got this scary smile on his lips. I point to the phone again, but he won't listen. He's so close now, I step back to get away. But he puts his arms out. . . . He grabs me.

"What are you doing? Put me down!" Her voice climbed to a plaintive shrill. "No, please!"

"It's okay, Kitty. This isn't real. You're just telling the story," DeMott soothed.

She shivered.

"What happens next?"

The child's brow furrowed. "He tells me to shut up. He puts a hand over my mouth and carries me up the stairs. When we get to my room, he pushes me on the bed. That's when he—No, stop!"

"Okay, Kitty. Take it easy."

The child started weeping in earnest. When DeMott's words failed to calm her, he deftly drew her to a better place.

"Shh, Kitty. The man's gone now. You're in the mall again. Tell me what you see?"

The child pouted. "They're closing. All the gates are coming down. Everyone has to leave."

DeMott nodded sagely. "The young lady has had enough. It wouldn't be advisable to push her further."

The prosecutor shook her head. "Our clock's ticking, Dr. DeMott. You sure?"

"It wouldn't be productive. And it might possibly be harmful to Kitty."

"No one wants to risk that," Kresky said.

Slowly, the psychologist roused the child from her trance. When Kitty was fully conscious and sitting up, Kresky showed her the artist's composite.

"Is this the man who assaulted you, Kitty?"

Everyone tensed. If the child confirmed the likeness, it could be put out over the wire services, distributed to law enforcement officials nationwide, flashed on television news shows, plastered on phone poles and bulletin boards.

Surely someone, somewhere would recognize the suspect and come forward. With any luck he could be identified and tracked in time to save his latest victim. It was even possible that the young actress, Sharon Sue Davis, might still be alive in the rapist's hands. A long shot, true. But stranger things had certainly happened.

Kitty held the sketch. There wasn't the faintest glimmer of recognition as she studied it. Finally, she shrugged and returned the page to Sergeant Kresky.

"No, that doesn't look familiar."

"Are you sure?" Kresky urged.

"Yup. I told you, I didn't really see him. The cap he wore was hiding his face."

Chapter 30

LENNIE

Police work was definitely not for me. I couldn't bear the pace. All the waiting and weighing and inaction made me itch. I liked my enemies out in the open, where I could battle them with something more than strategies.

On the ride back to the station house, Kresky caught the brunt of my frustration. "Why can't you put out Kitty's composite anyway?"

"Because it may bear no resemblance at all to the suspect. Last thing we want is to go off on false tangents."

"What about trying to get through to Kitty another way? Couldn't you give her truth serum or something?"

He eyed me balefully. "Doping kids with dangerous drugs isn't high on our list, Finn."

"How about a house-to-house search? Aren't there special dogs for that kind of thing?"

"Make you a deal, Finn. I won't tell you how to put out fires, and you don't tell me how to catch criminals. How's that?"

"I'll make you a *better* deal, Sergeant. I promise to get off your case the second you catch the rapist."

"I can't wait to hold you to that. Believe me."

As Kresky turned into the station house lot, I spotted the flash of back-up lights on Red's Blazer at the far end. Tossing a fast good-bye at the sergeant, I slammed out of his car and raced in Red's direction.

The Blazer quickly edged out of its space. Red was angling down the far lane now. I flailed my arms to catch his attention. But he barreled past, swerved out the exit, and sped off up the street.

Maybe he hadn't seen me. But on his granite expression, I read the snub as deliberate.

"Go to hell, Red," I told the dismal emptiness. "Who needs you anyway?"

The glum sky spewed pellets of frozen rain. The wind swirled in loud, lusty currents. Turtled deep into my jacket collar, I headed inside.

The firehouse was eerily still. My entrance went unmarked by quips or cat music. None of the standard clumps of people cluttered the halls. Checking the equipment bay, I noted that two engines and a ladder truck were out on a call. From the duty roster, I learned that Hitsig, Bartell, and several others had been sent for a refresher course in Hazmat. Shorthand for hazardous materials. Red and Wuss were at Company Three across town, running a seminar on Rescue for interested rookies. Dumbo and Studs were cleaning hose in the scrub room. Perriman and Deputy Raines huddled in the captain's office with several briefcase jockeys from City Hall. Joe Sprouls, a fresh-faced rookie with an impressive cowlick collection, manned the desk.

"Hey, Joe. What's up?"

He rifled through the mail and message slips. "Nothing for you, Finn."

"Tell me about it."

The next five hours felt like ten. No emergency calls. No interesting diversions. At lunchtime, I had a sandwich in the kitchen with the coffee urn. Afterward, during what was scheduled as unspecified training time, I studied for an upcoming EMT test on the vascular system. Finished, I cleaned and oiled the ladders used in this morning's fire and returned them to their assigned slots on the truck.

Checking my machine from the pay phone, I retrieved two urgent messages from Shelby. When I called back, she was in a major snit, demanding to know what I'd done to alienate Dell Ginzler's affections. Dell's mother had phoned to report that the boy wanted no part of me in the future.

"You did it on purpose so I wouldn't send you there anymore, Lennie. Tell the truth."

"The truth is that Dell wanted to play a certain game and I lost my temper. I feel terrible about it."

"What game?"

"It's not important, Shelby."

"Not important?" she howled. "Babe's hinting she might kick her overflow to TempAmerica, for God's sake. Are you trying to ruin me, Lennie? Is that it?"

"If there's any way I can patch things up with Dell, I'll be glad to. Why don't you tell that to Mrs. Ginzler and see if she has any suggestions?"

She puffed her disgust. "Damn it, Lennie. All this over some stupid *game*?"

"Let me know what she says."

"You can goddamned bet I will."

There were also three messages from Jack. What was wrong? Was I angry? Wouldn't I please return his calls so we could talk?

I spent several minutes holding the dead receiver before I settled it back in its cradle and walked away.

Restless and out of ideas, I indulged in a bit of aimless wandering. The firehouse was an architectural symphony in one note. Everything was square, spare, and numbingly neutral. The boldest stroke was the soft blue paint above the brick-based corridor walls. But poking around, I still found much of interest.

Glass-faced trophy cases chronicled the squad's long history of close camaraderie and fierce competitiveness in activities ranging from basketball to bridge. Framed newsclips detailed acts of outstanding heroism and wrenching tragedy.

Too many plaques honored colleagues killed in the line of duty.

When Perriman ushered out the visiting bureaucrats, I was studying the vintage squad photos opposite the elevator. After the suits were safely dispatched, the captain's political smile froze over.

"Are you trying to tell me we're overstaffed, Finn?"

"I was looking at the pictures, Captain. Noticing how different the uniforms were in those days."

"This isn't a goddamned history class. I just spent two hours trying to convincing those bean-counting bozos that there's no room for the mayor's fiscal ax in our personnel budget. I tell them we're shorthanded, working full-out, full-time, and then some. And what's the first sight they see when they leave my office? You mooning around like the poster girl for terminal boredom."

"Sorry, Captain. I've had a lot on my mind lately."

"While you're on duty, you're to get everything off but business, you read me? After that, go tell it to Dear Abby. Whatever bug you've got up your butt needs to be eliminated, Finn. And fast."

Perriman had never struck me as all that insightful, but this time, his aim was uncanny. I clearly was hauling around some ancient, damaging baggage. And nothing would please me more than to get rid of it. In fact, first thing this morning, I'd taken the first major step in that direction.

My meeting at the Rape Crisis Center was scheduled for six-thirty P.M. Arriving five minutes early, I joined two other women in the reception area. The older one was a central-casting librarian: owl-eyed and earnest with dark-framed glasses and drab hair huddled in a bun. The younger was a gum-cracking twenty-something packed in spandex. Five dangly earrings and a silver cuff rimmed each of her pendulous lobes. The right side of her hair was a dyed black plume, the left shaved baby bald.

Both women struck me as improbable rape victims. The kid looked nail-tough, the librarian as musty and forbidding as a long-abandoned house. But from morbid interest and personal experience, I knew that luck had far more to do with victim selection than appearances.

The other women were still waiting when Lila Sperling poked her pleasant face into the waiting room. She smiled my way.

"Come in, Ms. Finn."

Instead of her toy-cluttered office, the director led me to a colleague's spare space halfway down the hall. "We've got a little girl coming in at seven to meet with one of the other counselors," she explained. "I thought she'd be more comfortable in my room."

"This is fine."

All the essential elements were in place: green leather couch, tweed chairs, pole lamp, diplomas, psychology texts, therapist, head case.

"You said you wanted to talk, Ms. Finn?"

"It's Lennie."

"What can I do for you, Lennie?"

I wanted to tell her everything. I'd planned to. But when the time finally came, I simply couldn't find the words. They were lodged deep in my chest, a hard painful lump.

The center director waited patiently. But soon, I felt obliged to fill the crushing silence. "I'm worried about Kitty," I blurted. "Knowing there's a new victim must be so hard for her."

"I'm sure it is. But Kitty's getting all the support we can give her."

"Support can't take the fear away, can it? It can't erase the memory. Once a child's been hurt like Kitty has, the damage is done."

My eyes stung, and a lump of sorrow lodged in my throat. I took a tissue from the box Lila Sperling offered and blew my nose.

"The damage needn't be permanent, Lennie," she said gently. "The victim can choose to get rid of it."

"You make it sound like an ugly dress you can throw away. It's not that simple."

She nodded. "I know that. And I'm not suggesting it is. But pain that's kept buried continues to get in the way. Once it's brought out in the open and examined, it loses some of its power. With time and hard work, there can be real healing. But you have to be willing to go through the process."

"This isn't about *me!*" The anger in my tone startled me. Sitting back, I tried to release the trapped head of steam. "Sorry. It's been a tough week."

"I'm sure it has."

"Monsters like the one who hurt Kitty are never punished enough. It's the victims who suffer."

"The *survivors* have choices, Lennie. And if they've made unfortunate ones, they can always decide to change them later on."

I rose and grabbed my coat. "I have to be going now, Ms. Sperling. Thanks."

"Not at all. I'll be here whenever you want to talk."

Leaving the center, I checked the time. My next appointment wasn't for nearly two hours. In the interim, I could see to another vexing piece of business. Bracing myself for the unexpected, I stepped out into the freezing mist.

Chapter 31

DANA

"Is that really you, Dana?"

"Yes, Mr. Yurie. It's me."

"Amazing. Here I'm watching you on TV and it's you on the phone. Of course, the you on the set is coming from the VCR. Bet you figured that out, am I right? Of course she did, Lester. Dana Saunders is no dope."

"You said it was urgent?"

Becky was whimpering in the bedroom. Dana covered the mouthpiece and called to her. "Shh, sweetie. I'll be back in a minute." Impatiently, she returned to the phone. "What is it, Mr. Yurie?"

" 'Fraid I sorta run into a little snag. Or should that be 'hit' a little snag? I gotta admit I'm no damned good with grammar."

"What's the problem?"

"I dunno. Never was any good with words and parts of speech and stuff. Goes way back."

"I mean, what's the little snag, Mr. Yurie?"

"Oh, that. The thing is, I been hanging out in this coffee shop across the street from your lawyer's office half the day. I figure the firm will clear out at lunchtime, but no. They send out for sandwiches instead. Turns out I was right here when the order came in: coupla tunas on rye with mayo, a turkey club, few burgers, sides of slaw, and a ham-and-Swiss. Not real impressive for a fancy bunch of pencil-pushers, if you ask me."

Becky whined again. "Fascinating information, Mr. Yurie. But I have to get back to my daughter now."

"Sure, right. I just figured I oughta tell you I can't go in tonight. Dunno when I can."

"And why is that?"

"It's that lady lawyer of yours. She's still in her office. Got this guy with her. Big jock type. Young. Not much to look at, but whadda I know about guys, right?"

"All I can suggest is that you wait, Mr. Yurie. Ms. Eckhardt has to leave eventually."

Yurie snorted. "No she don't. You gotta see that office of hers. Got a pullout couch in it, a bar, TV, VCR, the works. Looks to me like she and Romeo ain't goin' nowhere no time soon."

Dana couldn't bear to think of her last best hope evaporating. From *Back Talk*'s background check on Valerie Eckhard, she knew the lawyer had been married for twenty years to a much older man, a Portugese shipping magnate who traveled frequently to tend shop. If Blowhard was conducting an illicit affair in her husband's absence, Yurie could be right. She might well be putting in many long, late nights at her office.

"Damn," Dana murmured.

"Say again, Dana? I didn't catch that."

"I wasn't talking to you, Mr. Yurie. I was trying to think."

"Thinkin' helps, I always say," Yurie agreed enthusiastically. "Speakin' of which, would you believe I got an idea of my own?"

"Mommy!" Becky wailed.

"Can you hold a minute, Mr. Yurie?"

"For you? You bet."

Setting the phone down, Dana hastened to her daughter's

room. Tucked in tight, Becky looked like a frightened little mummy. Her lip quivered.

"You said you'd sit with me, Mommy."

Dana leaned over and kissed the child's cheek. "I will, honey. I just have to finish up with this call. Give me five more minutes and I'm yours, okay?"

The child nodded bravely. "Sorry I'm being such a baby."

"You're not at all. You're being the very best Rebecca Meade in the entire universe, same as always."

A tear slid down Becky's pale, freckled face. "Then how come I don't feel the same, Mims? I feel all weird and icky inside."

"Me, too, princess. Must be those cheeseburgers."

A grudging smile tweaked the corners of the little girl's mouth. "I'm not fooling, Mommy."

"Well, I am. Dr. Gwen prescribed fooling four times a day, minimum. You may have yours crushed up in apple-sauce if you like."

Becky's smile broadened.

"There, that's better." Dana kissed the freckled nose and pointy chin, so like her own. "Be back in a jiff."

Yurie was humming when she picked up the receiver. "Sorry to keep you."

"I gotta get kept, I'm glad it's you doing it, Dana. So anyway, here's my idea."

Yurie proposed that Dana call Valerie Eckhard and arrange an immediate meeting. She'd have to plead some fake emergency, but Yurie had no doubt she'd come up with something convincing.

"I seen you with some of those *goombah*s in the audience, pretending you really care about what they got to say. That's another thing I admire about you, Dana. You really know how to phony up to people."

Dana chose to ignore the dubious compliment. "Your idea has merit, Mr. Yurie. I'll try to put the pieces in place. Give me your number there, and I'll call you back soon."

The way to Blowhard's heart was self-evident. Dana's

message was relayed to the attorney by her answering service. Valerie Eckhard rang back five minutes later.

"Glad I caught you, Ms. Eckhard. We've had a last-minute cancellation for tomorrow, and I was hoping you might be able to fill in."

The lawyer hesitated, then went coy. "Let me check." She returned a beat later. "I'm booked solid tomorrow, but for you, Dana, I'll move things around. What's the show?"

"It's on office environments. We're going to tape several prominent people at work and interview them about what they've done to make their work environments comfortable."

There was a muffled sound on Blowhard's end of the line. The lawyer giggled, then collected herself quickly. "Sounds straight up my alley."

"Great. Oh—I'll have to stop by tonight with my location scout. He'll need your offices to himself for about an hour. We can go somewhere for a cup of coffee while he works."

"Is that really necessary?"

"Sorry. It's inconvenient, I know. But he needs to do lighting and sound checks and take some Polaroids for the setup crew. If you can't manage it, I'll have to ask someone else. . . ."

"Not at all," Blowhard hurried to say. "When would you like to come?"

"An hour from now?"

"See you then."

Dana dialed Adam's apartment. She was about to give up after five rings. But before she did, the call was answered.

"Adam Meade's residence."

Dana cleared her throat to chase the shock. The voice was the unmistakable high-pitched whine of Adam's secretary. Very private secretary, it seemed.

"Hello, Jeanette. May I speak with Adam?"

"Sure, Dana. Just a sec. Adam honey," she called. "It's Dana for you."

Adam honey? So much for any pat excuses Dana might have tried to offer herself for the secretary's presence at Adam's home. If this was business, it was clearly the long-tailed, tree-swinging variety.

How could you be so blind, Dana Saunders? Did you honestly believe he hired that bimbo for her keyboard skills?

Adam's starched voice broke the thought. "Yes, Dana? What can I do for you?"

For starters, you can go to hell! "I have an emergency meeting. I'd appreciate your staying with Becky for a couple of hours, if you can swing it."

Dana winced at her unfortunate word choice. Apparently, Mr. Iron Britches could swing pretty well, given just the right little jiggly piece of inspiration.

"I suppose, if it's absolutely necessary."

"It is."

"I *do* wish you'd consider getting the child a nanny, Dana. These little emergencies of yours are getting awfully tiresome."

And so are you. "I have no time to discuss it now, Adam. Thanks for helping out. I'll be waiting for you."

Hanging up, Dana wondered if she should have warned him not to bring the twit. Hopefully, Adam would show better sense than that.

But if he had any sense at all, how could he possibly hook up with that brainless woman? *Not thinking with the stuff between our ears, are we, Mr. Meade?*

Pushing him out of her thoughts, she dialed Yurie at the coffee shop. "It's all arranged, Mr. Yurie. I'll be by for you in under an hour. I told Ms. Eckhard you're a location scout for the show. She and I will be leaving you in the office to do light and sound measurements and take pictures."

Yurie whistled. "I gotta tell you, Dana. I'm real, *real* impressed. You sure as hell know howta think on your feet."

"Thank you."

"I'm only tellin' it like I see it. Quick thinkin's where it's at. Speakin' of which, I'm gonna need equipment if I'm gonna pull off this scout thing. Light meter, sound meter, camera stuff. The works."

"Good point. I can provide you with a camera."

"No good. Gotta look professional."

"Maybe you can fake it with a case. I can bring you one."

Yurie snickered. "No sweat. I got plenty of time to run up to one of those discount places on Forty-seventh Street."

"It's too late for that. They'll all be closed."

"I sure hope so, Dana. You don't wanna rip off big stuff like this when a place is open."

Chapter 32

LENNIE

Entering Ernie's, I was disappointed to find Walt Brewer in Red's place behind the bar. Scanning the crowd, my disappointment turned to dismay. Hitsig slumped at a table in the rear in the company of Wuss, Nervy, Dumbo, and two nearly empty pitchers of fresh-tapped swill. Sober, Wild Bill is merely obnoxious. Drenched in beer, his loose-cannon mouth is prone to deadly misfire.

I edged toward the door, hoping to slip out unnoticed. But through a clearing in his inebriated haze, Hitsig spotted me.

"Hey, look. It's Catwoman!" he bellowed. "Here, kitty, kitty."

Caught, I attempted a desperate exit. " 'Bye, guys. Have to run. See you tomorrow."

"But you just *got* here, kitty baby," Wild Bill howled in mock distress. "Where you going in such a fat hurry?"

"Anywhere away from you, Hitsig."

His lower lip jutted. "Don't be that way, kitty cat. Come to poppa, now." He made loud kissing noises. "Come on, kitty. Pretty please."

All action in the bar had ceased. Every eye was fixed on the floor show.

Nervy and the others urged Wild Bill to give it up, but

Hitsig is a creature fashioned from the shallow dregs of the gene pool. As I continued toward the exit, he struggled to his unsteady feet and displayed his extensive repertoire of obscene gestures. Pumping fist. Come-hither finger waggle. Humping hips. Tongue bobbling. "Come *on*, kitty. Here, here."

"Cut it out, Hitsig," Nervy said uneasily.

"Oooh, kitty baby, you *know* what I like!"

"Have some coffee, Wild Bill."

"Coffee hell. All I want is some of that sweet pussy over there. No, wait! Where you going, kitty baby? Was it something I said?"

I pushed out the door. The temperature had risen, plumping the sleet like air-popped corn. A soft, white layer blanketed the pavement. Sparkling fluff frosted the brittle shrubs.

Several steps down the walk, I was stalled by a clamorous crash from inside. Curious, I strode back to the bar. Wild Bill was splayed in the center of the worn wood floor with a split lip and a startled expression. Red stood over him, florid and panting.

"What the hell was *that* for?" Hitsig wailed. His drunken tongue ran the words together like finger paint on wet paper.

"*That* was for fun," Red said. "Now stand up, and I'll give you the one you deserve for being a revolting, out-of-line asshole."

"What's wrong, Snapper? I insult your little buddy-boo?"

"You insult my species. Now get the hell out of here."

Hitsig wavered on his feet like a Schmoo. "You asking me to leave? Is that it?"

"No, Hitsig. I'm *telling* you to leave."

"Don't bother to apologize, Red. I'm out of here. Off like a prom dress."

Wild Bill staggered toward the exit. Trailing behind, Dumbo, Wuss, and Nervy pressed for damage control.

"Come on, Red. You know he doesn't mean anything by

it. He's just a jerk," Dumbo wheedled, ever the peacemaker. "Aren't you a jerk, Hitsig?"

"Don't be mad at him, Finn. He's not worth it." Nervy counseled.

"Apologize to Finn, Hitsig. You can't talk to a broad that way in the nineties," Wuss urged. "That punch hurt your hand, Red? Maybe you should put a little ice on it."

As he stumbled past, I noted the full extent of Hitsig's wooziness. Likely, he'd remember little, if anything, of this unsightly episode in the morning. Given his level of restraint, I imagined he frequently arose with jackhammers beating in his head and a mouthful of wobbly teeth.

Dumbo was the designated driver. The others piled into his Taurus wagon and took off. I turned to Red in mock exasperation.

"I don't know, Red. Here I've been itching for years to hit it off with Wild Bill and you step in and do it for me."

"Sorry." He strode away and started tying on an apron.

I caught him before he could duck behind the bar. "Whoa. Wait a minute. Don't walk away. I came here to talk to you."

"I'm late to relieve Walt." He refused to meet my gaze.

The bartender overheard "It's okay, Red. Take your time," he said.

Red glowered in response to Walt's good-natured grin, then turned to me. "What?"

"I'd like to talk to you alone for a minute, Red. Can we please go outside?"

Reluctantly, he trailed me out the side door. Despite the snow, which was falling harder now, the air was still and reasonably warm. Red was neither. The guy was coiled entirely too tight, still refusing to make eye contact.

"What's going on, Red?"

"Just forget it, okay?"

"Forget what? What did I do to you?"

"Nothing. Now if you don't mind, I have to get to work."

I caught his arm as he turned away. "I do mind. After all these years, I think I deserve to know why you're acting as if I don't exist."

He wrenched loose.

"At least look at me!" I caught his chin and prodded his face upright. With a start, I saw that his eyes were pooled with tears.

Angrily, he jerked away from my hand. "You want an explanation? Fine. I couldn't stand to watch the way you risked your stupid neck in that fire. Made me so mad, I wanted to wring it for you."

"Jeez, Red. I may have acted foolishly, but I certainly didn't do it to piss you off."

"Well, it did. You don't take care of yourself, it pisses me off big-time."

"I'm flattered, but—"

"And if you want to know, it pisses me off to watch you make googly eyes at that Sergeant Gorgeous George who keeps mooning around. He's even worse than that redneck professor of yours. Can't you see those guys are three-dollar bills? It's so goddamned obvious."

"Kresky, you mean? There's nothing between me and Kresky."

"You can fall for whoever you goddamned please, Lennie. There's no need to lie about it."

"I'm not. That's crazy."

"Yeah? Well, *you* make me crazy. So how about staying out of my life, and I'll do the same for you?"

I wanted to hug some sense into the irrational lug, but his words were cruel hands, pushing me away.

"I don't want that, Red. You're my friend. I care about you."

"Give it up, Lennie. It doesn't work."

"What doesn't work?"

"Us. this. None of it. Don't you get it? Don't you goddamned *see*?"

As he stormed away, I feared I did. But I didn't want to

believe that our friendship had been sentenced to death because of a temporary surge in Red's testosterone level.

Over the years, I'd felt plenty of romantic tugs in his direction. The guy was extremely appealing: cute, funny, sweet. Perfect crush material. But the last thing I ever wanted to do was risk what we had for a fling.

So now, we had nothing.

My Toyota was blanketed by an inch of gossamer fluff. I brushed the windows clear, slipped in, and worked the motor until it grudgingly caught. Driving away, I flipped on the radio to chase the stifling silence.

The deejay on the first of my two available stations threatened an hour of uninterrupted country "classics." First, a warbly woman carped about unrequited love in that poignant standard, "Pierce My Heart And Chances Are I'll Bleed For You." That was followed by an album cut of the timeless "Black Eyes Always Give This Girl The Blues." My only other choice on the dial was testing its civil defense alert signal.

The thought of listening to country drivel all the way to New Haven was unbearable. I decided Miranda's voice couldn't bring me lower than I already felt, so I popped in the special cassette she'd prepared for me before leaving on her latest tour. On the cover, she'd written, "In case of extreme loneliness, take side one and I'll call before you know it."

I expected to hear my friend sing, but after the tape's long lead expired, it was her speaking voice that wafted through the speakers: *"Hey, Len. If you're listening to this, you must be having one of those days. For what it's worth, I'm with you. I know having you along, in spirit at least, always means the world to me.*

"Is that corny enough for you, dear heart? Because if I have to go on and on telling you how lucky I am to have you for a friend, I'm afraid I'll get sick to my very delicate stomach. So chin up, dukes up, and come out swinging, will you?

"Oh, and whatever or whoever it is, do me a favor and take

notes. *I'm about out of song ideas, and as you know, life on the road always gives me way more indigestion than inspiration. Anyhow, speak to you soon. Love you, Len.*"

"You, too, Miranda."

I couldn't help but smile. That girl had always been a sucker for ulcer food, vampire clothes, and urban cowboys.

Bless her solid, predictable heart. I'd always been able to count on Miranda when I needed an ear or a laugh or a shoulder. If Red chose to bail out on me the minute things got tough or complicated, maybe he wasn't half the loss I felt. Anyway, there were other, more immediate puzzles to solve.

The Toyota veered and skittered on the snow-slicked pavement. I had to keep my mind on the road.

Chapter 33

LENNIE

Hilliard's department store is a stark, post-modernist structure, designed to resemble a gigantic landlocked ship. The fourteen-story building occupies a prime central slot in New Haven's business district.

I parked at the front of the staff lot. It was after closing hours and, the only remaining vehicles were a gunmetal Honda, a blue Jeep Wagoneer, and a flame-red Ferrari Testarossa with vanity plates bearing the initials EH.

Walking toward the employee's entrance, I gave the Ferrari wide berth. Frightfully expensive things like that make me edgy. I never know whether to feel reverence or revulsion.

On the one hand, the car is undeniably sleek, alluring, and remarkably engineered. Even Huck, for whom most people and things hold spare interest, salivates like one of Pavlov's dogs when confronted with so much as a picture of a bright red Ferrari.

On the other, for half the price, Ms. Eden Hilliard could have bought herself a couple of modest little Mercedeses or Jaguars, leaving a substantial sum to put to nobler uses. Of course, I had to allow that on the third hand, the woman was a known philanthropist, regularly infusing large sums into a variety of causes involving the hungry, homeless, and disabled.

Dealing with one hand too many, I set the question aside. It's highly unlikely that I'll ever personally confront the issue of how luxurious a luxury car is too posh. If I do, I'm confident I'll make a commendable decision.

As instructed, I entered through the employees' door. Following a series of marked arrows, I came to Eden Hilliard's private elevator. There, a bull-necked security guard checked my name and driver's license against a list of approved visitors. Wordlessly, he escorted me on the ascent to the top-floor executive suite.

The elevator opened into a generous reception area whose glass walls afforded a panoramic view of the city's snow-capped skyline. The guard led me across the marble tile floor, heels clacking. In a seating area at each of the four corners, eight leather Breuer chairs ringed an Aubusson rug. Beefy, the guard, motioned me toward the one at the left far corner.

"Wait here," he ordered. After I claimed the seat he'd assigned, he clacked across the floor again and took the car back down.

The elevator doors were polished brass with intricate art deco carvings. Lush plants in brass cylinders flourished in the glut of sunlight. As I sat pondering the interminable time it must take to clean the windows, the secretary appeared.

The young woman appeared crisp and efficient, even after what had probably been a twelve-hour day. She wore a well-tailored navy suit, a starched blouse anchored at the neck by a patriotic patterned scarf, and vivid red pumps. Her auburn hair hung to her shoulders like a satin drape. Artful makeup emphasized her large brown eyes and diverted attention from a mouth that was thin-lipped and severe.

"Ms. Finn? Come this way. Ms. Hilliard is expecting you."

Anxious to make a favorable impression, I'd dressed in brown gabardine slacks, beige wool turtleneck, and a heather tweed blazer in shades of rust and brown. The outfit was a favorite. Felt good, looked good. Approaching the CEO's inner sanctum, I enjoyed a surge of confidence. But a single look at Eden Hilliard reduced me to a dumpy, frumpy troll.

The woman was striking. She was tall and reed thin with taut chocolate skin, a rich spill of ebony hair, and cover-model features. Her smile was dazzling, her presence at once serene and unmistakably powerful. She was elegantly dressed in a white wool suit and gold jewelry, but a soiled housecoat, feathered mules, and hair rollers would not have dimmed her dazzle.

"Thanks for agreeing to see me, Ms. Hilliard," I managed to say without stammering.

"Glad to. Would you care for some refreshment, Ms. Finn? A drink, perhaps? Or coffee and dessert?"

"No, thanks."

"Please, make yourself comfortable."

The office was an enormous square centered by a free-form smoked glass desk. A conference area to the right held a rectangular black lacquer table and a dozen bentwood chairs. At the left, a casual meeting space was fitted with a fawn suede settee, glass-capped occasional tables, and tapestried armchairs. She drifted into one of those, and I took the one opposite her. As I did, I noticed that her left sleeve, poised on the chair's plump arm, was empty.

I looked away quickly, but the move did not squeak past her. "I was born this way," she said evenly. "Congenital amputee. My mother always thought it might be something she took early in her pregnancy. She felt horribly guilty, but I can't say it's ever really gotten in my way."

"No, I wouldn't think so."

The smile warmed. "How can I help you, Ms. Finn? My secretary said you mentioned Jack Chambless?"

"Yes. I understand you and Jack were close years ago. I'm

trying to get background data on him, find out what he was like as a young man."

Her shapely brow arched. "And why is that?"

My heart squirmed despite the numerous times I'd rehearsed the lie. The direct approach had been successful with Sally Deane. But I didn't want to risk having this crucial door slammed in my face.

"I'm doing an article on him for the New York University magazine. Major profile. Part of a surprise tribute the university's planning for some popular professors this spring."

"You play poker, Ms. Finn?"

"No, why?"

"Because you're a lousy bluffer. Now, would you like to tell me the truth or shall we adjourn this little meeting?"

My cheeks burned. "The truth is I can't tell you the real reason. Sorry to take your time, Ms. Hilliard." I stood to leave.

"That sounded true enough. No need to go."

"I shouldn't have come in the first place. When you speak to Jack, I'd really appreciate it if you wouldn't mention I came snooping around about him."

She motioned me back to the chair. "I'm not going to speak to Jack. I'm going to speak to you. There's not much to tell, but you're welcome to it."

She repeated what I'd already heard from Rabbi Deane. Eden Hilliard's parents had five children but never married. Her father, who suffered from sickle cell anemia, died of a stroke before the baby of the family was born. When Eden was eighteen, her mother perished in the crossfire during an attempted robbery at a neighborhood convenience store.

Left to care for four younger siblings, she'd accepted the help offered by a variety of interested parties, including the volunteer group from Sally Deane's synagogue.

"I was of age, but just barely. The folks from child protective services were itching to send my brothers and sisters to foster care. They assigned us the social worker from Hell, woman named Regina Crawshaw. 'Cross Whore,' my brother Billy called her. I pretended to disapprove, but I didn't really. Old bitch hung around like a bad cold, just dying to find some reason to get us split up and scattered.

"One night, Miss Crawshaw happened to turn up at the worst possible time. The baby was cutting a molar—hard. Billy and my sister Ardena were fighting to the death over who borrowed whose sweater and wrecked the thing. And my other brother, Cecil, had just come in from a fight. Boy looked like something out of a horror flick.

"When the bell rang and I saw it was that woman, I figured we were finished for sure. Fast as I could, I hustled everyone into the bedroom, held my breath, and let her in.

"Old biddy was poking around like she always did. Asking questions. Any second, she was bound to ask to see the other kids. But before she had the chance, Jack showed up and took over. Man was amazing. He sweet-talked that shrew like you wouldn't believe. Got her out of the apartment before she had a chance to get a look at the damage.

"Man was amazing that way. Always turning up in the nick of time. Regular white knight in shining armor."

"You must have been grateful to him."

"Oh, I was. *Extremely.* And he took *full* advantage."

"You and Jack?"

"Very much so. For awhile, I deluded myself into believing it was the real thing. The whole veil-and-gardenia. I found out otherwise the hard way."

"You didn't know he was married?"

She smiled sourly. "Married was the least of it. Turned out he was just using me to torment his parents. Aside from Jack threatening to turn Jewish, I was their worst nightmare, you see. Not just a black girl, but a one-armed, dirt-poor, Yankee, orphan, bastard black girl with four kids to raise. Talk about your grand slam home run." She shook her head. "Ever been used as a weapon, Ms. Finn?"

"I don't think so."

"I don't recommend it." She looked me hard in the eye. "And I don't recommend Jack, if that's your question."

"It's one of several."

Sitting back, she sighed. "I'll tell you the truth, Ms. Finn. When my secretary mentioned that you'd called asking about Jack, I was delighted. I saw it as a chance to pay him back for some of the hurt he caused me all those years ago."

"That's understandable."

"Maybe so, but it's also childish and ridiculous. Jack had a big, ugly problem with his parents, and I got caught in the middle. But his folks are long dead, and what happened between Jack and me is very ancient history.

"In a way, I should probably be grateful to him. After he dumped me, I turned all my energy toward succeeding on my own. Turned out pretty well, I guess."

"To say the least."

She sighed. "For the record, I don't think Jack set out to hurt me deliberately. All he really wanted was to hurt his folks. I was beside the point. But it really shouldn't count anymore, to me or to you. The past belongs back behind you where it can't do any more harm."

I realized this search was an exercise in inertia. I was running in place, going nowhere. The more I found out, the less I seemed to know.

Discovering that Jack cheated on his wife a quarter century ago honestly didn't add all that much to the picture. I could muster a decent head of pique about philanderers in general. I could embroider a big black mark on his seemingly perfect face. But I wasn't any closer to certainty about what any of it meant to me.

"Do you think Jack was capable of hurting someone deliberately Ms. Hilliard?"

She mulled that over. "Honestly, I didn't know him—the real Jack—all that well. Looking back, I think the only one who really did was Ginny."

"Who's that?"

"Ginny Bliss. You never met her?"

"No."

The blazing smile returned. "Then you're in for a treat, Ms. Finn."

"Where can I reach her?"

"Leave me your number. I'll call her tomorrow and try to set things up."

Chapter 34

LENNIE

Awake and restless, I decided to slip out early and stop for coffee at the Greek diner. But the instant I got downstairs, Mrs. O' called my name from the kitchen.

Dressed in her blue terry robe, cheeks vibrant, my landlady presided like a symphony maestro over a steaming stockpot. She stirred furiously, her fervent gaze darting between the pot and the open recipe book propped on a Lucite stand beside the stove. The room had the dense, earthy aroma of a rain forest.

"I'm fixing a bit of breakfast for you, Lennie. Sit down. Be done in a jiff."

"You shouldn't have bothered, Mrs. O'. I'm not hungry."

"That poor appetite of yours is part of what this is meant to fix. Have a seat, now. No arguments."

With a final swirl of the mixing spoon, she turned off the gas jet. Then, she scooped out a bowlful of gray-brown mush, and served it to me with an explanation. The loamy-smelling slop was a macrobiotic concoction, specially designed to restore inner harmony.

"Past few days, it's a dreadful aura you've been giving off."

"I shower every morning, Mrs. O'."

"Don't be trying to joke your way out of this, Lennie

Finn. Trouble is, your yin and yang are seriously out of kilter."

"My who and my what?"

She puffed her dismay. "Yin and yang: Principles of Chinese cosmology, they are. Yin's the female side, expressed in darkness, cold, or damp. Yang's the male, shown in light, heat, or dryness. When they work together, everything's hunky-dory. Problem is when they don't."

"Sounds kinky."

"Eat now, make fun later. Goes down best hot."

"Oh? Is that a yang thing?"

She eyed the heavens. "Now you can see why I pray for strength come Sundays, Lord. She's a weighty piece of work, this one."

I ventured a taste. The goop reminded me of honey-roasted topsoil. I downed what I could in deference to Mrs. O's watchful eye and fine intentions. When she briefly left the room to fetch the paper, I set my bowl on the floor and summoned Maniac. The mutt loped over, sniffed, and turned tail. Romulus and Remus seconded the motion, bounding after Maniac into the pantry.

"Some best friends you three are," I grumped.

Mrs. O' was coming back. Quickly, I spooned the remains of the gunk into the trash and buried it.

"Done so fast, are you?" She eyed my empty bowl with open suspicion.

"That was great, Mrs. O'. I feel better already."

The sky was pale and promising. A sharp sun crouched at the horizon. The air smelled wonderful, tinged with a heady hint of spring.

Perfect day for rescuing that kidnapped little girl. Ideal weather for nailing the bastard who took her and hurt Kitty. Being linked to those horrors was like banging my head against a wall. I couldn't help but think how terrific it would feel to stop.

Please, let it all be over soon.

I drove with the windows open, reveling in the chill,

fresh breeze. By the time I arrived at the station house, I was verging on drunk with energy and optimism.

In that spirit, I resolved to act as if last night's foolish incident with Red never happened. Probably just a mood. Phases of the moon. A momentary brain blip. By now, I bet he was thoroughly embarrassed by the lapse.

The duty roster had us together for the day on Rescue One, along with Wuss, who'd traded days off with Zulu. Retrieving my turnout gear, I found Red's equipment already positioned on the truck. I tracked him to the second floor, where he was rummaging through his locker.

"Morning, Red. Gorgeous out, isn't it?"

He studied his gear in rock silence.

"So. What do you think of those Giants?"

Nothing.

"Jets? Knicks? Rangers? State of the union? Grand Union? Genetically-altered geraniums?"

Uniform in hand, he strode toward the men's room.

"At least we had Paris," I told his retreating back.

At roll call, Perriman announced me and Red as the first pair slated to inspect the new Research Park chemical plant. I optimistically viewed the assignment together as another chance to break the choking ice, but Red refused to let me get near enough to try.

As soon as the captain dismissed us, Red aimed for the building's exit. Wordlessly, he loped across the parking lot and drove off without me. In the time I took to start my Toyota, he was out of sight.

I tracked the weave of back roads to Research Park, a sprawling industrial complex at the city's east end. Red's Blazer was parked and empty in a visitor's spot. I found him in the lobby, peering at a large silver vat as if the secrets of the universe were inscribed on its gleaming face.

"You could have waited for me, Red. I'm not contagious."

His green gaze lit on me and quickly pulled away.

"This is ridiculous, Red. You're acting like a child."

The foreman, a well-oiled company cog, appeared. His graying blond hair was parted in the middle, spouting waves that framed his wide-set, gray-blue eyes. He came equipped with a ready smile and genial manner. "You from the fire department?"

"Yes," Red said.

"'Don Allen." The foreman proffered a hand. "Welcome to Greystone Chemical. Proud to show you around."

"Larry Snapper," Red responded.

"I'm Lennie Finn," I told him sweetly. "But Mr. Snapper prefers to call me Mud."

At first, the man was wholly focused on pointing out the plant's safety features and procedures. From the scripted sound of his presentation, he'd done this dance many times before.

"—And here's the distilling area. We feature cold-washed vats, circulating three thousand gallons per hour at a constant ten degrees Fahrenheit. We've also installed the latest steady-state vapor containment system. Our computerized monitors have built-in fail-safe backup provisions. Any questions? I'll do my best to answer."

"I was just wondering how that water-cooling system would work on a hot-headed human," I said with a pointed look Red's way.

The foreman chuckled. "Moving on to the bottling section—"

"Actually," I persisted, "some people I know could use vapor-containment, too. Has that ever been tried on people, Mr. Allen? Or people substitutes?"

Red's jaw twitched. "Pay no attention to her. We had a fire call yesterday. I think she breathed too many fumes."

"If I have, they're coming from you."

The foreman cleared his throat. His smile held, but his eyes kept darting nervously from Red to me and back again. The tension between us was enough to spark a serious explosion, and our guide was clearly at a loss. Apparently, the plant's procedure manual failed to cover ways to handle an unholy mix of highly combustible fire fighters. He seized the first opportunity to usher us out the door.

"Thanks for stopping by, folks. Greystone Chemical is totally dedicated to furthering close cooperation between public agencies and private enterprise."

"You mean getting along and resolving differences like grown-ups? Fascinating idea," I said.

"Thanks for the tour, Mr. Allen." Red's face was the hue of his nickname.

"Right, thanks. It's really good to hear you've found fail-safe ways to prevent unfortunate explosions," I added.

For the rest of the morning, Red and I worked side by side in devout ignorance of one another, like machine parts. I found the exercise exhausting. Staying strictly out of his way took constant vigilance. Pretending not to care turned out to be harder still.

We'd just finished a devilishly complex do-si-do, totally avoiding each other while simultaneously checking gear in a space the size of a broom closet, when the intercom crackled to life. The voice from dispatch was crisp and urgent: *"Rescue One: Respond to vehicular incident, Four-six-two-seven Roxbury Road. Rescue One—"*

We were on the truck and rolling in under a minute. Wuss drove. Red flipped on the lights and sirens, slicing through downtown traffic.

At the scene, a line of flares led to a blue Dodge Caravan ringed by frantic people. A woman in a housecoat and an elderly man were struggling to jack up the van. A balding man in a sports coat crouched near the driver side on the pavement. At the passenger side stood a dazed-looking brunette clutching two small moon-faced boys.

We were the first emergency detail to arrive. I listened for the blare of distant sirens.

"What's going on?" Red asked.

"Kid's trapped under the car," the blonde with the jack called out. "Drunken bitch knocked him off his bicycle."

I followed the blonde's accusatory gaze to the woman

with the little boys. The wreckage of the victim's bicycle was at the side of the road fifty yards back. It was a pretzel twist of shiny yellow-and-black metal.

The kneeling man identified himself as a doctor. "I happened to be driving by when it happened. The van slammed the little boy and kept going. Kid got trapped in the undercarriage. He's still alive, but I can't say by how much. Haven't been able to get close enough to check his vitals."

Red dropped to the ground and peered under the van. When he stood again, his face was the blue-white of skimmed milk.

"We've got to get him out of there," he told us. "Kid has massive cranio-facial damage and who knows what else. Come on, Wuss."

The two of them went to the rescue truck for supplies. I peered beneath the car, and my stomach lurched.

"Hang in there, slugger. We'll get you out."

Swallowing hard, I went to the aid of the pair wielding the jack.

"It'll work better here," I told them, repositioning the jack brace nearer the center of the rear bumper. As the van's hind end started to rise, I passed the lever to the blond woman. "Keep pumping. I'm going underneath."

The doctor moved aside to let me through. "See if you can get a hand in his mouth and clear the airway," he said.

"Okay."

The van was about eight inches off the ground now. I scurried into the breach, pressed hard to the gritty pavement. The victim's breath came in thready rasps. His gore-spattered head remained beyond my reach. Squeezing through the cramped opening, I inched closer. The air was rank with oil fumes, hot grease, burnt rubber, the stench of fear.

"Almost there, champ."

At last I could touch the boy's shoulder. I worked my fingers along the slick quilting on his down jacket.

A wet, rattling sound escaped him as I strained to reach his face. My seeking fingers found matted hair, raw cheekbone, a mangled nose.

The car edged up a trace. Enough for me to wedge my fingers between the boy's teeth. I felt for obstructions. Opened the jaw. As I tipped his head back, I heard the clean rushing intake of a solid breath.

"Got it!"

But suddenly, everything lurched around me. There was a clamorous crash. Massive roar of cold, black terror. When it passed, I was pinned and immobile.

The scene cut to slow motion. Vividly, I felt my fingers in the child's mouth, teeth and secretions, palate and flesh, warm airstream. Everything else was blunt, dull, distant. Unmovable. Unreal.

I was dimly aware of the frenzied swirl of activity around me. Wailing sirens. The angry toss of words. Metal squeals. More sirens. Screamed orders. The sharp, piercing strike of tools.

In what was probably only minutes, the van was hefted off me and rolled aside. Gingerly, I tried to move. Everything seemed to work, though not without time-delays and shrieks of protest. I found several promising additions to my bruise collection. Thankfully, nothing worse.

Wuss and several medics crouched at my right. They were working on the victim, strapping him to a gurney. Two cops were questioning the young brunette with the kids. I caught her whimpered answers. Name Patsy Monahan. Age: twenty-six. The boys were hers, ages three and four. She swore she hadn't been drinking. The liquor smell she insisted must have been from the empty beer cans she was returning to the supermarket for her husband.

"That so, ma'am? You carrying them in your mouth?" one cop cracked.

Another team took statements from the witnesses. The van had hit the boy twice before he was sucked underneath.

It was going fast before the crash, definitely speeding. One witness thought it was veering as it went.

Suddenly, Red's face, pale and clammy, hovered over me.

"God, Red. Go sit down. You look awful."

"Look who's talking. What hurts?"

"Your attitude," I joked. But my near-death experience had done nothing to improve Red's sense of humor.

"Shut up, Finn, and let me check you out."

Gravely, he felt my bones for fractures. He watched as I moved my arms and legs in response to his terse commands. Peering into my eyes, he searched for signs of possible trouble.

"I'm okay, Red. Just bumps and bruises." Twisting away, I got to my shaky feet.

His face reddened. "No, you're *not* okay. You neglected to block the front wheels, Lennie. What is it with you? You have some kind of a death wish?"

"Not exactly."

"What then? What the hell's going on?"

Impossible though it felt, I desperately wanted to tell Red everything. Maybe that would clear the toxic cloud between us. But this wasn't the time.

"Give us a hand, Red!" Wuss yelled.

Hesitating a beat, Red claimed a side and helped ferry the injured child to the waiting ambulance.

Chapter 35

LENNIE

By the end of the day, I detected some softening in Red's behavior. Encouraged, I slipped a note into his locker, offering several possible ways to resolve our conflict. The checklist included dueling pistols at high noon and a macrobiotic eat-off. Among the more tempting selections was my full confessional over dinner at the restaurant of his choice (within reason) on me.

Whatever it took, I was determined to salvage our sunken friendship. An excess of caring seemed a truly ridiculous reason to go our separate ways.

At shift change, I dawdled near Red's locker, hoping for a positive response to my peace proposal. But before he showed up, I was drawn to the sound of a commotion from downstairs.

Tracking the cheers and whistles, I found nearly all my esteemed colleagues salivating uncontrollably in the parking lot. The source of their frenzy was the sleek crimson Testarossa idling nearby. Some seemed equally inspired by the car's contents.

"Would you get a load of *that*!" Studs gushed.

"And *that*!" mooned Wuss, pointing toward the driver's seat like a kid ogling puppies in a pet shop.

I muscled my way through the crush. "Excuse me, gentlemen."

"Hey, wait your turn, Finn," whined Dumbo.

Spotting me, Eden Hilliard lowered her window. "There you are, Ms. Finn. Have a minute?"

"Sure."

"Hop in."

Dozens of envious eyes widened as I slipped into the passenger seat. There was the sound of jaws dropping as Miss Hilliard slipped the Ferrari in gear and drove away.

Once we left the lot, she loosened her death grip on the steering wheel. "Quite a group. Must be something to work with."

I laughed. "Keep them away from beautiful women and fabulous sports cars and they're almost bearable."

"I was in town for a business meeting. I knew I'd be sure to catch you if I dropped by."

"You reached that woman?"

"Yes. Finally managed to run Ginny down late this afternoon. Her time is tight, but she's willing to see you if you can make it before eight. She's in Port Chester at this address."

I took the slip of note paper embossed with Eden Hilliard's initials. The street was a main road off the Hutchinson River Parkway, no more than a twenty-minute drive.

"Sure. I can go right now."

We'd circled the block. Approaching the station house again, she slowed.

"Mind if I drop you here? I always avoid visiting zoos at feeding time."

"Smart policy. This is fine. Thanks for making the contact, Ms. Hilliard. I really appreciate it."

A glint of mischief lit her eyes. "Ginny Bliss is one of a kind, Ms. Finn. If nothing else, I'm sure you'll find her entertaining."

• • •

Most of the grand old homes on King Street had been converted to commercial uses. Now they housed the nursing homes, nurseries, private schools, and sanitariums that flanked the meandering river of pavement separating tone-deaf Port Chester, New York, from tony Greenwich, Connecticut. New construction had sprung up to fill all vacant land space. Watching the numbers, I passed condominium complexes, office parks, convenience stores, package stores, and occasional buildings whose purpose was either undetermined or undisclosed.

One of those, a long brick rectangle fronted by an unmarked green awning, matched the number on Eden Hilliard's note. There was no doorbell, so I knocked. In speakeasy style, a disembodied voice demanded my name and the nature of my business.

The interior was spare and dark. Battleship gray walls and flooring gave the small anteroom a tomblike feel. The woman who appeared to greet me furthered the mood. Her complexion was talcum white, her hair the black of charred marshmallows. She wore a long black dress with a flowing hem and trailing sleeves. From her willowy throat hung an enormous silver cross on a black velvet ribbon.

"Ginny will be with you as soon as she finishes rehearsing," she informed me. "You're welcome to wait in the café."

If this was the warm-up, I hated to imagine the main event. As we passed through the connecting door, I tensed.

But the ambience inside was bright and festive. The cavernous room was centered by a scarlet-curtained stage. Surrounding it were concentric rings of small round tables. Each was set with a white cloth, polished silver, crystal stemware, gold-rimmed place plates, and a rose. Vampira directed me to a table near the front and soundlessly departed.

Soon, there was a rustling behind the curtain. The velvet drapes parted, revealing a stage flanked by countless colored spots. At their intersection, framed in a bubble of light, stood a tall, robust woman dressed in flame red satin. Her hair was a curly blond halo. Large gray eyes and dark brows dominated her face. A keyboard player, a guitarist, and a drummer sat at stage left behind her.

They played eight introductory bars of "Comedy Tonight," launching the star's performance. She danced; she sang. She portrayed a breathless kaleidoscope of real and invented characters: First Lady, aging screen star, toddler being potty-trained, Kate Hepburn, old man on a park bench, banana republic dictator. Her range was uncanny, her presentation priceless. Even after she stopped half an hour later, the room continued to thrum with her spark.

"Okay, fellows. That's a wrap."

The band lumbered out. The star performer strode my way and stuck out a hand.

"Eden sent you?"

"Right. I'm Lennie Finn."

"Ginny Bliss. Mind talking in back while I freshen up?"

"That's fine."

Not that she appeared to need freshening. She wasn't breathing hard or visibly perspiring. The hot lights and hotter performance had not drained her powerful batteries in any way.

I trailed her through a rear door to a musty office. Her costume changes were draped across the shabby couch. A makeup case lay open on the desk. Frowning into the mirrored lid, Ginny Bliss replenished her blush and shadow.

"Sorry you had to sit through rehearsal. Trio showed up late, as usual."

"I enjoyed it. You're terrific."

"That's what I keep telling my agent. But the man's dedicated half his career to keeping my abilities top-secret."

"Is this a nightclub?"

"Members only. *Very* private. Guaranteed to raise my obscurity to an all-time high. But the crowd's a bitch. And the pay's lousy. So how can I possibly complain?" She tortured her spider-leg lashes with a curler. "Which, I suppose, brings us to Jack."

"Eden Hilliard says you knew him better than anyone."

"You could say that. What's up with Jackie boy, anyway? Haven't heard from him since Nixon resigned. Or was it Reagan? I keep confusing those guys."

"Jack's wife died a few years ago. He's living in Wilton now."

"Imagine that, Jack a neighbor. Gives me goose bumps." She scratched her arm. "Then again, they could be hives."

"He wanted to be near his son."

"Little Mikey, you mean? Don't tell me that boy's gone and gotten himself grown up."

"Michael's married. Has a little girl."

Deep sigh. "Where's it go? I had a muffin and coffee and suddenly I'm forty-five."

"You knew Jack when he was a student?"

"Oh, we go way back. Want the lowdown?"

"Yes."

She chuckled. "The lowdown is he's low down. When it comes to Jack, what you see is definitely *not* what you get. Man's a born liar. He'll tell you black's white just for the hell of it. For example, I bet he put on the devoted daddy-and-husband act. Told you he *loved* Liz and doted on little Mikey, that right?"

"It's not true?"

"If it was, he sure had a funny way of showing it. Jack would just up and take off on them for weeks at a time. Not a word from him until he finally got sick of whoever she was and dragged his sorry ass back home. How Liz put up with it, I'll never know. Woman was a fool or a saint. Maybe some of each."

"You think that was part of his rebellion against his parents?"

Her ample bosom jiggled with laughter. "He give you that line about having an abusive daddy? Which others did he feed you? That he was a shy boy?"

"Actually, yes."

"That's Jack for you. Did he tell you the one about having a deranged sister who lives in loony bins and shelters?"

"He made that up?"

She lit a slim brown cigarette. "Let's see if I remember how it goes: Once upon a time there was a sorry little thing named Jillian. Girl was a big talent, but her head wasn't screwed on straight. So one day, she ran off in the Rotten Apple, where she wound up dancing topless in a dive. That the gist?"

"Why would he lie about something like that?"

Her broad shoulders hitched. "Why steal, cheat, set fires, and torture small animals? Guess Jack figured if he couldn't be the best, he'd try for baddest. Wouldn't put anything past him. Not a blessed thing."

None of this made sense. Jack a pathological liar? A raging delinquent? A budding sociopath? Shelby's investigator's report confirmed his current status as a model citizen. Could anyone really turn around that completely?

"How can you be sure those things he says aren't true?" I demanded of Ginny Bliss.

"Because I was there, my girl. Jack's daddy never gave him a single lick he didn't ask for loud and clear. There was nothing in the least bit shy about that boy. And as far as his baby sister goes, she was such a grade-A goody-two-shoes, it stuck in Jack's craw like a bone. Jillian was a picture-perfect little girl. Great student. Straight as they come. Apple of her parents' eye, too. Which left poor Jackie nothing but the pits."

"How about now?"

Her eyes glittered maliciously. "Now, she has to get ready for showtime. Nice meeting you, Lennie. Tell my brother Jack I said hello."

Chapter 36

DANA

Dana's face ached from all the unfelt smiles. For the second consecutive evening, she was charged with the unsavory task of keeping Valerie Eckhard out of her office and fully distracted.

Last night's plan had worked beautifully, except for one small, lethal hitch. While Dana entertained Blowhard Eckhard in a nearby Brasserie, Lester Yurie spent nearly an hour trying to break into the wall safe behind the attorney's desk.

As Dana's partner-in-slime described it, the installation was akin to Fort Knox, a welded-escutcheon, multiple tumbler affair with sate-of-the-art computerized timing devices. Though Yurie touted himself as an accomplished safe-cracker, he'd been unable to decipher the access code within the time allotted.

"One more shot and I'll have it, Dana. Guaranteed."

"How can you be so sure, Mr. Yurie?"

"Want the truth?"

"That would be refreshing."

"Happens I got an in at the manufacturer. Guy I roomed with years back at Lewisburg is head of customer service. If I call him at the office tomorrow, he'll get me the combination. We're real close."

"They hire ex-cons at a safe company?"

"We're all over, Dana. I got ins in places you wouldn't believe."

So everything was put on hold for twenty-four hours. Dana made further excuses to Valerie Eckhard, claiming that the mobile camera unit she needed had been diverted to cover a gas main explosion on the lower East Side. That meant the taping on the office environmental show would have to be delayed until tomorrow.

Blowhard made a grand show of being miffed at the inconvenience, but predictably, her lust for the spotlight far outshone her pique. She readily accepted Dana's questionable explanation that the location scout needed to return this evening for more measurements and photos, since they'd decided to expand the show's scope to include the firm's conference room and library.

"This is the last time, I hope," the attorney griped without feeling.

"So do I, Ms. Eckhard," Dana replied sincerely.

Back at the same Brasserie tonight, Blowhard was inhaling a Belgian waffle capped with whipped cream, chocolate sauce, and strawberries. Dana picked at her fruit salad, her appetite deadened by the numbing realization that Yurie could be caught.

The crook had remained philosophical about the possibility. "Don't sweat it, Dana, honest. If it comes right down to it, I can do a coupla years in a sleepwalk."

But Dana couldn't view things quite that calmly. Pulling strings was one thing. Pulling a heist was quite another.

"Any more questions?" Valerie Eckhard's mouth was crammed with masticated waffle, her lip capped by a rakish whipped cream mustache.

Dana consulted her hastily-scrawled notes. "You say you chose peach for the chairs because it's relaxing?"

"To me it is. The only color I like more is thousand-dollar-bill green. But it doesn't work as well for me on furniture. Clashes with my eyes."

Her eyes were contact lens teal blue framed by a disquieting sliver of barnyard brown.

"What about the art motif, Ms. Eckhard? Any particular reason you chose to go with Op?"

"I'm a realist and a sensualist. I like what looks great and feels better. How's that for a sound bite?"

"Just dandy." Dana eyed her watch. "Mind excusing me for a minute? I have to call the sitter."

Actually, Becky was with Adam again. Much to her ex-husband's chagrin, Dana had shown up at his apartment earlier to drop the child off for her regular weeknight visit.

Adam could barely mask his dismay. "Rebecca? What a surprise. I presumed you'd prefer to rest at home this evening."

Catching a whiff of Jeanette's flowery cologne, Dana's smile froze. "She wanted to come, Adam. She wants things back to normal. Don't you, honey?"

Becky held back. "Is it okay, Daddy?"

"Certainly. My—secretary—stopped by to do some work. We were just about to have supper. Delighted you'll be able to join us. Come in, dear."

"I'll be back for her at ten," Dana said as the door closed in her face.

Leaving Valerie Eckhard in the booth, Dana crossed to the pay phone at the rear of the restaurant. The call she really had to make was to Lester Yurie at Eckhard's office. The thief had copied the number from the attorney's private line. Dana was to ring twice and hang up, a signal that Yurie had ten minutes to finish up and clear out. After that, he was to go somewhere, wait an hour, then call Dana at home with the results of his search.

Shakily, she dialed the number. After the second double tone, she hung up quickly. Dana pictured Lester Yurie closing the lawyer's safe and collecting his things. He's going to the door now, she thought. He's letting himself out and locking up. He hasn't forgotten anything. Hasn't left any evidence of his break-in. The guy's a pro, Dana reassured herself. Professional scum.

Dana paid the check. She and Eckhard caught a cab back to the firm's office. Thankfully, the place was dark. From appearances, everything had gone according to schedule.

"Looks like your location scout's gone," Eckhard observed as she opened the door with her key.

"Guess he got what he needed and took off," Dana said. "Thanks for everything, Ms. Eckhard. I'll be back tomorrow with the mobile crew."

"You're headed uptown?"

"Yes."

"Park Avenue in the sixties—right?"

Dana stifled her annoyance. Obviously, Blowhard had done some information gathering of her own. "I have a stop to make first on Central Park South."

"Fine. I'll drop you off." With a wistful look around, the attorney locked the door to the firm. "Nothing here for me to do tonight. Guess I might as well go home."

Chapter 37

LENNIE

A cluster of cars crammed the drive. I couldn't recall Mrs. O' mentioning that she expected company, but the house was prone to spontaneous congestion. I ditched the Toyota on the nearest side street and stole through the yard toward the fire stairs.

From inside came the press of eager voices, bursts of hilarity, the heraldry of Maniac, the canine Paul Revere.

Cringing, I kept out of view of the windows as I crossed the snow-capped lawn. People were the last thing I needed right now. My mind was swarming with angry confusion. I needed to think, to sort things out, to figure out what the hell to do.

At times like this, I could fully appreciate my brother's preference for the other side of the looking glass. The nastiest surprise in Huck's circumscribed world was meatloaf, and faced with that, he could always fall back on peas and mashed potatoes.

I had no such comforting cushions from reality. Jack had lied to me about his sister and who knew what else. Jillian Chambless, a.k.a. Ginny Bliss, was a talented performer, not a pathetic emotional wreck. I could no longer rely on any reassuring assumptions I'd made about Jack. Up was down, blue was yellow, right was wrong. My shadow was suddenly six feet tall and male.

"Hi, Eleanora. I thought that was your car I saw pass by."

My throat parched fiercely. "What are you doing here, Jack?"

He was dressed in dark slacks, a blue shirt, and a sweater. No coat, but the cold didn't seem to faze him.

"Mrs. O'Callaghan invited me. She's having a fund-raiser for the new children's cancer research center at St. Joseph's Hospital. I have to admit, I hoped I'd get to see you, too."

"It's not a good time, Jack. Been a long day."

I turned to leave, but he caught my wrist. "Please, don't be mad. I know I should have listened when you said it was a bad idea for me to visit your brother. I'm sorry."

"It's not that."

"What, then?"

"I need some time to think, Jack, that's all."

Breaking loose, I hurried up the stairs. At the third-floor landing, I chanced a look below. He was gone.

The swelling crowd of doubts made me dizzy. I had to find my equilibrium again.

I freed the Halligan tool from the flower box and prised open the door. With a breath of relief, I strode down the darkened hall toward my bedroom. As I slid my key in the lock, I felt a sudden presence and a breathy whisper in my ear.

"Please, Eleanora. Let's talk."

"Christ, Jack! You scared me."

"Five minutes. That's all I ask. After that, I have to leave for Norwalk. Bunch of kids are meeting me to work on the rec center building. Framing inspection's scheduled for tomorrow morning. Probably take us half the night to get the place ready."

"I'm really tired, Jack."

"I know I can clear up whatever it is. Please give me the chance."

He clearly wasn't going to leave until I did. "All right. Come in."

I motioned him to the chair beside the window, then perched on the bed beside Hubby the bear. My phone machine was blinking wildly. How many of the six messages were desperate calls from Jack?

"All I want is to make you happy, Eleanora. Just tell me how."

Fueled by rage, I faced him squarely. "You can start with the truth."

"I don't understand."

"Neither do I. I met your sister tonight. She's working at a club in Port Chester. Her act's impressive. Sorry I can't say the same about yours."

He stiffened as if I'd slapped him. "Jilly? But how?"

"That's *my* question, Jack. How could you lie like that? *Why* would you?"

"But I didn't. I wouldn't. Jilly can be convincing, I know. But she's delusional. Can't separate fantasy from reality. It's part of her illness. I explained that to you."

"You told me she was crazy. Lost. That doesn't describe the woman I met tonight. Nowhere close."

"It's hard to explain her particular sickness, Eleanora. Jilly's very talented. And she can come across just fine, especially when she's taking her medication. But she's not fine."

Incredible. He was the portrait of sincerity. "I honestly don't know what the hell to think, Jack."

"Jilly's doctor can confirm what I've said. I'll call him right now." He crossed to the phone and dialed. Listening, he frowned. "No. No message." He turned to me. "Doc Rowan's not in. Soon as I can reach him, I'll have him contact you and explain about Jilly. Will that put your mind at rest, Eleanora?"

No, yes, maybe. "I guess so."

"Glad to hear she's okay. Haven't had a word from her in months."

"She looks great."

"That's good." He frowned. "Now, can I ask how you came to meet her?"

Lacking a reasonable explanation, I decided to punt. "I told you. She was performing at a club."

"Guess that'll have to do." Standing, he stared out the window. After a long silence, he turned to me. "What happened to make you so suspicious, Eleanora? Maybe it'd help to talk it out."

"When things don't make sense, I question them."

"Maybe so, but I've always felt you were holding back for some reason. As if you'd been hurt and didn't want to risk having it happen again."

"Everyone's been hurt."

He shrugged. "Yes, but if the hurt's bad enough, it can make a person shut down. Close herself off. That's the last thing I want you to do, Eleanora. I want to be part of your life."

Approaching, he circled his arms around me. But I held back firmly. Closed for necessary repairs.

"There are some things I have to work through by myself right now, Jack."

His lips brushed my ears. "You can't change what's past, Eleanora. Only way to move on is to put whatever it is behind you."

"I'm really tired, Jack. You'd better go."

"Please, darlin'. Don't shut me out."

I crossed to the door and opened it for him. "I'll call you."

He hung back. "Memories don't count, can't you see? They're nothing. You must forget the past, Eleanora. You must put it away."

I turned away from him, gazing pointedly at the hall. Finally, he took the hint and left.

Shutting the door behind him, I felt a vexing mix of regret and relief. Was Jack right? Did I keep myself locked away like some foolish treasure no one ever dared to enjoy? Was I really unable to put the past away?

Put it away—

That thought started my tumblers whirring. Abruptly, one of the long-lost pieces of my past clacked neatly into place. Suddenly, I realized that Jack held a critical piece of the solution. I couldn't let him leave and take it away.

Hurrying out of the room, I caught him at the bottom of the stairs.

"Jack—you forgot to kiss me good-bye."

Puzzled, he leaned down and brushed his lips against mine.

"I meant a *real* kiss."

As he complied, I raked my fingers through his hair.

"Mmmm. That mean you changed your mind, I hope?" he said softly.

"No, but things are getting clearer."

Racing upstairs, I went to my room and shut the door. Very soon, all this would be resolved, I thought. I already held the answer in my hand.

Chapter 38

LENNIE

Driving toward Westport, I cradled the resurrected memory in my mind's eye. The hairs I'd plucked from Jack's head were wrapped in a wad of tissue in my jacket pocket. I kept patting the lump to reassure myself that this was more than a wishful dream.

Westport's Larkspur Lane is shaped like a teardrop. Aunt Selia's brick-and-board Colonial occupies a central spot at the bulbous end of the block. Mindful of my aunt's aversion to unnecessary noise, I rapped lightly at the door frame.

"Yes?"

"It's Lennie, Aunt Selia."

"Lennie?"

I heard the click of turning locks, the rasp of chains dragging. The door opened, and she peered at me over dark granny glasses. "What's wrong?"

Predictably, my aunt was perfectly groomed and fully dressed. As a child, I suspected that she even bathed in her clothes and shoes. Now, I was certain she did.

Age had plumped and dulled her ever so slightly. But her composure remained flawless, except for the telltale blink.

"Nothing's wrong. I came to pick up something I left here. Sorry if I've disturbed you."

"Actually, I was having tea. You're welcome to join me."

"No need for you to bother."

"Not at all. Come in."

"I know it's late, Aunt Selia. I could just—"

"Surely you have time for tea, Lennie. It's been months."

The house has the look and feel of library stacks. Everything somber, musty, overly arranged. The drab green living room furniture is still plastered with crocheted antimacassars, though I presume that sitting on the furniture is still discouraged, if not punishable by death.

Following her toward the kitchen, my uneasiness mounted. My aunt is a human corset. Living here, I don't think I ever drew a full or easy breath. There were so many rules, so many invisible lines I couldn't risk crossing. So much about me was unacceptable: my age, my unthinkable presence in her house, my existence.

She retrieved the necessary china from the cabinet above the sink and transferred the tea bag from her cup to mine. All her moves were so damned predictable. Fill to half. Dunk twice. No cream or sugar offered. Selia was religiously opposed to both.

I took the bitter brew and sipped politely. No matter how anxious I was, this visit, like all things within these hallowed walls, would proceed according to my aunt's preference and direction.

"How's Huck?" she asked.

"Great, actually. He's started to talk."

Her brow peaked. "Is that so?"

"He's responded beautifully to a new method called Facilitated Communication. If you support his wrist, he can type his thoughts into a computer."

The thin lips pursed. "I would hardly call that talking, Lennie."

"No. I'm sure you wouldn't."

"The work? Is it going well?"

She never referred to my chosen career by name. No doubt she found the word too distasteful. I'd never forget her reaction when she first heard I was testing to become a fire fighter. *How utterly predictable, Lennie. You always were drawn to the most unsuitable pursuits.*

Firmly, I reminded myself that Selia's questions were intended solely to fill dead air. They didn't express any real interest, and she didn't honestly want substantial answers.

"Work's fine. Yours?"

"The garden show this May is shaping up wonderfully. We've gotten the president of the American Orchid Growers' Association as our keynote speaker," she gushed. "And of course, I'm looking forward to the Philharmonic gala. They've planned some truly outstanding programs for the Friends."

"Sounds wonderful, Aunt Selia."

She frowned. "Shall I warm that tea up for you, Lennie?"

"No. It's fine. I really should go."

"Surely, a few moments won't kill you."

Though it felt as if they might, I held my tongue. *Soon, I'll know everything. Soon.*

Sipping, her eyes went vague. I allowed my mind to drift as well. My aunt and I had always related this way. Split and distant. Oil and water. Jupiter and Mars.

Finally, she stepped to the sink and washed her cup. Swallowing my impatience, I followed suit, making certain that I used two squirts of liquid detergent: Selia's bare minimum.

"So," she intoned. "What is it you came for, Lennie? I don't believe I have anything of yours."

"Remember those things you kept of my parents'?"

"Some letters, photos, and jewelry, as I recall."

"Right. I hid them here years ago and totally forgot where I put them. Tonight, it came back to me. You mind?"

I didn't wait for her response. I crossed the hall to the back of the staircase. The wood planks appear solid, but the boards at the center can be prodded loose. Kneeling, I nudged until a rectangular panel collapsed into the space under the stairs.

Selia followed me. "I never knew about that," she huffed.

"Kids are the masters of secret hiding places. When I was little, I used this as my fort." I lifted the fallen boards and edged them out of the dark interior.

"You might have told me, Lennie. It *is* my house."

"But it was *my* secret." Groping deep inside, I found the battered old suitcase. Heart pounding, I pulled it out.

Please, let it be there. Let it be all right.

"Can't imagine what possessed you to hide that old thing."

"No. I'm sure you can't."

"You needn't be rude," she snapped.

I stood and lifted the case. "I'll be going now, Aunt Selia. Thanks for the tea."

Outside, I drew a long, greedy breath. The suitcase felt surprisingly light to me. Carrying it toward my car, I had the awful sense that the contents had somehow disappeared.

But that was impossible. Selia didn't know about the hiding place. From the dust, it was clear no one had touched the case since that awful night twenty-five years ago when I'd hid my angel bait inside.

I settled the case on the passenger seat of the Toyota and parked out of sight around the block. My hands trembled. From what Clarissa Pratt told me, I knew it was possible to extract DNA fingerprints from decades-old samples. All that mattered was preserving the specimen properly. Keeping it dry and cool.

Inside this old suitcase were the panties I'd worn the night of the rape. If the dried specimen on them could be compared to the DNA in the hairs I'd pulled from Jack's head, I'd finally have a definite test of his innocence or guilt.

The secret place under the stairs was perfect. I remembered crouching in my fort as a little girl. Even on the hottest days, that space was cozy and comfortable. Dry and cool.

The latches felt stiff with disuse. I forced them open. Inside, I found several packets—the love letters my father had written to my mother. Below was a jumble of faded family snapshots. Huck and me. Huck and Mom. Mom and Dad. All of us gathered on a picnic. At Christmas. At the beach.

Underneath those, I found the old family Bible and my parents' things. I held my father's Bulova watch, enjoying its heft. I fingered his wallet and the silver dollar-sign-shaped money clip. Mother's blue lace hankie had yellowed. The cameo was caked with grime. Her wedding band wouldn't slip beyond the second joint of my ring finger. Odd to think she'd always seemed so large and reassuring. But, those qualities had precious little to do with size.

I rummaged through the rest of the angel bait: Huck's ruined snapshot, the letter with the rain-blurred ink. At the bottom of the case was the chunk of ruby-colored stone I'd found on the walk that night. Obviously, it wasn't real. Something about the gleaming glass struck me as familiar, but I couldn't make a connection.

Bristling with anticipation, I lifted the only remaining item in the suitcase: a paper lunch bag. I must have put the panties in there.

Please, let it be a well-preserved specimen. Dry and cool. Dry and cool.

Carefully, I unfolded the crumpled top of the bag and dipped my hand inside to tug out the contents. With a sinking heart, I felt the edge of a plastic bag. The wadded cotton inside was stiff and covered with dense blue mold.

Tears welled up, unbidden. I'd longed to leave my aunt's house with the answers.

My Toyota caught my foul and darkened mood. It took five minutes of stomping and cursing to start the obstinate engine.

Driving home, I couldn't shake my devastating disappointment. I'd been so certain the suitcase would hold the key.

How could I have come away empty-handed? All those long-lost treasures had to have some value beyond sheer sentiment. One by one, I pictured the letters and snapshots, the jewelry, the handkerchief, the Bible, the painful reminders of that hideous night.

And suddenly, the real solution came to me. I'd left Aunt Selia's house with the key to the truth after all. It simply wasn't the one I'd expected.

The Road To Redemption

by Patterson Graham, Ph.D.

(Advance Reading Copy)

At the Cambridge program, client progress is continually monitored and evaluated. Rapid crisis intervention is a key element in our success. Many reformed rapists have been prevented from reoffending by the timely response of the therapeutic manager.

John's recent experience is a notable case in point.

At first, I thought I'd picked the perfect curative model, but I was wrong. Turned out this guy had a dark side. You'd think he'd be flattered that I chose him. Instead, it made him furious.

I don't even know how he found out. The model's supposed to be strictly secret. Maybe he got the idea from something I said last week in our therapy group.

After the meeting broke up, he cornered me. He threatened to take me apart if he found out for sure I was still hurting kids. He said he didn't want any part of me. And he didn't want me to have any part of him.

You should have heard the way he carried on, raging like a stuck bull. He swore he'd kill me if it kept up this way. From the look in his eyes, I knew he wasn't kidding.

Lucky thing he doesn't know the half of it, how far I've actually gone to step into his skin.

Luckier still that he can't step into mine. He can't know what I'm thinking, what I've planned. Half the time, I'm don't know myself until it's too late to stop or make a difference.

My therapist is the key. He's promised to help me find a substitute. The minute I do, this one's out. Hopefully, it'll be soon, before another bad thing happens.

Meanwhile, I have to be extra careful about what I say in front of him. When I start talking in the group, it's easy to let go and spill whatever's on my mind. After so many years, it's hard to hold back.

Right now, it's almost impossible. Nothing is going the way I hoped. All I wanted was to make her happy, but she keeps refusing me. The group could help me out with this. I'm sure of it.

But I don't know how to ask for help without asking for trouble. If only I could make him see the error of his ways.

Chapter 39

DANA

Dana was waiting near the phone. Staring hard, she willed it to ring. Still, she jumped when Yurie finally called.

"Hey, Dana. Guess what?"

"Did you get the name?"

"How would you bet? That I did or didn't?"

"Dammit, Mr. Yurie. Just tell me."

He sniffed. "Whatsa matter with you, Lester? Important lady like Dana Saunders got no time to dick around. Am I right or am I right?"

Dana felt ready to explode. "The name, Mr. Yurie? Yes or no."

"Well. It's interesting. That's for sure."

"*Please,* Mr. Yurie. If you have something to say, *say* it!"

Long pause.

"Mr. Yurie?"

"You hear that, Dana? That was the sound of me tryin' to kick myself, which ain't easy seeing how the leg bone's connected to the thigh bone and the thigh bone's connected to the hip bone and the—"

"Please!"

"Hey, sorry. I don't know what gets into me, goin' on and on like I do. Must be a case of the runs from the wrong end. So get to the point, Lester. Give the lady a freaking break."

"I'm ready to hear your news, Mr. Yurie. *More* than ready."

"Well good. 'Cause I got some."

She filled herself with air and exhaled slowly. "I'm listening."

"First thing this morning, I called my pal at the safe company. He was on a break, so I left a message. He called me back, but I was in the can, so I had to call him again, only it was lunchtime. Goes like that sometimes. Know what I'm saying?"

"You didn't reach him?"

"Did I say that? 'Course I did. And he called up the customer file on his mainframe and—bingo—I got me the combination."

Dana allowed a flicker of hope. "You found the release form?"

"You betcha. Thing was right between the stacks of hundreds and a sweet little stash of high-quality blow."

"I hope you didn't touch the money or the cocaine, Mr. Yurie."

"You think I'm stupid, or what?"

Both, she longed to say. But she resisted. "Go on, please. What was the name on the release?"

There was a sound of crinkling paper. "I wrote it down so I'd be sure and get it exactly. Here it is. The name was John——J—O—H—N."

"John what?"

"That's it. Just John. Guy signed that way and everything. Must be he goes by that. Like Cher, I guess. Or Madonna."

Dana held her temper hard. "No, Mr. Yurie. John is an alias. His real name must have appeared somewhere on that form. Or maybe there was a supplemental release cross-referenced on the original."

Yurie hummed irritatingly. "Nope. There was nothing about cross-dressing or anything like that."

"Where are you calling from, Mr. Yurie?"

"Same coffee shop, right across the street from the lawyer's office. I was starved, and they got this cheesecake you wouldn't believe. Thick crust, fat blueberries. In-freaking-credible."

"I need for you to go back to Ms. Eckhard's office and check the safe again. There must be a document with the rapist's real name. Check the release you found for numbers or anything that might indicate where she keeps his file." Dana couldn't keep her anger out of her voice.

Yurie sighed. "I'd do anything for you, Dana. You know that. But whadda you need his name for? You wanna invite the guy to a party or something?"

"I want him arrested, Mr. Yurie. I want him in prison, where he belongs. To do that, the police will have to know who he is, don't you think?"

"Way I see it, they can just go to his house. Guy'll tell them his name, sooner or later. Cops have their ways. Believe me. I—"

"You have his address?" Dana's voice sliced through his.

"Didn't I tell you that? Whatsa matter with you, Lester? You got your head up your ass, or what?"

Dana grabbed a pen from the holder on her desk. Her hand was shaking. "What is it?"

Yurie read her the street number and town name. "You got that, Dana?"

"I do." She hung up without thanking him.

Her throat parched as she lifted the phone again.

Before this night was over, Becky's attacker would be found and locked away.

Chapter 40

LENNIE

Mrs. O', Frank Murphy, and the antiques dealers were having a nightcap in the living room. Their silhouettes played behind the curtains. I saw the raised glasses. Heads bobbing like spring toys in a moving car.

The crowd from the charity function had dispersed. Thankfully, I wouldn't have to deal with Jack right now. I needed time alone to plan my next critical move.

Killing the lights and engine, I rolled my car to the end of the drive. My arrival went unnoticed by everyone except Maniac.

"Hush, girl," I rasped as I slipped around back. "Not now."

The dog stopped barking, though she could not have heard me and wasn't likely to listen if she had. Treading softly, I climbed the fire stairs to the third floor and dug my Halligan tool out of the window box.

I spent several minutes sitting in my room in the dark, trying to gather my thoughts and muster a reasonable course of action. But I was distracted by the glint of Hubby the bear's glass eyes. He seemed to be angling for attention, trying to save me from myself.

When I turned him facedown to eliminate that annoyance, my focus swerved to the answering machine. It was blinking frantically. The number six still blazed on the indicator.

Lowering the volume, I pressed the playback button. My blood chilled at the sound of Jack's honeyed drawl. He'd be at Mrs. O's house tonight, he said. Wouldn't I please agree to get together and talk? He knew he could fix whatever was troubling me. "I can't think of anything but you, Eleanora. You've got to say you'll see me, darlin'. You must."

The next two messages were also calls from Jack. I listened coldly, armored against him.

When the next call replayed, I expected to hear Jack again. But it was the sergeant: "Finn. It's Kresky. I'm afraid I've got bad news and worse news. Wendy Lister's body was found in a leaf bag in the woods near the Merritt Parkway. We've got a positive ID, but still no suspect. We'll be out in force tonight, trying to get a handle on this bastard. Thanks for the help. Sorry we couldn't make it pay off."

Shocked raw, I heard the beep ending Kresky's message and the robot voice announcing the day and time of his call. The tape reeled ahead to the next message. That poor little girl. When would this end? At least the news can't get any worse, I thought.

But I was wrong.

The fifth call was from Kitty's father. His voice was thick with fear. Kitty had run away, he said. Was she with me? Would I please call immediately if she was or if I had any idea where she might be?

Pulse racing, I listened to the final message. It was Lila Sperling from the Rape Crisis Center. "Kitty Dolan was extremely distraught when I saw her earlier, Lennie. She said she couldn't stand being with her parents. She insisted that she be allowed to stay with you. I have a feeling she'll head your way if she hasn't already. Please call when you get this message, no matter what time it is. Naturally, the Dolans are distraught." She left her office and home numbers, then repeated the plea that I call with any information.

I dialed the Dolans', but no one answered. No one picked up at Lila Sperling's home or at the crisis center either. Of course—they were probably all out searching for Kitty.

Why hadn't the child tried to reach me? Then it occurred to me that she might have. If she'd dialed and gotten my answering machine, she might have hung up and tried the main phone. Maybe she'd left a message with Mrs. O'.

Clinging to that slim hope, I raced downstairs. Mrs. O' had drifted into the kitchen, where she was washing the cordial glasses.

"Did you get any calls for me tonight, Mrs. O'?"

She cupped a hand to her ear, letting me know that she couldn't hear over the din of the running water. Raising a wet finger, she gestured for me to wait.

Reaching across her, I turned off the tap. "Did you hear from Kitty Dolan? Did she call for me?"

"The little girl, you mean? No."

"Are you sure, Mrs. O'? This is important!"

Drying her hands on her apron front, she eyed me worriedly. "What is it, child? You look a fright."

"Someone else could have answered the phone," I blithered. "Maybe one of the guests. I have to call everyone and check. Where's the guest list?"

"Easy now. The phone didn't ring once all night. No one called."

"But Kitty must have. She can't be out there alone. That sonofabitch will take her, too. Kitty will be the next—" My voice broke.

Mrs. O' put her arm around me and led me to the table. "Lennie, dear. What's happened?" she asked.

I squeezed the words past the painful lump in my throat. Mrs. O's face blanched at the news that another child had been murdered. But she looked almost relieved when I explained that Kitty had run away from home.

"Now don't go thinking the worst, dear. Chances are the child's off with a little friend, is all. You'll see."

Her comforting voice did nothing to ease my escalating panic. "I'm sure the Dolans checked her friends. Kitty told her counselor she wanted to see me. Why hasn't she called? If anything happens to her—" Tears streaked my face. I struggled to keep the dam of grief from bursting.

Mrs. O' gave me a tissue and another hug. "There, now. Weeping's not going to find the child. Let's try to think where she might have headed."

"I don't know . . ."

"Every child's got a favorite spot. My son Dermot's was the pond down by the sheep meadow. Mary Ellen always headed for the hayloft. If Collum was missing, I always knew to look at the church. What's Kitty's place?"

Starting with our first meeting on the roof, I reviewed all the spots I could possibly associate with Kitty Dolan: the hospital, the police station, the Rape Crisis Center. Since the assault, we had forced the little girl to relive that night of horror over and over again. How gruesome it must have been for her to study the mug shots, how terrifying the lineup must have been for her. How horrifying it must have been when the hypnotist placed her back at the site and moment of her attack. No wonder she so desperately wanted to run.

Suddenly it came to me. "The mall. That's her favorite place. And she could have caught the bus there. You're a genius, Mrs. O'!"

She flapped away the compliment and eyed the clock. "If it's there she's gotten to, you'd better hurry. They'll be shutting down within the hour."

"I'm going. Call—"

But Frank Murphy stood in the kitchen doorway blocking my path. Amusement played on his irksome face.

"Excuse me, Frank."

"Where you going in such a rush at this hour, Lennie girl? Looks as if your tail's caught fire."

"Get out of my way, Frank. I'm in a hurry." I bit out the words.

"Haste makes waste, I always say. Wouldn't you say that, Mrs. O'?"

"Let her go, Frank. Her little friend Kitty's run off. Lennie's on her way to find the child."

Frank shifted his weight and stood his ground. His eyes gleamed maliciously. "Just where are you figuring to do that?"

"She's going to the mall," Mrs. O' told him, ever the peacemaker. "That's the child's favorite spot, so that's likely where she'll be. Now let the girl go, Frank. Don't be a tease."

"Damn it, Frank. Move!"

He waxed innocent. "I'm just trying to save you the trouble . . ."

I elbowed past him, but he kept talking.

"You won't find Kitty Dolan at any mall, Lennie girl."

Something in his tone stopped me at the door. "How the hell do you know, Frank?"

He took his sweet time answering. "Because I spotted her out back no more than an hour ago. Kitty was talking to that boyfriend of yours. She went off with the man in his car."

Chapter 41

LENNIE

Jack's big stone house was dark and locked. No sign of his Jeep in the driveway. Could he really be holding Kitty inside?

I examined the door. The construction was solid-core, the jamb fitted nearly airtight. The lock was a firm, brass deadbolt. Without my entry tools, I couldn't see a way in. If I made too much noise, Jack might panic. He might hurt Kitty. I couldn't risk that.

The windows were no more promising. The sash bars were solid. I couldn't begin to squeeze through the narrow panes between the muntins.

Desperate, I started circling the house. But I saw no simple, soundless way to gain access. I should have called the police. Too late now. I didn't have time to go looking for a phone. Every second might put Kitty in deeper danger. *Damn it, Lennie. Why didn't you think!*

Rounding the deep shadows at the back of the old stone building, I spotted the soft glow seeping from the woods. Tracking it, I picked my way through the trees, wincing at every sound I made.

Closer, I saw that the light came from the playhouse. Two shadows wavered behind the shade: a man and a child.

Ducking, I raced across the clearing. Approaching the small building, I heard voices.

"*Please, please! Let me go!*"

"*I said, shut up!*"

There was a sharp striking sound and a hurt scream. "*No!*"

The monster was hitting her. Again, I acted without thinking. Racing forward, I tripped over a large branch. Sprawled out, breathless, I struggled to my knees and grabbed the branch. Then I dashed toward the door. Building momentum, I butted with my shoulder, as I'd been trained to do in an emergency. The wood splintered and gave. Racing inside, I raised the branch and readied myself to swing at Jack's head.

But it wasn't Jack.

The resemblance was startling. The stranger was the same size as Jack. He wore his hair in precisely the same style. He'd clearly studied Jack's expressions and the way Jack dressed and held himself. Even his drawl was a chilling copy.

"Eleanora, what a lovely surprise."

Numb with shock, I searched for Kitty. The child had ducked out of sight behind the toy chest. Now she got to her feet and dashed toward me. By the spare light of the hurricane lamp, I saw that her hair was tangled. Dirt streaked her face and clothes.

"Lennie! Help me! Save me! He's going to—"

Dropping the branch, I held her close. Poor child was trembling. "Shh, sweetie. He's not going to do anything." I turned to Jack's smirking double. "Who the hell are you?"

"Name's John. I'm an old friend of Jack's, Eleanora. Heard all about you from him."

"Come on, Kitty. I'm getting you out of here."

As I reached for her hand, he caught me by the arms. His grip was a sprung trap. "Now that's not neighborly at all, Eleanora. You just go on over there and sit awhile."

He shoved me so hard, I went sprawling. Recovering, I turned to the sight of him clutching Kitty by the neck.

"It'd be a crying shame if you went and made me hurt this pretty little friend of yours, Eleanora. I've grown real fond of her."

"Leave her alone."

"You just sit, darlin'. Do as I say and the child'll be fine."

I had no choice. For the moment, John held all the cards. I perched on the toy box, taut with fear and anger at my helplessness.

"There, that's better." John eased his hold on Kitty's throat. "Now we can all get acquainted. Any friend of Jack's is a friend of mine."

"How do you know Jack?"

"We met more than twenty years back at the Cambridge Center."

"The place in Greenwich that treats sex offenders?"

"That's the one. Saint Jack came into group after he got himself in some trouble with a little girl. Said he was drunk at the time. Swore he'd never do it again. Never did either. But he still comes to group from time to time. Gives him a chance to lord it over the rest of us."

My blood froze. *Was that me he was talking about? Was I the little girl Jack raped?*

Kitty whimpered.

"It's okay, sweetie." No time to dwell on the past. It didn't matter now. I had to get Kitty out of here.

Keep the lunatic talking, Lennie. Keep him off guard. "You look so much like him."

" 'Course I do, darlin'. Saint Jack's what they call my curative model. It's part of the Cambridge program. You pick someone perfect like the saint and act just like him. The doctors claim that'll help cure me."

Kitty was pale as chalk. I met her petrified gaze and tried to pass some mute reassurance.

Don't worry, sweetheart. I'll think of something.

The stranger snickered. "Problem is, they're wrong, Eleanora. I see a sweet young thing like this one, I . . . simply got to have her."

His voice caressed the ugly words. He ran a hand over Kitty's chest. My temper snapped. Enraged, I bounded across the room and pummeled him with my fists.

The stranger caught my wrists easily and held them. I tried to kick him in the groin, but he deflected my knee with his and tripped me.

I fell hard on the wood floor; pain speared my hip and elbow. Before I could stand again, the madman was over me. He held the gallon can of solvent.

He tipped the jug, dripping the contents onto my head and clothing. Horrified, I froze as the drops spattered my hair and jacket. The stench filled my nostrils. It was my rapist's scent: wood and chemicals.

Memory washed over me in a sick fever. *The man grabs me. He carries me up the stairs. He's throwing me down on the bed now. Huck—I see Huck's face. His eyes are wide with terror.*

"NO!"

"Oh yes, Eleanora." He reached for Kitty and leered. "You are the prettiest little thing, darlin'. We're gonna be real, *real* close, you and me."

Kitty screamed in terror as the animal nuzzled her neck.

"Leave her alone!" I scrambled to my feet.

As I did, John lifted the glass from one of the hurricane lamps, exposing the pink candle inside. He raised the wavering flame.

"Now, darlin', that's might flammable stuff you got all over you. If I was to get anywhere close with this little candle, you'd go up in a heartbeat. *Whoosh!*"

The fumes were making me dizzy. In vivid waves, I kept reliving that hideous night so many years ago.

He's pulling my blouse off, tugging down my pants. Stop!

John edged closer. The flame flickered, then flared. "Get down, Eleanora. On the floor."

Numbly, I obeyed. He was right. One spark, and I'd go up in lethal flames. I'd seen people burned alive. I'd never forget the horrid stink of scorching flesh. The wretched screams.

"That's a good girl, Eleanora," he crooned, his voice a sick parody of Jack's. "For that, you get to watch the floor show. Now you get down, Kitty darlin'. Lie on your back."

"No, please! Lennie, help! Leave me alone."

Leave me alone!

Her screams, everything, dimmed. I was stuck in a murky bog of memory. *He's on me. Pressing. Hurting me. I can't scream. Can't do anything.*

My body froze. Bile rose in my throat.

Don't look, Huck! Turn away.

It was all so unreal. The tear of clothing. A zipper opening. Sick animal moans.

John set the candle down on the toy box. The dancing flame was mesmerizing. I stared as it settled and swelled. I caught its lilting rhythm: *More than you know—*

Then, as I watched, the bobbing light was transformed. It turned luminous, became the firefly. Bathed in the stench of solvent and crippled by memory, I suddenly saw my mother's strong, hovering spirit.

It's okay, Lennie. Everything's all right now.

And it was. The nightmare released me. My darkest demon flapped its wings and flew away.

"Lennie, help!"

The stranger paused to unzip his pants and pull them to his knees. He was erect. Ready.

Before he could lower himself on Kitty, I grabbed the solvent container. The spray struck his face and spattered his clothing.

"Goddamnit!"

As he flailed about blindly, I splattered more of the reeking fluid all over him. He lunged at me, trying to grab the can. But as he passed the toy box, he caught a spark from the candle.

He went up in a thunderous rush of flame. Shrieking, he tried to beat down the sizzling blaze with his hands. It kept rising, engulfing him.

Drenched in flammable liquid, there was nothing I could

do to help him. All my training warned me that I, too, could become a human torch if I approached the flames.

Circling cautiously, I knelt beside Kitty.

"Come on, sweetheart. Let's go."

She recoiled, staring at the fiery mass. The flames were spreading, feeding voraciously. Eating the monster alive.

"Kitty! We have to get out! *Now!*" The fire was drawing closer. Shooting sparks. Burning with a white-hot ferocity. If I didn't move soon, the flames would take me next.

Kitty whimpered but made no move. I saw the fire reflecting in her eyes. It was straining toward us. Massing in a ravenous spire. The heat was enormous. The fiery beast could be building toward flashover.

I kept the panic out of my tone. "Okay, sweetie. Come on."

Bending, I hefted her into a shoulder carry. As soon as I had her in place, I raced toward the door.

Licks of fire trailed us by inches. I could feel the melting heat. My lungs were on fire, heart bursting. But I kept going. Only a few more steps. Nearly there.

Yes!

Safely out of the playhouse, I slammed the door to keep the demons inside.

Chapter 42

LENNIE

"Everything's okay now, Kitty."

"He . . . grabbed me, Lennie. I was coming to see you, and he forced me . . ." Violent trembling stilled her words.

I smoothed her matted hair. "It's over, honey. He's over. I'm taking you home."

We got in the car. But when I tried to start it, the engine hacked and died. I couldn't bring myself to drive the stranger's green Jeep, which was parked beside the playhouse. Even the car was a replica of Jack's. Too weird.

"Come on, sweetie. We'll call for help from the house."

As we emerged from the woods, I spotted the headlights barreling toward us on the access road. Preparing to face Jack, I found myself oddly at peace. Somehow, what had happened to me all those years ago was finally finished. At last I could walk away from it. And from him.

The approaching car stopped. A figure emerged. Not the one I was expecting.

"Red?"

"Lennie, thank God! Are you okay?"

"I'm fine."

Red turned to Kitty. "Hey, sweetheart. You okay? Are you hurt?"

"We're fine," I told him.

Red was shooting sparks. "Where's the bastard? I'll take care of him."

I turned to Kitty. "It's cold, sweetheart. Wait in the car and I'll be with you in a minute."

She hesitated, then did as I asked.

After Kitty was out of earshot, I gestured back through the woods. "God help me, Red, the bastard's already taken care of." Tendrils of flame threaded through Jack's pretty playhouse. The air was thick with smoke.

"What's burning? Did you call it in?"

"There's nothing left to save. How'd you know where to find us?"

He scowled. "I stopped at Mrs. O's to patch things up with you. She told me Jack had Kitty. I couldn't believe you'd come after them yourself. What the hell's wrong with you?"

His fury fueled my own. "Having a jerk like you in my life, Red. That's what's wrong with me."

He sniffed at me. "What the hell did you get all over yourself? You stink."

"So do you, buddy. And without chemical help."

The fire roared and spewed a burst of smoke. "What the hell? Tell me what's burning, Lennie. I'm serious."

"I'm burning, Red. Thanks to you."

At that instant, two more cars raced our way down the drive. Uniformed police, including Kresky, emerged from the first one. A woman and a man climbed out of the second vehicle. They were too far away for me to see clearly. But from the woman's aristocratic carriage, I knew it definitely was not Clarissa Pratt.

Red, drawn to the swelling flames, moved toward the playhouse. I walked over to Kresky and filled him in.

Afterward, I got into the car to talk to Kitty. "Sergeant Kresky has to report in to the other officers. Then he'll take you home."

"Can't you?" There was a hint of hysteria in her voice.

I gave her a hug and smoothed a wisp of hair back from her forehead.

"Not in this car, sweetheart. I'll come by and see you tomorrow. I promise."

For a moment, I feared she'd refuse to go. Then she nodded and stepped out. Kresky huddled with his colleagues for a couple of minutes. When he finished, he beckoned for Kitty. She gave me a hug, and she went.

Red came up beside me and sniffed again. "That's some kind of solvent, isn't it?"

"Leave me alone, Red."

"In case it slipped your mind, Lennie, that stuff's flammable. What is it with you? What's your problem?"

"*You're* the one with the problem, Red. You make me so mad, I could—"

And I did. Venting all my pent-up frustrations, I braced my hands against Red's shoulders and shoved.

He staggered back a few steps, caught his balance, and then swooped forward, clasping me in a bear hug. I struggled against him.

"You're such a pain in the butt, Red Snapper." I tried to pummel him with my fists, but he was too damn close for decent leverage.

"And you're impossible." His hand closed around my fist.

"Not half as impossible as *you*!" I freed the hand, backed away, and wound up to sock him.

"You're *twice* as impossible!" He feinted below the punch, sending me whirling.

"No, *you* are!"

"No *way*!"

Breathless and staggering, I threw up my hands. "I don't know how in the hell I can love a pigheaded ass like you, Red Snapper."

"That counts for me. Double."

That exchange left me momentarily speechless. Before I could find my tongue again, Red slipped his arms around me and kissed me. The move brought a rush of unexpected sensations.

I kissed him back. Seemed only fair.

The sound of a throat clearing broke our clinch. The woman from the second car had come up beside us. She was a commanding presence, incredibly poised and elegant. And *so* familiar. I thought I must be hallucinating from the fumes.

"Dana Saunders?" I croaked.

I'd caught her talk show a time or two. Mrs. O' was a huge fan.

"Sorry to interrupt, but Sergeant Kresky told me what you did, and I wanted to thank you personally." She tipped her head toward the burning playhouse. Spikes of flames strained skyward. The air was thick with smoke. "That man assaulted my daughter."

Another victim. My heart squeezed in pain. "I'm so sorry. Is she all right?"

"She will be. Especially now that I can assure her there's no way he can ever come after her again."

"I'm glad."

She tipped her head back and studied me. I knew at a glance that she wasn't the type you'd dare to cross. She had the steely strength to crush any opposition like a bug. "If there's ever anything I can do for you, Ms. Finn—anything at all—say the word."

"No, that's fine."

"I *mean* it."

"Actually, if it wouldn't be too much trouble, I have a friend who's crazy about your show . . ."

"She's welcome to tickets anytime. Come along if you can. It'd be my pleasure to take you both to lunch after the taping."

"That'd be wonderful."

"I look forward to it."

Astonished, I watched Dana Saunders stride away. She

slipped into the rear of the long, sleek car. The chauffeur slammed the door, then, unexpectedly, tipped his hat at me.

Red put his arm around me. "So, Finn. How about I take you back to my place for a spot of bubbly to celebrate?"

"What about my car?"

"I'll put in a call. Have the bomb towed and resuscitated."

"Sounds like a good plan."

He pulled me toward him. But this time I deflected the kiss. "You'd better not, Red. Remember. I'm flammable."

"Tell me about it."

He kissed me again. When we finally came up for air, he lapsed into his best Bogie voice. "This sorta takes the sting outa being occupied," he said.

I pulled him closer. "Play it again, Red."

"Oh, I will, sweetheart. Again and again and again."

ABOUT THE AUTHOR

More Than You Know is Judith Kelman's ninth novel. In addition, she's written articles for major magazines, including *Redbook, Glamour, Ladies' Home Journal*, and *McCall's*, and for the *New York Times*. She lives in Connecticut with her husband and two sons, where she is at work on her next novel, *Fly Away Home*.